Vanishing Worlds

Level 3 Letting go of the old -Annelies' Journal

I AM YOUR IDEA. ...E DAY YOU'LL LOOK FOR ... AND I'LL BE GONE

Published by: The Power of Words SA
Contact Details:
Website Author https://nadinemay.company.site/
Author's Blog: the End of Time: https://nadinemay.com/
Novel Blog: https://allrealityshifters.wordpress.com/
The Language of Light workbooks and journals: https://lightworkerjournals.wordpress.com/
ISBN – SKU 978-1-0672285-4-5
EBOOK ISBN 978-1-0672285-5-2
Previously published by Kima Global Publishers.
© Copyright Nadine May 2020
Cover Art by Author Nadine May

Table of Contents

Books by Nadine May

Awakening to our Ascension Series

Novel 1. The Reality Shifters – 2018 (Ingrids Journal – Romance)

Novel 2. Orphanage of Souls – 2019 (Richard's Journal – Romance)

Novel 3. Vanishing Worlds – 2020 - 2023. (Annelies' Journal – Psychic awareness)

Novel 4. Parallel Realities – 2025 (Tulanda's walk-in Journal)

Novel 5. Riddles of the Prophet's Game – 2026 (POWAH – the Guide)

The Language of Light – workbook in Full colour 2021

The Language of Light – workbook in Grayscale 2021

Meditation on the Language of Light 2021 (Full colour)

Seven. Doodle Symbology journals on the 7 Chakra channels in full colour or greyscale

The Body Codes of Light – workbook—(forthcoming)

The Self-Employed Housewife Book 1 – 2018 (novel)

The Self Employed Housewife Book 2 – 2022 (novel)

The story of the Group Soul, the Jaarsma Clan, and their awakening was downloaded over a period of twenty years. "Orphanage of Soulmates" was published in 2003 and republished in 2019. This award-winning novel was updated twice. "Vanishing World" has been re-edited and published worldwide.

Dedication/ Acknowledgements

This novel is dedicated to all the readers of our "Vanishing World. When I read the words of Mahatma Gandhi:

Your beliefs become your thoughts. -Your thoughts become your words.- Your words become our actions.-Your actions become your habits. -Your habits become your values.-Your values become your destiny.

The word 'destiny' completely describes what this novel is all about.

As I finish this third ascension novel, I have no more doubts about how I came to the material that makes it possible to write about such an awesome topic. I know now that the right people are in my life for the right reasons. That's why the words of Mahatma Gandhi showed me who I must acknowledge in this novel: the many people in my life who made a difference.

My beliefs were partly passed on by 'my parents' who, through their love, tried to guide my sister and me with theirs. I thank them for their unconditional love, especially my dad, who urged me to think for myself.

I rebelled against the thoughts surrounding their belief because of the words from the religious establishments. I thank all the writers of spiritual books for opening my inner knowledge through ignorance.

The words from preachers and well-meaning family members propelled me to study 'esoteric science' and quantum physics topics to turn my inner thoughts into words and actions. I thank all the writers of metaphysical books for awakening me to my inner truth.

When my actions became habitual, I learned the power of release from my husband of 33 years. Above all, I thank him for making me emotionally stronger.

Release from my past experiences that were not conducive to my 'intent' was difficult. Especially since who I am today is partly due to the lives of the people who shared mine for half a century.

Teachers always appear at the right time. Among the many teachers that have become part of my life during the writing of this novel are the many authors that I got to know through being a partner of Kima Global publishers

Above all, I am grateful to my soul partner, Robin Beck, my editor, proofreader, and publisher. No words can adequately describe the support he has given me to get my ascension project into the world of words.

After my dear soul mate of 22 years, Robin Beck, my publisher and the love of my life, passed from this physical reality, I asked for guidance, especially to finish my Soul purpose project, writing about our awakening to our ascension back into the higher realms through the genre of visionary fiction.

Robin was the kindest man alive. He passed on in January 2023, and it broke my heart. I thought the best was behind me, but during the staggering weight of despair and unforeseen circumstances, I needed to regain control of my Soul purpose by finishing writing the visionary five-stage novels about the Jaarsma Clan. That meant to republish all my books.

The duality of our lives and the power of perception gave me a chance to look back in wonderment and gratitude. It is that awareness that I try to bring with this novel, and at the same time, my grieving lifted.

Dedication

I dedicate all my visionary fiction writings by acknowledging Robin Beck, who, during the month before his passing, started

writing the first pages of the fifth novel in the Awakening to our
Ascension series: The Prophet's Game.
Nadine May - August 2024

Preface

The Chronicles of our Ancestors.

From the archives on our home planet, documented material describes what effect the transformation towards the state of oneness 6000 Earth years ago entailed. Our forefathers left us details of what it was like during the previous cosmic shift when their realities changed.

According to our records, the rule of darkness was oppressive since the dark forces were fighting for survival. The greed, anger, and envy genes that had infected human creations became a virus called 'belief'.

During Planet Earth's ascension into the light, the dark forces will again make their last desperate attempt to maintain their world dominance through this virus. Destructive belief thought forms (inorganic vibrations) that are absorbed daily by the human population through their physical body must be transcended within each individual's etheric light body energy grid before actual ascension can occur globally.

The enormous complexity of individual consciousness, influenced by an invisible energy field from birth into this world of duality, is severe.

It still surprises me how difficult it is to open up to our genetic akashic records. How many synchronicity moments have to occur in our lives to awaken past/future memories? For many, it never happens, but I was already very awake. I had already uncovered my sole purpose, why I was living and known as. Liesbeth. The founder and creator of the Jaarsma Clan saga channels the information in Annelies' journal.

In my journal, I will share what I have learned from Annelies' journal, both Hans and my husband in life as Liesbeth. I always knew Annelies was a gifted trance voice channel that brought forward advanced information from various light beings over the last few years. Her information has been changing lives worldwide for quite some time now, especially since her ascension workshops became available online.

While editing Annelies' journal into a novel, I discovered that being able to experience several lifetimes simultaneously depends on the amount of energy each individual has and how their life is lived. This conclusion has changed my life.

Annelies' journal has given my life as Liesbeth a new level of purpose concerning my spiritual path, and I cannot adequately express my gratitude.

As a walk-in, what I have learned has brought me incredible compassion for Earth's community. Each individual who has to cope with survival skills on multiple levels is entitled to get help when they ask for it. One mistake through this toxic virus will otherwise bring disaster, even Soul death.

This fragmented aspect of each individual managed to shatter every incarnating Soul for millions of years. It took on the role of the victimiser or the attacker. Emotions of guilt, remorse, fear, and relentless self-judgment did the rest. As a result, each human being has a huge task to accomplish when they choose to awaken their blueprint of ascension.

The Detrimental 'Belief' Program

Life on planet Earth's realm of duality seems more meaningful through having survived difficult experiences, especially in the early years. Then, a more vital mental attitude seems to develop compared to people who had it easy. Incarnations into a privileged society have their drawbacks. Those Souls lose hope far more quickly, and small matters bring about irritation, anger, blame, and ungratefulness.

People who are spiritually inspired and stay motivated regardless of life's obstacles must reach a level of emotional stability on this journey since their whole lives may well go through disruptions similar to those of the members of the Jaarsma Clan. The success of the lives of the people from the Jaarsma Clan depended on the following aspects:

I. Look for the divine in every experience of your life.

II. Aim to awaken to your blueprint (Soul purpose)by clearing your energy field daily.

III. Stay strong while establishing a link to your inner guide through telepathy, creativity, intuition and the power of LOVE.

IV. Release any belief program within the mind that is not conducive to entering into our immortal body of light

V Any healing is temporary until we heal and learn what happens during the transformation into our immortal body of light.

We from the 7th Astral Division are honoured to share the ascension journey with the Jaarsma Clan on planet Earth as it nears a cosmic shift. The need for enlightenment has indeed triggered more people than ever before. The right brain hemisphere of the human race is responding to our light frequencies as we expected it would.

Many of you know that these times would be difficult, but all you need is an intention to transcend in consciousness. Yes, there are challenging tasks ahead, so we feel that the Jaarsma story can help you, the reader, ascend to a new reality.

Namasté Tulanda

Prologue
The Realms within Realms

As above. So below.

<The levels of conscious awareness in Annelies' Ascension Workshop Game vary, with the five stages of awakening meant to prepare readers for their ascension into their body of light.

<Annelies' journey, translated into a human story most readers can relate to, was written to show that to be in harmony with the infinite, that alone will lift the veil on a Soul's journey into a human form.

<Humanity has once again reached the end of another stage in its evolution. Soon, very soon, your transformation will accelerate as your Planetary Soul enters an electromagnetic null zone.

<Every human being on this beautiful planet will perceive this shift differently. The truth will be apparent to you, 'the reader' who has chosen to ascend with planet Earth at this time.

<The planetary Soul will soon manifest the start of her ascension. That means she willingly enters a dimensional space and time zone that creates the makings of artificial time warps. Any virus that has plagued her will transmute. Instead, the movements of time going forward and reverse that established your three-dimensional realm in the human mind will create a light beam where high-frequency bodies can ascend and descend.

<You will experience that your three-dimensional universe, connected with many other universes, will interact and be raised to a higher dimensional frequency. There will be a connection between one planetary realm and another simultaneously in the same consciousness time cell. One species from one density can transfer into a different density level. That is how ascension will take place!

<We, the cosmic Time Lords and the Cosmic Hierarchy of higher angelic masters have listened to the appeal of the great planetary Soul named Earth. We all simultaneously agreed to grant this great being its ascension into the higher realities of spirit.

<The only species that have free will to choose to ascend with her or not is the human population; to stay with their beloved planet and travel inter-dimensionally to a different location within the creator's vast endless solar system, or they can decide to take their leave of the planetary soul named Earth and embark on a different journey.

<Annelies' journal will reveal to the reader which direction they are heading if they don't shake off the 'belief' virus. There is no right or wrong way. Many individuals will continue with the same evolutionary game by living in the human form, expressing the creator of it all as they have before, and staying ignorant of the opportunity to become a galactic citizen. Evolution is ongoing and continuous due to the omnipresence of the infinite.

<Many will stay unaware that all individual Souls are always pure consciousness. They will remain trapped in their physical form during the transformation. So be it; the choice must be theirs to wake up from the human dream. They have special permission to remain in your three-dimensional world. A NEW planet, of lesser vibration to that of the Earth, will be created,

where all those of the human evolution, incarnate and discarnate, who have proven themselves incapable or unwilling to emit more light, will be transferred. There will be NO re-embodiment on your planet Earth for any of them.

<I, the Jaarsma group Soul named POWAH, have been granted an opportunity to incarnate, as a guide, into 144 human Souls during the ascension process of this planet. While each particle of myself has been an individual choice to awaken to full consciousness, I was aware of how illusionary a three-dimensional world can be.

<In my last human incarnation, during the reign of the human spirit named Djehuti, my decision to depart from the royal court while my beloved Pharaoh was struggling to awaken to full consciousness had set off a karmic event that led to the destruction of Tel El Amarna.

<For this error in choice during that time, I will now be using this opportunity to set right what would have changed the evolution of man. Through this journal, I will take the reader on a journey on the third level of the awakening game, bypassing the mind trapped by the TIME matrix.

P.O.W.A.H

Cast of Characters

Apeldoorn - Holland
Annelies (Annie) Zwiegelaar
POWAH - Spiritual Guide
Ben: Husband – Detective
Fred: Brother - Bookshop owner
Quincy: Wife of Fred (New owner of Annelie's home)
Hans: Adopted son - walk-in
Liesbeth / Tulanda: daughter-Editor of the journals -walk-in
Half-way House
Peter: Otto's adopted son - Half-way House
Helen - Peter's wife
Toon - Half-brother – (the philanthropist)
Ingrid: Toon's wife - Journal the Reality Shifters
Sandra - Toon & Ingrid's baby daughter
Trevor - Uncle - Scientist
Leo: Ben's twin brother - Genetic scientist
Harry Brinks - Friend of Annelies and Mien
Tieneke - Harry Brinks' daughter - Trevor's partner -
author of The Language of Light
Body Codes of light – (workshop participants)
Gerrit: Half-brother
Adel Gerrit's wife
Richard de Jong: - Journal Orphanage of Souls
Sascia - Daughter of Ingrid –
Buttercup Valley
Otto: Half brother - Buttercup Valley -Jill - Otto's wife
South Africa
Mien - Ben's sister - a close friend
Nick du Toit - First husband of Mien
Jock & At du Toit – sons of Mien

Sonja - Mien's daughter
Katrina with her husband, John
Pat with husband Harrie
Ben van Dongen - Sonja's husband - Doctor
Debbie - Daughter of Ingrid
Dirk - Toon's pilot

Chapter 1
The Breath of Life – Soul Purpose

March in Apeldoorn

A loud crash made her almost jump out of her wheelchair. ANNELIES pushed herself away from her desk to have a look.

A branch had smashed against her home office window. Thank goodness the glass didn't break. She disliked cold, wet weather more than ever before, especially when the rain was pouring in torrents and the wind howled like mad, screaming, *"You have broken my spirit."*

She shivered at the idea that she had telepathically heard the gale-force wind speak since she had never felt such an intense, despairing tone. Her sensitivity had heightened; that must be it.

A cold, wet nose nudged at her hand on her wheelchair.

"Gosh, Joris, it's cold."

The pleading look in the Labrador's eyes made her smile.

"You are far too big to sit on my lap." Not to mention the mess he would make on her long wraparound skirt; BEN had bought it for her in Cape Town a week ago. ANNELIES loved Ben, her husband's gesture of purchasing an item of clothing for her to wear on the plane flying home.

Stormy nights feel cosy and secure when snugly curled up in bed. Still, being in their office, Annelies felt the despair from the wind, which just now shook her deeply, knowing that the emotions of the collective fourth-dimensional realm were engulfing her physical realm, now more so than ever. Did the air elemental, known as a sylph, just now speak to her?

The dancing words of her computer screen saver, SMALL THINGS MAKE BIG CHANGES, gave her pause. *"If the whole world is a stage and I play an individual role, how can I rewrite my script?"* That was the question she had asked in a dream. In the dream, she was an elemental being of light, communicating with a giant boulder. A shiver ran down her spine when she recalled that dream. *"There will be a natural spiritual selection,"* but then the visions from her dream changed.

"How could her body consciousness influence a different outcome during these chaotic times?" Annelies pondered, ignoring the fierce storm creating havoc in her garden. Her office looked bare, apart from the boxes. They would be settling into their new home in France in a week.

She saw that the central heating was on low, so it was no wonder it was chilly in her office. It could only be BEN who had changed the setting. Her hubby had a faster metabolism than hers.

The more sensitive she became, the slower her circulation, or so it seemed, unless her clothes were getting tighter. Her otherwise trim figure might have taken on some padding. Not being able to exercise or walk could be one reason.

Oh, how she now understood the danger of being in a reactive mind. How easy that can take over when the elite of the lower astral plane try to control the physical world through fear. That was the case at one moment when her accident happened. when they were running away from fear back in South Africa.

The sky had a reddish-dark glow. Had she honestly heard a desperate cry from the gale-force wind, or was it her imagination? "Forgive us", she nevertheless projected towards the dark clouds.

She wheeled herself away from the window and back to her desk to continue with her work when she spotted an introductory pamphlet left on the floor. Its words: The resurrection of matter made her recall Richard, the Egyptologist and his lecture that she had attended in Utrecht last year.

She leaned sideways to pick it up. Richard's topic confirmed his Soul purpose throughout his journals: to make an opening through the nearest astral realm by travelling out of his body. With the help of his brother Theo, they had mastered the art of resurrecting the power within physical matter.

Not for anything would she have missed his lecture. A calmness settled over her when she leaned back in her chair and recalled the scene in the lecture hall last year.

Utrecht - The Resurrection of Matter

A buzz of bewilderment had filled the auditorium when Richard showed the image that had plagued him for weeks.

"Ladies and gentlemen, I'm not here to convert anyone. There is nothing to convert to. I want to close this lecture with the following material and let everyone here absorb it as they choose."

There had been a buzz in the auditorium when she telepathically heard the words: *"We warn you, if you continue, the Jaarsma clan will come up for trial."*

Ben had heard it, too. They were both telepaths. She sensed that Richard had also heard it but had shrugged it off. She knew that he felt that his audience needed to be warned.

When Richard showed them the twenty-two tablets up close on the big projector screen, she felt a familiar energy signature near her. She had known then that Richard's older brother Theo, who had played a significant role in their lives for the last five years, was with them in consciousness. His physical departure still made her feel sad. It was through Theo's warnings that both she and Ben started to take note of the low vibrational shadow entities that had corrupted a large field of humanity's global awareness levels.

"Two other colleagues and myself were permitted to disclose the following discoveries," Richard had said. She had known who he was referring to.

Everyone in that lecture room was holding their breath with keen anticipation. She could have heard a pin drop; it was so quiet.

"You can see in the movie clip that the crystal skull communicates with the person inside the stone." Richard paused the video to point at a human figure resembling a hologram before the boulder. The gasp from the audience was electrifying.

"Her physical body has altered so that she can tolerate the presence of the skull to accomplish her intent. Please observe her body language. This individual is still both awed and terrified."

Someone had creatively captured the memory files from the universal matrix visually by creating a video enabling people to grasp Richard's unusual explanation.

"You can see how the crystal skull can resonate tones like the planet speaking." The moving film images that flew past held more information than words could reveal.

"Man learned over the centuries that these crystal skulls abide organically within each person's brain."

At that moment, the movie shows a light being hovering nearby. *"Richard, is that me?"* She had beamed. Her thoughts were out before she knew it. While the audience saw how the planet spoke to a human light body through the crystal skull, she at that time was in two places at once. The female human figure seemed to shiver while accepting a message.

Her adopted son Hans remarked after the lecture that more and more people would interact with the planet through telepathy when their vibrations within this physical reality expanded to a multidimensional awareness level. At the time, His explanation had gone over her head.

Apeldoorn

The reflection on her computer screen of a middle-aged woman in a wheelchair made her question whether the despairing feeling was her own. Hearing the strong wind speak was either a phantom of her imagination or her psychic sensitivity had returned....her screen saver slogan, SMALL THINGS MAKE BIG CHANGES, confirmed it.

The loud car door closing snapped her back into the present. The crunch of footsteps on the gravel outside their front door alerted Joris, the Labrador, to bark. Ben and HANS had arrived home. She had aimed to finish at least one chapter of her decoding workbook before they went out for dinner, so she settled herself at her keyboard and opened her word processor.

She tried to concentrate on her typing, but her neighbour's car radio was on so loud she could hear the radio announcer saying:"

"Hail, rain and strong winds battered the Netherlands Tuesday, felling trees, creating localised flooding and causing major road and rail disruption. The Dutch meteorological institute KNMI said wind speeds of more than 105 km/h caused trees to fall on roads and rail tracks, resulting in long delays throughout the country for commuters. More than 5 cm hailstones are recorded in the country's southwest."

Brrr... she was glad not to be living near the coast.

"At last, Annelies has started writing in her journal again," she heard Ben telling Hans in the passageway.

She wasn't so sure of that. Lately, she had woken up with more information meant for her decoding book instead. Her Soul purpose number five, The Breath of Life, had only now started to make sense, especially when she had started writing her journal in January, just before they left for South Africa.

Her decoding formulas seemed to hold some of the answers she was looking for, but why had she then not been able to foresee her accident?

The flight back from Cape Town was a sudden decision before the country was scheduled to go into a total lockdown to stop the spread of the coronavirus. The National Government had announced a lockdown across South Africa.

She sensed that Hans and LIESBETH knew what was in store for humanity during the coming years, but they stayed quiet about it. Ben and she knew this so-called "health Pandemic" was a financial pandemic with a sinister agenda. In early January, TOON had already told Ben, "If you want to control the minds of the masses truly, what better way than to create a worldwide economic collapse?"

Looking around the empty room that had been their office for many years, she noticed the vision board collage she had made after their return from South Africa.

It was the only decoration still hanging on the wall. Now more than ever, she needs to focus on her physical health. Never in all her life had she been challenged this way. Health was never an issue, but after the accident, she realised how much she had always taken her body for granted.

Her vision board was full of photos of her walking on the beach in Cape Town, taken only a few weeks ago. She had added earlier pictures of herself and Ben when they were both in their thirties, climbing in the Hogsback. How a vision board holding such good memories uplifted her mood is amazing. In response, she quickly beamed healing feelings of love down her legs into the feet. They were both in plaster. That felt better already.

Hearing the men talking to each other outside her office made her eager to carry on adding at least one page to her journal, **Vanishing Worlds**. Having two projects going at the same time was not unusual for her.

Typing out her own story at sixty felt somewhat presumptuous. How would she explain the terrors that had infected each Soul from birth into this world? The toxic intake into the human body, physically, mentally and emotionally, had doubled in these chaotic times.

She was born with the gift of clairvoyance, and as a child, she was also very telepathic but never recognized. It took her years of observing the energy fields of others to understand what the crystal skull had told the woman in Richard's video....

She had been the woman who had telepathically heard:

"A mass awakening on a global scale must happen for humanity to participate in the next dimensional shift."

She felt like a frozen statue at the time, hearing this coming from the crystal skull Ben had brought home last year. Typing the dialogue made her recall what followed:

"A new set of genetic codes has activated those proceeding into the oneness of co-creation. During an ascension journey, an initiate must slowly and cautiously prepare and awaken the appropriate nerve centres and learn to control them. To recalibrate your perspective on the outside world, you must adjust your genetic programming to reconnect with the fundamental principles of the divine mind and the universal Godhead.

She almost recalled it word for word, so it was essential to type it into her journal; it might make sense later.

She suspected that the next few years would be an excellent challenge for the human population on the planet. In this third journal, her contamination had to be exposed. That was the scariest part, but humanity would have succumbed to the lie if she didn't. The distortions were intertwined in each person's auric field, making it difficult to awaken fully.

Her telepathic dialogue with POWAH, her higher self-guide in the last few months before and after her accident, had helped her to come to terms with her immobility. She now sensed that he had spoken through the Crystal scull.

Joris suddenly got excited, wanting to leave her office now that Ben and Hans had arrived home, which interrupted her pondering.

The pressure of writing both her journal and her decoding workbook and coping with moving away from Apeldoorn while learning to get around in a wheelchair started to take its toll. She could feel that her emotional energy field was under stress.

The sudden change of colour on her computer screen startled her. Her eyes almost popped out of their sockets when she saw text appearing as if someone had sent her a PowerPoint slide.

<**Humanity is like one unified organism. While the world around you has been natural to you for centuries, including in this lifetime, your reality shatters and shakes. Your old world seems to commit suicide, and there is a sense of darkness and impending doom enveloping you all unless you all awaken! A human with a beast-like selfish nature is more animated by lower vibrations of vital energy than a spiritually developed person. A mass awakening on a global scale must happen for humanity to participate in the next dimensional shift "**>

How weird, as if the wind had reminded her of something. Those were the very words she had just added to her journal. She grabbed her mouse, and her screen turned back to page 24 in her journal. She wanted to check if the exact text was still there.

So much has happened since she started writing her journal last year. In her mind's eye, she pictured loving energy that could take on any shape standing behind her, embracing her. The way her mind had created an image of her guide had never changed. Only after she trained in the art of proper breathing did the sound of the name POWAH add a kind of solidity to her psychic awareness. Thank goodness that POWAH had always been near during many of her vision quests.

There it was. The text was still there.

<"Within the inner chamber of every individual being, within their world of imagery, there is an opportunity for humanity to devise a plan to create something new from the wreckage of each individual's manifestations. Vital energy from the spinal column, where it has its seat, is transformed into a low or higher vibration corresponding to the degree of consciousness of the person concerned, and only this transformed vital current is conducted into the body.">

She recalled what her reply was, and she decided to repeat the same message in later chapters. She would then question why she felt it was appropriate. She closed her journal file with one click and opened the page in her decoding workbook that she had been working on so that in France next week, she could hand a printed version out to her students, who would be participating in her decoding workshop. They would all have a copy of her workbook, **The Body Codes of Light**. Liesbeth, her daughter, promised to edit it so she could publish it online.

"Mom, when will you be joining us?" Hans peered around the door. His tousled, already unruly light blond hair was half-covering his face. Due to its paleness and nearly white hair, Hans' almost angelic face bears signs of supreme intelligence and powers of concentration. His mouth is well-formed and energetic, with soft corners revealing his tender love for every living creature. I love him from the moment he came into our lives.

"Soon, I promise."

Her inspiration kicked in as her fingers ran over the keyboard,

"Like the caterpillar who emerges from its decay as a great butterfly," she replied to POWAH a while back. She had been writing about her own Soul purpose number **five: The Breath of Light**[1]. She was keen to finish interpreting this Body Code before the men called her to get ready for dinner.

---

1. https://allrealityshifters.wordpress.com/the-22-body-codes-of-light-level-5/

Suddenly, a symbol of a classic Egyptian knot, found on the side of the Egyptian pharaoh's throne, swam before her inner eye. When these mental interruptions happened, she had learned by now to follow through on them by letting her body go soft and relaxed. Often, words would come if she just let them.

The symbol came back into her inner vision; something about the sacred breath that somehow cradled her physical body into a morphogenetic field that could bypass the third-dimensional realm.

"Is that how we can ascend our physical form?" she mentally asked POWAH, her higher guide both Ingrid and Richard had written about in their journals.

She needed to rest her heavy legs, plaster, on a stool. It wasn't easy to get genuinely comfortable, but after a while, she heard the following words, which seemed to be a reply to her question.

<Biological ascension can be like the metamorphosis of a caterpillar into a butterfly. Your human body will undergo the same transformation. The degree of consciousness of a living creature fluctuates up and down, depending on its emotional condition, within the etheric resurrection body of light. New possibilities arise by tuning higher Soul qualities to a Christ LOVE frequency. You will escape from the lower realms into a beautiful world beyond your imagination.>

POWAH's reply made her recall the decoding of the 22 vibrational layers in her Body Codes of Light workshops. They were important. It could remove humanity's mental programming. Every layer must be purified so that the Soul qualities to a Christ LOVE frequency can embody a human etheric copy body.

Joris' loud barking made her snap out of her contemplative mood. She heard Ben calling him inside.

She knew what she had just heard telepathically, but had she understood it? Annelies had seen glimpses of a higher world in her dreams. The scene reminded her of the movie Avatar by James Cameron. Gosh, more and more people must have seen what she saw in her vision quests.

She pondered in silence for a long time until her breathing became part of a melody. Then suddenly she heard POWAH's voice in her head saying:

< You currently lack a complete understanding of the context in which your technology operates. This insight will come, but it will take time. Rest assured that we are watching, waiting, and ever vigilant to protect your and our mission's interests.>

She swallowed hard and tried to speak; whether it was with her conscious mind or vocal cords, she wasn't sure which.

"Who are 'we', and what technology?" she mentally projected.

Again, she waited silently and felt as if somebody was trying to speak through her, but she wouldn't allow it. Her body was hers, and allowing some entity to take control of her body was not an option. Her telepathic ability was the only way she could interact with other conscious beings.

>The physical health wavelength the body code interprets shows us what an IAm is thinking and feeling at any moment. The degree of consciousness of a living creature fluctuates up and down, depending on its emotional condition, within the limits of an octave of vibrations. These fluctuations must not exceed the limits of elasticity of the nerves; if they do, injuries and sicknesses of a more or less serious nature occur, even after death.

> The vital energy from the spinal column is transformed into a lower or higher vibration corresponding to the person's level of consciousness. Only this transformed vital current is administered into the body.>

The need to record this message made her take action. As she typed the words that her mind was forming, describing the visions of her inner world, she was once again distracted by the howling wind outside. It was still cold for the time of year. She had not lasted long the few lovely days last weekend before Easter. Leaving Apeldoorn for good had finally sunk in. If only she could heal faster and be able to walk again.

"Annie, Hans has booked a table for dinner in half an hour." Ben had come in to fetch more boxes, and he brought her crutches, knowing she hated wheeling herself out onto their driveway.

"Just give me fifteen minutes. I must finish my interpretations chapter for the Body Codes of Light workbook. Has Liesbeth arrived?"

"No, only Hans. She has gone ahead with Tieneke to prepare everything for your decoding workshop, remember?"

Of course, how had that slipped her mind? When Ben left her alone, she suddenly experienced a déjà vu, as if she was reliving a reality that had already occurred before her trip to South Africa.

She had been sitting at her computer but on a chair as she did now. She had started her journal while a storm outside was howling just like it was now....

She had written about how to interpret auras. Only the power of love, compassion, and gratitude for being who she was, only those 'Christ' vibrations, would respond as the immune system did in a biological form. Only then would true healing take place....

Last year, she discovered that the great lie programmed into the cellular memories of physical matter was like a virus that could wipe out everything on a computer. Only an excellent immune system would be able to destroy any foreign invaders.

The tiny black holes and distorted vortices often seen in auras saddened her. That's what fed the shadow entities. It reminded her not to be too judgmental of others who were unkind or even cruel. She knew that these black holes in a human energy field were often doorways for disembodied fallen entities to get through. If enough of them occupy one's energy field, emotions like anger, grief, or irritation towards others would be irresistible, just like junk food is to unhappy people.

Suddenly, her feelings of déja-vu disappeared. What had brought that on? She leaned back in her wheelchair, contemplating. How best should she describe how dark forces enter one's energy field?

After Richard's lecture, she had never shared with Ben or Richard what the crystal skull had impressed as an image in her subconscious. It was the idea that the human aura or energy field was similar to space - like a universe with galaxies, stars, and black holes.

A rush of insights came to mind. She knew she had to share the telepathic dialogue with POWAH through the crystal skull last year while attending Richard's lecture in Utrecht.

Typing the words she mentally heard again spoken out loud inspired her inner reality.

<If you are the caretakers of the Universe, and there is only One Source and One Force that controls everything, then...

She recalled that she had further mentally asked as an afterthought:

"What is super light?"

She heard Ben and Hans chatting in the kitchen, so she quickly typed what the crystal skull had replied or instead shown her last year in a vision she saw at Richard's lecture:

<Super Light is the unseen force of Christ's consciousness in nature that science has ignored but has been fundamental to the mystics and metaphysicians for thousands of years. Different cultures have given it various names for thousands of years.>

She had mentally replied:

"Oh, do you mean chi, our life force, or Zero Point Energy?"

Suddenly, it all came back to her. Richard showed his audience a video clip created by Trevor that triggered her inner dialogue with POWAH at that moment.

<Yes, but in your reality, everything has an equal and opposite mirror image counterpart, the Yin and the Yang, right and left, matter and antimatter, the electron and the positron.>

"Is there a polarity in light?" She had been surprised at her reply. Then, more visions showed her that superlight is an unseen force in nature. The ideas streamed through her fingers while she was typing.

"Where does superlight come from?"

That was the last telepathic question she recalled from when she had been hovering near her physical body in the auditorium. She never received a reply. Her uncanny experience the previous year had left her speechless.

She typed it all down in her journal. Letting go of the old shifted her into the present. She stopped typing, leaned back in the wheelchair, and recalled a discussion with Hans after Richards's lecture....

Two evenings later, after Richards's lecture, she shared her telepathic experience with Hans. Their son was very aware, as crystal children are often. She had questioned him if zero point or space energy was super light, and that because super light travels at speed 10 billion times faster than light, she remembered asking Hans why, if this super light is so powerful, how come we do not feel it, or how come it is not detected scientifically?

He replied that higher frequency must have a corresponding, shorter wavelength because of its higher energy density. Hans reminded her of how to use this superlight through his auric field. Mentally, he could tap into this super light and transform this light energy into a vital life force. Then she understood what she had seen Hans doing.

He demonstrated it to Joris when he was hit by a car last year. The blue energy that had come away from his hands when he ran over

Joris' body had a fantastic effect. Joris immediately moved again and stood up, wagging his tail as if nothing had happened.

Seeing Hans performing a healing miracle left a profound impression on her then. Hans explained that anything transformed by superlight goes through a cellular transformation. Because the frequency is so high and its wavelength so short, its velocity is high-speed; it becomes invisible and goes through everything. Any object becomes completely transparent, like glass.

Recalling how Hans had instantly healed Joris brought on an emotional feeling. Why could she, or Hans for that matter, not have healed her after her accident?

She sighed in dismay at her lack of healing powers. What happened in South Africa brought up old, hidden mental blocks that must be exposed.

She intuitively knew that the accident had allowed her to eliminate distorted thought-form programs in her etheric copy body, as she liked to call it. So what had she learned so far? Only future healing by medical converters could change superlight into a vital life force. This new science would revolutionise the medical profession if they allowed it.

She leaned back in her chair, contemplating if positive thought might hold proof that a bright future was still possible.

"Annie, will you join us for a wine before dinner?" Ben mentally suggested.

The cursor on her screen was waiting for her quetional mind.

The italic text she had typed: *"If you are the caretakers of the Universe, and there is only One Source and One Force that controls everything of the topic I needed to address: how can I best describe dark forces in one's energy field?*

"I will come soon. I'm writing. I will skip the wine!"

It was important for her decoding students to understand this. Tieneke's Language of Light workshop made so much sense now that she had completed her mind drawings with their colour, shape and forms. She had combined Tieneke's symbol samples with the numbers of her decoding formula.

There was no reply, so she needed to accept the proses of her awakening. Today, she would describe these dark forces or shadows as a smell or a sound.... Emotions like anger, grief or irritability are like how a hamburger would smell to a rugby player after a match...or...the smell of pizzas to a group of hungry teenagers. These human emotions, and especially the reactions to them, become the attracter field for these dark entities. That's it. She had typed this all before! All of a sudden, her déja-vu feelings came over her again.

The Crystal Skull

Her journal had to include understanding what POWAH implanted through the crystal skull. She had lately found that out by looking into the energy field of trees and rocks while gardening. Hans' explanations suddenly started to make sense, not that that affected her life as Annelies, but it was enough.

Now she knows how to lay out her **The Body Codes of Light** workbook. Liesbeth would post the 22 interpretations online for readers to follow the meanings behind the codes.

"Mom, are you okay?" Hans' telepathic message brought her instantly back to the present.

"Stop snooping. I'm coming."

Lately, she found it more comfortable to have her feet up. Her feet were starting to swell up, which she never experienced before her accident.

She saved what she had written because she heard Ben calling Joris, who was still barking at somebody outside. She closed her computer after she had printed out what she had typed so far. She placed all the pages into a ring binder and tucked it behind her in her chair. This folder was with her all the time. She could only keep her ideas fresh by reading over them while she was a wheelchair user and away from her computer.

Since everything in the kitchen was packed in boxes, eating out was the only other option. Hans was helping his dad move boxes into their garage so the removal van would know how much stuff they had to fit in.

"Joris heard something or somebody. I'm sure. I'm glad he will stay with Ingrid and Toon while we drive to France." She remarked as she wheeled herself into the hallway.

Joris was, after all, Toon's dog, but since her half-brother was often out of the country, Joris lived most of the time with them.

The lashing rain reminded them of the latest viewpoints on rising sea levels due to the planet Nibiru. Not that any TV channels ever mentioned that.

Toon was more eager than ever to build communities on high ground levels around the planet. Trevor, her father's youngest brother, did not believe in the rising sea levels. He claimed they are scare tactics to put fear into the human population as they did with the global warming scenario. Still, Toon aimed for his communities to be at least forty metres above sea level, but that was not always possible.

Toon had the capital to do it, and that might have been one of the reasons why his life had been in danger last year.

"Ben, please close the door. Brrr, I'm looking forward to the sunshine in France." She hoped the weather would be better than in Holland, although Europe was experiencing frigid autumn weather. She would ask Hans again about the voice that seemed to have come from the wind. She wanted Ben to hear Hans' explanation repeatedly.

"Are you ready?"

"Yes, apart from taking my files with me."

Ben closed the office door and picked up her decoding folder from behind her in the chair, knowing what it was about....

He flipped through it in the hallway.

"When did you write this about the bluebirds?" Ben was always curious about how she gathered her ascension materials.

"I don't remember, but you said you saw a bluebird. Remember?"

Ben nodded, saying, "I did indeed. I wonder if it is an omen?" ...

"There is no such a thing as coincidence. I wonder what the bluebird stands for. He pondered." I'm talking about the vibration of five in connection with your Soul's purpose: The Breath of Life. Annelies grabbed her folder back to see what he was remarking about. Ben towered above her at six feet in height, which seemed huge now that she was seated. His hair was a dark brown with grey streaks, and his eyebrows were a lighter shade of the same. His well-proportioned frame still lacked any trace of fat.

"Oh, well, I'm using my decoding vibrations as a guinea pig. I am busy writing my journals and, at the same time, the **Body Codes of Light** workbook because they seem to overlap."

"So your soul purpose is The Breath of Life?"

"I took the symbolic number vibration from Tieneke's Language of Light workbook. I still have to add my interpretation. POWAH calls it the Christ impulse code vibration. I have chosen it as the Soul quality purpose vibration."

"Oh, interesting, I wonder what mine is?" It seemed he might be thinking or planning mischief when Ben smiled but quickly dispelled when he spoke or laughed.

"I have researched this before, but it hasn't yet written in my file." She winked. He wore his favourite outfit, an old pair of brown corduroy pants. She did not wear clothes for dinner, but she would not comment.

"When people don't remember their Soul purpose, would this coding, as you call it, help them to remember?"

"The interpretations? I hope so. There is more to it in the questionnaire they must fill in. They have several options to choose from."

Ben helped her with her winter coat and handed her her crutches.

"Yes, you said so, but how do you know that these transmissions, as you call them, are not just mentally inspired by you?"

His voice was rich and even calm despite being a detective, the gentlest of men. She loved the grey streaks at his temples contrasting his dark hair.

"I stopped questioning that. Whatever comes into my mind at any time, I just let it flow through my fingers as I type."

"Mmm, I can't wait to read that decoding book of yours," Ben said, kissing her neck. Now that Annie stood up, she was nearly as tall as him. In their twenty-two years together, Annie kept all her curves and grace. She tended to wear colourful flowing caftans, and much of her wardrobe was a stylish interpretation of a creative gipsy look.

"It's far from finished, but the idea is that they collect their interpretations together from what appeals to them." Annelies felt Joris' cold nose brushing against her knee above her plastered leg. He would need to be locked up in the kitchen before they left.

"The Breath of Life number vibration reveals at what vibrational rate I, as a person, have chosen to access through my willpower." She replied while taking a few steps towards the front door. She could rest on her one foot, which was in a big boot, but her balance was precarious.

"Oh, that is?"

"I'm trying to remember the right word POWAH used. I've typed it out. It's in my file at the back behind the blue plastic divider. The Breath of Life coding applies to a person who contemplates a lot."

"Oh, that is you."

"You think so?"

"Absolutely. You mull over things. I can see when you are in a contemplative mood."

"How so?

"Your body language is like a frozen statue; you are not there mentally; I mean, you turn inwards into your world." Ben beamed at her while holding her steady, helping her with her crutches. Hans spoke to Joris, telling him that they would be back soon.

"I'll remember that you said that, me turning inwards." She ruffled through his short-cut hair. "Come, let's go and have dinner."

"You must show Hans what POWAH told you about The Breath of Life," Ben replied, taking a deep breath. "May I take both your folders along?"

"Sure, why not? So you can read how I have ended some chapters with my interpretative paragraph that came from him in the same way that Ingrid and Richard had received his message." Annelies handed over her files.

"Oh, so it can be published on the website for readers to find out what their 22 spacings are in the Body Codes of Light workbook." Ben summarised

In a separate folder labelled **"The 22 Body Codes of Light[2],"** she had collected the transmissions emailed to her. Each symbol represented a chemical code but was associated with their ethereal double-copy or light body.

Ben took both folders under his arm and helped her outside to the car. He telepathically warned Hans to open the sliding door of the Volvo.

After dinner, Hans left them to go to his flat. He had lots of papers that needed scanning before emailing them to Toon. With all his many activities, Hans ensured that Toon would never get into trouble in the financial stock market, which was at the point of collapse. Hans warned Toon that more and more companies would

---

2. https://allrealityshifters.wordpress.com/the-22-body-codes-of-light-level-5/

be coming up with increasingly 'creative' ways of getting more money out of him—meanwhile, tremor after tremor continued to strike the world's financial system.

"Ben, what if the Financial Collapse parallels the Polar Shift?" She asked after Hand had left, and they were alone in the restaurant, waiting for dessert.

"What makes you come up with that idea?"

"Well, bees are not pollinating the crops anymore. Bees have a sense of geo-navigation but are deserting their hives. Something is awry." She had read that on the internet.

"Who knows? I want to read the transmissions you have discussed while we wait for the bill. Where are they?"

It was nice and cosy in the Pannekoek. Not all that busy, but then it was winter, and no tourist would visit Apeldoorn at this time of the year. The girl who served them was new. She'd never seen her before, and the requirement to wear a mask was also new. They had not followed that rule until now, wearing masks, but more and more people outside were buying into the fear-mongering bulletins on the news.

Ever since the ownership had changed hands, the vibe in the restaurant was not the same anymore, except for Richard's girlfriend's photography displayed on the walls.

"Yep, we live in the times to wake up. Look at the signs around us. I believe in intelligent design, much like Einstein, Da Vinci, and many other great Minds." She took the folder from him and settled next to him on the only settee in the restaurant. Liesbeth would create a link to the Body Code interpretations in her novel.

The 22 Body Codes of Light[3] – Level 5

"There it is. The body vibration code number five." For her Body Codes of Light workbook. Her Soul Purpose Code 5-The Breath of life

---

3. https://allrealityshifters.wordpress.com/the-22-body-codes-of-light-level-5/

"Heaven is between earth and sky, where bluebirds fly and die. I will not add that last italic paragraph about the bluebird into my workbook, only into my journal." She explained

"What is it with this Bluebird? Is it a sort of a symbol? Does it mean something else?"

She suspected seeing a bluebird in dreams could symbolize happiness and sadness, but Ben thought he had seen one in their back garden!

"I looked it up on a search engine. If one has a bluebird tapping on your window, something else is far beyond our understanding, such as "I'm your only friend ... not your friend, but your I Am.""

"Like guardian angels...?"

She shrugged her shoulders. She didn't always understand the whys or her intuitive hunches, but she followed them up.

"Well, what you have typed further must be your influence since that is so YOU!"

A spiritual researcher must embody the vibration of the Breath of Life for the Soul to awaken through the etheric immortal light body of the human form.

People who choose this vibration as their Soul purpose are often scholars, preachers, teachers, writers, and lightworkers. To them, the Soul quality of The Breath of Life means food for the questioning mind. Therefore, they must always ask for their higher self's participation.

"Mmm,...food for the questioning mind... I still wonder what my Soul's purpose is?"

"I'll look it up, I promise."

Ben paid their bill, and after they arrived home, she was glad to finally get into her warm nighty and bed. Her preparation before going to bed took a great deal of time, but at least she was more independent than she had been for the first two to three weeks.

She never thought it would be this scary to know what others would read about her and how weird she was—living in different realities simultaneously. She took a deep breath and closed her eyes, knowing she was participating in a virtual reality game where Time was also an illusion. She knew that when her mind recalled a past event, time stood still, or rather, she became the observer of her script.

Again, her déja-vu impressions took her back a few months into a reality that was no more when she had started her ascension journal, Vanishing Worlds – before their trip to South Africa....

Chapter 2
Forgiveness Motivation

Apeldoorn - Three months earlier

When Annelies' animated popup email announcer, the butler, said: "You have mail, madam", she couldn't resist clicking it. It might be an important email.

"Oh no, not another one of those!" She protested loudly, annoyed with herself for looking at emails now that she had made a start with the first chapter of her journal. Why had she allowed an interruption, no matter how minor? Was it an excuse to break away from her assignment?

"What, Mom, spam mail?" Hans questioned with humour as he entered his mother's office. He had specially come after work to see the artefact his dad had told him about and to drive them to Schiphol the following morning.

Reading over her shoulder, Hans' unruly mop of longish light ash blond hair, close to his mother's long dark hair tied up in a French roll, made them an odd pair.

"This email advert gets to me. Why do people get so... I had every intention of joining this healing workshop."

"Why do you need to attend a healing workshop?"

"Sweety, I'd like to experience what it is like to participate in a workshop now and then. It helps me to be in that space, listening to other facilitators. Last week, I received a fascinating email about a 'hands-on' healer. His course combines bio-energetic healing with brainwave technology. It sounded interesting. The person came with great credentials, but now I'm unsure."

She typed a flow of words in reply. Hans was still behind her, looking at her screen. At moments like this, when she reacted, she could almost type faster than she could speak. Knowing that her strong willpower was often her greatest enemy, she would probably regret what she'd said or written in the spur of the moment.

"Mom, let me first read what you are reacting to before you send it."

"Yeah, yeah, I'm reacting, aren't I?"

While Hans was reading, she was distracted by the bright flashing adverts on the email's sidebar. Those were indeed a giveaway. The sender even wanted to earn money through his emails!

"Mom, why do you subscribe to those newsletters?"

"I didn't. At least, I don't think so, but it came from Dirk, your uncle's pilot, so I opened it."

His mother didn't tolerate fools or dishonest people easily, so he was surprised since this email promotion smacked of competitiveness, which he had no time for.

"Hans, why do people need to advertise themselves like that?"

From: Dirk van der Linden

To: mailing list

Subject: Certified Human Anatomy, Physiology and Pathology Course.

A high Adept of the Healing Council of Orion, the Ashram of Lord Rama, will present a profound healing manual never offered to humanity.

The copy in the email was full of unbelievable promises. The bold-coloured text in the paragraph and the words used were all geared to convince the reader of the opportunity of a lifetime.

As Hans read her lengthy reply, Annelies needed to stretch, trying to scan his mind. Her body felt stiff, being chair-bound. She held a vision of a brisk walk around her garden.

Dear Dirk.

I was genuinely interested in the healing course, but for the one sentence, 'a high Adept of the Healing Council of Orion and the Ashram of Lord Rama.' that did it for me. I've decided against it.

Gosh, Dirk, Anton's earthly qualifications were enough for me, so why the rest? Many people already know DNA and light activations, healing and shifting resistant patterns and aligning the body and mind to our Soul's purpose. Many are interested in science and spirituality, but to advertise that he is highly adept at the healing council of Orion and the Ashram of Lord Rama is fiction or a new age term that gives our alternative way of thinking a bad name!

Let's get grounded, I say.

Every human is already a being of light operating simultaneously on a higher frequency of Light in another dimension of consciousness. We are spiritual light beings! Yes, many of us love the paintings and drawings that reflect mystical worlds that might include ascended masters who have fully awakened while living in a human body. Why is that? Is it because they are our mirrors? Who knows?

Can't we leave the metaphysical hierarchy and mumbo jumbo out of our ascension process? It was probably created by the very people (in or out of embodiment) who failed their ascension. Was it maybe to glorify themselves? Who knows. Again, I strongly feel that we give our psychic power away by doing that.

Dirk, I know you only advertise what people send you, but I felt I must be true to myself and express my reasons for not attending.

I wish Anton all the success with his workshop, and I'm sure he is as dedicated as they come. Please tell him that his human credentials are enough for me.

PS: I have full permission from the Healing Council of Sirius to say so.

"Gee, here I am, going on about nothing while you visit us. I never learn, do I, losing my temper through a simple email instead of beaming forgiveness." Hans kept silent but projected: "Stop snooping into my thoughts, Mom; you don't need to know everything,"

"Are you going to send it?"

"Probably not, but it felt good to write it."

"Really, how so?"

She leaned over Hans's shoulder, grasped her mouse, and moved the email into her draft folder.

"I know, I was reacting to something within me. It's my mirror, and I should know better."

"Mom, do I hear you feeling guilty because you should know better? You know that everyone can collect what he calls bio-energy to heal. Some use Ether instead of bio-energy, which is plentiful in the universe."

"I know that, but not all people know their abilities. Here is someone who projects some exclusivity. That gets to me." As an afterthought, she deleted her email.

"Mom, why are you reacting?"

"I suppose I don't feel I have worthy credentials myself. Thanks for reminding me." She telepathically replied while hugging him.

Her love and respect for her adopted son knew no bounds. The moment that she and Ben brought him home and became his adoptive parents, Hans filled their lives with joy. He turned out to indeed be a gift during her darkest moments. Often, during their marriage, when she and Ben argue over something, Hans is the gift that helps them get on with their lives.

"Hans, just now, I had an amazing Déjà vu. I heard the wind speaking. Is that ridiculous? It was as clear to me as when we spoke to each other. I can only ask you that. Dad would get worried that I've lost it, but you might have a different opinion."

It was windy outside, but had she truly heard words like: *"You have broken my spirit!"*

Her question to Hans was out before she could stop herself.

Hans was peering at her." Her body felt stiff even when standing. She had been sitting at her computer too long. Not that she got very far with her assignment since her decoding workbook had taken up most of her time.

"Mom, we were taught that the mysteries of every inhabitable planet, the laws, elements, and powers of that universe would be epitomized in the human constitution on Earth, meaning that everything outside of man had its analogue within."

Hans was staying for supper, so she should be in the kitchen preparing dinner, but his explanation was so confusing she had to ask:

"What you are implying is that what I heard was coming from within my energy field, my universe?"

"I remember talking about how even the angelic beings from Vulcan could only understand a small part of the incredible glory that was the origin of all things. When people have divine inspirations, they can temporarily overcome their limitations and glimpse the celestial brightness surrounding all creation."

Hans had a faraway look when he turned to face her. His flow of words was difficult to understand.

"So, what are you saying?" Hans had taken her seat because she was about to leave the office.

"Mom, your mind picked up on a timeless wavelength, and your brain interpreted it into words for you. I'm sure you will understand the meaning behind those words if you are eager enough to understand them."

She was still frowning at Hans' rather tricky explanation. Could that not be simpler?

"Mom, your spiritual nature is your visible material personality's invisible cause and controlling power. Thus, it is evident that your spirit bears the same relationship to your material body as the universal matrix of the objective universe. There is no separation, remember."

She shook her head in dismay. Hans's perception of their reality has gone over her head for now. Instead, she had better start preparing a meal for the two favourite men in her life. She left him at her computer since he wanted to look at his emails.

Joris must have heard her pottering about. He was trying to get her attention because he was getting in the way.

Hans was right; the star map they uncovered hidden inside a double wall of the Prinsegracht Hotel undeniably proved that all human beings are interconnected on an energy level. Her pondering while preparing dinner took her back some years to the moment when she had read the following text at the back of the star map...."**I am your idea, and you will be looking for me one day, but I will be gone.**"

Apeldoorn 2008

During the renovations to the Prinsegracht Hotel, previously an orphanage, her brother Fred and her friend Theo had been pulling away layers of old wallpaper, wondering what they would find underneath. When the men had gone for a coffee break, she had pulled at the last layers, only to find a long tube stuck in a hole made in the old brick wall. The tube was the kind used to hold maps.

The mystery that old maps often evoke stimulated her curiosity, so she broke the seal and pulled out a canvas painting, not a map at all.

Theo and Fred called her from the newly built dining room, telling her that her coffee was getting cold, but she had been mesmerised by the sentence on the back of the large oil painting:

'I am your idea, and one day you will be looking for me, but I will be gone.

The artwork had an Egyptian flavour due to the winged part bird, part human figure on top. Two big eyes below a round yin yang symbol at the top centre, between the eyebrows, made Annelies think of the third eye. The flat figurine balanced on the big bold 1888 added a mysterious flavour. Below the number spreading sideways, a map-like pattern of shooting stars took up the rest of the large canvas. What was the most startling for her was that she had seen this painting before.

It took a while for her to recall why the painting looked so familiar and suddenly created a déja-vu moment for her since she had never seen it in the flesh, not as far as she could remember.

Theo and Fred were equally curious about what the painting meant when they returned from their coffee break. Theo was interested since he had studied ancient Egyptian history, language, literature, and religious practice, but his major field was archaeology. He was a colleague of Trevor Zwiegelaar, a relation of Ben. They were both Egyptologists.

Fred knew a lot about old maps. For the last ten years, he had been an expert on ancient maps while running an antiquarian bookshop named The Power of Words in Apeldoorn. Her brother's private studies had shaped his philosophy similarly to Ben's twin brother Leo, the evolutionary biologist and genetic scientist of the Jaarsma Clan.

The map became the centrepiece of their conversations in her home in Apeldoorn, about 50 mi/80 km east of Amsterdam. Apeldoorn is still a reasonably large city with a relatively small business centre. It was situated on the edge of the Veluwe and surrounded by beautiful woods.

She had the painting framed between two layers of glass. The painting had no relation to the oldest known star map she had found online. It recorded a chronological study of a genetic lineage of the births that had taken place in two affiliated orphanages: the one in France, just over the border near Limburg, and the other in Apeldoorn.

They could all trace their birth chart and gradually unravelled their parents, grandparents, marriages, and children from these unions, and why finding the people who were now alive during these transition times was essential. With the help of Fred, Leo, Theo and Trevor's insights, she gradually combined their knowledge with the information she had received while living in South Africa.

The star map implied a revelation, especially about their own genetic and soul lineages on an individual spiritual level. All her genetic decoding workshops had evolved from these discoveries.

Apeldoorn January

Dinner was almost ready. She hoped it would be palatable because her mind had not been on her cooking. Gosh, so much has happened since she started giving her genetic decoding workshops. Looking back, she now knew that the star map contained the accounts, combined with the order of time, from 1888 until the presence of the incarnated group soul lineage of the Jaarsma Clan. She still saw each individual's genealogical and reincarnation map as an energy field divided into a grid pattern. It was through decoding this that her ascension workshops had been born.

Now, the time had arrived for all the research behind her workshops in a decoding workbook.

The howling wind outside and Joris' urge for her to feed him snapped her back to thinking about what to prepare for dessert.

Ben popped his head around the door and asked when dinner was ready. He had finished packing, telling her he had brought the metallic-looking artefact with the papyrus scroll found at Leo and Trevor's archaeological site in France into their lounge. Hans had promised to return it to his uncle Trevor the next day....

"What is Hans doing in our office?" Ben asked. His favourite working-around-the-house clothes made him look trendy compared to his business suits.

"Looking at his email."

"Mmm...How far did you get with your journal?" Ben washed his hands under the kitchen tap as if he was scrubbing before surgery.

"I've started but never imagined it would be so difficult."

"Really?" Ben turned to face her while drying his hands.

"I thought that you, of all people, would have no problem. You write for the website all the time and have given the decoding workshop so often; what do you find difficult?"

"To stay honest, I suppose."

"Joris, come inside, now!" Ben spoke in a demanding tone. "Gosh, I could have sworn I saw a bluebird in the trees, but it can't be. Holland has never had any sightings of bluebirds. Ben's comment about the bluebird reminded her of something she had heard. "Was that what he was barking at?"

"No idea, but I'm not going out again to see. There you are." Joris came rushing in as if he were fleeing from something.

"And now?"

Joris was panting from sheer fright. She stared at Ben, who was just as puzzled.

"He must have seen a ghost or something. There is nobody out there," Ben once again peered outside the back door. Except for the howling wind and the rain, nobody was there.

"Oh, I think I know what is troubling him."

"What?"

"You will not believe me or take me seriously when I tell you." Joris' memory must have a short timeline since he was now happily eating dinner.

"Come on, tell me."

It was so uncanny to explain that she experienced moments as if she was in a timeless zone. Flashes of the past or future rolled into one. It was a weird sensation. She wondered if there was something she should be worried about.

"When I was in the office writing, I heard a loud crash, so I got up to see." Ben was waiting for the punch line.

"I heard the wind saying: *You have broken my spirit.*"

Ben raised his eyebrows but kept quiet; then he shook his head.

"Oh, Annie, please, we have not done such a thing. Humanity might have collectively, that could be true, but do you think Joris heard that as well?"

"He heard something or somebody. I'm sure. I'm glad he will stay with Ingrid and Toon while we are touring in South Africa."

Gosh, she suddenly had a déja-vu feeling again. How strange. It was as if she had said it before..."Oh, forget it." She scolded herself when gooseflesh trailed down her spine.

"Ben, please close the door and call Hans while I dish up dinner. I'm looking forward to walking in the sunshine in two days."

"Are you packed?" He asked. At that moment, a weird feeling came over her again, as if she knew he would ask her that. Ben's question had happened before, another déja-vu.

"Mostly, apart from my laptop and handbag."

Ben closed the door and peered into the pan on the stove. Then he picked up her decoding folder, knowing what it was about....

"This is your workbook, not so?"

She knew what he would ask ... "When did you write this about the bluebirds?"

A chill ran down her spine. Was she losing it? She grabbed her folder to have a look. There it was; she had typed it but couldn't remember when or why.

I don't recall when I wrote that, but you said just now that you saw a bluebird not so?" "I know what you are going to say next." She beamed

Ben frowned, looking up..."I wonder if it is an omen?"

"You said it, just as I knew you would."

"I'm serving dinner. Let's forget about bluebirds." Oh gosh, something was strange. She couldn't remember when or why she added that comment about bluebirds in her first chapter.

"It will come to you; it always does."

Ben returned her folder and telepathically warned Hans that his dinner would get cold.

After dinner, Hans returned to his parent's office, but he had mentally overheard his parents questioning what the symbol of a bluebird stood for. He knew that the natural habitat of the bluebird is open fields, prairies, and meadows with few trees or shrubs. The bluebird seemed to have materialized in Holland, where they don't usually appear because the realms between the time zones were merging.

The wind spoke the story of the bluebird, revealing to him that planet Earth was created to host lifestreams connected to the universal Matrix. This Matrix is like a school for Creator Gods of light.

He and Liesbeth were Interplanetary walk-ins, ready to prepare and guide the Jaarsma Clan towards inter-dimensional realities....

Hans Jaarsma

He stretched his long, thin body under his mother's office desk, recalling when he knew that as an earthling, at least in body, he would never be like an Earth human.

Hans knew that he was an oddball. Others saw him as a somewhat aloof character with no real ambition except to express his wit and humour while serving his time on Earth. Lately, life has become more attractive. Occasionally, he would still get involved in the intricacy of 'being human on Earth', but never for long. After all, he hadn't lost his ability to see other worlds parallel to this one, even if his human mind had distorted other twin realities into fractals. Being simultaneously aware was often troublesome. To experience the level of awareness that most humans held onto, which was a limiting cognition through the sensory organs, he had to be both an individual and view the collective with the totality of the infinite.

Hans understood that his adoptive mother learned early in life that dishonesty could give or cause problems. What troubled her most were people's hidden agendas. Like himself, she also knew what was happening in people's minds. He loved her dearly, and she was never domineering over him as long as he communicated verbally or mentally about what he wanted from her. Then, she was as mild as a kitten.

He was equally proud of his adopted dad, who was often away on an undercover assignment but stayed integrity in his conduct towards his colleagues in the police force.

He knew that he was an interplanetary soul who incarnated as a 'walk-in' instead of entering this reality through birth, but he never knew that there was a term for it. He needs to inquire with Liesbeth whether she thinks their story should included in Annelie's journal. He remembered who he was before he 'walked in'. He was ten years old, or at least his human body temple, when the memories of his natural home started to penetrate his daily awareness on the school playground.... He should share his experiences in Liesbeth's journal.

He looked back at His Mom's computer screen because her moving screen saver, SMALL THINGS MAKE BIG CHANGES, held the key to part of her success or failure. Her own emotions, locked away by the grief she held onto in this lifetime, were just a mirror reflecting great suffering from previous incarnations. Many of her readers would feel empathy and hopefully release useless distortions from their energy field. Her major pain-body had surfaced, especially now that she was writing her awakening journal. These distorted cellular memory codes had to be released. He was not allowed to interfere too much before the time was right, but now that she had finally started on her journal, he knew what she would discover during her assignment.

Hans knew what was still to come, but it was not for him to remind her that what is not actual can never become real if she didn't give it any power. He knew the prophet's game rules.

He saw on her taskbar that she had written an article for the website titled: Are we living during the end of times[1]? That powerful statement alone made him wonder how deeply his mother's mind had reached into the shadowy corners of her emotional filing system. He would read her article. Her office was already showing signs of clearing out. The chilly temperature added an empty, hollow feeling.

When Ben and Annelies returned from their overseas trip, they decided to leave Holland for good after the latest incident when his Dad had been attacked. Knowing what was ahead of them, Hans hoped that together with Liesbeth, his life partner, he would be able to protect them without interfering. Many dark shadow entities would aim to prevent them from clearing out distorted genetic codes. That was probably going to be challenging, especially for Liesbeth. She was far more emotionally affected, being a woman.

He sat down again to look at his email because he had left his iPhone at his flat. Through Google, he could link to his Gmail account. Several emails had come into his inbox. He would read them later on his cell phone, especially the one from Trevor, his biological dad, although no one knew that. Ben and Annelies were to find that out in due course.

He knew where the artefact and the papyrus scroll his dad had brought home came from. The scroll could be perceived as a recorded library book containing ancient Sumeria's information. The author was a member of the Jaarsma lineage during the Akhenaton dynasty. The rock told a very different story. It had the twenty-two necessary genetic codes that would restore humanity's original immortal body blueprint, and that alone could shatter the scientific community. This technology would become critical without changing the genotype.

---

1. https://nadinemay.com/2013/12/20/are-we-living-through-the-end-of-times/

Unsubstantiated discoveries were ignored, but a great awakening became imminent as humanity approached the final stage of its evolution—each person who still perceives him or herself as a separate individual instead of their I. has little time left to wake up. The distorted thought forms now rife will keep them trapped, or somewhat asleep, due to the persona (EGO)program outside the extracellular[2] substance embedded in tissue cells.

"You will not be alone, as you know." His teacher had said.

When he finds Liesbeth, he recognises her as Tulanda, who joined him in fulfilling her assignment. His and Liesbeth's mission had started in earnest.

During the following years, the speeding up of time would create havoc around the planet when the cloak between time zones disappeared.

Together, they wrote the article: 'Can we break the death habit?'[3] to prepare as many visitors as possible.

He was about to get up from behind the PC when Annelie's screen saver changed to the word Forgiveness, and after a few bounces, that word became another symbol of light. Unconditional Love. His mom wanted to be reminded of the ten most powerful Soul qualities, so she made it a screensaver. Not a bad idea. Most of his mother's traumas in life and the feelings that surrounded them must have already flared up. He knew that more distorted belief programming was still blocking her true potential and would come to the surface. Her journal writing would do that, and he was not allowed to interfere. That was his lesson, to stay at all times in the moment. His mother's cellular awakening probably started with the kidnapping saga they had all heard about on New Year's Eve.

---

2. https://www.merriam-webster.com/dictionary/extracellular

3. https://nadinemay.com/book-illustrations/lightworkers-articles/liesbeth-tulanda-a-walk-in/liesbeths-articles/can-we-break-the-death-habit/

Times were now speeding up. He knew the artefact his dad brought home was meant for his mother. She was the holder of the Body Codes of Light, but she had not yet realised that fact.

He would drive them to the airport the next day, but before his parents would once again set foot on the oldest continent on the planet, it was essential to unlock Annelies' memory codes. The metallic key that had come up from deep within the Earth's iron core had surfaced for a reason, as with the papyrus scroll found nearby in the underground tunnels in France. Both he and Liesbeth knew what it was about.

His elders knew she would be ready to receive the awakening codes when his mother asked how humanity had lost its multidimensional awareness.

The catastrophic events predicted that the collective mind of humanity would soon experience would bring up primary post-traumatic stress syndrome in many people. His mother's Soul motivation code stood for the soul quality of forgiveness. How very appropriate. He knew she had received the interpretations through her email, or so she thought.

He knew that only certain chosen ones could work with crystals, and they had to meditate for several years before they were even allowed to touch a crystal skull. His mother, in her past life, had earned that privilege. She had become a great Healer and Priestess who knew the secret of the magical Dragon: to keep the Earth and the people in balance.

When his Dad told him what an effect the artefact had on his mom, he felt the need to ask her herself before they embarked on their journey to South Africa.

He opened the page where she had stored the transmissions. His mom had typed in her decoding workbook: There are 22 keynotes anyone must embody to achieve immunity during cellular transformation. For my Soul Motivation vibration code, I've chosen Forgiveness.

Her Soul Motivation Code 1-Forgiveness[4]

For her Body Codes of Light workbook, she copied the text for her inline 22 body codes of light. So, this information was going to be separately published online.

The last paragraph in italics seems to be his mom's telepathic notes meant for her journal. Hans shifted out of his reverie when Liesbeth telepathically told him that she and Tieneke had arrived at Half-way House in France. He'd better join his parents in the living room for dinner.

Chapter 3
Unconditional Love Quality

Apeldoorn – January

Annelies looked up at Hans, thin, wiry, quick and agile, and with a constantly moving body, as he joined her in the lounge. She loved his unruly mop of thick, ash-blond, almost silver hair that Liesbeth threatened to cut very short. His expressive, very blue eyes, surrounded by skin colour as if he had spent his entire day on a surfboard, gave him an almost angelic look.

"Were there any emails from Liesbeth? Not that I think you two need to email each other."

"Where's dad?"

Ben was outside inspecting the damage caused by the storm and checking if something had scared Joris. They were all aware that the weather patterns were drastically changing. Much colder and more extreme, but for them, the rising sea levels were a serious concern. Toon predicted this could become problematic for Holland because 50% of the Dutch population lived at or below sea level!

"Please come inside, Ben; Joris is scratching the door paint. I'm sure the next owners will see that when they move in!"

A strong whooshing wind came rushing in when Ben closed the sliding door to the patio. Gosh, she had to grab the vase of flowers to prevent it from falling.

"Don't tell me we are heading for an ice age."

"It feels like it, but no, I don't think so," Ben replied as he stamped his boots. For years, she remembered playing in the snow during January and February, but the rising sea levels were a different story. "Now, Mom, tell me your visions from the Matelic artefact. Dad told me that they had upset you?"

She looked at Ben's short, wet hair that had matted to his head as he ran his hands through it. His eyes were a striking blue no matter what he was thinking. She was still shivering from the cold air that had blown in. In a few days, she would feel the sunshine. Although some packing was still waiting for her, she started to look forward to spending these coldest times in South Africa, where it would be lovely and warm.

"Yes, when I woke up this morning, I was still having fear attacks." It still amazed her how feelings somehow seemed to cross different realities quicker than mental images.

"I think that my dreams were affected by the rock, but that was at first just my idea. I wasn't sure then, but now I understand more."

"Were you aware that your mind had seen visions while you were holding the artefact Dad brought home? I know that was the plan for you to get some information from it."

"Yes, probably. It directed me or brought on a strong hunch. It might sound crazy, but it felt like it was messing with time."

"What do you mean?" Ben asked

How was she going to put it into words that there were moments that felt like being timeless? "I don't know how to verbalise it."

"Please, Mom, try; it's important."

"OK, as I was closing down, it started buzzing. Creepy, as if it was alive."

"Why didn't you call me?" Ben called out. He was packing his hand luggage at the dining room table in the far corner of the lounge.

"You were already fast asleep."

"Last night, instead of directly accessing anything from the artefact, my mind projected visions as if I was looking into the past that had created the future, or so I thought."

"You mean it felt like a prophecy?" Ben suggested.

"If a prophecy is an emanation sent forth by a higher being through the medium of my intellect, then yes, it is possible. I know that my mind projects my visions, but still, I question what is real and what is not."

"Nothing is real, Mom, so ultimately, all thoughts that portray a dysfunctional world are meaningless since every split away from the ultimate Godhead seems to create more levels within the realities where separation is experienced. It could have been a vision from the Earth's causal plane."

"Do you mean that each reality bubble we create is still united in a unified causal realm, accessed in our dream state?" She always could ask Hans difficult questions. His replies were always original. Hans got up and walked around the lounge. He could never sit still for long. His long legs seem to need movement.

"Every created universe fragmented further into galaxies, each evolving. In our world on Earth, where duality is at its peak, even within our mental illusions, our reality bubbles can be seen as having many levels within that fragmentation. It all depends on the awareness level that each vibrates towards."

She needed to digest Hans' reply before she could carry on with such an intellectual discussion.

"Gosh Hans, yes, that does make sense. Everyone on our planet is like a universe, another closed system."

"Now you've both lost me. How can I see myself as being a universe?" Ben's response alerted Joris, who started to wag his tail. They all laughed.

"Look at his innocent face. Is that not pure love looking at us?" Annelies cuddled him as he was about to jump on the leather couch.

"No, Joris, that is not allowed, you know that."

"Does he?"

"Yes, Ben, I'm sure he does. I know you keep quiet when he sneaks onto the couch, pretending nobody sees him, but he knows it the moment I come into the room, don't you, Joris?"

The young Labrador knew all adored him.

"Mom, what were your visions all about? You still have not told us." Hans sat down again, studying her with his bright blue eyes. Her aura was subdued, as if she could not deal with something that had shocked her.

"At first, I think...the metal object, while holding it, showed a glimpse of our future. Visions, especially driving between massive domes where people had formed whole communities....then they changed...."

"The second vision somehow left me with a great deal of anxiety."

"Did both visions feel like being in the future to you?" Ben asked, raising his eyebrows while Hans was in thought. They were both eager to hear what she had picked up from the mysterious, heavy, round Matelic-like keystone, which seemed to have an alien feel.

"What was its message? Can you remember?"

"Hans, it's always the same, like you said at the dinner table on New Year's Eve. It felt like It's all to do with 'programs' stored in the nucleus of our body cells."

Last night, Ben had pushed a heavy metallic-looking rock Leo had given him carefully across her desk. Ben was warned not to touch the artefact unnecessarily in case it distorted her vision. Leo had researched its origin for days and was convinced it was otherworldly.

Annelies' psychic ability to sense or 'read' the history of an object by touching it was well known to her family. She had ignored the warning by countering, "What could happen to her?" because her intuitive nature told her to pick it up. She was stunned at the weight and ice-cold surface.... Then the rock started vibrating...She had almost dropped the rock from pure creepiness.

Ben explained how it had come into his possession and why he had left her alone and gone to bed.

The silence in the lounge brought her attention back to both her listeners. They were waiting for her story....

Then she told them of her experience.... They didn't interrupt her.

"As I was holding the artefact, it started buzzing. When the vibrations travel through my arm into my body, and the tingling sensation travels up and down my spine, it is as if a drug has taken hold of me." She knew that letting go would not be an option.

Then, she saw herself standing in front of a massive stone door. In the centre was a hollow that she knew held the key to the science of healing....

She had been sealed off from the world above so she would be alone. She, the priestess, would be buried alive unless she could find the key to discover the secret of immortality. If she failed, she would die a pauper's death.

She then heard the words of the teacher...

"The key is hidden around all physical bodies, but owing to the shortness of human's lifespan and the length of the work that will awaken the light from within, my symbolic art, originally revealed to man, has been sealed forever."

Somehow, she knew that she had failed and died alone from starvation.... She had no idea if she could have found the secret, so the feeling of despair stayed with her until she fell asleep....

Both men were looking at her in awe. Ben might have been somewhat sceptical at first. She couldn't blame him for that, although he once told her that his twin brother Leo knew of many drugs that stimulated hallucinations, so he shouldn't be all that sceptical. Lately, they had discovered that the mysterious clinic near Halfway House was using psychedelic drugs on people. It was the same clinic where they had found her half-brother Toon's wife, Ingrid.

Hans knew what she had experienced had come to her at just the right moment. He said so to his dad, which helped. Ben had great regard for Hans' unusual psychic knowingness.

"Was that it?" Hans asked.

"So, if we can maintain our awareness levels and understand what it means, we would not only change our own lives but influence much of what others experience around us not so? Potentially, we could all activate the shift that will change humanity's outcome." Ben said after mulling over Annelie's story.

"Hans, it was as if...it was life?"

Instead of following Ben to their bedroom last night, she gently rested the artefact on Ben's side of the desk. She had a strong hunch when restarting her computer. Her psychometry skills had left her with a feeling of urgency. She knew or had strong feelings that, somehow, her brainwaves were picking up information related to her decoding structure. She intuitively knew she needed to trust her inner intuition. Was this a test?

Her soul quality number was the vibration of six, the quality of Christ's force of unconditional love. She knew it to be necessary, so she should include it in her journal. How Liesbeth would re-edit her journal was not up to her.

She read her interpretations of the number six vibration, taken from her workbook, but suddenly, the artefact she had placed on Ben's desk started to glow. Before she could forget the words she heard as a whisper, she started typing them into her separate file, **The 22 Body Codes of Light.**[1]

She was unaware of being an initiate, but after her mental impressions, which was like hearing a whisper, she again tried to get an impression by letting her fingers caress the ridges of the metallic-looking stone while concentrating. Instead of the vibration she had felt before, it now felt like just a lump of heavy metal. It stayed silent....

She left the men in the lounge while she cleared the table in the dining room. Tomorrow, they will be dining on the plane.

It always helped when she heard others voicing their understanding of topics such as theirs. There were so many ways to perceive what they experienced as being accurate.

"That doesn't sound so bad, that is if that was the message, Annie," Ben commented when both men joined her in the kitchen.

They still lived well despite the economic depression and the fact that there was no longer any income from the Hotel. Ben's early pension paid the bills. She intuitively knew that life on Earth, how they knew it, would change, but how that would work out was still unclear. Now that France and Germany were also bankrupt, and Holland was close to it, the fact that the hotel had gone and the insurance claim would take years to settle made it almost a relief to be free of the work the hotel had created. She'd always wished for more time to devote to her ascension workshop project, and now she'd got it!

"Mom, why do you have feelings of anxiety?" Hans asked, back in the kitchen.

She switched on the dishwasher while Hans carried a tray of coffee and stroopwafels into the lounge. Lately, she had been wondering if she should make significant diet changes. The way they ate could not be that healthy.

"Hans. I'm not sure, but somehow, I feel there's still a dark force trying to sabotage my intent, and I wonder how they achieved that.

---

1. https://allrealityshifters.wordpress.com/the-22-body-codes-of-light-level-5/

I know that is impossible because nothing is real, so why should I react like I did?"

Hans didn't immediately respond to her question, but she sensed something

"Maybe because the future only exists as a morphogenetic field of possibilities, and our actions in the present create it moment by moment. Was that also part of the message?" Hans asked.

"I'm not sure. I need to give that some more thought."

"Oh dear, what is a morphogenetic field?" Ben asked.

"Dad, it's a field of energy of a certain frequency, created by all visible and invisible living species within and on our planet. It's our immortal body of light. All living species, man, animal and plant, have consciousness, and Dad was warned not to touch the artefact unnecessarily in case it distorted Mom's visions. Leo had researched its origin for days and was convinced it was otherworldly."

"Oh, so...is there a link between the relationships of morphogenetic fields and our memory and intelligence?" Annelies summed up, thinking of the inner voice she had heard coming from the artefact that had surfaced from the bowels of the Earth.

"Yes, there is. Our brains may not contain memories and knowledge, per se. Still, scientists will soon develop devices for tuning in to relevant sections of our morphogenetic, etheric fields around our human body. That is what the artefact must have done with Mom."

That was a thought. Both Ben and herself would have to think that through.

"Explain that to me further?" She asked

"This morphogenetic field could have affected Mom's neurological network that controls her memory files."

"You mean...a bit like the one hundred monkey syndrome. When a hundred monkeys learn a new trick, others on different continents follow the same behaviour?" Ben was perceiving this energy field differently than she did.

"Oh, Dad, you are more evolved than a monkey, but yes, theoretically, the memories of every human, ...and other entities, ... would be available to anyone capable of tuning into their sixth-dimensional energy fields."

"Even rocks, boulders or crystals?" Ben winked at her.

"Mom remembers that the true mind of human beings is part of the cosmic intelligence that pervades nature, but due to artificial intelligence infiltration, we know how easy it is to be sabotaged or even occupied by another mind."

"Did Trevor translate the engraved text from the ancient scroll?" She asked, knowing both men corresponded with her father's younger brother.

"Only the sections Richard and Ingrid had received," Ben replied. Both men perched on the breakfast counter stools as she finished her kitchen duties.

She loved those conversations because they stimulated her intellectually. She knew that it was nothing compared to her psychometry experiences, authentic or not accurate, that was different. In all its many forms, the word consciousness may be the primary playing field of human evolution. So, were they evolving? She hoped so.

"Okay, so you are implying that if all people thought and acted similarly, this would create a field of similarity for all people?" Ben's question promptly gave her an aha moment.

"That's it. Morphogenetic fields play a great role in the idea that when humanity, at one point in time, goes through a dramatic collective shift in consciousness, we evolve as a united species."

Hans smiled but kept silent.

Joris kept nudging her with his cold nose against her legs as if to say. "Where is my dinner?" he was always hungry like a puppy.

When she cleared the dishwasher, both men offered to help. It was a nice gesture, but she would rather they stayed where they were, perched on the high chairs at the kitchen counter.

"Dad, there are many different morphogenetic fields that have contributed to the creation of the world we are experiencing now, which, as we know, is caught between the polarity of good and bad."

That was an understatement, thinking back to all the criminal activities of the past year, not to mention what had happened to her fourteen years ago in South Africa.

"Annie, why did you say each individual is a universe, a closed system?" Ben asked while helping himself to the last stroopwafel in the packet on the counter. Had she said that?

"Mmm, it seems that the secret of immortality is encoded within the nucleus of our body cells." Gosh, was it not the message she had heard intuitively?

"There are different people and groups who are different in their thoughts and actions. Because of this diversity, there are many different morphogenetic fields, or as I call them, reality bubbles. I thought of the human body because I am working on my genetic decoding workbook. It makes sense why distorted thought forms play a role in our lives."

"Mom, that is an interesting angle regarding healing."

"Why so?"

"Well, our physical bodies are only an aspect of what we truly are. In reality, we are beings of light and energy, but you know that. "

"Hans, that might be true, but I also thought that our physical bodies don't exist, that everything is an illusion. I don't grasp that concept, but you have often mentioned it." Ben chipped in.

"Well, let's say that our bodies, and we have several, are shaped by our human consciousness, which is a duality-orientated thinking device. Our etheric body still vibrates in the fourth dimension because our thoughts and intentions symbolically create a cause-and-effect pattern, but it is still holographic. It's still a hallucination. It's to do with how our minds make us perceive space and time."

After Hans' rather intellectual reply, all she saw in her mind's eye was a grid sheet from her workbook with the twenty-two spacings. "Annie, what did POWAH tell you about these times?" Ben asked. The very name POWAH made her recall how long ago she had experienced having her higher guide around her all the time. As a young child, she was introduced to an infinite light being. Not that she knew that at the time. To her, this being of light was an angel that grownups talked about. She knew intuitively she was part of this great light being, but this knowledge was more like an emotion. She had no words for the feeling. As a child, this egg-shaped luminous ball looked like a lady, but as she grew older, the 'she' became more of a 'he'. When she learned to read and write, the tune of this light entity sounded like the word POWAH, so she gave her guide this name.

"POWAH said that we must study the twenty-two clues he left behind. They show us that there are special moments when we must be alert. Only then can we awaken the energy map of our life? Only then can we awaken our trapped intentions. I didn't understand intellectually what that meant, but somehow I knew it to be true."

"Mom, there you have it. POWAH always used the number 22 in all his interactions with us. Ingrid received 22 excerpts, Richard found 22 tablet translations, and you have reminded yourself about what POWAH hinted at. Then we know what the Jaarsma star map has shown us: that every number interpretation will help individuals to be alert and aware of the fabric of the everyday world that seems extraneous to the interaction of the moment."

"What are they? I mean the twenty-two clues, do you know?"Ben asked. "

"No, not really. It's a genetic trigger of some sort. But I'm sure I will grasp it by the time I've finished the journal, hopefully with the help of Liesbeth." She winked at Hans.

"Mom, you have to write it independently; Liesbeth will only transform it into a script like a story. Like she has done for Ingrid and Richard, but you know that."

Both Ben and herself had heard Hans' thoughts about her assignment. According to instructions from POWAH, she had encouraged Ingrid and later Richard to write down their experiences in the first and second stages of awakening. They all experienced both levels, but the ascension card game required documentation for each of its five stages.

"But, when you read Ingrid and Richard's journals, they have already participated in your mother's workshops, as if you have already finished your workbook, Annie."

"Dad and mom still have to write down whatever is important to her, but in our higher self reality, we have already done the work."

They both looked at Hans for further explanation.

"Sweety, why did Liesbeth imply that I have finished my workbook? You mean it's because our time concepts are an illusion, so everything happens simultaneously?"

That reminded her that she still needed to pack her laptop away to work on her journal and workbook during their three-week stay in South Africa.

"Yes, Mom, you've got it. Liesbeth rewrote the journals into novels outside of Earth's time. She did that for a good reason. You, of all people, should know that. Remember what happened on New Year's Eve? I'm off to bed. Dad, we have to be up early, remember."

Hans would stay in the spare bedroom because he would drive them to Schiphol Airport in Amsterdam the following day. Ben went to their bedroom, and she went to her office to close her computer and pack her laptop to take with her on her trip.

The episode during that New Year's Evening again played repeatedly in her mind....

New Year's Eve.

All her favourite family and friends had come to celebrate New Year's Eve. So much had changed in the lives of everyone that evening. That evening, Ben told her he had booked two air tickets to South Africa.

*"Where are your thoughts? I have beamed and beamed, but nobody was home!"*Ben beamed from their bedroom

When she was daydreaming back in time, she had blocked him mentally. *"I'll be up soon. I've let Joris out for his last pee while I pack my handbag."*

It was wise that they both had a good night's sleep before a long flight, but after their conversation with Hans, her mind had stayed active.

In a flash, her mind recalled when Ingrid, Richard and Liesbeth had joined her ascension workshop.

It felt like ages ago. It was incredible that everyone could trace their ancestral lineage through the star map. At the time, Ben had said that he had probably read somewhere on the internet how each person was, on average, only six steps away from knowing any other person on Earth.

She should be going to bed, but somehow, she had an intuition to Google it as if the artefact had urged her to investigate her hunch.

She opened her browser to see if she could type in: Six degrees of separation. Lots of options came up. She clicked on the Wikipedia page. Above the heading, she read an interesting sentence:

SixDegrees.org is about using the idea that we are all connected to accomplish something good. I hope Six Degrees will soon be more than a game or a gimmick. It will also be a force for good by bringing a social conscience to social networking.

"Annie, when will you join me?"

"Soon, go to sleep." She was now wide awake.

Under the heading 'shrinking world' she read:

Any two people can be connected through a maximum of five acquaintances. The characters create a game out of this notion in their personal story. A sudden chill came over her. As if somehow she was made up by someone?... As if they were all part of a game!

Back in the kitchen, Hans explained about brainwaves and that if one holds an intent, what effect can that have on a person? We all unconsciously identify with our authentic selves, including conscious and unconscious elements in our working memory. Intent heals, he added. She had not understood his brainwave explanation, but now, the idea that she was part of a game, who then rolls the dice?

Last year, POWAH told her to compare her interpretations with Ingrid's excerpts and Richard's tablets, which they had both written about. What this six decrees idea had to do with her decoding still eluded her.

Annelies got up and took Ingrid and Richard's journals from her bookshelf. She had kept their manuscript for that very reason.

There it was: Ingrid had received excerpts but had no idea who had sent them to her. She always thought it was either Trevor or Leo who had found a way to hack into her computer at work. Not that she ever said that to her at the time.

She had questioned Hans about it after Ingrid and Toon's wedding. Toon told her that Ingrid had even received an excerpt while flying in his private plane! There it was. Their 'program' existed in every dimension simultaneously.

The metallic artefact began to buzz as if to say carry on. Gosh, was it alive? Why was Ben not here to observe this mysterious rock with her? She should have called him, but somehow, leaving the office was not appreciated!

"Okay, I hear you" She beamed at it as if it was alive.

There it was, excerpt three, but who had sent it to Ingrid?

Program Planet Earth[2]

Sound & Colour[3]

She clicked on the link and read POWAH's message online to Ingrid.

She returned Ingrid's manuscript and found Richard's when a paper fell out.

Tablet 3 with the link Sound is the Primary Basis for Creation[4]

What had POWAH implanted in her mind? Her soul quality number six must have something to do with it. That she was sure about.

Her Soul Quality Code.6-Unconditional love [5]

The sixth verse read: Ye who can visualize patterns in the night—will realise meanings that shall awaken thee to the truth of light. Wow, was that addressed to her?

At that instant, text appeared on her screen like before, as if someone had sent her a PowerPoint slide.

During her bath ritual last night, she meditated on the artefact, but this time, she asked her higher mind for guidance. She needed a good night's sleep without scary dreams.

When she turned off the light, Joris was already in his basket in the kitchen.

His tail wagged as if to say, "Good night."

The wind seemed to have quietened down. All the suitcases were in the hallway, so she added her laptop and hand luggage.

---

2. https://allrealityshifters.wordpress.com/powah/the-reality-shifters-excerpt-3/

3. https://allrealityshifters.wordpress.com/powah/the-reality-shifters-excerpt-3/

4. https://allrealityshifters.wordpress.com/richard-de-jong/tablet-3/

5. https://allrealityshifters.wordpress.com/the-22-body-codes-of-light-level-5/

She switched off all the lights downstairs, thinking that all the packing and preparing for their move away from Holland on the first of April when they returned from their holiday.

She looked forward to the trip. She had overheard Ben speaking to Toon earlier today, and it was something about a surprise.

As she climbed the stairs to their bedroom again, she wondered why she had awakened this morning with horrid feelings.

Then she remembered her dream from last night. She was glad that she had shared it with both men today.

Was the metallic artefact on her bedside table from the past or the future? No, she wouldn't go there again.

"Finally, Annie, may I remind you that we are not sleeping in a bed tomorrow night."

"Are you still awake?"

"Yes. I've been thinking about the artefact. Leo wanted to know every detail of whatever you could come up with or sense when you held it. He believes you know what secrets are in this unusual rock formation."

"Well, that might be, but having remembered that I was locked up in some underground dungeon with no way to get out was horrible. I hope I'm not having nightmares from it."

"Come to bed; you must be cold. What did you do with the rock? We must not leave it locked up in the house."

"I packed the artefact in a box for Hans to return to Trevor. It's on the floor near the front door." She replied our loud

"Good girl."

"I know, and we must get up early to check in at Schiphol at ten-thirty." She repeated what he had said earlier.

Ben switched off the light after she settled in bed next to him.

"Come, snuggle up. We will enjoy ourselves, and let's not think about all the preparations we need to do before we leave Holland for good. That can wait.

Chapter 4
The Higher Self Observer

Johannesburg – Cape Town

The ever-changing scenery of the South African landscape that flashed past the Rovos Rail train's windows reminded Annelies of the times when she had lived in the little village called the Hogsback. Travelling by train then was nothing like this....

The luxury coach did indeed live up to its reputation. The magnificence and splendour of their private suite reminded her of a movie. The finest bed linen, marble tiles, and gold fittings are in their en-suite bathroom with a shower. A huge double bed and a lounge area. The sheer luxury of it all was such a contrast to the real world out there.

Her reflection in the window was kind. She hadn't yet lost her gipsy look. Her long dark blond hair, casually held together by two long wooden pins, gave her an ageless appearance, not Dutch. Her trim, tall frame was the only part that gave away her ancestry. The way both Ingrid and Richard described her in their journals made her smile....

A flicker on her laptop announced an email. Being connected to the internet while travelling in style was handy. Instead of working on her decoding workbook, she opened the email.

FEEDBACK - ascensiontopics.com
Name: Dawn Meeuws
Email: DawnMee@gmail.com
Subject: Our Soul Purpose

Dear Annelies,

How does one know one's Soul Purpose? If we have all chosen what we want to experience, why is there turmoil and strife in the world? Rumours are going around that are unbelievably evil. Is it due to the final throes of negativity and destruction or the grounding of a new world in all its splendour and glory as heaven on earth? Do we not all play a part in the initial setup and act on it? I know our peace prayers are powerful, but sometimes I feel I'm living between different worlds in these times of great transformation.

Many thanks

Dawn

P.S. When can we follow your decoding formula online?

She knew all about living in between worlds. The so-called physical reality – the one her five senses instantly documented – and her psychic world that she accessed with her sixth sense—the infinite silence of reality within all, from where all creation originates.

Before she could honestly reply, she would have to come up with the right words. How should she verbalise the different realities and how various levels of reality exist within the mind, separated by several time frames, like multiple universes? Dawn, whom she didn't know, must have read the latest article:'The God/Goddess Within' published under her name.

Our two Higher Self and Guide Spacings[1]

After reading her online article, she had to read up on what she wrote. In her decoding workbook:

"The most important numeral tones are found in the fifth-level decodings. There are three vibration codes: Soul Purpose, Soul Motivation, and Soul Quality frequencies, followed by the two angelic tunes of the Higher Self and the Guide frequency codes."

If you intend to discover me's' riddle' or Game's' riddle'. It's the highest sound vibration of accumulated experiences you have chosen to reincarnate with at birth,

The idea behind the decoding exercises is that each individual should start to recall their Soul's experiences from this and other

---

1. https://allrealityshifters.wordpress.com/the-two-higher-self-and-guide-spacings/

lifetimes to release distorted impressions. Tieneke's Language of Light workbook came at the right moment in her life. By practising the release of distorted memory files in their database, each person can replace these shadow-type energy cords with soul qualities from the divine.

She had to reply as clearly as she possibly could. If people could start hearing their sound signature, or at least intellectually be aware of it, then their transformation would be a lot easier.

Dear Dawn

Thanks for your feedback. Dawn, the vibes of all the vowels in your full name on your birth certificate hold a unique vibration. Your actual lifestyle can often conceal this sound signature, your present emotional situation, or any other external circumstance.

Her lifestyle had adjusted the moment she knew her Soul's purpose. It had so changed her perceptions about what was real and what were the illusions she often still reacted to. So she typed:

Yes, our future dramatically depends on renewing our perceptions about our world. People have always created their reality based on religious beliefs or the trends during each period. During these times, our priority is changing our perceptions about our thoughts. See your reality, the one you are in at the moment through choice, already having the potential to be the actual blueprint of who you truly are. Then, contemplate that our realities have merged because your email arrived in my inbox.

She was aiming to put into words how awakening can be so unexpected. Hers lasted only a few moments, but it was enough to know who she was: an energy-light being who had chosen to play the human game.

Each individual's reality is within an energy field. See it as if yours is within a balloon. The veil that holds your colourful pulsating vibrations together has an individual tune, but the real you, your I Am, is the light body that shines from within outwards. Some call this your Merkabah.

Each layer of colour interacts with the reality you are in while your consciousness interprets your world through your biological computer, your brain. The more awake you are, the more you can control your reality.

Dawn, accept that your mind can never create a world of harmony if your inner world holds the distorted codes of disharmony. The word 'awake' stands for light, which you embody within your energy field, so if you become awake, your light body will shine outwards. If we all, as human beings, evolve, adding more light while keeping an open mind during these times, then our global community field will be able to ascend.

That is how she understood what it meant, how to add light frequencies within one's energy field, the body of the Soul. Her consciousness could free itself from the time zone that held her physical world intact for a split second.

She would always recall her awakening moment and how, for a fleeting moment, trillions of energy bubbles interacted with everything and everybody, merging and dividing like a biological cell that holds the idea, the blueprint of whatever it wants to become. It's like the seed within the apple's core with an apple tree's potential.

The rhythmic noises of the train travelling on its tracks had put her into a contemplative mood.

The darker the shadows within each energy field, the thicker the disharmony in that person's life.

If anyone knew that they, in the blink of an eye, could have seen what she experienced, they, too, would be motivated to awaken fully, just like she was. Still, she knew that her perceptions were hers alone. It could not inspire others; she could only share it in her journal.

The landscape outside the train window, her laptop, and the private coach were all an illusion from a different perspective – but very real once you were part of it.

She could hear and see beings from early childhood that adults couldn't. Queeny, her ginger cat, saw them too. The light beings that were always around people were very comforting. Especially when she was with people who were very angry or even fighting, in those moments, she would see their shadows that took on the same shape as the person the shadow belonged to. Then, the light beings would disappear. It was as if the shadow people scared the light beings away. Queeny would then often tell her to call them back silently.

Her passion for her ascension journey was ignited when she understood why these shadow people were trapped in this darker reality. She was shown how spiderweb-like strands wove themselves around people's energy fields. She developed a removal tool by needing to remove the shadow-like strands around herself and others. At first, she practised decoding ideas about her family, and slowly, over many years, her ascension workshops came into being.

She saw how each spider web strand was like a timeline hooked into the matrix. This matrix was like a gigantic ball of string. Each cord was controlling the period of each reality within multiple universes.

The website came into existence much later. Since it was a joint effort, she did not receive all the website feedback in her inbox. Other members of the Jaarsma Clan, who also wrote articles for the website, received mail as they all perceived their reality differently. However, every email addressed to her had to be answered truthfully. Every visitor was like a family member or a soul mate.

When each individual's shadow seems to take control, there is a need to become our inner observer. If we can keep the light shining within us during those moments, we will keep our vibration up. Those who have reached the third stage of awareness level in my ascension workshops will reap the rewards. Inevitability: We will all make the progression, but those who are aware will leap at a faster rate.

Across from her, Ben saw her typing away. He asked if she was working on her journal.

"I'm replying to feedback from the ascension topic website."

His short-cropped hair gave him a boyish appearance. He still had that intriguing air about him. He was the same height when she wore heels but appeared taller due to his broad shoulders. He never lost his sex appeal for her. He took her psychic gifts seriously, although, as a detective, his world was not always coherent with them.

The forest fragrance from the polished woodwork in the luxury coach reminded her of times in South Africa when she had been living in a forest with the woman who had re-awakened her psychic skills by showing her multidimensional universes. It was when Ben had found her again.

It was so easy to drift into her past; now, it was just memories.

To enjoy the last moments of their train journey, she typed down her last inspired thoughts before they disappeared.

Once we reconnect with the light body of our soul, where all our experienced realities are stored away, we can grow and expand, ultimately dazzling our limited sense of self.

What more could she add? There was so much more....since they were living in extraordinary times. Leo called it the end of times.

Dawn, In a sense, anyone who is in denial and keeps saying nothing will happen will be correct in saying so. They will go right on with their low-vibrational living and dying, birth and rebirth, lessons and growth. Their reality link is outside the universal matrix. That is their choice, and in the process of their doing so, the experimental nature of Earth's history will manifest.

Ben's cell phone interrupted her thoughts.

"Zwiegelaar speaking."

She tried to listen to who that could be. Who knew that they were in South Africa, apart from her family? With difficulty, she brought her attention back to her email. She had to stay focused.

Dawn, If your soul's purpose is to expand your consciousness beyond your perceived reality, you will be shown how to increase your vibrations. You have to move beyond the old creation myths. Only then will you realize that the cosmos is unconditional love, from which we are inseparable. Once we understand that, we know our Soul's purpose.

She had promised herself that she would work on her workbook and journal during this trip. Dawn's questions kept her focused on the task she set herself. It was helpful to reply to emails.

Thanks for asking about the 22 decoding formula, as you called it. Our number vibes or sound codes create a kind of timeline grid pattern that we all have around our energy field, knowing this will remove our shadows. The more light we bring into our energy field, the faster we can all transform back to our original blueprint, which is also genetically immortal, like the light body that encloses our spirit.

There was still so much that needed further investigation. Interpreting the understanding of how to recognise the twenty-two sound codes that influence the special moments in one's life was a challenge. These moments are, in truth, the initiation steps that each soul has chosen to experience. By translating her sound codes through writing her decoding book, she could create a program on how to reawaken one's soul memories. So she typed:

My decoding formula starts with 22 vibrational spacings. Each person has a unique melody that vibrates according to the colour rays. I have created a grid pattern image on the website. In the Language of Light workbook, you can see how it appeared in Tieneke's mind. The twenty-two string endings are all connected to the universal matrix. I use the term "spacings" in my workshop to refer to the same thing. Each "spacing" is represented as a card to add a gaming element. It allows us to interpret the melody that each person has chosen to embody. These twenty-two major archetypes are the leading tonal vibrations of your Blueprint.

Writing her journal was quite a task, as her workshop students Ingrid and Richard had done before her. Soon, she would gladly hand over what she had written to Liesbeth, who would edit her story into a novel, as she had done for Ingrid and Richard.

P.S. My decoding formula will be published on the website when we return to Europe.

Namasté

Annelies

She clicked send and closed her laptop, packing it in the inside pocket of her hand luggage on wheels. She had given herself plenty of time to publish her decoding formula without putting a date on it.

"That was some reply." Ben's remark was said with a smile. She had threatened to complain the moment he spent too much time at work during their holiday break. She got his hint.

"It was important. It's only an email. Unlike you, going to meetings with undercover agents during this trip."

He kept smiling, but she knew he was hiding something from her.

"Who called you just now on your cell?" A knock on the door broke their private moment. The purser wanted to know if they needed a taxi at Cape Town station. They were to be met by family, so there was no need for transport.

When Ben thanked him for his service with a handshake that included his tip, she reminded him of the customs of gratitude in different countries.

The rhythmic train noises had a hypnotic effect on her. Did it affect her brain waves, she wondered? It felt as if her contemplations reached a deeper level.

The Hogsback

It was a glorious day with a cloudless, crystal-blue sky. The landscape nearer Cape Town took her back to South Africa's most sacred place at a height of 1300 metres amid the peaceful Amatola Mountain range: The Hogsback. Its incredible magical energy was said to have inspired Tolkien, who later wrote Lord of the Rings. Her fascination with his work was ignited when she learned the deeper meaning of Tolkien's writing. Primarily, the major obstacles that were encountered by his main characters were as follows: They so reminded her of what had all happened to her friends and family last year. There had been significant obstacles. Tolkien stated that men became dominant and influential in the Middel-Earth in the fourth age. It was then that the fading of the elves began. If the fourth age marks the bridge from the fantastic fictional pre-history of the Earth to our known history, she then suspected the fifth age would be a golden age.

He initially described Middle-Earth as a fictional early history of the real Earth, but instead, his story reminded her of the Lemurian times.

Cape Town.

Ben was again engrossed in his newspaper. Whoever phoned didn't seem to disturb him, but the call brought her back to what happened the last time they visited South Africa....

"Ben, are you.... I want to ask you something."

"Shoot. I know what kind of mood you are in."

"Oh, what mood is that?"

"Your philosophy mood. Am I right?"

"Mmm, I suppose so. Ben, if each reality field had a timeline – with a beginning and an end – then would every individual's reality not be influenced by these beginning and end restrictions within that timeline?"

"Good grief, that is a deep question. Are you mulling over the times we are living in? What do you mean by a timeline?"

"You know the grid sheet I use in my decoding workshop." She reminded him. "The threads that form a grid pattern around the human aura?"

Ben still frowned, trying to follow her reasoning, no doubt.

"I call these threads timelines, remember. The thicker the web of threads, the lower a person vibrates. Now, I just wondered, why did the end of a cycle for our early ancestors have to be accompanied by a major cataclysmic event?"

Ben shrugged his shoulders. "Ingrid and Richard have written about planet Earth's program, which will soon end. It's not that I believed that in a physical sense, but you know, as I do, that ideas are changing. What is perceived as being the latest concepts are often thrown overboard the next day."

"I know, but aren't the ancient scripts that Trevor and Richard translated implying the same thing?" She replied.

"Yes, their message seems to come across as if they knew what was coming, but they still seemed to have needed to warn us by leaving their summary behind for later generations."

"You mean for them it was too late?"

"Well, maybe it is our message that we left behind for ourselves. Who knows." Ben reflected as he put his newspaper down and sat relaxed opposite her in their train coach.

"That idea must have come from Richard. He had speculated something similar." She knew that the symbolic text had them all puzzled. Especially since they had all been approached by the same energy light, her POWAH. She had written extensively about POWAH on the Jaarsma Clan's website, but had they all fully understood what they were heading towards?

"I can relate to the idea about the matrix you asked Leo about once, that an intercellular substance might be the timekeeper," Ben remarked.

"That's right, and Leo's reply was: The timekeeper prevents everything from happening all at once." She recalled.

"So, if the past and the future are present, could we travel in time?"

"Mentally, we already do." Ben summarised. He picked up one of the magazines she had purchased in Johannesburg and read out loud:

"According to the Mayan Prophecies, the 5,000-year Fourth Age will conclude in 2012. A new, unified global reality that we are now in is the beginning of the sixth night, 2019 - 2025. How did they know that?"

She was surprised at Ben questioning the article since he was not all that into prophesying assumptions. She leaned over and took the magazine from him. In the back, she had read an article on UFOs. Many see the coronavirus pandemic and economic meltdown as either a wake-up call to faith or the takeover of the transhumanist movement.

"Listen to this: Zecharia Sitchin's writings suggest that we must prepare ourselves for the return of an alien race, who created us some 300,000 years ago." She waited for a comment, but Ben had received an SMS.

"Mien just confirmed that she will be at the station in Cape Town."

"Ben, did you read the part that an Alien race would land soon?"

"Well, so far, the visitors from the 12th planet, the Anunnaki, have not landed on Earth yet", he grinned while studying the clouds that flew past; "I feel in my gut that it is all a hoax, this alien invasion." He looked at the UFO magazine again.

"Who knows, we may be approaching the truth about extraterrestrial existence will be revealed. Ben added. But not in the way some internet sites profess to believe." Ben shook his head, adding that the topic surrounding the end times was so rife around the globe that it had awakened much uncertainty in many people.

"This is a very controversial magazine. It also says something about the Hopi Indians. Their philosophy steers the reader in a similar direction as the Mayans. They also mention a shift into the Fourth Age. They focus on keeping the planet in balance during another polar shift. They believe that the ancient pyramids on the planet were built for that reason and that people would survive the polar shifts within these pyramids." Before their trip to South Africa, she had asked her uncle Trevor, the Egyptologist, the same question. His reply had been:

"Many quantifiable scientific indicators are proving that the Earth and the Solar System are going through changes which have never previously occurred in recorded human history, but it has never proven that the pyramids were some sort of hiding place."

Leo, Ben's twin brother, added: "Scientists have no idea what the impact will be to the planet's electronic and electromagnetic power grids, and they don't know what it means to the human immune systems. When you are in South Africa, read up on the myths and legends of Africa about twins. How they bring fortune or misfortune to families and communities." She knew that Leo never suggested something without a reason so that she would investigate.

She had come across the horrific story while surfing the internet; how, in May last year, as many as 50 whales had beached themselves in Kommetjie, near Cape Town. She had asked them both about their thoughts on beaching Wales.

"Annie, the lines of navigation that the whales have always followed have shifted and now lead them onto a beach. When they took them back out into the water and set them free, they continued to align themselves with the same magnetic lines, and in following them, they ended up on the beach again. So yes, it might have to do with what this coming polar shift does to the planet's electronic and electromagnetic power grids."

"Ben, do you recall that conversation with Leo and Trevor on the day we transferred the deed of sale of the house?"

"You mean the discussion about the polar shifts?"

"Yes. I got up to make coffee, but you three carried on about Indigenous peoples who believe that when the earth goes through what science sees as a magnetic reversal, it also will be a great shift and cleansing of the Earth's consciousness. Do you recall what Leo's or Trevor's reply was?"

"Mmm, let me think. I remember that it all sounded a bit far-fetched, especially about...Leo implied that nothing will hold all the magnetic patterns in place. When we awaken from this shift, what becomes consciousness will be our truest nature, our truest essence. At the time, it sounded like Leo was coming up with that happy note. Why are you asking?"

She ignored his question, instead asking him: "Did Leo think there is a correlation between consciousness and magnetics?"

"I can't remember. You came back with coffee and stroopwafels. That I do remember clearly."

"Trust you to react with your stomach."

"Watch out, girl. I will otherwise show you what I also still react to."

"You wouldn't dare. We will soon be in Cape Town."

Ben's glint as he observed her still affected her. During those moments, both their reality bubbles merged.

Day after day, she reminded herself that the global awakening would be relatively easy and even exhilarating if she could ride this tidal wave of change within her reality. She glanced out of the window and sensed that they were getting nearer to Cape Town with its famous Tafelberg.

"Ben, do you also feel the difference between the energy and the temperaments in Johannesburg and the people in Holland?"

"Mmm, probably, due to the fever surrounding the ANC campaigns. There is a lot of political instability within the leading party."

She still recalled her reaction to SA's energy levels during the early nineties compared to the apartheid years.

"That was because of the elections in 1994, my dear," Ben responded to her thoughts.

During her first visit to South Africa, her outlook on life was influenced by her angry energy. She hadn't been able to shed her grief.

"But Annie, remember that visit has also changed our lives?"

Ben was observing her as he beamed his telepathic dialogue. "Oh, I know. So much has happened since then."

Their second visit to South Africa was clouded by her horrific experience, which had instilled in her overwhelming emotions of fear. It had temporarily sealed her from her sensitivity. Instead, the locals' passive, almost despondent levels matched her own. It had taken many sessions with a therapist back in Holland to get her fear levels down to an average level. It had almost stopped her from coming on this trip.

To take her mind off their previous trip to South Africa, she browsed through a Cape Town brochure with a photo of an attractive young teenager displaying her jewellery on a creative market in Cape Town. How beautiful her world had been until the age of 16. How incredible it was when the nature, animal, and mineral kingdoms came to life through humanity's consciousness. No wonder she was so drawn by the words of songs from the late Michael Jackson and John Lennon: 'Heal the world.' They were all reminders of how her physical reality came into being by just thinking or mesmerising.

As a child, this knowledge had unconditionally been accepted as her right. Only when things around her started to happen without her immediate influence did she begin to lose her sensitivity. She had looked for comfort in her relationship with her cat Queeny, who was getting old, and the trees in her parent's garden estate. They stayed consistent. Thinking back, she now understood why her sensitivity skills had gradually numbed.

It took many years for her to get back to her observation mode, where she could feel, smell and hear how people created the world they experienced. Today, she recognized when she started feeling emotionally separated. Then, her physical reality became the mirror of that experience....

"I'm still convinced that humanity has now arrived at an obstacle course," she had a foreboding about it." What do you think?"

"Who knows?" Ben got up from his lounge chair to visit their luxurious bathroom.

"The people in your ascension group would agree with you. I can embrace challenges because they are said to serve a purpose." He replied from behind the closed door. "I've had enough of this train journey. Too many Japanese tourists are frightened to catch sunlight on their skin. I'm eager to get on with business before I can truly relax and think about pleasure."

As she surveyed their luxurious private coach, she knew that people like herself who had suffered from panic attacks and anxiety must still keep practising positive self-talk exercises.

"Annie, on this holiday, let go of all the obstacles that might still haunt you" Ben pleaded telepathically.

She tried hard to switch off, not to think about all the chaos and conflicts of last year's dramas. She knew that having been given glimpses of several possible scenarios to do with the reality she wanted to create for herself, she, of all people, should know better. During the years after her dreadful experience in Cape Town, she started to understand how her manifested skills could ever work without assistance from the elemental kingdoms within her universe.

When she allowed for the vibes of people's emotional energies to interact with hers, she knew that their level of vibrations could still affect hers.

Only having a genuine desire and an intent to ascend from this lower reality level would help her overcome the obstacles. Tolkien had fictionalised so well a world that they experienced as being real. Like Tolkien, when he wrote Lord of the Rings, these images must have also been inspired by the peaceful beauty of the Hogsback.

Her incredible experiences at this particular place had to be included in her journal, for it was the birth of knowing that awakened her to her Soul Purpose.

To have the intent to expand her consciousness beyond the old creation myths. To broaden her reality bubble with illuminated light, holding on to that intent had already changed her world.

She realized that the cosmos is woven with unconditional love, binding every manifestation of life. It mattered not that each individual's beliefs shaped their reality bubble. What matters is to know how to influence one's reality. That was also the core information her journal would address: that every life experience, no matter what beliefs, would undergo a closure ending with death or a full awakening. POWAH showed a clear demonstration of both paths.

"Annie, have you packed your bags?" Ben was closing his suitcase. "We will soon arrive at Cape Town station."

"We still have an hour, don't we?" She hoped to be able to revisit the Hogsback during this trip if only to rekindle the special moments when she had been shown what the times of the great awakening leading up to and beyond 2020 could be like.

In South Africa, she discovered her higher self and learned how individuals can reshape their reality to reach their full potential. Her decoding workbook and Richard's journal, Orphanage of Souls, outlined the energy of this fourth vibration. The genetic code of her Higher Self was number three. The keyword was I'm grateful for my Inner Power from the Solar Plexus.

Her Higher Self Code 3-Inner Power [2]

"Sweety, relax. Why are you so uneasy?"

Ben looked at his watch and checked the arrival time on their tickets. He insisted on wearing a timepiece since it had been a gift from her many years ago. She watched him with her inner eye and saw that something was troubling him concerning her as if he was carrying a heavy load on his shoulders. Had his wristwatch brought back memories?

Ben knew she was observing him with her third eye because he tried to subdue his energy field. If only he would share what was genuinely troubling him.

"Annie, have I met your approval? I feel as if I've been screened."

"Oh really? Then you must know that you can't hide anything from me."

She realized that Ben had worries connected to what had happened to her fourteen years ago, so denying it was pointless.

---

2. https://allrealityshifters.wordpress.com/the-two-higher-self-and-guide-spacings/

They had less than three weeks to clear out some past baggage on an energy level. Hers were very different from his, so she needed to be extra alert.

Ben had received an SMS, and she saw him frowning.

"What the..." "Nick is arrested in connection with, or being the middle man selling arms to Zimbabwean security forces."She had overheard Ben's inner dialogue and wondered who had sent it.

"It's from Jock."

He was Ben's nephew, her friend Mien's firstborn.

"For the last two years, your half-brother Toon has been steadily transferring his wealth into tangible forms, such as land and other assets, as you know. Nick tried to borrow from him through blackmail, and now Toon has been investigated."

Nick, Mien's first husband and her children's dad, was not likeable.

"What, do they suspect Toon has anything to do with Nick Du Toit's wheelings and dealings?"

"Jock knew that the Mail & Guardian indicated that assault rifles, as well as 9mm handguns, had been sold by South African interests to the Zimbabwean security forces. He suspects his dad was involved."

"Oh, what has that got to do with us?"

"Toon, the financial beneficiary of so many community projects, has been linked or mentioned in a report by someone on a fact-finding trip to Zimbabwe. He described the latest revelations as 'alarming'.

"Who is he, someone we know?"

"I suspect this individual is the same person who has been behind all the dramas at home."

"You think it has to do with Toon?"

Ben was clearly on edge, pondering how to reply to her question.

"The barely surviving financial institutions are under increasing pressure, and Toon always said he didn't want his wealth to disappear from some bank's computer."

Ben was very into conspiracy theories that sinister forces controlled banks.

"We both know that Toon's intent is honourable. He sees further than most people. He knows that the seas are going to destroy the coastlines of most countries, not to mention the lives that are going to be lost by the tsunamis due to more and more earthquakes, so what is new?" She replied with a shrug.

"Leo's viewpoint is that the people linked to the Jaarsma Clan's mission on Earth will show what to do and where to be when the time comes to evacuate."

Ben was on edge; that was very clear.

"You mean from Holland because it is mostly below sea level?"

"Partly, yes, but Toon is getting into building these floating structures in a big way, so he is not interested in finding anything that is not conducive to the transformation call of the Jaarsma Clan, of which you are the head of the Clan." He winked at her, knowing that he had said that teasingly.

"Annie, let's not even spoil our holiday over this. Instead, let's remember the good times we can both recall while on this visit."

The train had slowed down, but they still had twenty minutes to relax and ponder. Annelies' mind drifted away to the time she lived at the Hogsback. She observed him affectionately, knowing that he remembered the day like yesterday when they had found each other again...

Her higher self-observer lingered on, aiming to awaken her conscious mind... by whispering...

"When in doubt, take those quiet moments in your lives as an opportunity to engage your Higher Self, and most likely, you will sense the answers given to you."

Chapter 5

Her Instinctive Guide Frequency

Ben's memory script

Sooner or later, it was bound to happen. Leo's discovery and Trevor's archaeological find simultaneously could not be coincidental. It now became more apparent to him why the coming years are significant.

Jock's SMS took Ben's mind back to the conversations he had one evening the previous summer with Leo and Trevor. They had been staying overnight, but Annelies had to address some problems with her hotel. Leo and Trevor were discussing people's behaviour under stress in their living room. When these two had tried to explain to him that the thought sphere of the human mind is located in the Earth's magnetic field and that this magnetic field has been weakening dramatically over the last ten years, he thought that was useless information. It did not explain criminal behaviour in the people he dealt with.

"In physics, there is a parameter called 'Schumann's Resonance'. Ever heard of it?" Trevor had asked.

He vaguely recalled that it had to do with electromagnetic resonances because he replied:

"Aren't short-term earthquake predictions measured by electromagnetic resonances?"

"Correct, while for many centuries, it was constant around 7.80 cycles per second, during the last 7-8 years, it has risen to 11 cycles per second and continues to increase dramatically. If you work it out mathematically, this year will likely have 13 cycles per second." Trevor speculated about the effect this had on human consciousness.

"Mmm... I've read that there is a steep increase in a pattern of traits and behaviours, especially in western men, who suffered from NPD, Personality Disorder," Leo said. He asked if any criminal behaviour could be influenced by the speeding up of this electromagnetic wavelength.

Both Leo and Trevor wondered, shrugging their shoulders.

"When this resonance is 13 cycles per second, the Earth's core would stop rotating. With the magnetic field gone, our mind is gone. When I say our mind, I mean our memories of our past actions." Leo commented further.

"That would be handy for many people, especially criminals." He responded that he was thinking of the big players in the criminal world, mainly the two individuals who crossed his path this year. They had strong political connections and were both greedy and power-hungry. Then Leo had concluded. "In the dharma, we say, 'Mind is Karma'. All actions start from our minds. The mind is nothing but a storehouse of our past life experiences from which all our actions emanate."

"Meaning that when this electromagnetic field disappears, our present reality will vanish?" Trevor had summed up.

He had wished that Annie were there. This topic was so up her street. He was often blown away by those two, especially since Annie had practically dreamed of the same scenario.

That same evening, he had reminded them both that since Annie's decoding workshops had become known, anyone related in some ways to what she called the Jaarsma Clan was now being investigated. Having a detective mindset, he had been searching for a motive for the dramas they suffered last year.

"Not everyone from the Jaarsma Clan is related." His twin brother replied quietly.

"Because the human energy field acts as a blueprint of the physical body, sooner or later, a depleted or unbalanced field will create physical problems, except when a person knows how to speed up their energy field.

What is so different about us?" He had beamed to his twin brother *"It might be that they suspect that we of the Jaarsma Clan have found a remedy, or we carry a gene code that stops this depletion from happening."*

"Do we?" Trevor questioned

"Probably. Anyone connected to the Jaarsma Clan seems to have more developed psychic abilities, including gene particles in the DNA."

He had been stunned by what these two had shared with him that evening. He had asked them both if Annie knew about their suspicions. They hadn't told her about the gene code idea since they didn't want to introduce any negative, controversial, but plausible ideas into her mind. Then could have been the reason for what happened to her fourteen years ago....

Ben's Last Assignment

Ben knew that the train was getting closer to its destination, and that brought him back to the present. Leo and Trevor encouraged him to take on this last assignment to get to the bottom before it was too late. What he would find out on this trip had to do with what had happened fourteen years ago to Annie. She had no idea what his assignment was. He had to keep a mental screen up when he was investigating. He knew she could still detect that he was hiding something by the vibrations in his aura, but if so, she had not questioned him.

Ever since he told her about Leo and Trevor's discoveries, he had been more aware of a dark force starting to show its true colours....how and why their reality would vanish and what they would try to do to stop this from happening.

Hans was aware of it, and Toon had been informed of their speculations just before he offered them the luxury train ride tickets at their New Year's Eve party. All the chaos in weather patterns and the criminal and political dramas on Earth were minor events compared to the real issues at stake. There was no way he could share the knowledge about the infiltration of a dark force with his colleagues. They would think he had lost it.

Ben's ability to be in tune with human thought waves, especially when they were of a low vibration, made him more determined to hide them from Annie, silently staring out of the window.

He tilted his head slightly as if to catch the voices better. There were always noises in Ben's head, all natural to him, and they had been there since childhood. Leo was just as telepathic because their brainwaves were linked. His twin brother held the balance with him by tuning into the lower thought waves while Leo kept their connection to the higher frequencies. Leo's mental signature allowed him to feel every single cell, every electrical impulse, every atom of breath within his own body. A low, disordered dialogue now overshadowed his hearing senses. Occasionally, words would form, like breathy whispers from across a void; he could blend his reality with others.

At moments like this, while watching the scenery from the train window, he could now clearly distinguish whispering from the couple they had met over the previous evening's dinner. They were angry. The female was obviously in charge, as he suspected. The couple followed them as they entered the arrival hall at O.R. Tambo Airport in Johannesburg, Gauteng, on their way to their booked train cabin.

His detective alertness never slept. What was strange was that this couple had every intention to be spotted, or so he thought. They were hardly blending into the background.

He had not said anything to Annie and would keep it from her as long as possible.

Like him, she also admired the South African landscape that flew by. She was still a pretty lady at sixty. Her profile reflected in the train window was so peaceful. He didn't want to alert her about any possible danger. It would only spoil the start of their holiday. She knew he was on his last undercover assignment before his retirement but had only consented to join him on the trip to South Africa after promising not to spend all his time away from work.

He was surprised that she wasn't aware he suspected being followed. Or had she, but decided to switch off from it all? She seemed to do that lately, especially after all the dramas they both experienced in Holland.

"Dad, Mom, time is fast running out for anything and everything born of darkness. Lower vibrations of vital energy animate humans with a beast-like selfish nature!" Annie instantly sat up straight.

"Hans, is that you? Ben, did you get that?..."

He nodded. He had also heard their son's telepathic reminder while concentrating on the couple's mental noises. He questioned how they had managed to share a dining table with them.

"What is Hans warning us about Ben, something I should know?"

He tried to keep his focus on the couple's conversation. They clearly showed to him that the underworld wheels were in motion again. He had hoped to spare any unpleasantness with his investigation into dangerous cults. That was why he had accepted Toon, Annie's very wealthy half-brother's offer of treating them to this train journey, believing it was a last-minute booking so they would be safe, but he now was not so sure.

"You know Hans; he thinks we will be swallowed up in dark Africa" " he replied, shrugging his shoulders and acting as if he was not alarmed.

Annie looked at him, smiling because it had made her happy that they had telepathically re-connected with their son. He sensed that her philosophical mood had changed. She had lightened up, and any feelings of fear had dissipated.

Forty-Five Years Ago

The first time Leo introduced Annie to him, she had just turned fifteen. Five years his junior. Never had he seen a more alluring, sexy, beautiful girl in his whole 20 years. Time retracted back like a vacuum, and he became the observer of his film script.

That same year, just before he met her for the first time, he and Leo had made a pact together, a sacred oath, that neither would ever risk destroying a woman the way their father had their mother. Their father had loathed his twin boys because they took up all their mother's time and received her smiles and love. Their father had not been capable of loving without possession, jealousy and fear.

He remembered the first moment he had laid eyes on Annie like yesterday. She stood tall, reaching for a book on the top shelf of the library at the Orphanage in Apeldoorn. Her long, shapely legs from under her shorts had made him blush. He had come to her aid; her green eyes had stared at him.

They saw each other at least once a week. Ben had made sure of that. He was five years older and felt very adult-like. They went out for many months before they became intimate. He was her first lover. Now, being aware of what an insensitive upstart he was then, he could still throttle himself.

Four months later, after lovemaking, he told her that he planned to join Leo on a trip to Tibet after he had graduated. She had turned into an ice statue. He was sure it was the right decision. He had to let her go, he convinced himself. She deserved an average, more caring man. He had never shared his telepathic skills with her, but his close connection to his twin brother and the pact they had promised each other troubled him, so he broke off their relationship. He knew that Annie was psychic, but so was his mother, and it got her killed. He didn't yet trust himself, knowing that violent behaviour is often a family trait.

After she told him that she wanted nothing to do with him ever, to forget about her and to get on with his life, he knew what emotional pain was all about. He never understood then what truthfully made her react like that. They were always mentally very in tune, but from that day on, he thought he had lost his ability to read people's minds.

She had managed to keep the secret that she was pregnant from him, and he only heard about it many years later. That was in itself hurtful enough. At first, he had started to believe that she had betrayed him with someone else. When he heard that her baby girl of one year was kidnapped, his anger about a betrayal had turned into compassion for her grief. He truly learned how having beliefs or distorted perceptions can destroy one's life.

While they were touring Tibet, Leo heard from their sister Mien that he was the father of Annie's baby. When he came back to Holland and joined the police force, she had gone. She had left for South Africa on a student working tour....

As the years flew past his memory screen, like a timeline of realities, they stopped at several points, as Annie called them.

Annie had several affairs that he knew of. One was with her financial sponsor, Harry, who helped her buy the Prinsegracht Hotel. Her brother Fred and half-brother Toon, besides him, were the only ones who knew about her significant loss. Being in the police force, he investigated the case himself in his spare time but came to a dead end.

When they returned from Tibet for good, he was determined to win Annie back. He should never have broken up with her. While Leo's research interests included Zen Buddhism practices, he earned an MA in criminal psychology and became a detective in Den Haag.

After years of being devoted to science under an abbot's supervision, Leo became a monk. He started to specialise in genetic and environmental influences on criminal behaviours, while Leo took a post as a genetics researcher in France, which involved the science behind ageing. During the wintertime, being summer in South Africa, he took an extended leave to search for Annie.

Being twins, they always maintained a strong telepathic connection during their very different careers. While Leo focussed on the aspects of Tibetan medicine, including their culture, religion, art and literature, he collected a vast amount of evidence that showed how the criminal justice system had become a new home for individuals with psychological problems.

Although his memory of a young girl was mainly the vision he had kept alive all those years, he had seen later photographs. His sister Mien often wrote about her South African friend because they had shared accommodation in Cape Town. He never paid much attention or looked at the photos, only a few years later when he learned that his sister's friend was the same Annie he could never forget, had he recognised her from the snapshots.

He tried to discover what had happened to Annie, but Mien had no idea. After the birth of her son Jock, Annie disappeared from her life. They had drifted apart since Mien married Nick du Toit.

He approached Annie's parents, but someone had told them that she had gone into the mountains in South Africa to live a reclusive life and would only write when she could. They never understood her choices and prayed their daughter would be looked after.

Nineteen years had passed, and he never could get Annie out of his mind. He needed to close that chapter once and for all since he would turn forty that year. He would celebrate it during a hiking trip in the Hogsback.

On his birthday, he walked into the only supermarket in the Hogsback, and they bumped into each other. He was speechless while she stared at him, smilingly congratulating him on his birthday. He had stepped forward and held her close.

From that day on, they were never apart. Several times, he tried to persuade Annie to come home with him, but it was Nadifa, the woman who was her best friend and also her teacher, who explained why Annie was not yet ready to embrace the outside world.

One evening, Nadifa told them about some aspects of their possible futures. He was at first sceptic, but she did share some profound ideas. Since she reminded him so much of Leo, he agreed to some of Nadifa's suggestions. He participated in some of the very esoteric rituals, which claimed to open his third eye. They were both reminded never to reveal their heightened awareness until the right moment had come and only with those who could communicate telepathically.

He stayed with Annie for several weeks, and only after she shared her grief about the loss of Tessa and found out how much research he had done about the kidnapping case did she return home with him. Nadifa had shown them that they had a lot in common. They understood their genetic and soul connections and why they had chosen to be together in this lifetime. At first, he just went along with it by listening. His education and further training in the police force proved to be an obstacle. Still, after his first out-of-body experience in the Hogsback, he was ready to accept that other parallel realities would play a big role in both their lives.

Annie was eager to take her spiritual knowledge to the outside world. It was hard for her to say goodbye to Nadifa, who had become like a spiritual mother to her and was her devotee. During the last evening, when everything was ready for them to leave the mountain, Nadifa prepared a special herbal potion. After drinking it, they both had a profound mystical experience. It completely altered his outlook on life.

When they settled back in Holland, they married and adopted a young boy from the same orphanage where they had met for the first time. It was closing down. They both needed to raise a child since Annie could no longer fall pregnant. Fourteen years ago, he found out why but kept it from her.

Annie started to research her workshop material from the Western point of view in earnest while he was away a lot on business. He'd known that Annie had met Theo de Jong during the renovations of her hotel.

Several months later, Trevor met Theo Jong. They were both Egyptologists and shared their passion for ancient artefacts. Trevor and Leo were already investigating the ancient and not-so-ancient concepts of gateways to other dimensions for one reason – Leo had a hunch that if humanity could awaken to an inner journey to or see into different worlds, they could find a way to ascend from this reality. Ben realised that Annie had a Soul connection to Theo, a younger man.

He didn't know then that Leo, Trevor and Theo had been speculating outlandish theories on the star map that Annie had found. They had stumbled on a plot so devious against the human race that he would never have believed it, but now, while taking on this last assignment, he suspected his Soul's purpose. To expose the dark forces and bring them into the open.

Leo spent most of the year 2017 as a researcher at a private clinic in France near Toon's estate and founded Genetic DNA Sciences, a small company that developed genetic screening tools. Leo often stayed with them in Apeldoorn since he liked Annie's cooking.

One evening, Trevor and Theo had joined them for a drink. Their conversations were about an ancient text engraved on a papyrus scroll. They wanted to show it to Leo, who had been visiting them. Trevor and Theo's theories came from a shortwave radio frequency utilized by the world's intelligence agencies for transmitting secret messages. They had recognised the patterns on this ancient papyrus scroll to be similar to an electronic soundboard system used today to improve people's mental capabilities. According to Leo, they had also reported improvements in energy, mental capacity and transparency, where colours and objects around them were suddenly more colourful, bright and sharp.

"This, in time, could become the key to world peace." Theo acclaimed in joy. His reasoning was simple. The volunteers in these experiments would undergo a reconciliation effect due to balancing their brain waves.

"This process would enhance human nature's spiritual and artistic side".

He started to like Theo and realised how much Leo and Theo had in common. They were like father and son. Their relationship helped him overcome his fear of losing Annie to Theo. Their relationship was on a soul level while their own were physical, and they both had chosen to fulfil their Soul purpose together.

Because of Leo's previous work in psychology and on enlightenment or mystical experience, Trevor, Theo, and Leo started to work together. Trevor speculated that if one could create a perfectly balanced brain wave condition, they would see into other worlds.

That would relate to the mystical writings and traditions of humanity and to the mathematics of nature itself. They would have discovered an inter-dimensional doorway.

Sadly, Theo had been diagnosed with liver cancer. They suspected that their research had something to do with his unfortunate illness. Theo left his job as a travel agent, which he hated anyway, and moved to France to die.

Leo, Trevor and Theo were pioneering a new method of balancing brain wave patterns. Theo had insisted he be used as a guinea pig since he was terminal. Leo shared that the past shamans balanced the waves using entrainments, such as banging drums or flicking lights on and off, which is still practised today.

There was a spiritual science behind what Leo and Trevor were discovering in their underground laboratories below Toon's Valley of the Gods project.

During the construction of Toon's large project last year, the building of the Valley of the Gods amusement park in France, Trevor had started to discover a far more sinister plot behind the Particle Accelerator.

Leo overheard a conversation between researchers at the CERN Particle Accelerator in Switzerland. They believed their Accelerator could recreate conditions like the "big bang", which brought time and space into existence and created baby black holes and wormholes, elements that offer travelling backwards in time to bring in dark entities behind the one world order and transhumanism.

Leo began sharing the philosophy of Rudolf Steiner. At the same time, Trevor expressed his suspicions about the writings of Zecharia Sitchin and Erich Von Däniken after discovering that the notorious Nasi movement supported both authors. The sinister plot behind the depopulation agenda started to make sense.

After Theo passed away, Toon got shot, and Ingrid kidnapped, they explained their conclusions to him. If only Annie and he had shared their experiences at the Hogsback. He realized why Annie had not been told what was happening and regretted not recognizing the connections sooner. Leo explained that Annie had to wake up to them herself and that science and spirituality had to merge simultaneously.

Leo left Genetic DNA Sciences in 2019, a year after his company was sold; he joined Trevor and Theo's younger brother, Richard, full-time in their underground laboratories. Leo still maintains that the greatest medical geneticists of the 21st century are to be found in the Far East. He has never married.

Last year was a tumultuous time for their friends and family. After Liesbeth edited Ingrid and Richard's journals into novels, he realized how their lives had inspired a fictional plot. He began to recognize the significance of Annie's journal. He still couldn't accept that they were all responsible for the events of last year: the destructive fire at The Prinsegracht hotel, his nephew's eye injury while trying to save his daughter from the fire, Leo's harrowing experience of being buried alive due to an explosion that uncovered ancient tunnels near Paris, the attempt on Toon's life, and his wife's kidnapping ordeal. Yes, last year had been disturbing and tiresome; it reminded him of what Nadifa had told them years ago.

"You will both be tested during the end times when the dark masters are adept in keeping lightworkers separated. The dark masters want to re-energise the delusion program. They will do this through propaganda to manipulate the world and take power, which traps many followers in fear for their livelihoods. The lie, the deception is their primal focus programmed into the masses during the transformation years."

Nineteen years ago, her warnings had sounded very dramatic. Still, the most recent event was last year's New Year's Eve party when they discovered that their long-lost baby daughter Tessa had grown up as a woman named Liesbeth, a friend from Annelies' ascension workshops.

Cape Town

A knock on their door shook him out of his reminiscing mood. Their purser handed him a packet of pamphlets, a map of Cape Town, and a booklet that included all the good restaurants in Cape Town.

"Let me have a look. I want to see if some of my favourite spots are still in business."

They were now travelling past the outskirts of Cape Town. Annie got up to stretch her legs and redo her hair in front of the mirror in their bathroom. He would always be proud to have her as his wife. When he read Ingrid and Richard's journals after Liesbeth had edited them into novels, his taking part in their lives made it even more evident why they had to be re-written into fiction. He started to understand how vital Annie's journal was going to be. He could still not come to terms with the idea that they all were responsible for what happened last year, but they all needed to look within themselves to get answers.

The shouting in the corridor made him jump up to listen with his ears against the compartment door. He saw that Annie was looking at him, frowning. Ben tried to telepathically overhear the argument of the odd couple a few train coaches away while resting his ear against their door. Still, he could not follow their shouting in Afrikaans. Intuitively, he knew that last year's drama was still not over.

All he could pick up was, *"Stop worrying; he's already eating out of the palm of our hands."* He still didn't know who the 'he' was, but he sat back and managed to calm down by staring at the City Bowl's many railway tracks running parallel to each other as they approached Cape Town's station. He sensed at that moment that Leo was tuning into him, sending him comforting impressions that seemed to arise from tones best described as living with the ebb and swell of an invisible, limitless sea.

"Leo, we seem to be confronted more than ever by our 'dark' issues. Is there a 'deadline' on dealing with those feelings, attitudes, emotions, addictions, etc., or should we acknowledge them and we will outgrow them as we evolve into 5D existence?" He mentally asked. Leo was far more awake than he was. Because they were twins, each interacting with each other's light and darkness. He chose to tackle the shadow side by studying criminal behaviour, while Leo chose to explore the light side within them both.

"Ben, the darkness had not reckoned with peoples reawakening, which will let us shake loose from its control. This triumph for us is doom for the darkness. With all the evidence that their end is inevitable, the puppets of the dark forces will not accept defeat as long as they can arouse fear and panic."

Leo did not seem to be his usual calm self. Did he wonder why? He instinctively knew the global appearance of swine flu was related to what Leo was beaming.

"Ben, Nick du Toit was arrested in Switzerland last week on fraud charges connected to the bankruptcies of several companies, but there are rumours that he still has connections with his family in South Africa. Be aware. "

It was Toon who had sent the second mental message. He always knew by the telepathy signature of a person who it was.

By Annie's expression, he knew she had also picked up on Toon's telepathic warning. He wasn't as good as Annie at seeing auras, so he stopped trying, but wondering if the two telepathic warnings had something in common. Nick du Toit was his sister Mien's ex.

"Ben, does what Toon just projected have anything to do with your undercover assignment?"

He was surprised that she asked. He never revealed what case he was in. He shook his head, hoping that would satisfy her. He could feel she was looking at him from her inner eye, but he knew how to conceal his energy field. Nadifa had shown him how, because of his line of work, he was in contact with people who held a lot of anger and cruelty in their field, and these energy waves might stay in his if his soul library had recorded the same vibrations from past lives. If so, she would read them, which would only unnecessarily burden her.

Outside the window, he saw that they had almost reached their destination, Cape Town, one of the most beautiful cities in the world.

He knew that his thoughts would greatly influence what kind of experience he would have on this trip. The distorted energies he had left in this continent had to be released for him to evolve, so they had to learn the art of bending their realities. Leo had made that very clear. Annie's Soul Purpose was to write a map-like program where everyone calling to ascend this third-dimensional realm could recognise the awakening stages. For him, his Soul's purpose was to be at her side.

"Ben, you aren't hiding anything from me, are you?"

The shouting in the corridors had stopped. The train was slowly moving on its tracks while many on the platform were waving at people on the train. Their purser had told them not to leave the couch until he was there to help them with their luggage, so they both stayed seated.

"Annie, I don't always tell you everything, so trust me. I will tell you if you need to know my assignment." He beamed

She nodded and settled herself while looking outside...waiting for the porter's knock on the door.

She instinctively heard the observer's voice in her head whispering....

<The Gift you have received on your Soul's Journey is the gift of intuition. Know that you are conversing with your intuition and subconscious self.

<You will highlight how intuition can help you combat people who are after death - a marker of your Soul's journey.>

It was too late to open her laptop again, but she hoped to recall what her higher guide POWAH was channelling to her, knowing her code was twenty-two. Instinctive was her Soul Guide master number.

Her Guide Code was 22-Instinctive through the Heart Chakra.[1]

Who was the marker of her Soul journey? Was it Theo or Nadifa?

---

1. https://allrealityshifters.wordpress.com/the-two-higher-self-and-guide-spacings/

Chapter 6
The Gift of Intuition

When the Pupil is Ready, the Teacher Appears

She could sense that Ben was uneasy and that the shouting outside aggravated this feeling even more. After hearing Toon's telepathic warning, Ben denied it had anything to do with Nick du Toit. She suspected that that was not entirely true, but she knew better than to ask. He would never share anything to do with his undercover assignments. He seemed to have a knack for diminishing his energy field, so she couldn't read it.

During this train ride, she had seriously gone over in her mind the twenty-two initiation periods that POWAH had shown her. While travelling in style, she wanted to use these last moments to recall her memories of what had led her to South Africa the first time, especially to work out when she got the inspiration, still vital to this day, to hold ascension workshops.

When was her number one soul vibration of having motivation activated? These days, she is rarely upset for the same reasons she was a few years ago. What caused her upsets was not that things went wrong but that she expected them to go a certain way. Her expectations went unfulfilled.

Her childhood, teens and the period after Tessa's abduction were life experiences that had prepared her for what was still to come.

It took her years to realize the flaw in her approach to life. Now, she must practice having no expectations, only knowing that Spirit will fulfil her wishes with a complete awakening. It's necessary to document these moments in her journal; her soul's motivation with the power of number one.

The Diary of a Soul's Journey

As a young child, she encountered a highly evolved light being, which she perceived as an angel and felt deeply connected to. Over time, the being's appearance and gender perception changed. When she learned to read and write, she named her guide after the sound of the being, which resembled "POWAH."

On her decoding chart, his vibration was the number twenty-two. It was the same for Ingrid, but in Ingrid's life, her guide had only appeared to her when she was in her forties. Being a master number, she recalled what she had written in her decoding workbook about having a master number for the guide code: 22 – Intuition through the Heart Chakra[1]

Having a master vibration as a Guide in your decoding can mean that your intuitive sense is heightened by having chosen this to wake up faster than others.

That did apply to her, but she must have gone on a different path during the early stages of her life. She knew many people detoured due to their positive or negative experiences. Since her Higher Self represented her Masculine principle, and she knew hers was the root vibration of six, she somehow felt that her connection to her Higher Self was cut off when she was seventeen...

She was fifteen, and Ben was twenty when they first met. Her mother was visiting an orphanage in Apeldoorn. It was one of her charity duties, so she thought at the time, but years later, she learned why she was a regular visitor there. Her mother had given birth to a baby at fifteen, but her parents forced her to give it up for adoption. She never found her baby boy. History seemed to

1. https://allrealityshifters.wordpress.com/the-two-higher-self-and-guide-spacings/

have repeated itself because her world had shattered when she was seventeen....

Her First Trip to South Africa

She never truly fell in love with any other man after her affair with Ben. He had wanted to travel with his twin brother before having a serious relationship. She was far too proud and hurt just to get married because she had his baby. She decided to do it all on her own. She lost contact with Ben, so he was not there when Tessa was born.

After Tessa's disappearance at one year of age, and the police had given up searching for her, she became rebellious. Her telepathic sensitivity kept instilling more distrust and hurt within herself. The only way out was to shut them up verbally. Exposing outright what people were thinking, instead of what they pretended to say, didn't make her many friends. She started to hate seeing colour flicks shooting off someone's aura when they were blatantly lying or hearing a distorted energy tone when a lie was uttered. She knew that people started to dislike her for it.

Five years after she lost Tessa, her parents talked her into joining a study workgroup that included a working holiday for six months. She chose South Africa.

On this trip, she met up with Mien Jaarsma. She was in the same group that had travelled to South Africa during the apartheid era.

Mien was the first person she met who spoke her mind and, at the same time, managed never to upset people. They became the best of friends. She was her best teacher. Mien worked as a cook for a posh restaurant in Sea Point while she found a position in a recruiting agency in the centre of town. They shared a room in a boarding house to save money for travelling.

Mien often spoke about Nick, the waiter she'd fallen in love with. She had no interest in having a steady relationship, preferring to go out with many guys. When it came to the point that they wanted sex, she quickly exchanged them for a new companion. She broke many hearts.

Mien was very serious about Nick, and one evening after work, the subject of marriage and children came up. She told a sad story about her family, especially about her dad, who had an alcohol use disorder and abused her mother. She had one sister and two brothers. When she mentioned her twin brothers, Leo and Ben, it was as if an iron rod had stabbed her in her solar plexus. After confirming that Ben, the father of her baby, was also her brother, she confided everything: Tessa's abduction and the police's failure to locate her. Now that Mien knew her background, Mien understood why she was not interested in a serious relationship.

Their friendship was solid until she met Nick du Toit at a bar in Cape Town. She had warned her friend not to fall for this Nick, explaining what she picked up mentally, but Mien would not listen.... She understood enough of psychology to know why Mien had attracted an abusive man in her life. He was probably a carbon copy of her alcoholic father.

What she didn't know was that Mien was pregnant. Nick was the father. They married at a registry office without any family or friends present. During that time, she had to acknowledge that keeping secrets away from close friends was painful for them. Mien had hurt her by not sharing her predicament of being pregnant.

Over the years, her bossiness and abrupt behaviour have isolated her from people. When Jock was born, she had visited Mien in the hospital on her day off but seeing a baby brought so many memories for her that after that visit, they lost further contact. Gradually, there was nobody left to turn to.

She didn't want to return to Holland but lost many jobs because of her temperament, so she moved away from Cape Town. Her only option was to become a hermit....

Meeting with Destiny

She had been waitressing and looking after the administration at a small local hotel in the Hogsback for a year when she heard about an eccentric woman called Nadifa.

The hiking crowd in the hotel mentioned a mystic called Nadifa several times. One of the Dutch girls overheard her speak to a staff member and knew by her accent that she was Dutch. She wanted to see if she knew many people who lived in the Hogsback. When this girl kept speaking about this psychic woman living in the mountains, she asked the hotel staff if they knew of a Dutch woman named Nadifa.

They all knew whom she was referring to. They called her spooky. Why Spooky became upset became apparent after she overheard the kitchen staff gossiping about her. One of the kitchen boys had gone to her with his young child for healing.

He vividly explained in Afrikaans how Spooky had held her hands over his young son's body while he was shaking from a fever. In his animated style, he told them in the kitchen how a blueish light had streamed from her hands. The reaction from the listeners was full of fear, but it had gripped her attention. She wanted to know more about this woman, but their boss had walked in. With his usual abrupt manner, he broke up their conversation.

She was now very keen to join this hiking group on her day off, so she organised a guide from the village that could show them where this woman lived.

Eight people were in this Dutch hiking team—five guys and three girls, all around her age or younger.

They had been walking, following a trail for at least two hours, when they saw smoke above the thick, dense forest. Their tour guide, a black boy from a nearby village, pointed at a narrow path through the woods. He shook his head, and all he wanted was his money. He was scared to go any further.

They were too excited to be alarmed by his fear, so they paid him and followed the trail through the forest. After about ten minutes, they came to an abrupt stop. The trail had come to a dead end. A large tree trunk blocked the track, but they spotted steps to climb over it, which they did. At first, they only saw lots of trees and ferns, almost covering up a narrow trail, but they hiked towards it when they heard the sound of falling water.

She had heard of waterfalls and had been to some, but this noise came from a much more significant or higher drop. Then, one of the men spotted a wooden swing bridge erected over a rocky stream. He checked to see if it was safe, and one at a time, they crossed it.

When she walked across, she felt almost like she had returned home. She felt that a higher source had destined her residence in Hogsback. She had been meditating for the last few months, asking for guidance. She would often wander off away from people to be by herself. During those moments, she started to feel a loving presence from within.

***

The years flew backwards into her past when this rather colourfully dressed but weird-looking woman suddenly appeared from nowhere. Everyone on the hiking trip knew she had to be the mysterious mystic. She had the presence of a very old soul.

"Well, it took you all a long time to get here. Did you pay Skip?" She asked, addressing them as if she had been waiting for the whole group.

They explained that Skip, the black boy, had been too scared to stay with them and, yes, that they paid him. The fact that he was scared didn't seem to phase the woman. She just nodded and made a sigh for them to follow her.

They arrived at a rather large rondavel after what felt like half an hour. When they came closer, the view took their breath away. They could see far into the distance. They were overlooking the flat plains of Africa far below. The view was outstanding. It was as if they were high up on a tropical island in the desert.

"Welcome to Rainbow's End," Nadifa said.

Her rondavel cottage was built with natural rocks, wood, and brickwork. The aroma of cooking gave everyone a warm welcome as she invited them inside. They left their hiking gear outside and stepped into a round room decorated with colourful wall hangings, some of which were in leather. The artist had lived briefly in Hogsback and had given them to Nadifa as a form of payment for helping her make a very important decision in her life.

When Nadifa looked into her eyes, it was as if she had overheard what she had been thinking. At first, her penetrating stare took her by surprise. She felt as if the woman had walked right into her body as if they had melted into each other. From that moment, she knew she would not return to the hotel with the others.

The feeling was gone without warning; Nadifa hugged her as if she had been a long-lost relative. The others were all speechless. So was she. It felt good to be wanted again. She had missed having any emotional contact with others. She would also never forget the first question Nadifa asked; "Annie, did you bring some spare clothes with you?"

The hiking group waited in total amazement for her reply. She explained that she joined the Dutch team on her day off from her work at the hotel. Nadifa just waved her hand as if that was immaterial. Instead, they were all asked to join her on the patio for something to eat.

Each got their turn to talk to her, and the day was over before they knew it. Nadifa decided that the group would report to the Hotel manager that Annie was not returning.

"Annie will come to fetch her personal belongings by the end of the week," she told them. Nobody ever called her Annie, except for Ben....years ago.

Nadifa left her on her own for the first week. At first, she ensured that she earned her keep until she gave up and let go of her fierce need for independence. She asked why she was living with her. Nadifa said, "When the pupil is ready, the teacher arrives."

Nadifa took her back to her childhood, establishing that POWAH never left her during her difficult years. Over a few months, she did lots of regression therapy, covering the most challenging period. Then, with her help, she learned to accept that her baby girl would never be found.

It took several more months for her to be confident enough to face the world again and to be social in every kind of company.

Nadifa introduced her to her body avatar through cellular memory healing. Her training in the often hidden esoteric mysteries had started in earnest.

She also assisted her in developing her inner eye to study the energy field around nature and animals, and later, she was taught to interpret the human aura.

Nadifa showed her how to recognise the initiation periods in her past lives. Those were the moments when more Soul qualities would enter one's present lifetime, and she took her back into the first astral realm near the Physical reality; in that Astral realm. Nadifa shows her a preview of the life she could live as Annelies. Nadifa made her recall several previous lifetimes, or so it seemed to her then. She only later understood why the mind had translated it as a past life. The human mind cannot interpret anything out of time. Nadifa said that she needed to train her mind

***

She returned to the present for a split second, having just arrived in Cape Town. She was startled by her admission. That was when she must have connected with her Higher Self-vibration, the soul quality of inner power. She couldn't look up what she had written about the number three code vibration since her laptop was already packed away. She knew the number three stood for being grateful, but she would look it up later.

"Are you having an aha moment?" Ben beamed, smiling.

"Yes, it was Nadifa who, years ago, showed me how a morphic field comes into existence. Remember our conversation with Hans back home?"

"Something about the sixth dimension, but I still have no idea how geometric structures create this reality," Ben said.

"It's through sound, which is the property of the seventh dimension. That is what Nadifa was trying to explain."

"Was that what your aha conclusion was about?"

"I was looking at the fields outside while thinking about the time I lived in the Hogsback.." She questioned if crop circles had ever appeared in South Africa, and she then linked Nadifa's warning: that she needed to train her mind to see the five platonic solid life forms that make up this three-dimensional world.

"My mind is so busy. It must be because we are back on South African soul."

"What connection do crop circles have with what Nadifa tried to teach you back then?"

"I will only share it after I have figured out how to bypass time."

"Mmm, please do so." Ben got up to use their private bathroom. Nadifa had shown the twenty-two significant periods she needed to recall before her life work would be complete. The order of the light body codes didn't matter, but once all were decoded, she would know her destiny. She had awakened in her what the qualities of her Soul purpose were in this lifetime. The four Christ forces, called by Nadifa, are balance, consciousness, service, and education. Years later, she understood that these were the language of light qualities that Tieneke, a younger friend, had introduced to her years later. She remembered what Nadifa had told her, that the right people would come into her life when she needed them to fully awaken so she could leave this physical reality in her etheric light body.

She came up with the idea of giving a workshop whereby people drawn to the ascension movement would recognise their own 22 major turning points.

During that time in the Hogsback, she learned to reawaken feelings of compassion and understanding for others unaware of their psychic powers through her emotional healing. During this time, she also realised how judgmental she had been of people not speaking the truth. She had falsely pretended she was fine when European visitors asked her why she lived such an isolated life away from her family. She had reacted to the mirror that she had seen in others!

She had written to her mother several times during the years that she lived in the Hogsback. One time, she flew back to attend her Dad's funeral, but she didn't stay. Fred and Toon tried to convince her to come home, but she was not ready to pick up her life in Holland.

Meeting her Soulmate

The local community were still scared of her since they associated her with Nadifa. Especially after she moved in with her, she had always respected the local community because she was far more in tune with their thinking. She rarely spoke to them, not wanting to insult their spiritual intelligence by being false. It made no difference what education they had; the less academic, the better.... She had narrowed her social circle to a few people who at least could listen to themselves. She made South Africa her home.

She was thirty-six when Ben tracked her down. Ben had booked a hiking tour, hoping to meet up with her.

She had been shopping at the only grocery store in the village when she saw him. At first, she thought it was just her imagination because it was Ben's birthday, so it had to be a coincidence to see a man who reminded her of Ben. At first, she wasn't sure if he was her Ben. She hadn't seen him for so many years.

She could see that the man was just as startled. His response was simultaneously elated and cautious. By this time, her clairvoyant sense had reopened because she saw the familiar golden light particles streaming off Ben's shoulders.

"Annie, is it you? Or am I dreaming?" She heard.

I can hear you...Ben, what made you come here of all places?" She replied mentally.

"To find you, why else?"

"Happy Birthday," she replied aloud, unsure if she genuinely heard his mental projection. Ben took her in his arms. They embraced each other and held on for a long time. Several locals were reluctant to leave her alone with this strange white man. Only when she introduced Ben to the shop owner did some people in the shop greet him as part of their community.

She was somewhat nervous when she took Ben home to introduce him to the woman who had saved her life in many ways. It was so important to her for Nadifa to like him. Instead, they were both welcomed well before they entered Rainbow's end. She could have known that this woman would have known that Ben had returned to her life.

Nadifa insisted that Ben stay, knowing he would plead for her to return to Holland several times.

Ben was introduced to the lifestyle she had lived in the forest for several years. At first, he was polite but sceptical, but when Nadifa showed him how in tune she was with nature, how she could make birds sit on her shoulders, and how she could heal the ailments of the local community when they would visit her, he started to listen genuinely. Nadifa's wisdom, humour and insight into what caused the distortions of a criminal mind, since that was Ben's passion, was a revelation to him. Their training further enhanced their mental connection during those weeks.

On their last evening, Ben woke up to his Soul purpose energy. Nadifa had prepared a drink for them, which she knew was her final gift to both of them. She had prepared Ben for it, and he was eager. Nadifa had already explained to them that this last induced mystical experience was her parting gift and would never be repeated. During the weeks Ben stayed with them, he had learned enough about her to know that she despised charlatans. The sorrow she felt for leaving this woman was very difficult to overcome, but she knew the time had arrived for her to face the Western world and blend in again as an average Dutch woman with no special psychic abilities.

Nadifa often stressed that it was essential to never use their awareness in any way if it was not conducive to their Soul purpose. Hers was to teach the genetic decoding program during the last years before the great shift. Ben's was to be her support, for only then would he be able to recall his unconscious misconduct his Soul had filed away.

She warned them that they would be tested to see if they were worthy of living a life of integrity by using their psychic powers. Nadifa also stressed that they should never use their gifts to enhance their lifestyle or psychic powers to heal or save a loved one from their karmic lessons unless they were already awakened enough to receive it. If they did, they would immediately lose these psychic skills.

***≈

Now that the train had stopped, she quickly made notes on the train's stationery about the four initiations she had recalled. Her guide awareness was the first. The motivation of her soul vibe, number one, with the soul virtues of courage, leadership, determination, and individuality, helped her to understand why she wanted to stay with Nadifa and learn what to do with her life. Her Soul's quality of motivation and the energy of forgiveness linked her to her Soul's purpose for the Breath of Life. These two Soul qualities helped her discover how to create a twenty-two initiation game, which later became her stepped decoding formula. She reconnected with her Higher Self's power when she was introduced to her body avatar through Nadifa's cellular memory healings. She had already felt the energy of her Higher Self during her meditations, but understanding why she had chosen the life of Annelies did help.

Ben saw her writing feverishly on the train's notepad. He asked what she was doing, but she ignored his question.

She promised to write in her journal during this holiday, especially about the third awakening stage. She would have plenty of time during the periods Ben would be away, doing what he needed to attend on this trip.

Annelies now recalled their last trip to South Africa. Her major obstacle had come into her life fourteen years ago. Could she have prevented all the drama? The experience she had during that trip with Ben still makes her shiver. Once again, she had to stay sharp and in tune with her intuition to prevent her premature death while her Etheric body was targeted. Her Etheric body code was eleven, a master vibration.

Her Higher Emotional\ Etheric Body Code 11-Direction. She had included what POWAH had implanted in her mind.

<The etheric body of an initiate with this vibration frequency did not originate on Earth. Your etheric body sees and knows

things before they happen, often explained by chance or coincidence. This belief is related to synchronicity and will influence your life direction. **Your emotional field has chosen to interpret projections of living light from Source Consciousness.>**

When Tieneke showed her that the Soul quality of 'direction' was what had caused her to be very vulnerable years ago, it now made total sense. She had lost her direction in life for so many years. Fourteen years ago, her ascension calling had not yet awakened.

"Have you planned anything with Mien while I follow up on some of my appointments?"

"No." She had hoped Ben's detective work was minimal. "I would rather do some writing during that time."

Her finger tapping on the window ledge with the train rhythm reminded her of a song. Ben glanced at her sharply because she recalled the music playing at the restaurant fourteen years ago.

"I know. The Way We Were by Barbra Streisand."

"You remembered it too?"

"Your tapping helped." Ben looked again at his watch.

Good grief, she recalled what that song had done to her then. It had activated her emotional or Etheric body code. If only she could open her laptop again and read what she had interpreted in her decoding book about the higher emotional field number code eleven.

"It is your higher emotional memory that provides the heart with impetus, fuels the brain, and propels the corn plant from seed to fruit to give it direction."

Startled, she looked at Ben. Had he? No, he was not in a telepathic mode. Who had just mentally planted that sentence in her mind? Was her memory speaking back to her? Could that be possible?

"Oh, I can't wait to stretch my legs or go for a long walk."

Ben had picked up a copy of Time magazine. A photo of a drug user triggered her recollection that individuals lacking purpose in life often have stimulated etheric bodies, fueling their addictive nature..

Knowing that the physical and Etheric/resurrection body are intimately connected, it was her friend Tieneke who, last year, had shared how doodling can strengthen the Etheric body.

She tried to quieten her busy mind by looking out the window at the many people crowded on the platforms. During their train journey, she had occasionally spotted a village or town in the distance, but nothing like the squatter camps she now saw. However, she had never travelled on this route towards Cape Town.

Everything about the last station they passed before their final destination still showed that poverty was still very rife in South Africa. From her posh window seat, she had observed how an older woman tried to keep a toddler from running away amongst the sea of waiting crowds. Poverty must surely be one of the main reasons most of the human population has never progressed.

Had physical ageing on planet Earth carried the secret beyond physical immortality so well that it had even fooled scientists? Had she truly interpreted the genetic codes that could regenerate the human cells back to their original blueprint? Was it so easy to consciously embody the soul's qualities in one's everyday life so the endocrine glands and their hormones can be restored and re-activated to their true spiritual functions? Her research on the ascension topic motivated her to get to the truth, but she often still questioned, why her?

She also wondered when, in this reality, they would experience the holographic medical beds that some internet groups talk about. Her feelings were somewhat troubled when she read about all the technologies that might be available soon.

"Annie, what time are we meeting Mien?"

Ben was not in a holiday mood but preoccupied during the train journey. He was going through his stacks of papers again, which made her suspicious. Only his safari outfit, dating back from the last time they were in South Africa, gave away the fact that he was a typical tourist.

Did men still wear those, she wondered, imagining a better, more youthful-looking outfit? He was, after all, still a dish at sixty-five. Ben was very fit and strongly built. Even his posture was of a much younger man. He so well matched her powerful willpower. Not that he showed that side of himself very often. As a detective, he usually fooled people, giving them the impression that he believed everything they told him.

"Ben, Mien will meet us in the main hall under the clock. Please don't tell me you have scheduled an appointment immediately after our arrival?"

His mind was occupied by the case he was investigating. What had given her the idea that it would be different this time?

The 27-hour journey of 1 600 kilometres travelling in a world of grace, elegance and romance had not relaxed Ben. Toon, her half-brother's generous gift of this trip, was truly an experience for her, but it only seemed to trigger uneasy feelings for Ben.

"I'll be glad to get off this train, that's all. I'm eager to have some meetings behind me before I can truly relax and enjoy South Africa." He responded to her through the closed bathroom door.

As she surveyed their luxurious private coach, she knew how to meditate and lower her mental thinking. Going into her depressing past had kept her mind too busy. People like herself who suffer from panic attacks and anxiety must keep practising positive visualisations.

"Annie, on this holiday, let go of all the obstacles that might still haunt you." she heard. Could it be? Was it possible that Nadifa

was communicating with her? Had she recognised her telepathic signature?

She tried hard not to let her mind return to all the chaos and conflicts from last year's dramas. She took a deep breath and repeated positive affirmations to herself. Ben observed her with sadness in his eyes when he came back from the bathroom.

"Annie, can't you ...We are going to be fine. Honest. What happened years ago is never going to be repeated."

Ben had also picked up on her anxiety levels. Their telepathic connection had saved her life fourteen years ago, so what was she doing to herself now?

Moving from Holland's cold, wet and windy climate into a warm, almost tropical temperature must have triggered some of the shadow entities she was still harbouring in her energy field. Changes on the physical level often brought up unfinished business. Since this illusion would soon be over, she felt somewhat irritated with herself for being unprepared. She, of all people, should know better.

They both recognised that awakening people are often seized by doubt, ridiculed or hunted, threatened, or even killed. Ben's brother Leo, the genetic scientist of the family, had spelt it out in one sentence.

"Science, technology and religions can heal, or those three developments can kill. Annie, it all depends on the Soul of man."

She had asked Leo what place religion had. Intuitively, she knew that the dogmatic traditions of many religions often instigated horrendous outcomes.

"The split between science and religious belief programs, during 2000 years of human history, has probably stifled humanity's evolution on intuitive levels. " Leo had replied.

Her life work, mapping the ascension journey of the Jaarsma Clan, had clearly shown her several crossroads. Several pathways could lead many souls to their evolution or devolution. Was that why everybody who, in some way, was related to the Jaarsma Clan's intent was opening themselves up to be persecuted? It was probably more to do with the fact that many negative thought forms were now coming to the surface. So, plenty of mirrors were coming up for them all. At the same time, more fear energies had to be overcome. The dark forces wanted to stay alive, so they used every opportunity to create as many obstacles as possible. Trevor was very much into that way of thinking. It might have some truth to it since so many people around the globe were at war.

Seeing her reflection in the window, that of a colourfully dressed elegant woman who still managed to make heads turn, made her feel better. She smiled at herself because she truly felt at home in the luxury of their deluxe suite, with its classic earthy African décor, but it had made little impression on Ben.

"Please, Ben, why don't you put those papers away in your briefcase and enjoy the last bit of this fantasy world."

"Annie, this luxury is all distasteful for me, especially knowing what is out there. I know that both worlds must exist hand in hand, but it's so unbalanced. Toon must have paid handsomely for all this."

She had a good view of the luxurious bathroom from where she sat. Ben's gesture pointed at their twin beds, which had been efficiently made up, while they enjoyed their breakfast in the dining car. That was the last time she had had an opportunity to greet the other passengers before they all disembarked in Cape Town.

Their private butler, a lovely African who had attended to their every need, had indeed reminded her that they were all actors on a stage.

"Ben, do you still feel that that odd couple were there to keep an eye on us?" "I know they made you suspicious. Did they follow us from the airport in Johannesburg?"

"If you mean the older man with that young chick, most definitely."

"I hoped you hadn't picked up on my thoughts; sorry." Ben beamed as he snuggled up close.

Ben rarely shared his views about people, but he did so after they had visited the lounge carriage, where people relaxed between meals and later returned to their private quarters. He was clearly in an irritated mood.

"Gosh Annie, most of these people, I mean the few Europeans, whom we shared an after-dinner conversation with over coffee, they are all great actors; they all lie. What a pompous crowd."

"I know that, but Bennie, most people are not aware of it themselves. It's called being social, you know that." Had they behaved any differently? Their last interaction with other passengers had also irritated her, but who was she to hold any judgment, especially about the young woman who was clearly out of her element? She had sounded very false. The man, who could easily be her dad, was a smooth talker, and she was just arm candy, nothing more. She had gazed at their auras when they were under the impression that she was daydreaming during their conversation. His was of a lower vibration since there was hardly anything to see. There were wave patterns that she had not seen for a long time. People who lacked compassion, who were capable of cruelty to others, had that kind of signature. Hers was somewhat brighter but still very diverse and complex. She had found them both puzzling and disturbing.

"Bennie, my intuition tells me this princess is not intelligent enough to act two roles." She knew that this couple had been on his mind.

"Believe me, she is good at it. She is the one in control, not him. Do you know when Toon booked this train trip?"

"Ben, you should know that I was not even aware that we would be flying to South Africa so soon. When did Toon give you the train tickets?"

"Mmm, do you think Toon had already booked this private deluxe suite? I can't imagine you can book it at the last minute." He summarised instead.

"Ah, you know what Toon is like. He had probably booked it for himself long ago, but you know the rest since Ingrid came into his life. Come and sit with me. Relax and be in the now moment." She was determined to enjoy the posh decor with its polished wood smells while it lasted.

"OK, you win; move over so I can sit up close. I'll show you what being in the NOW moment feels like, shall I?" Ben's loving strokes made her feel all soft and warm.

"Is Mien fetching us from Cape Town station on her own?"

"No idea. I spoke to Jock, but very briefly." Ben mumbled, "So they must know I'm not Toon." His uneasiness about that odd couple had to be taken seriously. For him to be so suspicious made her wonder why she had not picked up anything. It must be because she wished for a lovely time as a tourist, nothing more.

"Are you, like me, getting paranoid? I know what happened fourteen years ago to me, and it will still affect many levels, but I need to deal with it. It was maybe foolhardy to join you on this trip, so please don't get anxiety attacks. That is my department."

"I'm well aware of that, Annie. That is why I see things that are not there." He held her tight, encircling her as if to say I will not let you leave my side.

"Ben, do you still suspect that some elite group is trying to stop our theories by ridiculing them all, especially my workshops on immortality? I find that so hard to swallow."

Ben had been reading an online document about Hammarskjold's death on the Observer South Africa page, so she wondered if his mind was elsewhere.

"It's far more complicated than that, Annie, and you know it. Anyway, just now, the porter will call us."

Ben closed his iPhone and got up to get his things together. She knew that for her, this trip was more than a holiday. It was to release all the programmed beliefs that manifested years ago, to make them disappear forever.

She was also looking forward to seeing Mien again. They had so much history together. What would it be like visiting all the places with such vital memories? They had to be included in her journal. This trip was probably some energy detox. Bad or sad memories are also just as toxic for the human body.

"Ben, do you think we have the time to visit the Hogsback?"

"Why not? I'd love to. That place has great memories for me to remember." His expression said the rest.

"We have an open ticket... not so?"

"Yes, but may I remind you that we made many plans for this year. Let's not stay away from our home in Apeldoorn too long. We have to pack and sort out what to keep and what to leave behind."

"Do we have to?"

"What, leave things behind?"...Ben was shaving in the bathroom while the train was stationary when he replied. "We decided to move to France and for you to run the guesthouse, and I want...well, you know."

She sat back and recalled rows of tin shacks that were an endemic part of the South African landscape the nearer you came to a big city. This luxury train must have a different track since she had not seen any tin shacks on its route.

The owners of this train ensured that no wealthy tourists saw the poverty still around. South Africans who lived through the turbulent later years of apartheid all intuitively knew that the country's leadership was morally bankrupt, let alone deeply in debt.

"Ben, look at that crowd on the other platforms."

There was a knock on the cabin door, and they both looked at each other *"That must be our porter"* Ben telepathically beamed, but instead, as he opened the door, the smooth talker cried out ", Why are you both hiding away?"

She could see that the young woman was standing behind him. She hoped that Ben would not invite them in. "Don't worry, they won't get past me."

Surely the hoity-toity princess didn't know about their ability to communicate telepathically?

Ben was making small talk while she pretended to read a brochure on Cape Town. Where was their porter? The man's slimy voice above Ben's more profound, more cultured way of speaking got to an almost shouting pitch. Their dark shadow vibes were all stirred by an electrical force, their ego energy.

"Can you not join us for the last drink? I want to discuss Nick du Toit, abandoned by all the big players behind the coup plot."

That name gave her a jolt. So Ben was right; they knew far more about them.

"The only person I'm willing to discuss with is the one willing to stand up in public and tell me the truth about himself. That is all I have to say on the subject. Let's leave it at that. We are on holiday and uninterested in getting involved in your rescue scheme." Ben's voice was firm while he gradually closed the door.

"What was that all about?" She beamed since the silence after Ben had closed the door was nerve-wracking. Where there should have been sounds of footsteps walking away, there was silence. Then they heard other people in the corridors talking to them. "You were right, but what is their connection to Mien's ex?" From now on, she would only telepathically ask questions.

"Nick is in jail and wants bail money. I suspect this guy is the same man that kidnapped Ingrid last year." Ben beamed.

"Gosh, if you are right, they know you are not Toon?" She hoped they would lose them for good as soon as they were off the train. There was another knock on the door. The porter grabbed the big suitcase and her smaller laptop from them this time. "Let's try to give them the slip, shall we?"

She glanced at the luxury coach that had indeed lived up to its reputation, but she was glad to get off the train...

Chapter 7

We are all Divine Union Beings of Light

When Timelines Cross

Cape Town station's oil and diesel smell, mixed with the odours coming from the crowds, told her that she was in Africa. Ben was on edge, so she suspected he had an appointment with people involved with crimes in Cape Town. Now more than ever, she truly hoped that this trip was his last one as a detective. Ben had promised that he would retire after they returned to Holland after finalising everything, and they would then move to France.

The noises outside the corridor told them many other passengers were leaving. Thank goodness they travelled light. Each had a briefcase on wheels, and she had her shoulder bag. Ben was managing the big suitcase on wheels that they shared. The faster they could disappear into the crowd, the better.

The platform had porters and other staff wearing vibrant green uniforms lined up. Everything went in style, welcoming the Rovos Rail passengers to Cape Town. Ben was trying to avoid any unpleasantness. He pushed their trolley while she greeted some familiar faces they had met over dinner. The odd couple was not among them.

"Do you think that Nadifa is still alive?" Ben asked as they walked away from the platform into a long station concourse. Gosh, he must have followed her reminiscing. She was sure since she suspected Nadifa had telepathically sent her a message.

"Probably, she was not all that older than we are now, or ...we will see. I never found out what age she was when I lived with her. What does your intuition say?" In the meantime, they both wondered which way to walk, left or right. Many people were walking in both directions. There was a lot of trading going on. "No idea. She was rather ageless, come to think about it." Ben was trying to phone Jock on his cell.

Why had she never questioned that? Ben was right; she could have been between 50 - 60. Nadifa claimed they could get all the sustenance they needed from the sun to survive. Some of their conversations about the laws of physical immortality had truly generated a passion to pursue her everlasting life from within. Not that she was scared of dying, or ageing for that matter.

Nadifa had reawakened her childhood abilities to see and hear non-physical realities. Only then did she start to understand how, because this human life is rooted at the very heart of materiality, death had become a deeply programmed human race belief on a cellular level.

"Oh, Ben, I think I see them. Let's go left where the clock used to be."

They were both practically running. Annelies couldn't remember arriving at the main hall where the departure board used to be took this long.

Mien would be just outside the main hall, where they always met years ago. She hoped that it still looked the same.

Cape Town station was not what she remembered at all. She recalled the interior of the old Railway station. Above the train indicator board was the famous clock, which was always their favourite meeting place. That was where they would meet. They made their way through the crowds. Ben told her that Jock had explained that the station has two main parts, local travel platforms and the other side for national departures. He warned them not to go sightseeing as if they were in the mood to explore! She felt like a fugitive running away from danger.

Ben wanted to see the old 'Blackie', the first old locomotive on display on the national side that he had seen on the brochure, before their reunion with his family. She never knew Ben was so interested in old locomotives.

"Annie, I have some memories that go far back to do with Blackie, but you are right, let's look out for our family."

"Do you think it's true that Cape Town station has the reputation of being a hotbed of crime?"

"We were recommended to stay close to any security guards, so let's do that."

"Who are they? There are so many different uniforms around."

"Never mind. Let's look for that clock."

The weather was warm and sticky for the time of day, and every tourist dressed as if they had been to the beach. Cape Town remains one of the world's most naturally beautiful urban locations, nestled between the Atlantic Ocean and the stunning heights of Table Mountain.

"Ben, come quickly!" She had spotted the odd couple because their auras were hyperactive. They were looking out for someone. Hopefully, it wasn't them. Ben pulled her behind a partition.

"Gosh, can you believe it? I was lucky to spot them amongst all these people."

"Annie, let's wait inside there." He pointed to the Ticket Office. Let's see if anyone knows where we are."

"What are we going to do there?"

"I'm about to send Jock a text message, but I hope his cell isn't monitored.?

"You can't be serious?"

"I am. Just trust me, Annie."

Ben wasn't kidding. What did he know that she was unaware of? No movie on terrorism, highjacking, corruption, or a plain police drama had her prepared for this stressful experience. It was for real! They were standing in line, pretending to be waiting to be served. Ben typed an SMS while she remained looking for that weird couple.

It was almost their turn when Ben's cell ringtone reassured them that they were not alone.

"Ben here", he nodded at her, confirming that it was Jock. "We are at the Ticket Office, but I see no old locomotive, as far as I recall." Ben was listening while frowning. She could see that the couple were arguing as they walked past. Probably angry at losing them.

"Oh, I see. Yes, we are..." Ben saw them.

"You mean we need to follow a walkway towards Golden Acre?" She was rolling her eyes in frustration.

"Yes, I understand. We go down the escalators." Ben repeated the directions so that she would remember Jock's instructions.

"Past Clicks...a pharmacy...past a stationery shop towards...yes, I'll see you there." Ben closed his phone. He mentally told her that Jock was still trying to find parking under the shopping mall. Meeting them at Golden Acre, in front of the Wagenaers reservoir, would be better.

"Annie, we will move from here in five minutes. Let's move out of the queue. Pretend to wave at someone while I have a good look if anyone is watching us."

She did what he asked. A young Asian woman with a toddler looked surprised when they let her move forward closer to the ticket office.

Ben tapped her shoulder, "Let's go." They stepped out of the queue and walked down a long passageway into the terminal, which reminded her of Hoog Catharijne in Utrecht. Modern and colourful. Their luggage was now getting cumbersome as they tried to blend in with the crowd walking towards Golden Acre. There was a lot of noise, mostly from the announcements, which were deafening.

This run-down station reminded her that all the renovations in Cape Town had been done for the 2010 FIFA World Cup. She felt as if she was walking into a movie set. The changes compared to what she remembered about Cape Town station were impressive.

"Have we lost them?" She asked, peering over her shoulder.

"No idea, let's just get to the escalators."

"There they are, what now?"

"We go down and outside, I think?"

"Didn't you say past Clicks?" She remembered that Clicks was a large department store with a pharmacy.

The escalator took them upstairs, and they followed the crowd through glass doors outside. There were so many street vendors! To top it all, they were bothered by various traditional herbal doctors offering healing miracles.

She was mesmerized by every imaginable kind of clothing, bright jewellery, kitchen implement stalls, herbal medicine and blankets.

"This is all wrong; we must go back. I'm sure we need to go under the street."Ben said.

They returned through the glass doors when a poor-looking man asked if they were lost, but Ben kindly declined his help.

"Look, there is Clicks." She pointed.

Suddenly Ben grabbed her by the arm. He nodded for her to see what he saw. The odd couple.

They both saw the magazine and stationery shop and dived inside. You couldn't miss the odd couple and the woman who must have had trouble walking in high heels. They were both angry. With an almost mesmerizing intensity, she interpreted their fiery energy with a shining metallic gleam, displaying a determination that would not be limited by kindness or mercy.

"Thank goodness Annie, they are running toward where we came from."

While hiding behind a bookshelf, a title drew her attention.

"Is Biological immortality an absence of ageing?"

She never believed in a coincidence, so instead of pretending to look for a book, she took the book off the shelf and read the first page.

Scholars believe the high emphasis on immortality originated from a series of Sumerian legends and poems. They were gathered into a longer Akkadian poem. The most complete version existing today is preserved on 22 clay tablets.

The essential story revolves around Enkidu, who is half-wild and undertakes dangerous quests with Gilgamesh. Much of the poem illustrates Gilgamesh's search for immortality after Enkidu's death.

Before 3000 B.C.E., the Sumerians invented a script that was impressed with their clay writing material with the sharp edge of a wooden stylus. Thus, the symbol had a three-dimensional look and was called "cuneiform." Initially, the symbols were pictorial. However, by 2700 B.C.E., the pictorial text had given way to phonograms – a symbol representing a syllable; the outward form of the symbol was simplified, and it assumed a stylized appearance.

"Ben, this reminds me of Richard's translations of the twenty-two tablets!"

"Annie, please let's move out of here and find Mien." Ben had picked up a newspaper with screaming headlines:

A medical journalist has recently filed criminal charges with the FBI against the World Health Organization (WHO), the United Nations (UN) and several of the highest-ranking government and corporate officials concerning their attempts to commit mass murder via the swine flu.

She kept reading about the Sumerian gods Anu, Enlil, and Enki, who were the gods of the sky, wind, and water.

"Ben, listen." She whispered. "Enlil assigned junior divines to do farm labour and maintain the rivers and canals, but after forty years, the lesser ones rebelled and refused to do hard labour. Instead of punishing the rebels, Enki, the kind, wise counsellor to the gods, suggested that humans be created to do the work." Ben hadn't heard anything she'd read. It was a thick book, at least 500 pages long, but after she had looked at the table of contents, she was hooked.

Ocean Currents and a New Ice Age - Did the Ice Age Exist?- The Earth's Orbit and Wobble - The Visiting Comet - Wandering Poles - Mysteries of the Inner Earth and Subterranean Worlds.

She took the book to the counter and paid for it. It's going into hiding, which motivated her even more to write a map-like procedures awareness program where the awakening stages can be followed by everyone with a calling to awaken fully.

"Annie, let's find the ruins of Wagenaers Reservoir. Jock must be there by now, and I think they walked back in the direction of the station hall if we are lucky."

"What do these ruins look like? I can't remember ever seeing them."

"I believe that it's the oldest remaining structure in South Africa and can only be viewed on the bottom floor of the Golden Acre."

Ben took the large suitcase while helping her to turn her laptop bag on wheels towards what he believed must be where he would see his sister. They were both eager to see familiar faces.

"There they are!" Gosh, they are all standing in front of several huge boulders!

Both Mien, Jock and At were glad to see them. Seeing Jock all grown up reminded her how long ago it was that she had last seen him. Gosh, he looked at the spitting image of his dad. Very groomed, intelligent and at the same time jolly. She hoped that the resemblance stopped there. There was no time to peer at his field; she would do that later when all the hugging and greetings had been done.

Fourteen years ago, he was more like his younger brother At. Jock now gave the impression of a young man who had passed his wild years and was now ready to take up responsibilities. He was dishy. She wondered if he had a girlfriend in tow. Years ago, when she saw him last, Jock looked just like At today. Long dreadlocks, an earring, worn jeans and a tattoo. She wondered if he was a Rastafarian?..."Don't," Ben warned her. While At was talking into his cell phone, she read on a display board that the ruins above the massive boulders were built by Zacharias Wagenaar on Table Mountain's Fresh River in 1663.

"But Dad, my story is bound to collide with your belief systems, picture of reality and boundaries.

"Still living in the Newtonian world," Al replied frustratedly. She raised her eyebrows at Ben, standing before the glass partition. He ignored her and instead read out loud. "How the original shoreline was there before the foreshore was reclaimed from the sea." It reminded them both of Holland. Then Ben turned to Jock, who seemed to have something on his mind, because they moved away, speaking in private.

At was trying to rebel against something his Dad must have proposed or schemed. Nick had a habit of popping up in all the wrong places. Was he not arrested? Could people use a cell phone in prison? His timing was once again unfortunate. She wondered what At's comment about 'Nick's picture of reality and boundaries' was about. Feeling uncomfortable was not her intent, but Nick du Toit brought back scary memories.

"I'm glad to see you, my friend. Is Nick in town?" She whispered to Mien. They walked through a door that took them to a parking garage. Ben looked back, but the couple were not there.

She thought Nick was in jail. Mien looked tired. It was not like the last time she said goodbye in Holland. Her smart tracksuit could not hide Ben's sister's stress levels. Her aura was vibrating like a tight violin wire, out of tune.

"Come, let's not spoil our get-together. Are you joining us, or have your plans changed?" At's mother asked, ignoring her question about Nick.

"Oh, Mom, don't. I told you I...never mind" At took her laptop suitcase from her and limped towards a large motorcar in the parking lot.

"What is wrong with At? Has he injured himself?"

"Yes, he crashed his motorbike. He's lucky to be alive." Jock's tone clearly showed that there was trouble between the two brothers.

She peered at Ben, and his expression of concern clearly showed that he tried to keep something from her.

She couldn't imagine that Nick would uphold any belief system except if it would benefit his pocket. Had Toon not mentioned that Nick had been arrested? That comment from At collided with what she knew about Nick. What was At trying to explain to his dad? Since Mien hadn't said or commented, she wouldn't ask.

Beggars suddenly surrounded them, all eager to carry their bags. Some of them were no older than ten or twelve. Poverty had not lessened when the ANC came into power. Mien commented that poverty had grown worse for many people. Jock gave a few kids apples that he had taken from the van. Then they all climbed in a large seven-seater Volvo Toon had left for them to use when he was not in South Africa; Mien saw her surprised look.

"Annie, giving money is not a good thing to do since many children are addicted to tic, glue-sniffing or other drugs. Food and healthy snacks are better to hand out."

"I will remember that on this trip. So you keep apples in the car for that reason."

"Yes, seeing abandoned hungry children in the city is heartbreaking. It is the responsibility of parents to know where their children are, but so many parents have died of aids." Mien spoke in a somewhat despairing voice when they settled in the car.

"Tannie, it's not all that bad. Lots of black people's lives have improved."

She had to smile when At still used the word Tannie. So very Afrikaans. Jock called her Annelies, so he seemed more English-orientated. She never had considered that two brothers could be so different.

She would always regret never seeing Liesbeth, their only daughter, grow up.

Jock moved behind the driver's seat while At explained about South Africa, including the 2010 FIFA World Cup, many years ago and how many jobs that had created.

"Not to mention the cost, "Jock added to the conversation while he drove outside the parking bay through Cape Town's traffic. The sunny temperature lifted her spirits when they drove away from the station. She was determined to make the most of this short holiday.

"That's true, but it had given the City of Cape Town a unique opportunity to improve its infrastructure and market itself to the world." At replied. His more alternative, softer nature was seen and heard in his talk, compared to Jock's smart modern looking dress code.

"I've read on the plane that Cape Town is desirable for leisure and business travellers, investors, and residents. That must surely be good for business?" Ben addressed Jock since he sat next to him in the front.

She and Mien sat behind while At settled between their luggage in the back. It was a strange feeling to be back in the town that held so many scary memories for her.

She could see that much had changed in the city—lots of new buildings. The Waterfront, the Mother City's working harbour, set against the spectacular backdrop of Table Mountain, was truly impressive. She had never seen it the last time she had been in South Africa.

Over dinner at the Cape Town Waterfront, Jock and his mother were enthusiastic about their innovative model of sustainable living. Jock and At were both managers and part owners of this community, which consisted of five other families. She and Ben were listening to two people who seemed to have found their passion. At told them that recently, the community had started a permaculture food garden. For a fleeting moment, she again picked up that there was friction between the two brothers. She opened her inner eye to see what was going on between them. Her interpretation was about hurting, but who was insensitive to who was unclear.

Jock turned his back to his brother and carried on explaining to Ben how a type of water harvesting and a modern sanitation system had improved their already energy-efficient buildings. The central point was used for water harvesting within their sustainable village settlement.

Mien had been very quiet over dinner, picking at her food. Her two sons, each in their own way, were entertaining young men. At would be twenty-three and Jock thirty-two, both on the same day but years apart.

She remembered when she was at their birthday party fourteen years ago. Jock had come home from college. At never went to a boarding school like Jock. She wondered if that had made them so different.

At the end of dinner, after coffee, she'd heard enough. She would see for herself what their community would be like. Ben paid for dinner. He insisted, knowing that their Euro currency stretched much further regarding entertainment.

Back in the Volvo, Mien expressed her concern about the self-catering cottage she had booked for them since they had been travelling in great luxury, but she knew that Ben would welcome a more down-to-earth place. All she wanted was to be driven to the place Mien had booked for them.

"How far is the cottage by car from here?"

"About forty minutes. Depending on the traffic. We will be there just before dark. I stay in a room attached to the main house, with its entrance, and the boys are staying with friends nearby." Mien replied.

Titanya's cottage

When they arrived in Clovelly, it was pitch dark. The balmy weather outside felt welcoming after the air-conditioned car. The street and house lights on the other side of the valley, between Clovelly and Fish Hoek, had an almost fairytale appearance.

The holiday cottage was higher up against the mountain behind the main house. Trees surrounded it. Thank goodness Mien's sons trailed their luggage up the cobbled stepped pathway, past at least three water features. The lights around the back property revealed a cute cottage that truly lived up to its name. Titanya was the queen of the fairies.

"Annie, we were lucky to have this cottage for two nights. Everything is fully booked this time of the year." Mien remarked, following behind her as they climbed the steps.

"Oh, we are staying over one more night?"

"Yes, Ben asked Jock if we could book something for two nights since he has a meeting with somebody in Simons Town."

Ben was already ahead, making sure she could not say anything. She climbed another set of wooden steps up towards the cottage while Ben and Jock were already seated on the cottage's private deck. The view was outstanding. The twinkling lights from the houses on the other side of the valley created a magical atmosphere. A huge boulder below hid the main house from the view of the wooden deck. Mien's private room in the main house was past the giant boulder. She wanted to see what her room looked like.

This time, they had to walk down narrow steps chopped out of the rock to get past. Her front door also had a name. She wondered why they had named the room Love Rock.

"The first owners during the sixties had named it Love Rock, after the huge boulder," Jock replied. She wondered if he was telepathic! Mien's room had a double bed, a small kitchenette inside a cupboard, and a sliding door that opened to a full bathroom.

"The owners of the main house are away overseas. My friend is looking after this property and felt you two should enjoy a day's rest before we drive to our community." Jock added when Ben explained his appointment to her mentally:

"Annie, I didn't want to upset you, but you knew my trip was partly business concerning criminal investigations." She groaned. "Nice move, cowboy."

"Are we going to meet your friend? If not, thank her for the use of the cottage."

Mien wasn't sure. She didn't know the owners personally, and her friend was an estate agent always around and about. She said goodnight and climbed back up to the cottage.

Ben was under the shower, so he could've heard her coming in, but he was still talking to somebody. Their big suitcase was open on the single bed under the staircase.

"Who are you...Ben, your phone will get all wet!"

"Here you talk to Toon."

"What, on the cell phone?"

"Hi, Annie, how was your trip on the train?"I've not been able to reach you telepathically, that is why. Our mental connection seems unstable."

"The journey by train was very comfortable, thanks to you." *"I can pick up your thoughts. Toon, is everything alright there?"*

"Ben said that you are staying over in Clovelly. That must be near the golf course."

"No idea, we arrived in the dark. How is Ingrid doing?"

"Getting big. Did she tell you that we are having a baby girl?"

"No, I didn't know. How does it feel to become a father."

"Oh, Annie, I'm so excited. I don't want to travel away from home anymore, but after our little girl is born, I want to take them far away. Probably up to Buttercup Valley."

"Has anything happened? Are you starting to feel unsafe?"

"Annie, please tell Toon... why we are using cell phones. " Ben beamed the rest.

"I heard that. Ben, did you get my SMS? I could not reach you mentally, but now I feel or pick up your signatures."

Annelies knew he had not received hers. She wondered why. Ben took his iPhone from her so she could take a shower. She heard him talking to Toon, but the rushing water and her lack of concentration to listen mentally were not there.

The Language of Stone

Annelies woke up with a jolt. Her body felt stiff, like a corpse but alive! Ben's rhythmic breathing skipped a beat because she suddenly sat bolt upright in bed. Her emotions of panic and despair still lingered. Her dream still flashed by like a film script. She was in a speeding car that was out of control, in a world beyond

her wildest dreams; fantastic, but...the emotions of intense fear
must have made her jolt back into her body.

At least it proved that she'd just woken up from a nightmare. The
light starting to peep through the curtains showed that it was still
early, maybe 5 or 6 o'clock. Gee, why was the feeling of fear or
sorrow so strong?... Even now, her body was still shaking. The tears
of regret were stuck in her throat. Her emotional state was in an
uproar. She could hardly breathe, as if something or somebody
wanted her out of control.

The images that passed her mental vision made no sense. It was
like seeing the world through the multifaceted eyes of a dragonfly.
Each facet showed her a different scene. "What should I believe?
Which reality?" She thought. A voice deep beneath her psyche's
layers replied: *"A journey with or without purpose stays meaningless. You will
stay asleep if you believe your hallucinations are real. Believe nothing."*

At least her pounding head brought her firmly back into her body,
away from an unknown world, into her bed next to Ben.

Looking at his sleeping face brought back feelings of gratitude.
Whatever happened, Ben was her anchor in life. His total loyalty
in every situation she got herself into was a blessing.

How was it that a nightmare could have such a hold on her? Had
she been externalising a vision that she had witnessed internally?
What gave her that idea? Not more than inches from her inner eye,
the vision of a massive rock face in her dream had been waiting for
her response....as if it could wait no longer... Gosh, she had to stop
herself from being consumed by negative thoughts. It was easy to
see the worst in a situation instead of a positive solution.

"Get back into the present", she scolded herself. "Getting into 'the
moment' helps if some action follows. *Annie, you'd better practise
what you preach to your workshop students."* Talking to herself all her
life had often been ridiculed until Ben returned to her life. He took

her inner discussions with herself seriously, and they strengthened their telepathic skills.

She settled into a lotus position under the duvet, with Ben still fast asleep beside her. She prepared herself by travelling over her body from her toes to her knees while watching her thoughts fleeting. Thoughts like that an opportunity might not occur for thousands of years...or that tranquillity was necessary.... or thoughts like, was it not already too late...but who was thinking now?

She dropped back onto her pillow when feelings of despair once again tried to consume her. What if her dream was a warning?

The sight of Ben's profile reminded her of the rock with a human profile that she had seen in her dream. Had it spoken to her? Could stones, rocks or boulders hold onto man's external worldly outcome? Those visions! She still vividly remembered what had been said in her dream:

The shift is upon you. It is time to wake up and announce your presence within this realm. Your life purpose begins with humility. Having shaken off the beast, you can now get down to work.

Africa was not always as you now know it. It was once part of a great southern continent called Gondwana, which comprised Australia, India, Antarctica, South America, and Madagascar. I have stored memory from about 300 million to 183 million years ago. These energy sediments comprise the Karoo Sequence, which now covers nearly half the surface area of South Africa.

With her inner eye, she still saw every detail of how things looked then.

"God doesn't kill people; people who believe in God kill people", the angry crowd shouted. How could these timeless events concerning her past or future still be in the making while she was wide awake?

"Calm down, girl, your dream world is nothing more than a de-cluttering process. Everyone can 'see' what is stored there in our spiritual world."

She sensed that Nadifa's familiar energy signature was near, but somehow she could stay invisible.

The panicky feelings slowly dissipated by reminding herself that even her dreams were an illusion. Nothing was for real. She was not even real. Only her bodily senses created an illusion that she was real. By externalising, what appeared to be an internalising experience was therefore fruitless. Or was it? Her dream felt so real! Where had she been? A part of her was thrilled at remembering being in what seemed like another dimension. So what use was it to her if it was all meaningless?

<Annie, you'd better pretend you are real while penetrating your veiled dimensions of consciousness. During these times, many will re-discover the three-fold function of the mind and the qualities of their true inner self, the soul.>

She heard POWAH replying to her thoughts! How real was that? It was still early, well before six. The distractions of the day would not take up much of her time if she used them wisely. They had made a breakfast appointment at a bakery named Olympia at 9:30. It was now six o'clock. A good shower would clean up any possible negative energy. Talking to herself gave her inspiration to face the day.

She was keen to have a stroll in the garden before breakfast. What she could see from the kitchen window looked promising.

After her early morning shower, her mind had settled. Ben was still asleep, so she dressed downstairs and left the suitcases where they had left. The cottage had a fairytale feel to it. Especially last night, they discovered a switch under the wooden staircase leading up to the main bedroom. Hundreds of little lights transformed everything.

During the day, these little bulbs were by the ivy and leaf decor. She could see a fairy castle behind the big tree from the kitchen window by daylight. It inspired her to go outside to explore the terraced garden.

The huge boulders scattered over the mountainside property were in her dream, but she was intrigued enough to investigate instead of dwelling on it. Mien had said that the owners of the main house below were on a European trip so that she would have the garden to herself.

Thank goodness for her sturdy walking shoes. There were so many steps and cobbled pathways that once she stepped off the wooden deck, it would be easy to fall if she wore the wrong footwear.

She admired three small ponds on the lower level, below the grassed terrace. From there, steps led into an enclosed seating area. Six wooden stools are attached to a round wooden table under a thatched roof at the centre. Maybe they could all have lunch in this enchanting picnic spot this afternoon.

More curved steps took her up on the way past the grass terrace. She now had a full view of a fantasy castle with lots of toadstool-shaped towers, and tiny fairies were leaning out of windows and balconies. She was greeted by two large sculptured fairy pillars painted like the colour of gemstones. It made her recall a dream from long ago about the temples at Abu Simbel, of the two giant monuments of Ramesses II and that of his wife, Nefertari, surrounded by palm trees and ferns.

The energy in this garden had a higher vibration due to the singing birds and butterflies as if the natural spirits were holding a festival. In this wonderfully tranquil spot, she reconnected again to planet Earth with all its beautiful creatures from the plant and animal kingdoms, the insects and the unseen nature elementals that she knew so well from her childhood.

What had aspired the artist? Probably the traditional folk tales of fairies, goblins and spirits who inhabit secret woodlands and rocky places. She would love to have met the person who had created all this. She must ask Mien if her friend knows them.

Ahead, she saw a quaint bridge and a stick-paved pathway inside the fairy garden. On the left, a child's Wendy's house is hidden under a flowering hibiscus. Turning right, she passed a miniature goblin house and another sculpture as intricate as the real wooden Wendy's house.

She saw a small sandpit as she followed the swirling path on her left. Straight ahead, two big red toadstools greeted her after she ducked under a thick ivy-covered arch. Now she had a choice: on her left, she would arrive inside the towering castle, or if she turned sideways between another thick ivy arch, she would end up on a deck made from tree branches. She could not resist and stepped onto the small deck made for small people.

The view was splendid, overlooking the terraced garden, including the stone path from the main house to the gate in front of the property. She turned back and saw two colourful dragons, part of the castle, completing her fairy garden expedition. This fantasy playground would enchant every child. The garden was magnificent, with a small plot of green grass bordered by tropical succulents, an olive tree and lavender bushes, making for an excellent exercise place. She started with breathing exercises by guiding her consciousness into different body parts.

She recalled how she had a group of neophytes dressed like her in the same clothing in another life.

All of a sudden, a mist-like veil came over her. Before losing her balance, she quickly returned to the fairy garden and sat on the fake grass inside the fairy castle. She tried to regulate her breathing until it became a calm, rhythmic pulse. A weird sensation came over her as if she'd been here before....

<If you examine your inner space, you discover it is like outer space. It comprises vast amounts of nothingness, but that's not exactly correct. The sub-atomic world of electron behaviour gives credence to the belief that psychic abilities function on

this level of reality, the realm of higher consciousness where the Gods dwell. When your higher mental body is looking through your eyes, those are the eyes of your lover, friend, teacher, companion, and God/Goddess within.>

The mist was lifting, and she wondered what to make of this that POWAH had implanted into her mind, knowing that every thought, emotion or mental state has its corresponding rate and vibration mode.

Her Astral Vibration Code 8-Divine Union[1]

She recalled the first paragraph in her decoding book:

The Mental feminine energy of the eight vibrations of the divine union can give you the strength to achieve your life's goals. This frequency tends to stir or harness anger that can manifest in a stressful situation.

In what way was the number code eight of her Astral body code associated with her logical intellect and her left hemisphere? That is the clue she now needed to awaken to. Her code stood for divine union, and she always thought that Theo was her twin flame, but he passed on.

Knowing that all her manifestations of thought affect the minds of other persons, would Ben understand what she had just experienced?

She got up and peered in the direction of the cottage. Her body felt stiff as if she had been running uphill. She was about to return to the cottage when a familiar mental signature crossed her mind.

"To have a love affair with yourself is as close as you will ever come to feeling the Soul quality of Divine Union Annie. Then, there is no fear, guilt, judgment, or love. When you truly want to embody this Language of Light quality, there can be no room left for feelings that do not support this quality."

---

1. https://allrealityshifters.wordpress.com/the-three-higher-emotional-astral-and-mental-spacings/

Only two people she knew had that feeling to their mental tone. Theo, whom she knew had passed on, and Nadifa, who might still be alive.

"Nadifa, is that you?"

There was no telepathic reply. Annelies would know if it was Ben; his signature was familiar to her. Instead of calling her telepathically, she heard him calling her out loud.

He waved at her from the top balcony of the cottage. The birds must have awoken him. She took a different route to the cottage, past another picnic spot under a big tree.

"Exploring, are you?" Ben called out from above her. The creative atmosphere had uplifted her spirits and released all the energy from her upsetting, de-cluttering dream.

"Don't you agree that every moment we encounter must have a meaning," she asked when Ben joined her on the cottage's lower deck. Together, they admired the view over the ocean.

"Sure. The gardener and artist must have dreamed all this." Spreading his arms wide "before it manifested itself."

"This place so reminds me of why I decided to come with you on this trip. " she beamed while serving orange juice outside.

"Really, what wisdom has this place awakened in you?" Ben's humourous tone said enough. She loved the glint in his eyes as he spoke, knowing that, for the first time, he relaxed.

"It's about the power behind our manifestations. Just as a poppy seed or a flower bulb must have an exact picture or representation of what it must express, so must we hold an exact vision of what we desire to attract into our lives, don't you think." Ben was studying her while sipping his juice.

"Whoever is responsible for this garden must have had that intent and desire," she added with awe.

"Hi there, you are both already up and about." Mien came strolling up the stone pathway from the gate. Her colourful sleeveless top on her sporty pants made her look young. She must have been up before her or gone out while exploring the garden.

"I booked us a table at the Olympia Cafe, and At is already waiting for us," Mien climbed and bounced up onto their wooden deck. All she truly wanted to do was write, relax, and meditate in the fairy garden with nobody around.

Tomorrow, she could make their breakfast, but then she realized that she had better do some shopping today.

"It's a trendy place, so we'd better get going." Mien was clearly in a hurry. At least she was far more herself, like in Holland, primarily when she had run her own Pannekoek restaurant in Apeldoorn. Her energy field had calmed down to the usual rhythm she was familiar with. Ben's nephew Richard had told her that Mien wanted to sell her restaurant in Holland. That had surprised her. She wanted to spend time with her close friend to discover why and what her boys were up to.

"Okay, let's go the way we are. Mien, will we be coming straight back?"

"It's up to you. We can take a stroll up Kalk Bay's main road afterwards. It's packed with antique stores, coffee shops, galleries, second-hand bookstores and restaurants."

"That sounds like a good plan. Ben, what about letting us ladies do our thing while you, Jock and At take a drive in the Volvo unless you have other plans." *"I got your hint. Yes, spend time with her alone while I entertain the boys."* Ben winked at her.

"While you two go visiting shops, maybe At and Jock will show me Kalk Bay harbour. I read that it is still one of the best places to buy fresh fish straight off the boat."

"Slim plan. Annie, get your bag and a hat. It's going to be a warm day." Mien liked the idea of shopping with her.

While Ben got their cameras and other tourist gear, she took the tray inside. He locked the cottage doors, and they followed Mien down the path to the gate, which took them to the parking bay.

"It's not far. We can walk."

It took them ten minutes to get to the Olympia, where At was chatting up a young waitress. Jock waved at them from a corner table. The place was packed full. Mien had not exaggerated. The boys had kept three seats for them, but some people waiting for a table did not appreciate that.

After breakfast At, Jock and Ben walked to Kalk Bay harbour while the two women set off to explore the shops. They would meet back at the Brass Bell Restaurant for lunch, where the boys had parked the Volvo.

Chapter 8
Cutting Cords with the Past

The Hunger of Our Dark Shadows

There was so much to see. Annelies felt like she fancied treating her friend to a colourful scarf and found a lovely necklace for herself.

"Mien, do you want to sell the Pannekoek?" They were browsing in a plant nursery and coffee shop where Mien wanted to treat her to ice cream.

"Yes, I'm selling the restaurant to my friend Nel. We will stay partners until she can buy me out. I want to travel after the boys are more settled in their project."

"Sonja seems to like it in Holland. Is she going to stay permanently?"

"I suspect so. Sonja seems to have found someone, a doctor. I hope that he is the right man for her."

"You mean Ben van Dongen?" She had already suspected that something was going on between them. She had spoken to him earlier when Toon was in the hospital and later when Richard was at the burn unit recovering from his dreadful ordeal.

"Yes, him. What do you think?"

"He's perfect. You will like him. He has an open mind."

"Yes, I thought so. Annelies, how much contact do you have with Harry Brinks now that your hotel has burnt down? Is he going to rebuild it again?" Mien's question completely threw her. She didn't even think she knew him.

"It all depends. We are selling our house to Fred and Quincy. That way, I can repay my portion of the loan to Harry. It's time for us to leave Holland. We don't know where we will end up, but we will stay at the Half-way House in France for now."

"I heard something like that from Richard. Will Ben be retiring as an undercover agent?"

"I hope so, but you know Ben, he will probably take cases freelance, as he is doing now."

"Is he on an assignment in South Africa?"

"Yes, he is, although I'm not supposed to know that. Ben keeps telling me it's connected with Nick, but I don't believe that. He is holding something back from me."

"I didn't think that was possible." Mien smiled. She was right. Ben could never keep something from her if she used her physic abilities. However, early in their relationship, they promised each other that they would not abuse their sensitivity unless necessary. She wanted to ask Mien why her two boys had such a heavy cloud hanging between them, but something held her back. Mien was a very private person. Prodding about issues she had not yet shared meant to stay private was inappropriate. She would tell her in her own time.

"It's almost time to meet them at the Brass Bell. Let's go." She was about to pay the waitress when Mien intervened.

"This is on me, but thanks for the offer and my scarf."

It was busy on the pavement as they strolled past the second-hand junk shop. It was there, looking across the road, that she spotted the same odd couple that they had been running from at the Station. She pulled Mien inside while pretending to be interested in something.

"You've got to be kidding?"

Mien was reacting to her picking up an old, rather dusty-looking box with old photographs of Kalk Bay during the twenties.

"Since when have you been interested in old stuff?"

"Sorry, I thought it was something else," was her flimsy excuse when she put it back. They walked outside again, following the road to the Brass Bell. The couple had gone.

"Three hours was not long enough," Annelies complained after they found all three men drinking beer on the terrace two metres above the crashing waves. She had bought several gifts to take home. Annelies had visited some places before but had forgotten how interesting Kalk Bay was.

Ben kept looking at his watch during lunch. He and Jock had an appointment later in the afternoon. With whom they didn't elaborate, Annelies wouldn't ask.

After lunch, they travelled around the False Bay coastline to a beautiful spot, about 15 minutes past Simons Town, where At parked the Volvo. Strolling hand in hand with Ben was like holding onto someone on a tightrope. *"What is troubling you?"* Although the massive boulders next to the walkway were breathtaking as the surf cascaded over the rugged natural terrain, a tense air surrounded the group as if some dark, cloudy energy field had entered their auras.

"Jock got himself into some financial difficulties. He asked if I could join him at his meeting." He squeezed her hand as if to say, stop worrying. Intuitively, she knew that was not all of it. *"Is Mien's ex involved?"* She tried to shield herself from the deep shadows associated with Ben, Jock, and Mien. The only time she had been feeling this way was on the train near that funny couple. At seemed to be the only one who was cheerful. He pointed at the foaming waters as they rolled over the rocks next to the walkway. The filtered sunlight pierced the water and illuminated the sea bottom. *"Yes, Nick is involved. At and Mien do not know, so don't say anything before our meeting."*

The surf's sound and the seawater's clarity made her thirsty. There was a thickness to the water as it slickly flowed over the rocks. It was like some crystal in motion. As little water sections would begin to foam from minor turbulence, they added variety to the smoothly flowing textures. She kneeled closer while the others strolled on. Strangely enough, the movement reminded her of the genetic DNA coding program.

The moment she contemplated her writings, a similar mist-like feeling came over her, like what she had experienced in the Clovelly cottage fairy garden. She felt spaced out, away from the others. The sensation that POWAH was near, while she was temporarily in a null zone, all happened instantly. She never fully understood why his signature felt male, but somehow, his loving energy surrounded her in the flesh, and she believed it to be true.

<Annie, your Emotional youth code is the etheric layer where you keep the records of all your incarnations. It's the vehicle through which you go to the retreats at night and while you are in your Now moment. The God program is accessed here. It is the realm that humanity has to bypass to ascend.>

She was startled by the stream of thoughts that, for a moment, had stopped time, or so it seemed. She needed to remember these words, for they belonged in her decoding workbook.

"Why do I feel that I've been warned?"

That was how her emotional body interpreted this message.

<It's your body code calculations that will reprogram the matrix of your blueprint that is influenced by your intent. Use your mind while observing your feelings when archetypal forces seek a human vehicle. Instead, let them pass through you because your cellular regeneration will have started. Cutting emotional cords>

What was her Emotional youth code again? The eleven and eight root number codes made key numbers nineteen, ten, and one. Forgiveness.

"You mean the Soul quality of forgiveness, and now my Emotional youth spacings of forgiveness will help me to bypass the fourth into the fifth dimension?"

Her Emotional Youth Vibration Code 1 Forgiveness again [1]

<Remember there is no injustice in the universe and that all people are in the best possible condition their karma allows them to be in. You must also not lose sight of the fact that before coming again into this world with a new baby body, your physical blueprint is chosen as karma dictated. Your preset life circumstance, as well as your parents and your specific life course, is your choice.>

In the corner of her eye, she saw that At also sat on his haunches, leaning against a boulder further down near the surf, speaking on his cell. Why had POWAH chosen this moment to communicate with her?

Mien was sitting on a bench overlooking the ocean, so she stood up and joined her. No words were spoken between them. Ben was talking to Jock, but she couldn't eavesdrop. Why she was attracted or was almost possessed by 'POWAH's energy presence nearby when all of them were strolling or sitting down staring at the sea puzzled her, but for now, she would just trust in the mystery of how the numeral interpretations from her decoding book could awaken her super-conscious.

Mien appeared to be dozing next to her, so she relaxed and went with the flow.

She knew that in other lives, she had also contemplated the same topics that she was now busy with, but maybe not to the same

---

1. https://lightworkerjournals.wordpress.com/forgiveness-symbol-art/

extent. She hoped the memories from other lifetimes would soon surface so she could understand herself better.

"POWAH if our karmically based etheric pattern determines what kind of emotional propensity we have, as well as what our mental habit patterns are, and what our physical strengths and weaknesses are, through our genetics; if nothing is by chance, why do people have sudden accidents?"

Her telepathic question was instantly answered as if she already knew her question.

<Annie, you cannot experience true healing unless you have healing of the cause and core behind the condition, which is transmutation and healing at the level of the etheric blueprint first. Healing begins at the level of the spirit, which is etheric.>

She hoped that POWAH was not implying that she needed to have an accident first to let go of her own karmic but mental habit patterns. She peered sideways at Mien, but she had her eyes closed. She could see other people's etheric bodies. Mien's outer energy layer looked like a sea of sparkling points, a spider web of dynamic energy.

<Correct, and each spark or point of light on this web is a point of focus for vital, sustaining forces to flow into the denser physical body. For most people, this vibrational resonance is invisible to them.>

She wished she was near her laptop. There was so much work to be done. Instead, she was distracted by the intrigue playing havoc around her. Could she sidestep the drama that was playing out?

"Jock, it's time to go. At, please take care of the ladies while we walk down to the coffee shop where we are meeting the people who want to speak to Jock."

"Oh, people I know?" At was surprised and probably irritated for being left behind with the two women.

Jock turned while Ben walked on.

"I'll tell you about it when we meet up again."

"Ben, be on your guard, please."

"Don't worry, love. I have you to remind me why we are here."

"Oh, why are we here? Don't tell me, I think I know."

"See you in an hour. Oh, and Annie, I am surprised, but At will tell you."

Then Ben's signature was gone. They must have arrived at their meeting place. Ben was probably talking to people ignorant of what took place on an energy level.

<Annie, always remember that etheric or energetic healing only works by changing and transforming the patterns and imbalances from within the cellular, energetic, dynamic self of your genetic patterning or lineage. Whatever you experience, your blueprint is forever changing, ever-moving, ever-growing and expanding in form.>

"So what you are telling me is that what happened to me fourteen years ago was karmic?" POWAH's telepathic hint somehow seems to be directed at her. She thought she couldn't begin to understand, but she was sure that was why they were in SA.

<From our perspective, your karmic patterns and repetitive habit-forming programs can be removed and realigned. This can be achieved with the Soul body's permission. Most actualized diseases or accidental traumas can be traced to hereditary factors genetically and through your environment. The thought patterns of yourself and others, as well as your own beliefs and core beliefs, are the keys. Through fear, you can use your expression to distract your focus for a split second.>

"Mmm, I wish I could see my etheric field. Would it not be more helpful if people could see their energy bodies?"

<They can; you can imagine that you are layers of energy waves.>

She closed her eyes and started to see herself as an energy being. At first, she was unsure if she saw her own or intellectually what she imagined she saw; lots of colour waves were spinning and circulating. She felt her energy resonate when she thought about what she saw.

<The time has arrived for humanity to become the masters of your world.>

The voices of approaching people on the sidewalk broke her vision spell. 'POWAHs energy signature became a fainter impression, and then he was gone.

Mien looked startled at her as if she had been asleep and just woke up. She asked what time it was—to her surprise, only five minutes had passed. At came to the bench saying that he was thirsty, so they slowly walked past cute shops towards Simon's Town waterfront. At knew of a coffee shop near to where Ben and Jock had their meeting.

She hoped it was Ben's only meeting in Cape Town, no matter his surprise, but that was probably wishful thinking. His mind channel was closed, so she couldn't spy on him unless she forced it open, which she would never do without his consent.

Mien wanted to know how far she was with her genetic decoding workbook. Instead, she asked what the surprise was that Ben had been hinting at. At shook his shoulders.

"Ben received a phone call at the Kalk Bay harbour. Only after the call was finished did he tell Jock and me that he had been speaking to a person named Liesbeth. Who is she?"

"Oh, has something happened?" Ignoring At's question.

"No, but Liesbeth told Ben she would join you both soon."

"Really, on her own, or is Hans with her?" Her joy at sharing this country with them would make it a memorable trip.

"That we don't know. What has Hans to do with...oh, is Liesbeth Hans' girlfriend?"

"Liesbeth, are you and Hans both joining us?" She had to send a message before she could reply At telepathically.

"You asked me who Liesbeth was. Has your mother not told you?" Mien shook her head. That did surprise her. Surely her finding her lost daughter after all those years was worthy enough to be talked about? The moment these thoughts were out, she felt terrible. She can still hear Nadifa telling her. *"Too often, we have expectations of people that they just can't live up to."*

"Sorry, Annelies. I've just been back for a few weeks, and so much has happened that I never told the boys what happened on New Year's Eve. I was not there, remember?"

"Gosh, you are right. Who told you?"

Mien said that Sonya had phoned her with the news the following day.

"What happened? Who is Liesbeth?" At asked, "I think mom said that Hans had finally found a woman friend. We were surprised. He never was interested in women, so we...

"Good grief, you thought he was gay?" She had picked up his thoughts.

"Well, no, but he was so different. We met him a few times with Toon when he was here on business, and then Hans never showed any interest in women, so..."

Annelies realised suddenly that Mien's children probably never knew about their uncle's affair with her at their age. Nor that she had a baby at sixteen, and the kidnapping drama. Not many people knew about it, and her best friend was never one to talk about others.

"Mien, I'm sorry. I...never mind.At, Your mom never told you about me having a baby at sixteen, did she?"

"Mom. did you know?" At turned to his mother and glanced at her as if he saw her for the first time. "Gosh, at sixteen! Wow, that must have been quite a scandal in those days!" At's expression clearly showed that he was impressed.

"That's enough At. No, I never told you boys because Annelies is also my best friend, and I only heard years later that your uncle Ben was the father."

"Does Jock know?"

"Probably not, and don't tell your brother. Let them do that themselves if it comes up, will you." Mien was uneasy about something that had nothing to do with Liesbeth and Hans.

"OK, Mom," *"Mien's worry is far more severe. Yes, Hans is joining me."* Liesbeth's telepathic reply confirmed her suspicions. *"Is there anything I must do now?"* A telepathic two-way communication took just as much mental energy as a verbal conversation. She had lost the thread of their conversation when she noticed that Mien was trying to get her attention. It wasn't nice of her to mentally move away into a world of her own.

"Shall we order something to drink, or do you want to wait for the men to join us?"

"I'd love a cappuccino."

"At, I want to introduce Annelies to the people you have talked to me about."

"Are you serious?"

She wondered why At had responded to his mom with surprise after he made a sign for any waiter to come to take their order.

"What people, Mien?"

Their conversation came to a dead halt when the waitress approached them.

"I'm sorry. Did I miss something just now?"

At shook his head. He showed true interest in her ascension workshops by asking her about it again. She still knew too little about him to share her whole ascension project. Instead, she scanned his energy field and was disturbed by a schism mark she had only seen once. A participant stopped attending her decoding classes after a few weeks. Wim, that was his name, had the same markings. His aura was riddled with them. Now would be the right time to feel POWAH near her.

She became aware of a familiar frequency. She knew that others could not smell, see, or hear into other dimensions, but she could under special circumstances in the present moment.

She heard 'POWAH's words, or at least as she mentally translated them to be, like hearing a telepathic conversation.

<Send protective light around yourself. No one in your reality is not so pure. They cannot seal themselves from their shadows.>

At was still waiting for her reply, but she would rather wait for their drinks to arrive, and allow 'POWAHs energy to diminish.

<Send protective light around yourself. No one in your reality is so pure that they can shield themselves from their shadows.>

She tried to sound as intellectual as possible without freaking him out. At listened while she was thinking about what to say next.

"You mean at birth?"

"Yes. How the Soul only partly connects to a baby's mind and why an individual Soul chooses its genetics for this lifetime." At nodded and asked how her decoding would reveal that.

"It's not as simple as that. Every cell is made up of two invisible ingredients: awareness and energy. When the transition of a Soul being is translated into words, it sounds fantastic, but we are talking about a new understanding of psychology for the times to come, which is being anchored now."

Mien had not responded out loud; instead, she heard her telepathic question.

"Annie, do you know whom Jock and Ben have a meeting with?"

She was startled. Could Mien?

"Mien, you can communicate telepathically? Can you read my thoughts? Since when?..." It took a short moment for her to grasp

Mien's mental question, wondering if she had honestly heard her reply. At was still waiting for her to explain further.

"At, during the first level of my decoding classes, some participants were not ready to carry on. The reasons are not always clear, but somehow they were stopped from carrying on."

"Do you know why?"

"No. Or at least I don't think I know."

"Oh?"

At was waiting for a better explanation.

"Some people will link to others and experience a strong Soul recognition; you know whom I speak of, don't you?" Mien told her that Toon had often talked about Ingrid to the boys.

"Mmm, Ingrid and Toon, you mean. I suppose I find it difficult to mix a romantic encounter with anything of a spiritual nature."

"Why is that, do you think?"

"Don't know. How does one know that a person you are romantically attracted to is a Soul mate or twin soul, like Toon and Ingrid? I'm sure Mom and Dad must have been attracted to each other in the past, and look at them now."

Mien's raised eyebrows spoke of surprise, but she kept silent. At, was her youngest, and Annelies couldn't remember how old he was when Mien separated from Nick.

"He was ten. It's the first time that At is mentioning our relationship. I've tried to avoid Nick's wheeling and dealings with the law, but he has been spying on the boys. I know I'm not very good at telepathy, but you can receive and reply mentally. I think I'm good at projecting but not so good at receiving."

"Are you in contact with your father?" She asked instead of replying to At's question about Soul mates. She wondered if he had attracted a fragmented Soul schism that didn't belong to him.

"Yes, we meet occasionally. But he's now in jail, waiting for his trial date. Jock is more in contact with him than I am. We have a different outlook on life. I want to follow what you are exploring; Mom knows."

"I didn't know that," Mien replied

"Tannie, do you believe in UFOs?"

She raised her eyebrows as if to say, aliens. "Are you asking me if I acknowledge that there are other intelligent beings amongst us?"

"Do you?"

"Sure, we are all multidimensional beings, but humans are the masters of this physical reality. But that's not what you're asking, is it?"

At was holding something back. She wondered if he had been contacted in any way.

"You mean that there are no aliens among us who are physical?"

"That depends upon what you perceive as being an alien." The waitress asked if they wanted to order more from the menu, but they all instead waited for Ben and Jock to call them when the meeting was over and where they would meet up.

"We live in changing times. By changing, I mean our reality is about to change. What always appears solid or physical will soon merge with higher frequency waves, for the lack of a better word.

Let me explain. Hans told us that the electromagnetic fields give our third dimension a solidified effect. When this field expands, we can soon differentiate between Astral influences and higher dimensional interpretations."

The waitress took away their empty cups, waited until she was gone, and then continued.

"There will be people who feel that they are contacted by beings who are more intelligent or more powerful than they are. It can be a traumatic experience or an enlightening one. It all depends on the individual's state of awareness."

At looked puzzled, looking at his mom.

"At we are living at a critical time in history. Our capacity to overcome the world's ecological and technological difficulties today depends on one fact."

"And that is?"

"When people express only one side or the other of an issue, their minds are split. Fundamental dogma or holding onto beliefs does that."

"You mean when we still believe in good or bad, right or wrong, or...I'm better than you, and so on."

"Yes, our world of duality will soon be no more. During the closing years, excessive rationalising will frustrate and over-amplify 4D beings.

Both At and Mien wanted her to explain further.

"Many dark entities will try to stop human creativity, or what we call "awakening to their truth. Why? Because they do not want the higher worlds to penetrate 3D."

"But many people are waiting for the gods to return. You say they are being stopped from coming into our reality by lower beings?" At asked.

"No, the dark forces do not have to do anything for that to be prevented so long as religious groups create a split within people's perceptions between good and evil."

"Oh, you mean if we keep believing in a world of duality, we will not ...ascend?" At nodded.

"That is indeed the obstacle we all have to overcome. From the time a body is born, that is, from the time a "self" EGO dwells in it, the body develops a power of resistance corresponding to the average degree of consciousness of the spirit dwelling in it."

They all looked somewhat puzzled. She had probably confused them.

"At , we all have to undo the unresolved layers of history that will be dredged up for the final appraisal. That means each individual needs to release judgment about others." She said the last sentence with a smile since she was unsure if she could release or cut any emotional cords.

"Mmm, I'm starting to see why you keep hearing that what we do to others, we do to ourselves. Am I right?"

"Very good At. I was not that aware when I was in my twenties. Gosh, Mien, this son of yours is very awake!"

Mien was chuffed with At for being so open.

"Gosh, Mom, don't you think we should order something else? People are looking for a table, but our table is empty. What could be taking them so long?"

"At is right, Annie. Ben and Jock must be held up."

"Annie" Ben telepathically called out. *"You and I may not know the truth about our past, but we feel you are in danger."*

Her whole body turned stone cold. What was Ben referring to? First, POWAH warned her, and now Ben. Gosh, were there karmic memories from her past that would now come to haunt her? Looking around, she couldn't even imagine that there was any danger. The sun was shining. She was overlooking one of the best beaches on the Cape Peninsula, Boulders Beach. *"Ben, where are you?"*

At said to his mother that he often wondered if his brother was a Soul mate. At and Mien reminded her of how she perceived having a Soul connection with someone. How could she be talking about a spiritual topic when much darker energy was creeping around them simultaneously? Her emotional body had picked up on energies of fear.

"Annie, we won't be safe until we discover who or which group is behind all the Jaarsma Clan's terrible ordeals. We know that the forces of evil threaten to stop us from fully awakening. I didn't fully appreciate to what extent we are all still manipulated and controlled by them." Ben's mental confession gave her gooseflesh.

"Excuse me, but I need to visit the ladies." She needed to get away to connect with Ben. Where was he? Why did she feel that Ben was mentally warning her... She left their table with a flimsy toilet excuse, leaving Mien frowning.

The chatter from the other occupied tables outside Simon's Town's waterfront sidewalk seemed to interfere with their mental connection. She sensed that Ben was talking to someone while communicating with her on an open channel! He would only do that ...

"Annie, I have seen the results of a private research report investigating mental programming and de-programming. Remember that we live in an unstable reality where deception has become an integral part of the framework of our society."

Thank goodness, they were both entirely in tune, recognizing that the freedom of the mind is the first freedom from which all others are derived. She studied her face in the washroom mirror while washing her hands. She concluded that she couldn't trust anyone, not even herself – especially not herself. It turns out that there's one thing even more disturbing than forgetting one's past: resurrecting one's ego shadow program.

"Annelies, are you alright?" Mien must have been aware of her distress since she followed her into the ladies.

"Yes, well no, but ...did you leave At to settle our bill?" *"Are you telepathic?* She beamed while observing her face in the mirror above the washbasin.

Mien's expression told her that she tried to pick up her thoughts.

"Annelies, I know you asked me a question. I can sense it but I am not good at translating impressions into words. I get a sense, a feeling, nothing more. I suppose I'm not good at receiving."

Mien made a gesture with her hands as if to say: *"Did you hear me?"* She nodded.

"Wow, that is amazing. What did I mentally say to you?"

She repeated the words she had heard while trying to pick up anything Ben might want her to hear.

"Annelies, how does it work? Why do you, Ben, Leo, Toon, Ingrid, Hans and Liesbeth all interact that way?" Mien whispered, just in case someone was listening.

Whenever the emotional or astral aura overrides the mental aura, the soul quality of love and compassion can partially replace the mental aura to maintain sensitivity at a higher and more acute level. In this case, her emotional placement on her decoding tree was guided by the soul's quality of compassion.

As a mental body code, this frequency of four brings compassion relating to high morals, traditional values, honesty, integrity and inner wisdom to the foreground to master, building solid foundations in an incarnation.

"Mien, the main reason for our mental telepathic powers of communication is not known to us so far, but you must have been aware of Ben's telepathic communications with Leo, his twin brother." She spoke softly, wondering if there was someone else in the ladies. There were three doors, but they had not opened.

"Yes, I always knew they had a mental connection, but my two boys do not have that sensitivity, and neither does Sonja, so far as I know."

"The fact that we, I mean if we have any relation or connection to the Jaarsma clan, apparently some form of plan or program was born." She replied in a low tone while applying lipstick. That was what they had been after fourteen years ago—her DNA. Why only hers was never clear, but her horrific ordeal had left memory scars she needed to let go of.

"What do you mean?"

Mien forgot why she had followed her into the ladies. A young mother with a toddler came in, and when they left again, Mien took a pamphlet out of her bag and gave it to her.

"You want me to visit the big tree?"

"I have read that telepathy exists not only in humans but also in animal and plant kingdoms. I can verify that. I have a solid rapport with the big tree near Storms River, on the eastern Cape border."

Mien's face in the mirror clearly showed how serious she was.

"Really? How does a tree communicate to you?"

"My intuition, I reckon. I sense that the tree is having a sort of rapport with me. Lately, I have had a great need to revisit the tree. I would love for you to join me."

Her nerves had settled by now, and she liked Mien's suggestion.

"Okay, yes, let's go together. I would love to visit the big tree. Mien, I will write or explain how a certain feeling must be developed with light in my decoding workbook. That is why we work with the Language of Light."

"What do you know about..." Suddenly, Mien covered her ears as if she tried to stop something. Then she looked around, checking the doors to see if someone else was in the ladies' toilets. One door was locked.

They both jumped in fright when a cell phone gave away that someone else was in the ladies' behind the third door. Both stared at each other with big eyes, waiting to hear, but the flushing system drowned a muffled voice. They both had been conversing in Dutch, so whoever had overheard them might not have understood them. Mien grabbed her by the arm, and they ran out of the restroom....

Chapter 9
Titanya's Cottage

How to Choose the Right Actions

As they returned to the table, they saw that At was talking to someone on his cell phone. "I will ask, a moment, please." He covered his cell phone.

"Mom, how long did Jock or Uncle Ben say their meeting would be?"

"Why, who are you talking to?" Mien replied.

Annelies hoped to spot who had been in the ladies' toilet with them. Their waitress passed their table, asking if they wanted to order something else. She asked for the bill.

At, finished the call, ignoring his mother's question.

"Can you remember where your brother parked the Volvo?" Mien asked in a short tone.

"Gosh, why are you both so...nervous? Mom, I thought you wanted me to contact the group of people I told you about?"

"Something has happened to your brother and Uncle Ben. Please let's get to the car, and I will explain."

"Okay, this way."

After At had chatted to a waitress he seemed to know, they followed him back to the parking bay.

"Mien, what do you mean? Something has happened?" Annelies whispered, still not knowing how good Mien's telepathic skill was. She had just spotted the Volvo when Liesbeth suddenly beamed:

"Mom, throughout history, a dark force has manipulated and ruled the human race through various secret societies, religions, and the occult. We just heard that the humanoids from the outer worlds are now in complete control of our technology and the national global economy through the Council on Foreign Relations. That is why we will be with you as soon as possible."

"At, what are your friends all about? I mean the people that you want me to meet." He had opened the Volvo's door for them both to get in. Simultaneously, she telepathically replied to Liesbeth, *"I'm so glad you are joining us. Never mind the reasons."*

"It's a small group searching for missing people in South Africa. They are helping the police but not part of the police force."

She recalled reading part of an article about abductions last evening while they were waiting to pay for some purchases from a local shop in Kalk Bay. She had been surprised to find a newspaper on very alternative topics given away for free and had said so to At.

"I told Ben about them. I found them online after receiving their newsletter in my inbox." At waited for them to settle into the car before he got into the driver's seat.

"Do they publish a paper locally?"

"Yes, Tannie, but only four times a year. It's costly, why?"

"I think your uncle picked up a copy from one of the local shops last evening just before we arrived at Clovelly."

"Has he read it?"

"I don't know. I did, but only part of one article about how innocent people continue to suffer unspeakable horrors at the hands of humanoid scientists."

She wondered if Liesbeth was following their conversation. She and Hans could tap into a vast reception field, regardless of distance.

"Is this not that conspiracy publication you and Jock keep arguing about?" Mien asked.

What was brewing between the brothers had to do with belief differences. She would be relieved when they were all safely united again. Liesbeth's warning and At's comments made her uneasy.

At's drumming fingers on the steering wheel felt like a swarm of angry bees.

"Mom, many people who are driven by fear are likewise engaged in barbaric practices. As if that is not enough, many innocent people end up as food for the insatiable dark forces appetite for biological enzymes, hormonal secretions, and blood."

She was shocked by his angry tone. Neither had heard what Ben telepathically told her, but Mien was worried. She leaned back into her seat, trying to focus on seeing lots of light surrounding both Ben and Jock. There was no reason to alarm At and Mien just yet. It would only feed At's turbulent temper.

At had turned around, and his expression was serious.

"Tannie, I'm interested in your work but believe in aliens. Until now, I've only told Mom that I remembered being abducted last year."

She knew her response was important to him. She wondered if the off-world encounter was in his Akashic records. She wanted to inspire him to do shadow work to uncover the elite's plans in the Astral realms. It reminded her of her Physical Youth Vibration Code 21 of Consciousness.

"Stay in your intuition mode, Mom. Rather, be in tune with your soul's quality of consciousness to inspire and hold a positive attitude."

For a split second, Hans' telepathic interception took her off guard.

"Are you referring to the Biblical 'Book of Revelation' theory, which predicts that only those who accept the 'Mark of the Beast' – a laser tattoo or debit card – can buy and sell goods? She asked while beaming, *"Ben, where are you?"*

"First, I would like to hear the story of your abduction. Not now, but maybe later after Ben and Jock have joined us."

"I will never tell my story in front of Jock. Forget it. He will only ridicule me, and I have had enough of that."

"Who else made you feel that way, your dad?"

"No, my sister Sonja. I thought of all the people she would believe me" It was said with such a painful tone. Sonja must have hurt him. "At please understand that Sonja might not have accepted your story because she sees so much pain and suffering caused by people's mistakes. Your abduction story might just have come at the wrong time."

He kept silent, staring ahead while still drumming his hands on the steering wheel.

"It's already well after six." She added. Annelies sensed that they were all starting to feel uncomfortable.

"Mom, now is the time to practise applying all the Soul qualities you have already decoded, especially the powerful energies of forgiveness. Often, people's shadow sides feed on these anxiety emotions."

Hans' telepathic communication always comforted her. She shared her wish for a moment of silence to send positive energy to Ben and Jock with Mien and At. They all joined in, and she felt her inner power and unconditional love driving her forward."

She took a deep breath, knowing that through The Breath of Life's language of light vibration, her Soul purpose and higher self frequencies were on the same wavelength. The symbolic drawing expressions she had given all these light particles now came in handy. All she needed to do was visualise and use them for the good of all.

"There they are, finally" At pointed towards some street vendors selling souvenirs.

"Thanks for waiting. Please At let's get out of here." Ben called out as he climbed into the front while Jock got into the back of the Volvo behind them. At turned on the engine and drove away onto the road towards Fish Hoek.

"Mien, can you suggest a nice place to eat? I will tell you all about our meeting over dinner."

"Annie, your energy of light made all the difference. It's amazing how effective that was. It gave me more energy to save the moment."

"Were you both in danger?"

While studying a pamphlet on the South Peninsula, Ben's expression gave nothing away.

"That has still to be seen. So far as Jock is concerned, he got himself into trouble by borrowing from a loan shark. Why he didn't approach Toon is still beyond me. His dad has gambling debt, and Jock has been held responsible for the payments."

"When will Liesbeth and Hans arrive?" She asked out loud, but nobody seemed to know. Ben shrugged his shoulders.

"At why don't we go to that Indian restaurant in Fish Hoek? You know the place, I mean." Mien seemed to know Fish Hoek quite well, so she asked Mien if she had ever lived on the southern peninsula. Years ago, they had shared a room in Sea Point, and later, she knew that Mien and Nick had moved into a ground-floor flat in Rondebosch after they married.

"No, but I rented a flat with a friend while he was still studying and working as a waiter at the Brass Bell. I visited them as often as possible when Sonja worked at Groote Schuur Hospital. Before Sonja and I left for Holland in September, we rented Titanja's cottage for a month. That's how I know of the place."

At found parking on the main street in Fish Hoek. It was a beautiful evening. I would have loved to go somewhere with a view, but Indian food sounded fine.

"Can we go in there the way we are dressed?" She looked at Mien sideways. They were both in knee-high pants.

"Oh, I didn't think about that. Maybe we should go back to the Brass Bell. Then we can stay as we are. Sorry, but do you mind?"

"That's fine with me." At replied. "We can sit upstairs. Tannie, you will love the view from there." At skilfully moved out of the street parking and drove towards Kalk Bay. Jock had not said a word.

After At had found a spot to park, they walked through the subway under the railway line to the restaurant. It wasn't quiet when they came closer, but At knew the staff and the waiter showed a table upstairs in the pavilion. She could not have chosen a better place with a view right over the ocean. After the waiter took their orders, Ben settled himself, ready to explain their meeting.

"I have been asked to investigate two cases of corruption. One has to do with money, and the other is a more sinister abduction case. Whether it's a decoy that the controlling elite is now using, since they are getting worried that more and more people are starting to wake up to their tactics, remains to be seen."

"So you also believe that aliens are controlling our world?"

"Don't worry too much about the possibility of extraterrestrial life; likely, our world's monetary system would still influence any advanced beings.." Ben paused to collect his thoughts.

"As a family, we have been temporarily trapped by loan sharks. I will let Jock further explain that one."

"Loan sharks, why?" Mien called out in surprise.

"Jock, will you explain that to us."

She felt sorry for Jock. His self-assured posture when he had greeted them at the station had now changed. She could see in his aura that many distortions had risen to the surface. Now it was up to Jock to release his programmed feelings of failure. That seemed a major obstacle he had to bypass to move on.

"Mom, I foolishly used a loan shark to pay off Dad's gambling debt. I didn't want to tarnish the Jaarsma Clan, including Toon."

Jock elaborated some more. Mien and At were silent. Their expressions said enough.

"Jock, why didn't you tell me? After all, I know your father better than any of you. He will do anything to avoid his responsibilities. Why did you think you needed to bail him out?"

"Mom, I wasn't going to at first, but they, whoever they are, made me responsible for his debt."

"Now I understand why you were so secretive the last few weeks." At replied."You could have told me. You know my thoughts on money issues. Everything we have been taught by economists, universities, and other so-called 'experts' regarding our monetary system is only related to its effects, not its causes."

At's manner of speaking reminded her of rolling seeds inside a rain stick. The moment you turned it, it sounded like a waterfall.

"Where the money comes from is never discussed; it is glossed over so that most of our population does not ask any questions." He added.

"Guys, let's get back to our meeting with two roughnecks who were completely unaware of what we knew. They are like..."

"Robots, no doubt." At interrupted Ben. "The 'greys' use people's addictions of greed and lust for wealth and power to bring about their evil plan to control the Earth."

"Jock, I want to hear your part of the story first", she interrupted at At's domineering reply. Jock was about to say something, but their waiter brought their orders. They ordered a bottle of plain water for the table.

"We were so busy with our last project, which cost more than we budgeted. I was in the wrong space. I'm well aware of it now." Jock had mainly addressed his brother.

"At first, I tried to ignore the threats I received through my cell phone and emails. I tried to talk to Dad just before they arrested him, and his reply was to approach Toon." They could all feel the resentment Jock felt towards his dad.

"I'm sorry, mate. I am." patting Jock on the shoulder. "I'm not sure how I would have reacted if Dad had told me once again to let Toon pay for his addictive nature. He can now rot in hell for all I care!"

"At, please don't say that. Nobody needs to go through hell to take responsibility for their actions."

"Tannie, he deserves it. It's not the first time he has bled us dry financially. Mom, what do you say?"

"I understand how you feel, At, but we must learn from this. There must be a reason he is in our lives like he is." Annelies was proud of her friend. She said so, but what did this whole affair mirror to all of them?

"You mean it's the shadow side of us all?" Both Ben and her looked at each other.

"Yes, I heard Hans' message, too, about how often people's shadow sides are feeding them feelings of anxiety." He beamed with a wink.

"At, the problem facing most of us today is that if we react in anger, hate or feeling hurt, its more difficult to cast off our belief systems," Ben added.

"What do you mean?" At asked.

"If Nick and any others have created their reality, and we believe it, I should say we have allowed theirs to mix with our realities." Ben winked at her. "How are we doing so far, you think?"

"Okay, I can go along with that.... but I still believe that aliens know how the human mind process works. They intentionally keep us in the dark for their gain." At, challenged Ben.

"That is your belief, At. You create your reality bubble. Ignoring what's not supporting your viewpoint and instead emphasizing what supports your perceptions is playing the human game not so?" She wasn't sure if she, at age twenty-four, would have understood Ben's reply, but somehow both Jock and At were already far more awake than many others of their age. She waited with interest.

"Okay, I get it, but if more and more people are awakening to the fact that they are slaves to mortal enemies and have been tricked and betrayed by their "leaders" who sold them out, what would the best action be?"

She smiled at his quick reply.

"What do you think they will do, knowing that their alleged 'public servants' are willingly or stupidly carrying on plundering, bringing hard-working people to bankruptcy, and ruining their lives and country?" Ben asked.

At, was mulling over Ben's question. Since the veils between dimensions or levels of consciousness were getting thinner, other beings aware of this could feel threatened, compassionate or want to take control. Liesbeth and Hans would have a better understanding of the situation at hand. Nevertheless, their conversation was getting away from what happened at their meeting.

"Please, can we get back to our dilemma? Ben, what was the result of your meeting? I take it that you have refused to pay up?" She asked out loud. *"Were you tempted to use your psychic powers over them?"*

"I diplomatically told them what they could expect in return if they used fear tactics through using violence or physical destruction to Toon's property. "

"What was their reply?" She wished she could time travel and return to hear how Ben responded to their threatening behaviour.

"Strangely enough, at the end of a fruitless meeting, they were both suddenly overtaken by stomach cramps as if they had drunk or eaten something wrong. They had to run to the loo. I suspect they were having the runs." Jock added.

Mien's mouth hung open, and At started to grin.

"What did you do? I mean...you didn't?" she beamed to Ben.

"That was good timing, I'd say. What had they eaten?" At asked.

"No idea. We each had a Windhoek Light. I only paid for our drinks on the way out at the till. We left before they got back." Jock replied.

"Annie, I did nothing. I just visualized what would happen if lots of dark energy particles streamed out of their field away from them. It must have had a major detoxing effect."

"Let's believe in divine intervention and leave it as is. I'm tired and would not mind having an early night. It's already after eight, so is anyone ready for dessert?" Mien suggested.

Both At and Jock felt like something sweet, so the rest joined them. Her intuition told her that more dark shadows within them would come to the surface to be reckoned with during these times, but as long as they stayed optimistic about the outcome, all would be well. She looked around, studying the people at the other tables. How many were aware that Armageddon is about clearing the distorted layers on a cellular level? All the intense pain and sorrows that humanity, as a race, has genetically accumulated had to be released. Would her genetic decoding program do enough of the cleansing on a cellular level?

"Tannie, you wanted to hear about my abduction experience, or do you think that it's just my own belief?"

"Okay, tell us. We will all listen without interrupting you."

Their dessert had not yet arrived, and maybe At needed to get his ordeal out of the way.

"When did this happen?" Jock butted in. "Sorry, carry on."

"Last year in May. I was staying over with a few friends after we had been to a party. It was right here in Kalk Bay. It was the smell that had woken me up. At least that's what I think it was."

Nobody said a word in reply.

"I was paralysed, completely unable to move, resist or speak. I thought I just had a bad dream, but when I felt touched, I got scared."

The waiter came back with their dessert. It gave them all a chance to mull over what At had told them so far. She wondered if the crowd he was staying with was the same people looking for missing people. *What crowd are you referring to? What missing people.* Ben beamed with a worried expression.

"Tannie, did you ever have an out-of-body experience? That is what I had. I'm sure of it." At looked at her as if to say, you will understand!

"I was floating out of the room. I tried to wake up, but as I said, it was as if I was paralysed. I heard a voice as well, like whispering, but it was the smell I could not place. Yuck!"

"What did they say? I mean, could you hear people speak?" She couldn't resist asking. As At was telling his story, she tried to look into his energy field, and what she saw must have come from his memory files. There were symbolic signatures that she couldn't interpret.

"The voices were soft and ...I suppose gentle. They repeatedly reassured me that everything would be fine and that what they had to do was necessary and for some greater good. It was the smell that disturbed me the most. I could smell that they were lying. I said so, but I could not hear my voice."

They could all see that At was living his whole ordeal again.

"Please believe what I'm about to tell you. It's not some fantasy. " His voice had dropped to a whisper.

"I later remembered seeing three figures wearing strange suits. I can't remember being taken into an alien craft. I found myself in what seemed like a garden, although it felt indoors. While there, I was compelled to have relations with a lovely woman. She seemed completely real."Jock's expression looked doubtful, but he kept quiet.

"All I know is that I felt stiff when I woke up. I thought at the time that my legs were still numb, but when I felt them, I almost cried out from the pain. My legs felt badly bruised. As if I had fallen from a great height and landed on something between my legs."

Both Ben and Jock pulled faces from sheer horror. She had finished her dessert, and Mien had as well. She could tell by her expression that Mien had heard At's story before.

"It was still dark, but I had to see for myself if I was bruised, so I got up while still feeling the pain inside my legs. In the bathroom, I was frightened at what I saw in the long mirror. I looked like a battered victim. I was blue and purple all over the inside of my legs as if I had been fighting while riding on top of a charging beast. I never said a word to the others. I was too ashamed."

They were all quiet. What At had experienced must have been very real to him. She wondered if anyone had seen the bruises.

"I spent a long time trying to convince myself that I had a dream, but it was so vivid that it took at least a week for the bruising to go away. I turned to the internet for answers, something I had never done before, and that's how I found the group I now belong to. They are a great group of people and have become my friends. They suggested I take photos of the bruises if they were still visible. They believe that the aliens might have restrained me because I resisted while they were somehow taking fluid from me."

At had whispered the last piece of his story. He was concerned should anyone other than they could overhear him. The sounds of the sea were so strong that there was no way anyone from the other tables could have followed At's story.

"Do you have photos of your bruises?" Ben asked.

"Yes, but I wished I had taken photos directly the next day. I never thought about doing that."

"I would love to see them and meet up with your friends. Let me settle the bill and get out of here. We will have our coffee on the deck of our cottage. What do you think, Annie? Is that OK with you?"

"Great idea. Let's go."

At greeted some people he knew as they left the Brass Bell. The boys gave the busker in the station subway some coins. They seemed to know him, too.

It was still warm for the evening. Having coffee on the deck would be fantastic. Jock took over from At to drive back to Clovelly. She saw that he had squeezed his brother's shoulder in the parking bay. That was the best outcome of that day. The two brothers were once again friends.

Mien must have also seen it; her eyes were wet, but she smiled.

The energy of forgiveness is a powerful force, but seeing it in action was more healing than anything else. Whatever it was that had been brewing between the brothers had gone. At forgave his brother for his stupid action of going to a loan shark, and Jock showed compassion for his brother's ordeal and probably understood now better why At was so involved with this group he often talked about.

They arrived in Clovelly, parked the car and unlocked their private entrance gate. It was dark with no moon, but a few lights automatically turned on as they passed them on the pathway up the side of the property towards Titanya's cottage. She could hear frogs and insects buzzing around. Looking back far in the distance, against Fish Hoek mountainside, the thousands of lights from the houses on the hill twinkled like a starry sky.

While the men organised the table and chairs on the wooden deck, Mien joined her in the small kitchen while she made coffee.

"What are your thoughts on At's experience," Mien whispered.

"I can accept that he indeed experienced an abduction, and I was pleased to hear that At found these people after his ordeal."

"You mean if it was the other way around, he might have imagined it?" Mien was shaking her head as if to say: there must be a better explanation.

"No, it's not that, but many 'groupies,' no matter what draws them together, create a kind of egregore, like a unified thought-form. That energy might be responsible for a lot of unexplained phenomena."

"You mean it is still an illusion from a higher point of view, but from our awareness level, is it for real?"

"You could say that, yes. I would rather take the approach that whatever I experience is a personal experience. It's real for me and the people with whom I share the same wavelength, so to speak, but I can also accept that there are people who do not see into my world, so for them, my world or what I experience does not exist."

"I've seen At's photos. These bruises were real."

"I'm sure they were. All we can do is unify our energy projections of love and compassion and send that into this reality. It's difficult to bring that kind of action into our world of matter, but even matter is energy." How would she explain that so many realities all interacted with each other simultaneously? She could sense and sometimes even see into different worlds, but she still needed to ground herself in this 3rd-dimensional reality to keep her balance and survive physically.

When they joined the men, they talked about global warming.

"I agree that modern-day politicians should not fool themselves into thinking that humanity has a big impact on climate change. Our recent climate change stems from natural causes." Ben replied to At. They must have moved away from the topic of alien abduction.

"But what about the prolonged droughts, melting ice caps, heavy flooding, and unpredictable weather patterns? Climate change effects are already wrecking lives in Africa; how could we make a difference if we can?" Jock asked.

"I'm not denying that artificial pollution makes global warming worse. Our greenhouse gas emissions have probably slowed, but I don't think we are solely to blame. Global warming, or cooling down, has been a natural phenomenon since the beginning." She thought she knew Ben's perspective on the global warming scare, but now it seemed to fluctuate.

"At I feel that no one disputes that the climate is changing. Some even suggest the weird weather is caused by Nibiru or planet X. More recently, the Little Ice Age was a period of cooling that lasted several hundred years until the 19th century, when global warming began. So, there is no dispute that the climate changes constantly."

"Gosh, Annelies, you know a lot about the subject. Where did you learn all that? Mien was impressed, but quoting something she had read on the internet and Toon's input about it at the time made a lot of sense. She was not trying to impress anyone with her knowledge, but what she had not added was the Hopi's prediction that the sea would turn black. Her half-brother, Trevor, speculated that a black sea could be the effect of a massive oil spill. That could be disastrous for sea life on the planet.

"I only know what I have read, Mien. I'm just repeating an article I've read on the internet. That doesn't make me an expert on the topic."

"Still, there is plenty of motive for people to want global warming to exist! The most obvious one is money." At could not resist adding his point of view.

"So you say it is a naturally occurring event blown out of proportion?" Jock tried, like Ben, to see both sides, that neither At nor Ben was incorrect.

She knew the solution to many human questions was concealed in the three higher physical body codes she would teach in France after their relocation from Apeldoorn.

"At, the belief program one chooses to incarnate into during these times has to be released within each of us. It has to do with finances, religious beliefs, or health issues. As long as these perceptions still separate people from each other, they are stuck into their belief program."

"You mean belief patterns that are against unity consciousness?"

"Yes, Mien, any beliefs that uphold dualism are keeping us trapped in this third dimension."

"What are they? I mean, we are all still here, talking about weird stuff, I say." Jock was getting bored.

"Jock, just listen, the Jews still wait for the Messiah, and the Christians believe Jesus is coming back soon. Muslims believe their saviour Allah has already come to the Dome of the Rock. Fundamental Christians believe that 144.000 chosen people will be saved and everybody else will die in a holocaust. Who benefits by keeping these beliefs alive?"

Nobody said a word after Ben's comments. She could see the energy around each person on the table was very electric.

"Oh, I see." At spoke up. "Now I get it. The awakening movement around the planet, especially on the internet, all say that Christ or Allah is already within us; we are all united and always have been. Tannie, you say that the elite, whoever they are, will want to stop that knowledge?"

"Exactly. The people of the world are split into believers in separatism through terrorism. Something must happen to stop this madness."

"Where do the 144,000 ideas come from?" Mien asked.

"I feel that the 144,000 in Revelations has to do with the first wave of the rapture/ascension. If you link that number to my decoding book, where I mention the 22 Soul qualities each of us has to awaken to, then maybe the number 144 has a different meaning."

"You mean it's not referring to 144,000 people?" Mien replied.

"No, I think it's referring to the number of human lineages in the world today."

"You mean that we are the 144th generation on the planet?"

"Something like that, yes. I will explain that in my next workshop."

Jock and At took the Volvo and went home. They would join them for breakfast and leave for the community near George at lunchtime. Mien was also tired and said good night.

They were lying safely in bed that night, both wide awake, listening to the strange sounds from the garden not far in the distance; the howling of a wolf created an unsettling feeling as if the two sounds should not coexist.

"What is the story behind the wolf? Did Mien ever tell you?" Ben had the same thoughts.

"No, we must ask her tomorrow, but please tell me what happened at your meeting." She snuggled in his arms, and Ben kissed her hair. Feelings of gratitude that he was safe next to her didn't stop her mind from speculating. She knew he had used his psychic powers to escape the two men this afternoon.

"It's hard not to react when you practically smell danger. It was Jock's angry state, more than anything, that made me do it. I had a look into their energy fields. There weren't any Soul vibration qualities present. I felt that if they suddenly forgot their mission due to their bowels needing to be emptied fast, that would lower the chances of a fistfight because Jock's temperament was at boiling point. That would only do more damage."

"Well, you didn't harm them; you just temporarily stopped them from acting out their violent tempers."

"Let's hope that is the last we will hear from them. I want to meet the group that At mentioned."

"You mean about them searching for missing people? Or are you interested in where they stand regarding the possibility that there are non-humans amongst us?"

"Both, I guess. Look at what man has accomplished in the last hundred years with science, computers, space travel, etc. Now imagine a race with technology a thousand years ahead of us that had lived before, but all traces have been wiped away. Why?"

"I agree, and Mien said that she had seen the bruises. I also find it hard to believe that At just woke up thinking aliens abducted him. Why would he choose to fake such an extraordinary claim?"

"Who knows? We all need to transcend the obstacles that afflict our bodies and minds. Having an abduction experience must be similar to obstacles such as having an accident or being criminally harassed against your will." Ben was far more aware of what happened in the world regarding criminals. She knew all about wandering spirits lost in the lower astral realms trying to hook into people's energy fields, but she had little experience with non-human entities. People like Liesbeth and Hans, who could remember living in another world, were just as affected by this reality.

"It sounds like a horrifying experience, and many people have not yet come to terms with it. But where does that leave us? Are we being persecuted due to our intention to wake up fully?"

"Annie, throughout history, people have been unjustly ridiculed, harassed, and even severely punished for their views and ideas that didn't fit the currently accepted beliefs. I'm sure our Jaarsma Clan's experiences will be questioned. That is why Hans and Liesbeth will be here next week." Ben snuggled up to her.

"What ideas do you have about our removal of past distortions left behind in this southern African soil?"

Annelies knew of one life she had to work with; at least, that is what it felt like after reading Richard's journals. She had an awakening.

"I have no idea, love. I'm not like you, who remembers other realities. I know that both Leo and I must have chosen a very abusive father and a mother who seemed helpless. I plan to talk with Mien about how that affected her life."

"Well, she has attracted an abusive relationship herself. What was your other sister like? You never mentioned her."

"Wilma was headstrong. She left us all for good when she married Richard's dad Anton de Jong, without my dad's blessing."

Ben was sad about his sister, who had vanished from their lives.

"Annie, I'm aware that the number of Soul quality symbols a Soul can receive in any given lifetime and stored into our body of light is dependent upon the quality of experiences received in past lives, but it's not often that I'm aware that I have unfinished business that has not been resolved."

"I'm convinced that raising our awareness levels is the only way to solve the problems everyone faces today. Therefore, our Soul energy must be motivated. That will allow people to discern the difference between what is real and what is an illusion." She contemplated.

When POWAH showed her how the vibrations of a name could show her why she had chosen the three youth codes in this lifetime, she didn't understand it. The sound originated in the sixth or seventh dimension, according to Hans. He had tried to explain how creation starts with a sound. During this trip, she needed to understand why some people never show interest or even question who they were, yet a person like At was mesmerised by it.

She wondered what his three youth codes were. The decoding of her three youth codes gave her some insights.

She had not yet finished her decoding examples but remembered one of the three codes and what it stands for, recalling POWAH's signature energy she translated into words.

She had written that these codes would re-activate an individual's genetic and etheric blueprint.

"Ben, with each new birth, a person chooses a new geometric pattern for the first seven years. Then the three health codes during the following fourteen years reveal why each person chooses the genetic codes from their ancestors."

"How would they know?"

"People are starting to ask why and how they must let go of the programmed beliefs they came into this world with."

So you say only people who are questioning who they are. Apart from their physical identity?

"Yes. POWAH said it is because the Language of Light operates on a resonance basis. Higher quality symbols can only be received by embodied souls who resonate at a higher frequency or octave in this present lifetime, conditional on the person's acceptance of the change."

She recalled being born with the Physical YouthVibration souls quality Code 21 -Consciousness.

"Mmm, yes, but...How does that all relate to your idea that our embodied soul energy must fully awaken before we can ascend?" Ben mumbled, yawning while switching off his bedside light.

"Gosh, Annie, can we go to sleep now? We had a rather eventful day. Let's start enjoying the rest of our holiday."

"You mean let's go with the flow?"

His question had surprised her big time. "Have you read my article?"

"Which article?" Ben's sleepy voice replied, allowing himself to start dozing off.

"Hey, why did you ask me that question? Don't go to sleep now." Shaking him had an immediate effect. He turned towards her, observing her with an intensity that reminded her of their courting days.

"I liked what you typed...that Self-realisation simply means remaining as your-Self...that the real I Am is consciousness devoid of identity with form."

She had to think about which article she had written that sentence. It could only be connected to her workbook.

"Yes, it was sitting on your laptop: The twenty-two spacings that form the energy body of your soul." It was often weird how she could barely remember what she had written.

"Annie, I'm now going to sleep unless you have other ideas?"

"You are far too tired for other activities, I'm sure?"

"Never, I'll show you."

She glowed with pleasure, knowing that love had many faces.

Chapter 10
The Emotional Temple of Youth

The Garden Route

The drive to George, past the heart of the Garden Route, had lifted everyone's mood. They stopped at several spots to admire the green, forested mountains and the inviting Southern Cape coast. Nothing could overshadow their feelings from the day before, or so they thought.

Both At and Jock had proudly talked about their joint community project while they shared driving the Volvo. They aimed to manifest a conscious, supportive and self-sufficient eco-village.

They arrived near the turnoff towards Glentana just before George late in the afternoon. Ben spotted a sign pointing to a restaurant on the outskirts of George, where the hubbub of modern urban living still mingled with an old-world atmosphere.

Jock's cell phone shattered the tranquil energy so often felt around natural beauty. He said it was an unknown number. The two hoodlums had recovered from their runny stomachs, but how they knew that they had left Cape Town was scary. At parked the Volvo in front of the Alpine Inn, a 3-star graded Hotel.

"Is there a tracking device on the car?" Ben asked.

"Yes, of course, there is. Do you think...?"

"No, not necessarily, but I can't recall mentioning that we were leaving Cape Town."

"Oh, dear. Nick might know." Mien sounded horrified.

"When did you tell him, Mom?" Jock asked as he opened the sliding door for them to get out.

"I didn't. Dad phoned me just before we left for Cape Town and wanted to speak to Jock. Then he asked if Ben and Annelies would visit Crystal Cliffs. I never thought to keep that a secret. Should I have?"

"Why phone you, since he has my number," Jock said in disgust.

At admitted that he would also have told his dad that they were going home if he had been asked.

The cloudy sky promised rain, or was she smelling the ocean?

"At can you see the sea from your community?" Aiming to change the topic, they entered what looked like a typical German restaurant next door to the Alpine Inn.

"Mmm, we can rule out that the top controllers gave that information to them so that it might have been Nick," Ben commented as he pulled out chairs for the two ladies. *"Do you know who the ringleaders are?"* She beamed. After all, Ben was undercover on an assignment.

"Annie, to my knowledge, only Toon and Hans know about me being here to investigate a case which has nothing to do with these loan sharks. So far as my office knows, I've taken a vacation to be with my family in South Africa."

"Let's enjoy our dinner and not fall for the evil threats, Jock; they are just spreading fear," Ben suggested out loud while studying the menu.

"I will try, but I'll feel happier when we return to Crystal Cliffs."

Jock's admission that he still felt he was a fugitive reminded her of the third awakening stage. During her workshop, participants would decode six number spacings. The three youth spacings hinted at their Soul purpose in this lifetime. Hers were the vibration of two and twenty-one, and she recalled POWAH's comment very well.

Her six-card spacing on the third level was a mixture of soul qualities of consciousness, unity, truth, illusion, forgiveness, and prosperity.

<As a physical youth code, this consciousness vibration is often seen as an enthusiastic person who inspires others and fills them with a positive attitude and energy. Art plays a big role in their early lives.>

While the others were studying the menus, her mind took her back to what she had written about the three present spacings at the start of the decoding workshop. They have the opportunity to change depending on the decoding individual. However, when correctly interpreted by each player, these vibrations in the three youth spacings could trigger a difficult awakening period. It all involved letting go of old beliefs, behaviours and thinking patterns. Releasing emotions like anger, desire, or fear from the past and letting go was a challenge.

Was she ever going to achieve that? Lately, she had been even more aware of her bodily senses. By only being the witness, the observer of her life, did she stay in the present? Lately, she even had visions of being inside her body.

She tried to order something from the menu that was not a meat dish, but the food was traditional German home cooking, including Pizza, spare ribs and baked German bread. Ben and the boys ordered Weissbier while Mien ordered a Savanna light. It reminded them both of the good times past. Mien told them how they discovered that drink when they shared a room at Sea Point. She settled for a salmon salad.

"Tannie, you asked if you could see the sea from our property. Yes, you can, but only from our community deck, which is set up high. Then you can see the Indian Ocean. There were some existing buildings when Toon purchased this largely undeveloped farm. It's before you reach Glentana, next to a private nature reserve and only 20 minutes from George Airport."

"Where did the name Crystal Cliffs come from?"

"We named it so because steep trails lead between the cliffs and the sea. We have no private beach. Many people come to Victoria Bay or Herold's Bay for that, or they go on a cruise to Seal Island. Especially people who like deep-sea fishing and scuba diving." Jock looked at his brother when he mentioned scuba diving.

They were all tucking into their food. More people have entered the restaurant, so German food must be popular.

Jock spoke on his cell to the two retired but very active couples that were living full-time at Crystal Cliffs, warning them not to talk to anyone who might ask about any visitors they might have.

"How did they come to live in your community?" Mien had never shared much about her children's project with her.

"Toon knew Harrie and John from years back. John is a Capetonian, and Harrie is Indonesian but born in Holland. At first, Toon had asked if they would keep an eye on things since he invested in the boy's eco-village in the Southern Cape. Harrie has a lot of building skills, and his wife, Pat, will tackle anything, as long as she can be outside working in the garden."

"What were their reactions Jock, about us arriving?" Ben asked. He was still mulling over what further development could be expected; that was very clear to her.

"Jock, are they aware that you are blackmailed?" Ben's voice sounded like a detective questioning a suspect.

"No, but they know all about what happened to Toon, and they know about Dad. John worked for Toon years back."

The boys seemed to like them, which was a good start.

Mien's marriage to Nick and their father's connections had not helped the boys run a community. Instead, it brought harmful elements into their plans because they initially approached their father for financial backing, not knowing that Nick was a scaly character and suspected of being involved in arms deals. On an energy level, they kept their attachment cords with their father intact after Mien divorced him. During her long-drawn-out legal battle, she returned to Holland and started the Pannekoek coffee shop in Apeldoorn. Now, she felt ashamed for warning Toon not to get involved with Mien's children because of the bond they had with their father years ago. Her best friend was very offended when she found out.

"Annelies, they all look forward to meeting you, especially Katrina, John's partner; she is interested in your work." Mien touched her with affection. She was forgiven.

"Is Katrina Dutch?"

"Yes, and she and Harrie knew each other before Harrie married Pat, who was also born in South Africa."

When Mien was on familiar ground, her naturally wise but humorous self was in full play. How anyone could settle back in Holland after living such a free life in the open was a mystery to her.

"Are both couples South African residents?"

"Yes, they are. When Toon got involved by investing in the boy's project, they decided to stay permanently on the farm."

"When did they decide that...very recently?"

"I booked Sonja and my plane ticket to Amsterdam last year."

It was after the fire that their friendship had been reinstated. Mien was her best support at that difficult time.

"Oh, that reminds me," Mien added. "I received an email from Sonja. She has met Ingrid's daughter, Debbie. Sonja's new doctor friend, Ben van Dongen and Debbie's boyfriend, Vinny, knew each other."

When Mien was back in Holland last year, running the coffee bar, she got close to Ingrid's daughter Sascia when Richard was in Hospital. Sascia worked part-time at the Pannekoek in Apeldoorn.

"So Vinny is over Sascia?" Ben commented.

"Oh yes, that relationship was never meant to be." Mien replied, "When Richard was in the Hospital, Sascia had a tough time. First, the injuries that Richard sustained from the fire. Then the funeral of Sammy, which she organised."

"Who's Sammy?" At asked.

"Richard's little girl from his first marriage. Sascia attended the funeral while Richard was in the hospital. Did you know that she miscarried?" Mien turned to her for confirmation. She nodded. Richard had told her when he was very down while still in the Hospital.

"Who are these people you both talk about? Who is Sascia?"

"Sorry At. I keep forgetting that neither of you has ever met Ingrid's children from her first marriage."

"Who is Vinny?" Jock asked his mother.

"Okay, let's start from the beginning. Ingrid, Toon's wife's three children are Sascia, Debbie and Jeroen."

She smiled because At cringed his face at the name Jeroen. They had all finished their dessert, but both At and Jock wanted to hear about their family in Holland. She hoped that both brothers would meet them if they would come to Holland for a visit. It would be suitable for At to meet Richard and learn from him that not all 'out-of-body' experiences were terrible or even harmful.

"Sascia and Jeroen are twins. Sascia is Richard's partner, and Vinny is a good friend from Richard's university days." She explained, winking at Mien.

"Oh, now I get it. Sascia went out with Vinny before she met Richard. I remember Sonja telling me that Vinny had just discovered that he has a brother named Niels." At had been making scribbles on a serviette, which reminded her of the star map.

"That is correct. Niel's father is Gerrit, who is my half-brother. " She had to laugh when Jock threw his arms in the air. She hadn't added that Niels' mother has an Indonesian background like Harrie.

"Annelies, how many half-brothers do you have? I knew that Toon was not your real brother. He was adopted, not so?"

"Correct. Our mothers were good friends, and when his parents died in a car accident, my parents took him into their home. Otto is my big brother, and Fred is a half-brother, but the three of us, Toon and Fred, grew up together. Otto had already left home.

"Why is the name Otto so familiar?" Jock asked.

"Otto's wife Jill was married to your Dad briefly before my time," Mien replied.

Ben called for the waiter to bring the bill. He had been quiet during the explanation of the Jaarsma Clan.

"Where have your thoughts been?" She beamed. While they were talking about the Jaarsma Clan, she distinctly felt that Ben had put a mental shield up so she could not connect to him. But why?

The waiter, who came from the Cape because of his accent, knew At. They had been scuba-diving together. It was the first time that she heard At speaking Afrikaans.

"Annie, I have been in contact with Leo and have not listened. He warned me that what was a natural time relay would soon change. There are already many places on the planet where people and animals will soon experience the different levels of density, and how this reflects on our immediate future."

She was not sure what to make of Ben's train of thoughts, but she was sure he would explain them the moment they were on their own.

She knew their reality might soon vanish because of time speeding up and the diminishing density levels between timelines, but how that would be experienced was still a mystery.

When they walked back to the Volvo, it was already dark.

"It's a real shame that you'll arrive at Crystal Cliffs in the evening, but we will have to take you both on a tour tomorrow morning." At promised.

The following morning, Annelies spotted a walking trail up the dunes behind their rondavel, where they were booked. It was still early, but she had not slept all that well, so the moment the sun peeked through their window, she got up to look outside. Ben was stirring, but she let him sleep. She had always been more of a lark, while Ben lately seemed more of an owl, getting to bed well after midnight.

She followed the wooden steps up the gently rising dunes. On the top step, she looked down at a small camping area accessible from the road. Further away on her right must be Glentana, which At had mentioned.

There were only two small tents visible. Annelies wondered if they were also guests. She got a good view from the top, overlooking the entire ocean from a distance. The setting reminded her of Titanya's cottage, except this was the Indian Ocean instead of False Bay.

The sound of the surf and the chirping voices from a few seagulls inspired her to meditate on the top step.

This morning, she had again awakened from a dream with a jerk. In her dream, she had fallen and hurt both her feet. What her sudden anger in her dream meant had unsettled her. Now was the right moment to silence her lower ego so she could get an insight into the meaning of that dream.

<Annie, remember that you leapt out of nothingness. Focus on the interchangeability of mass and energy and the spontaneous creation of particles from nothingness. That is the way the universe works. Get used to it. You didn't construct it; you find yourself here. You are all approaching an ultimate mystery, something that defeats your scientist's attempts to probe and investigate.>

The cluster-like words triggered images of a sudden eruption out of nothing. What was POWAH trying to convey to her?

<All existence has exploded out of nothing, and then consciousness formed galaxies, stars, planets, minerals, life forms, and human cultures. Emptiness is the source of everything. Things arise from emptiness and exist inseparably with emptiness.>

With a startled jolt, she simultaneously heard a car approaching and heard Ben calling her. It unsettled her that she suddenly heard POWAH as her internal voice while unprepared. If only she had her laptop, pen, and paper to clearly write down the words she had heard. It was as if she was being prepared for something while asleep but forgot to remember it. His energy was gone, so she got up and walked down towards their rondavel, where Ben was greeting a man in a Land Rover.

"Welcome to our Safari adventure. I will be your tour guide on an excursion into the unspoilt nature of Crystal Cliffs." At spoke to them from the back of the open Land Rover. The driver was a sturdy guy in his mid-fifties, wearing a t-shirt and sunglasses. At introduced them to John, the Capetonian, Katrina's partner. They all suggested that Annelies sit beside John inside the cabin while Ben climbed into the open back as if they were going on a safari.

"Mom has prepared your breakfast on the deck of our community building." At shouted for her to hear. "Pat and Katrina will join us there." The road was sandy, almost gravel, so At and Ben had to hold onto the cage-like frame on the back of the Land Rover.

"You don't have animals, do you?" She looked sideways at John, who had not yet said a word, but she could hear At laughing at her question, and while bending down, peering into the cabin, he replied,

"No, not yet, but we will have if we let John get his way. He was a ranger at safari parks his whole life, and this is his Land Rover."

"Well, what I have seen so far is incredible," Ben remarked from the back. "When was Toon here last?" He asked no one in particular. John's face broke into a smile.

"Last year. The cottages were not even built then, only the main building." John replied as he slowed down. Not long before, they saw what John meant by the main building. The main structure's lower wall was constructed using natural stone. The top story was a circular timber building with a long winding wooden path that gradually sloped up and took them to the front entrance. Mien greeted them from a wide-open doorway. Tall palm trees in pots on either side created an outdoor feeling. The top structure was made of tall glass and wooden panels. A thatched roof covered the round section. A large wooden deck surrounded the whole top story.

"Welcome to our humble beginnings. Has At already shown you around, or would you like to have breakfast first?" Mien introduced Katrina, the tall blond woman in shorts who was pretty. Her face looked familiar. Pat was an older, skinny woman. They both stood up from their wooden deck chairs.

"We heard so much about you both; it's great to finally have more members of the Jaarsma clan visiting our community." She felt that Katrina's greeting was well-meant, and she took an instant liking to her, but why she sensed that she had met her before was puzzling. Katrina said nothing about knowing her. She was probably around her mid-forties, of middling height, average build, her skin rich and tanned. Her face was oval, and her eyes were hazel, younger than John, who looked much older.

John joined them, asking Katrina if Harrie and Jock had already left for Victoria Bay. Two black girls from the local community served them a continental breakfast.

"Everything you see on this table is from our garden. We also have chickens, and we make our bread." Pat told them proudly. She seemed more reserved. Her dark hair lay flat on her shoulders.

Some would have called her beautiful but for the melancholy look on her face. Often, when experiences of joy and happiness have not outbalanced bitterness or great sadness, then what was once a beautiful face would be destroyed by ageing. She appeared to be in her late fifties. She wondered what her husband Harrie was like. Having an Indonesian parentage could not have been easy living in South Africa during the apartheid era. Mixed couples were not encouraged in those days.

They spent the rest of the day exploring. The incredible passageway of towering sandstone cliffs left them both in awe.

"The plant diversity is unbelievable, according to Pat. Some plant species are known all over the world." John explained.

After lunch, Ben joined the men on a trip to George while Katrina and Pat had work to do, leaving her alone with Mien.

"Gosh, I can't imagine you ever want to leave this place. Where do you stay?"

"My apartment is still in the original section of the main building. I'll show you later. Jock and At share a two-bedroom rondavel that they built themselves."

"Who owned this before Toon bought it, do you know?"

"It belonged to a family trust. John was one of the owners, but he could not buy out the others. When they met with the boys, he and Katrina lived near Kruger Park, running a safari business. Jock was on a course learning about Ecovillages while At was writing an article on permaculture."

"Are there more people involved? I see two tents and some cottages near where we are staying."

"Yes, some people are just visiting friends of At. Harrie and Pat are now also permanent. A few single people are camping on the property. They are learning how to set up a village like this." She had seen other people being shown around.

It was late afternoon with thunder and black clouds rolling across the sky when Annelies and Mien strolled back towards their rondavel.

"Can you ever see yourself living in a place like this?" Mien asked.

"What in South Africa? Visiting maybe, but I first have to get over my feelings of anxiety that I have buried in this Southern tip of Africa."

"You mean what happened to you fourteen years ago?"

"Mostly yes, and some information I need for my decoding work has to be assembled...sort of."

Ben had come to investigate a case that was somehow connected with what happened years ago, so she had allowed herself to go into her past experiences. ...Mien's question took her back.

***

Fourteen years ago, when Mien was going through her divorce, Ben wanted to be there for her, and she joined him, leaving their adopted son Hans with Trevor. Mien had three children by then, two boys and a girl. That trip had not turned out the way they planned it. From the second day, things had drastically changed.

They had been at a restaurant at Constantina Nek when she had eaten something that she had an immediate reaction to. Much later, they concluded that she had been poisoned. She had been taken away by ambulance to the nearest hospital. Then she had disappeared. Only weeks later, after Ben had found her, with the help of Leo and Hans, did she learn that Mien had returned to Holland to start her own business in Apeldoorn. A year later, her children wanted to go back to South Africa. They did not want to settle in Holland, so Mien became a swallow, travelling between the two countries and avoiding the cold, wet winters in Holland.

***

"Mien, I have chosen to bury it for years, but I can't anymore."
She now increasingly understood how important it is to release
harmful memory files. They would otherwise be triggered by any
current experiences at these times while approaching a major
consciousness awakening. Any unfinished experiences would affect
how anyone's perceptions cope or adapt. Any psychic abilities
would also not awaken during the global consciousness shifts if
there had been no clearing.

"You know I was so bitter and angry during my divorce; I never
realised that you had both come just to be with me. I remember you
warned me about Nick, but I was too absorbed in my dramas and
didn't want to see you." Mien said in deep regret.

"That was why I never knew that you had been poisoned and taken
away in an ambulance. Only afterwards, when it found you weeks
later and Ben brought you back to Holland, did I learn about your
disappearance. The rest I heard from what the ambulance man told
us years later."

"What ambulance, man? Who was he? When...?"

Mien's confession took her entirely by surprise. They were both
resting on the steps of their rondavel. The men had not yet returned
from George.

"When Sonja was working at Groote Schuur Hospital in Cape
Town, a girlfriend came home with her on one of her weekends
off. Her dad picked her up from our home the next day. He was
the ambulance driver who vividly remembered being on duty years
earlier when you were brought in. He said he even tried to talk to
you."

"What did he tell you about...how did he know it was me?"

"That's what we asked him. Sonja had told some of her nursing
friends about her aunt, who had disappeared from the Tygerberg
hospital during the nineties without so much as an explanation or a

reason. You can imagine the impenetrable mystery that surrounded your disappearing act."

She felt her throat closing up. She would instead have used the word survival.

"This all happened when I left with the children for Holland. Later in Holland, I heard Ben had revisited the hospital, the morgue, and the police stations repeatedly, but no one knew where you were." Mien saw that her face looked grey from shock.

"Oh, Annie, I'm so insensitive. I never knew that you were...I'm so sorry..." Mien hugged her, which was unusual for her. She was emotionally very reserved.

"Did Ben ever speak to this ambulance man?"

"Oh, no. What I just told you only happened years later when you were in Holland, busy running your hotel."

They were both silent for a while, each with their thoughts.

"I was abducted. Like At's story, I was never asleep; they were not aliens. That is how I remember my experience. I escaped from a laboratory kind of room next to the morgue just before they were going to cut me open."

"Are you kidding me?"

"Only Ben knows my story. I've never been brave enough to go under hypnosis to recall my experience."

"Would you want to?"

She couldn't reply, knowing what could happen if she opened Pandora's box. How safe was she from the people from whom she escaped fourteen years ago? It still gave her nightmares.

"I've not found the courage to expose myself to what my mind must have locked away. Part of the reason why I came with Ben to South Africa was to visit Hogsback. That is the place where I might gather enough courage to confront my abduction head-on."

It helped. If only Annelies could find Nadifa.Would she still be there? Mien was silent for a while. It was getting dark, and there was still no sign of Ben.

"What made you go and live in the Hogsback so many years ago? I never understood that then. Was it still because of your feelings of grief you could not let go of?"

"Gosh, what made you ask me that now?"

Mien waited for her to reply. She knew why: Mien having a baby while hers was taken from her had been too painful to swallow. She had done a disappearing act then, but that was voluntary.

In great detail, she recalled the view from the one-roomed cottage she rented from Nadifa. It overlooked a forest of azaleas, rhododendrons, daffodils and many other species of European plants, not to mention a profusion of berries.

"I knew that my life needed to take a different turn. I started to dislike myself because I had become bitter. I had heard that many artists and alternative people had found a haven in its green and lush environment. So I hoped to find myself there again."

"And did you?"

"Oh yes....and more. That is why I want to go back there this time. The energy was very healing then, so it still might be."

She had excellent memories of the many walks over the rocky paths that led through an indigenous rainforest towards waterfalls that sparkled down the cliffs. It was easy to fantasize about misty rainbows leading to pots of gold and fairy hideaways.

"Some believe that the Hogsback is the home of fairies, elfin and forest folk. What do you say? Is it true?" Mien asked jokingly.

"Have you ever been?"

If Mien was hearing her thoughts, she was then not projecting hers.

"No, but I would love to. If you and Ben are planning a visit to the Hogsback on this trip, can I come along? Unless you'd both rather go on your own?"

It was true that she had never envisaged going back there with anyone else besides Ben, but then maybe not.

"I'm unsure if Ben has the time to visit the place. If not, then we could go together."

"Thanks, I would love it. We together, I mean. Maybe we can drive up by ourselves, and Ben joins us later? When is your return flight to Holland?"

"We have ten days left, so it all depends on Ben. Where are they?"

"Good question. Let's go to the main quarters and see what Pat and Katrina have cooked for supper. Who knows, they might already be there, having a drink on the deck."

Pat and Katrina were in the kitchen of the main building, preparing dinner.

"Hi there, glad some of you have arrived. Where is the rest of the Jaarsma Clan?"

"Have the men not come back from George?" Mien asked. Pat pulled her cell phone from behind her apron to look at the time. Annelies wasn't going to wait. Instead, she would use the time to do some internal networking.

"Ben, where are you? When will you be coming back from George?"

They would never misuse their telepathic connection by eavesdropping on each other or when one was occupied.

"They are late. Let me phone Harrie." Pat must have got her husband on his cell since she was nodding, but she could not pick up any thought projections from her or her husband; only Ben's mental signature came through.

"We have been held up. Jock was approached by a girl whom he thought he knew, so we are still waiting for him at a local bar. I've already asked if Hans can locate him. Don't worry and say nothing to Mien just yet."

"They are all having a drink at a local bar in York Street, waiting for Jock, who was called away by a girlfriend," Pat told them after she had spoken to Harrie.

"I'm not aware of any girlfriend, but then I will probably be the last one to be informed," Mien replied, smiling. At least she knew that Pat had confirmed Ben's telepathic reply.

"Come, let's also enjoy something to drink on the deck. I have made some popcorn since Pat and I have to watch our waistlines."

Pretending not to be concerned was not easy. If Ben had found it necessary to contact Hans, he was as uneasy as she was. She chose a chair nearest the glass panel because she felt a presence behind her. Katrina was chatting about the staff, who all came from Thembaletho nearby.

"Annelies, may I ask you something?" Pat's expression was studious.

"Sure, is it something serious?" The fleeting image of a person was still there, near them like a shadow.

"Katrina says that you believe we can be physically immortal. Have you ever met someone who has lived longer than, say, two hundred years?"

She was so taken aback by being asked that question and hearing the word belief. The word 'speculating' instead of 'belief' would have been less direct.

"Pat, it is a grave mistake for anyone to think it is necessary to meet an immortal to become immortal. The key to your immortality is never to be found in an external location. It is always present within us." She could see that her reply did not sink in.

"Trust in your Immortality, Pat. Remember that the original doubting Thomas died. Some Immortals will refuse to meet you until after you become immortal yourself. Several breatharians on the planet have very uplifting information to share." She added with a smile, thinking of Nadifa.

"So you say you must just accept it as your truth and never ask for proof?" Pat replied.

She understood Pat's feelings of doubt. If only they would experience, or at least since their observer as she often did. She could feel her energy blending with the rhythmic pumping of her heart and the steady rise and fall of her lungs. Lately, she could see or sense other energy bubbles around every creature with a life force, especially disembodied human Souls. Her being human gave her an extra insight into how perceptions play a significant role in each individual's energy field.

"Pat, when you think it is important to find an Immortal, you are making a judgment, creating separation, and building a hierarchy. These three cardinal sins create and perpetuate death in society."

Mien was attentively listening to their conversation, while Katrina was eager to share her thoughts because she placed her hand over hers, asking:

"You mean we are already doomed before we even question the idea?"

Pat was quick to respond as if her replies were already waiting. She was not yet ready to confront her own beliefs.

"The answer to that would involve explaining how much energy each person could draw in or lose due to fear or doubt energies."

That would be a lecture in itself. She would instead add that into her workbook.

"It has been discovered that during puberty, our bodies are programmed to activate the death hormone in the pituitary gland. For any healing method to be truly effective and successful, the death hormone must be deactivated. However, it is our beliefs that prevent this. Any belief stored in our cellular memories is not easily activated." It reminded her of physical youth spacing Soul Quality of Structure.

"So, when companies advertise a rejuvenation facial cream, that only works if you believe in it?" Pat replied in a suspicious tone.

"Adopting a decoding program will help each individual on their awakening journey. Such as bringing your Soul qualities into your everyday lives."

"You refer to your decoding workbook, but not so?" Katrina asked.

"Yes, but that is one way. When one has attained personal harmonization to the degree that one exists in health, happiness and harmony within oneself and with all life, then one can become naturally more compassionate and charitable and turn our attention to the global game, the service agenda, if you will, if they have not already done so."

Emotionally, she knew that she had a lot of shadow entities from her ancestral lineage that needed to be released. Her emotional youth code of nine that she had chosen in this incarnation symbolised the Soul quality of unity.

"When we look in the mirror, the real self is always there. We are all already Immortals. It's therefore essential to meet your own Higher true Self, not another Immortal. The Age of the Guru has gone." She meant giving energy to a teacher, but she was unsure if they understood her.

"That I can accept. I never have been drawn to become someone's follower." Mien added her part.

"The achievement of physical immortality is always a solitary initiation. It's solely between you and the infinite source. No intermediary is involved. Any initiation is attained through individual effort and then tested and strengthened in society." It reminded her that her dark sea of awareness levels was often just around the corner, waiting to be journeyed through.

"It's the testing that I wonder about. How is one tested?" Mien asked. At the same time, she added telepathically, *"Sorry, my friend.*

It was out before I knew you were tested, weren't you? Fourteen years ago?"

"You mean that you might get very ill or have an accident, and then you have to keep your faith?" Pat asked.

That was one way to look at it, but she didn't think it was always necessary.

"See it this way. Every Immortal is like a star radiating a pure, creative life force in all directions. Stars do not get bored. Only those who do not understand life get bored. If physical Immortals live amongst us, they profoundly understand life's laws. Life is the most exciting thing going on in this universe."

"Thanks, Mien, for reminding me of my tests. Yes, I needed to understand the laws of life and light years ago." She beamed on an open channel, hoping that Mien would pick it up or at least intuit it from the words in her mind.

"I like that, that life can be exciting. I met someone in Holland who reminded me of that very same thing, but will we ever truly understand the laws of life and light?" Mien winked at her friend.

She had tapped into her telepathic wavelength! Now, it just needed to get stronger.

"Oh, tell us. I bet you it's a man." Pat probed when John appeared.

"Are all the men back?" Mien asked, looking up at John and ignoring Pat's suggestion.

John shook his head. He seemed a man of few words.

"Annelies, where did the idea of death originate from? Do you have any idea?" Katrina must have even given her ascension work some thought to ask that question.

"Mortal laws are laws of restriction based on fear. They deplete energy. Immortal laws are principles of positive, creative, and expansive activity. They attract more energy. It's those two opposite energy laws where we experience the testing. That is why it is important to keep any feelings of fear, anger, or revenge at bay."

"That's all very well, but what about our survival instincts?" Pat remarked, looking at John for some support.

"There you have the answer to your question. The belief in death originates from the birth of our survival instinct. Our need to stay in our physical reality is programmed into every cell that shapes our body. The way we see ourselves in the mirror confirms it."

"But that survival instinct is also present in nature and animals," John added. Katrina smiled at him. He had at least joined their conversation.

"Yes, that is how we perceive it to be. If we look at the phenomenon of non-biological life, we have learned more about the laws of physical immortality by comparing them..."

She could see by their expressions that some had not been following her reasoning. Either they perceived reality differently or were still operating from a fixed viewpoint.

"Let me explain it through using the word animism. It's a philosophy that says that life permeates all things. The rocks, the wind, the sun, the stars, life is everywhere because everything has a soul." Annelies felt that their attention span had been exhausted. Mien and Katrina might still follow her topic, but she felt drained. That was a sure sign to change the subject.

"Ah, you've lost me. Where are these guys?" Pat's reply had verbalised her suspicions. Before these deep questions were fired at her, she had asked for her Higher Self to overshadow the energy of her persona just in case her ego mind would reply.

During the whole debate, she felt that the energy of a light being hovered behind her, as did a shadowy figure.

"There they are; I see them from a distance. They seem to be speeding. Look at the dust that approaching vehicle is creating!" Pat was pointing at the dirt road. A car that looked like a Land Rover was racing towards them when, at the same time, a sudden noise from a helicopter, at least what looked like one, was flying very low over Crystal Cliffs. Suddenly, a feeling of fear and real danger threatened to envelop her. Both the energy entities were gone.

The flying craft could have been from a science fiction movie. It had a very futuristic appearance.

"What is that? I've never seen...." John was just as astonished

"Do you have a helipad on the property?" She asked Mien, denying her anguish.

"No, not yet, we didn't have permission. Toon tried, but...Look, why is At frantically waving at us?"

"Get inside. Close every door and window and stay low." AT shouted from the back of the Land Rover, while the driver parked the car under the deck.

They grabbed what they could from the table and ran inside. A tall but lean and muscular Indonesian man wearing a faded grey sweatshirt, wrinkled army pants and high lace-up boots came running up the walkway, closing all the double doors as he went. His coloured complexion reminded her of Niels, except he was much taller and leaner.

"Where is Jock... and Ben?" Mien shouted over the noise of the hovering alien-looking craft's engine.

"Ben is getting help. Jock has been taken prisoner." Harrie replied. His eyes observed her, knowing that a proper introduction would be out of order. He appeared to be a lot younger than Pat, but that could be because Pat looked old for her age. Funny, he was just as familiar to her as Katrina had been at first glance. He was not the type to mess with.

The smell of fear permeated every fibre of her being. Gosh, was this another test? She tried to slow down her breathing by inhaling deeply. They were all inside when she saw through the glass panels that two figures had been lowered to the ground, while the strange-looking helicopter hovered not far from the main building.

"Come on, everyone, follow me." At ordered.

The sound from the aircraft became almost hypnotic; it reminded her of her childhood days when she and her mom would take the tram to town. A strong déja vu feeling came over her. Had this happened before?

The noise took her back to when she used to make up stories while the scenery through the tram window flashed as if she was looking at a movie. She had never seen one but heard about it. Her father forbade his children from watching TV or going to the cinema. He warned them that screen projections would interfere with their minds. He believed that the programs were all coming from an dark source.

Mien pulled at her arm, "Come, Annelies, what's wrong?"

"Sorry, but for a moment, I was somewhere else." Why did she remember that now?

They followed At down the circular staircase into a basement room with building equipment. She confirmed by following but wished she was brave enough to stay where she was. Running down a winding staircase into a dark basement did not inspire feelings of safety. Two men in black suits stopped Harrie, Katrina and Pat. They suddenly appeared from the other side of the basement.

At stopped abruptly, so the rest bumped into him. Annelies didn't see the last step, so she fell.

The pain made her scream, but more from anger at having an accident.

"Oh, Annelies, are you alright?" Mien turned, trying to get her up. John was behind her, helping her to stand up. They all forgot their fear for a moment, but that soon returned when the two male figures in black-like diving suits roughly pushed them aside. John shouted at Pat to get help and Katrina to run away.

"Lady, if you think you can pull a stunt on us like this, you are mistaken." That voice! As if a computer was talking.

At leaped onto the man's back but was seized by his friend, who then punched him, causing him to collapse. Mien yelled at him to flee and got slapped. Pat tried running away, but the same guy was quicker; he dragged her by her hair into a corner. Annelies was in a lot of pain, but his threatening, metallic tone made her even angrier. This time, her anger was aimed at the man in the shiny black jumpsuit. If looks could kill, she would have succeeded.

"How dare you use that tone with me. How dare you come in uninvited, threatening us all as if ..." She took a deep breath. "You are not worth even losing my breath over." Her contempt spoke volumes. She tried to get up and put weight on her feet, but the pain made her feel faint. Something was wrong with these two men. She never picked up any mental noise or images...There was no internal dialogue? No feelings.

"I have to...I can't walk." She whispered.

Harrie lifted her before they could drag her, forcing her to walk. John attacked the guy who had dragged Pat by her hair, but one heavy return blow knocked John out. He fell, tripping over At's still unconscious body. Her horror at seeing blood on John's face made her turn, looking over Harrie's shoulder. That was when she saw the emblem on the black helmet: a swastika within a yellow star-like symbol. Then everything went black before her eyes.

When she came to it, she was tied down like the others. She must have been out for at least a few minutes. They were now all tied together with orange nylon rope. It happened so fast that no one knew Katrina had escaped except Harrie.

For the second time in her life, she could smell fear. It oozed out of all of them. The first time was fourteen years ago. She felt so disappointed in herself that she reacted angrily instead of staying calm. Her behaviour took her back during her teen years and later after Tessa was kidnapped. If this was a test, she had failed miserably.

Chapter 11
Our Belief Programs

When Darkness is Threatened by Light.

Mien cried, not knowing what was wrong with At. John sat up to spit out blood and teeth, but it was getting too dark to see anything else. Pat was more worried about his heart, telling him to stay calm. Annelies was trying to move her feet away so no one could accidentally touch or even sit on them. They were very swollen; she could feel them.

Both attackers swore black diver's gear with hoods and huge black-framed spectacles. There was something weird about them. As if...No, that couldn't be... The one guy that John clobbered had lost his glasses. She tried to make out his features when the moonlight highlighted his face. His eyes were big black...Ugh...no, it must have been too dark.

"We know one of you got away, but my mate will find her."

His voice had an evil, hollow slant but was very human. The other one with glasses on moved close to Harrie's face. Only now did she notice Harrie was separate from the rest, leaning against the wall.

Harrie struggled to keep his temper; his aura was shooting flaming darts. His feet and hands were tied behind his back, making it impossible to move, but she knew that he tried.

"Mom, stay calm. Tell the others to lower their fear levels. It will only feed your attackers. Remember that your mind's mental projection forms your reality according to your emotions. Mom, your senses are in

action mode, draining your energy." Being reminded of her emotions calmed her down.

"Hans, where are you!"

"Arriving at Cape Town late tomorrow evening. We'll try to get a connecting flight to George. Toon's travel bureau is onto it now."

"Is Liesbeth with you? Be careful Hans, who are they? Are they human? Where is Ben? Thanks for reminding me. What do you mean by feeding them?"

At least At was moaning. Annelies was glad for Mien's sake. John and Pat were still in shock. Pat's shoulders were still shaking while Harrie tried to calm her down. He whispered that he was free of the rope but to keep quiet about it.

Instead of dwelling on their predicament, she settled into a sitting position with both legs stretched out on the ground – leaning into the corner. If this highjacking scenario was a test for her, she could accept that, but why the others? She took a few deep breaths and tried to silence her mind. All she allowed herself to hear was heavy breathing coming from the others. Then, a stale metallic smell tried to occupy her thoughts. Where did that come from? *"Annie, be in the now",* she scolded herself. She now watched for thoughts that would sneak in if she let them, almost waiting for them to arrive. The longer the silent waiting period, the better.

Annelies felt her heart beating in her throat. When she heard the whispering, it took her back.

His voice seemed to crack, like it had a little hitch in it, the way her dad's voice used to thicken, while his hands were up to her skirt, feeling the nipples of her teenage breasts getting hard under the soft touch of his lips when she was that important to him when he was that important to her when nothing else mattered.

Aah…What was that all about? What ghastly memories had she woken up? It could only be from another lifetime. She was caught off guard. *"This is nuts,"* she sighed… Again, she listened to the silence. She felt her breath suspended in her lungs. The others were utterly quiet...and then she suddenly had a remarkably clear connection.

The two attackers were whispering on the far side of the basement. She picked up that they didn't know what to do with them. At least, that is what her intuition told her. Instead of hearing any mental dialogue, she could almost hear a metallic device speaking, as if her physical hearing had become sharper!

"Now what? The boss is going to be pissed. What are we supposed to do, run after the one that got away, or..."

"Annelies, can you hear what they are whispering about?"

She nodded at Mien. When the man's cell rang, it gave them all a jolt.

"Bruce," he said into the mouthpiece. "Yes, yes." He listened. "No...not yet.... Yes, that can be arranged...No, there will be no difficulties..."As he spoke, his companion kept making hand signals. "Yes, I hear you." His angry whisper added more drama, ignoring his buddy. He listened for another minute while nodding in At's direction.

All she hoped was to be left on the ground until the pain in both her feet had settled.

"No...one got away...a woman...I'll tell him...yes...got it." He closed his cell phone and gave orders with sign language for all to understand.

The other man approached At, who had fully regained consciousness. She let out a yelp when he kicked her left foot sideways to get nearer to At.

At tried standing up but found himself tied to John. Harrie pulled at her waist to warn her about something when...all of a sudden, she was roughly pulled up onto her feet.

"I think my feet are broken."

"Come on. Don't mess with me."

"Let me help." Harrie jumped up to half-carry her. His immense stature towered over both men, even when he took her arm and draped it around his neck. His being tall helped. She sucked in her breath as if to hold in the stabbing pain. Every step was agony. "Where to?"

Both men were at a loss for words, seeing Harrie get himself free, but decided to let Harrie support her towards a doorway she had not seen before. She tried to project a lot of light around them, hoping that her mental energy would have a soothing effect on both abductors. Then she thought of Ben's trick.

The second man dragged the others through the doorway into a smaller room by pulling the rope. They all tried to stop it from hurting.

"What do you want from us?" Mien was courageous enough to ask.

"You will find out. Just do as we say, and nobody gets hurt."

At was about to say something, but John urged him to stay silent.

"Good advice"....she heard one hissing.

The small room must have been used in the past as a sort of living place. The others were told to sit on the old sofa while Harrie carried her to the corner of the floor. Then Harrie was threatened with a pistol and ordered to stand near a window after he first gently rested her against the wall. How would she ignore the harsh treatment that had made them all into a weak, subservient mess? It made her gasp for air.

Now, they tied them all together, except for Harrie. He was standing while they tied his ankles firmly to the same rope and his wrists behind him and onto the rusty mental burglar bar of a small window.

Both men left the room, locking the door behind them. It was by now pitch dark.

While their ordeal played out, she had mentally activated the bowel movements of both attackers, hoping she would have the same effect as Ben had. Her feet felt swollen to three times their size. Even a slight touch was painful now that the rope was tied around them.

"Annie, can you get Harrie to turn around?"

All she could see was the silhouette of a man's torso bent as if in pain in the moonlight. Harrie's back was arched as he struggled against the restraints. Was Ben on the other side of that window?

"Harrie." She whispered. "Can you turn to look out of the window?"

The others were also aware that somebody was outside the window and knew their predicament.

"Annie, tell Harrie to move away from the window so I can shine a torch inside."

She knew that pulling the rope around Harrie's ankles would injure her feet even more. Suddenly, Harrie moved as if he was free! Someone had cut the rope around his wrists. She whispered to Harrie what Ben had projected to her.

"Tannie, how do you... The rest was smothered by Mien, who covered At's mouth with her hand.

The others stayed silent, but they all froze. Someone had turned the key. A figure stepped through the door holding a torch.

"Jock!" Mien's urgent whisper trembled with relief.

"Stay silent; we don't know how many are around..." Jock whispered to them all. At that moment, a glass broke, followed by swearing.

"Ben, is that you?" She saw someone through the window.

"Jock, how did you get inside?"

He must have escaped. Had Harrie not told them that Jock was taken prisoner?

Harrie untied the rope around his legs and hers. Then he freed the others. John whispered to Ben outside how to get in from the basement side.

"Are you all alright?" Harrie lightly touched her feet. "Annelies hurt her feet. They might be broken." He whispered to the others while trying to help her up.

"We have to get you all out of there fast before they discover we found you. John, your Landrover is hidden under the deck. We pushed it for the last few metres, hoping no one would hear us."

Jock's urgent request spurred them all on. Harrie had already lifted her while she used Mien's shoulders as a crutch. The others followed Jock as quickly as they could out through the door into the basement in the direction where the attackers had come from. She heard someone closing the door behind them. She kept her mental visions of both men's internal digestion organs, even adding the feeling of heavy cramps to make sure.

They were near the Land Rover when Ben suddenly appeared. He must have seen that Mien and Harrie were carrying her.

"Annie, are you hurt? Are you in pain? Gosh...how?"

They all scrambled over the wire cage at the back of the Landy as fast as they could while Mien opened the passenger door, climbed in and held the door for her. With difficulty, she slid onto the seat with the help of Mien.

"Jock jumped behind the wheel and started the engine. The noise from the motor made them all cringe.

"Katrina got away ...." Harrie told Ben from the back of the Land Rover when they heard a shout in the distance.

"She managed to get to your cottage and got Jock on his cell." They all heard Ben over the noise of the engine. "She said she would take the bike and get away."

"We think she must have got away," Jock added.

As Jock shot away from under the deck onto the gravel road towards the highway, she wondered why Ben was staying behind? She did not see him jump into the back of the Land Rover.

"Annie, look after yourself. I'm fine. I must stay behind to find out who is running the show without them knowing I'm around."

The Land Rover sped on, and when she turned to look through the back window, she saw that they were all on the floor in a heap. Only Harrie was standing, holding onto the sides while bending over them. He saw her looking and winked. She again tried to remember where she knew him from.

"Oh, Ben, why can't we escape or look beyond this illusional reality? Why do all our mental perceptions so influence us?" She beamed while grabbing hold of the dashboard to keep upright because the Land Rover was bouncing over the rough road at a terrific speed.

She should know better. Why could she not move beyond her mind? It often felt like she had two minds, and one of them always seemed to get her into trouble.

"Annie, I feel partly responsible for you feeling guilty. I seem to have stirred a lot of people into reacting. I know that we must each work on our distorted, misinterpreted reality bubbles, but remember that my job is not all that conducive to that aim."

She wondered where Ben was hiding. How could he, on his own, affect their predicaments? Not that she had any idea what corruptive energy was driving their drama. At least Ben knew his work was inappropriate if he wanted to fully awaken and hold onto that intent. He needed to slow down; he had better still leave this job.

"Yes, I promised to resign, but I must find Katrina. She never started the bike, so she promised to wait for me while hiding behind her cottage."

Jock turned onto the freeway towards George. He seemed to know where the Hospital was. She agreed to have X-rays taken of both her feet, and John and At might also need some attention.

"Are your feet broken?" Jock asked.

"I hope not, but they are very swollen. I don't know how I could have damaged them so badly. It was only one step, so maybe they are not broken."

"I will go past the emergency and see if there is someone there who can have a look. I hope we are not followed."

"Are we...who are they?" Mien reacted in horror. She had not been aware that they were chased.

"As far I can see, no. Do any of you have a credit card on you?"

"No. My bag is in our cottage. Why?"

"None of us have bags with us. Don't you have yours?" Mien asked.

"Mom, I need to book us all for a B&B. It's already after eight. I don't have that kind of money on my card, and we can't go back."

Jock must be getting nearer the hospital because she saw that he started looking for Langenhoven Road.

"There it is." Mien pointed. "Let's see if you have any broken bones, Annelies, and we'll take them from there. Thank goodness it's a warm evening. I hope Jock's racing has not shaken the others in the back too badly."

They turned into a parking bay, and she saw steps towards glass-panelled doors.

She opened the car door to see if she could see her feet in the entrance lights.

"Wait here, Annelies," Harrie suggested as he jumped from the back onto the pavement. "I'll see if I can organise a wheelchair."

Harrie arrived back with a wheelchair, and Jock carried her out of the Landy into the chair.

"Gosh, they look sore. They are so swollen. Are you in pain?" Mien placed her feet on the footrests and rolled her up the ramp and inside together.

The nurse on duty took one look at her feet and phoned the x-ray department, while someone else wanted to know all their information. She realised that having no bag on her, or any papers, passport or document to prove who she was, had created a problem. Mien explained where they lived, and in the meantime, Jock spoke to Toon on his cell. She was not even sure if they had any travel insurance. Ben had arranged everything like he always did. John and Pat were escorted to the outpatient section.

"Let's take you to our emergency X-ray department. We'll sort the rest out later." The nurse suggested as she wheeled her away from the others into a lift. Inside, she pressed the up button, asking where she was from and how her injury had happened. How was she going to explain that? Surely the whole drama had to stay a secret? She knew that Ben and Jock both agreed not yet to involve the South African police until they had first found out if it was a vendetta pursued against the Jaarsma clan.

"I fell or tripped. I never knew there were more steps down, so I just fell onto my feet." The young girl nodded and wheeled her out of the lift into an empty passage. She parked her in front of a closed door. The nurse said she would be back soon.

There she was, all alone in a wheelchair. How fast someone's life could change.

Finding someone who could operate the X-ray equipment took a while since it was after hours, but finally, two people arrived. After they took several photos of both her feet, she was wheeled into a doctor's office and again left alone.

The hospital noises gradually faded now that she had the time to assess her situation. When these two people jumped from that alien-looking craft, some other energy force had taken control of them through fear. Something did not add up.

What did Jock, Ben and Harrie know? It was Harrie who had said that Jock had been taken prisoner. Those were the words he used. She had never asked by whom at the time, but now she wished she had.

After what felt like a half-hour, a tall, middle-aged man wearing a long white coat over casual clothing greeted her with a smile, introducing himself as Doctor Beck.

"How did your holiday injury happen?" He asked as he switched on a wall lightbox and stuck her X-rays onto it. She wheeled herself closer, and he stepped aside for her to see.

"I only slipped on one step that I had not seen." Hoping that her freak accident would prove to be minor.

"Look at your left foot." She was horrified to see that a bone on the side of her left foot was broken. That reminded her of how the attacker had kicked her feet out of the way. The doctor studied her right foot, but she could see nothing. Knowing that most of the pain was in her right foot, she wondered.

"Yep, your right foot has sustained a more complicated injury." he pointed at what looked like three cracks across the arch of her foot. "I'm afraid that putting any weight onto your right foot is out of the question for the rest of your holiday. I strongly suggest surgery on your left foot for now." He looked back at her, waiting for her reply.

"That bone needs to have a pin inserted to stay together, but then at least you can put your weight on it after two to three days. Your right foot has to be into a cast." He phoned someone while letting her adjust to his diagnosis.

How would she get around if she was not allowed to walk? An operation on her foot? Was that all going to be possible?

Someone arrived with a big boot that came in two parts. The nurse first bandaged her left foot and fitted the boot, showing her how it worked with a pump to make it tight. Then, she had to lie on her stomach on an examination table so they could bend her right knee. In that position, they made a cast under her sole behind her injured right foot and halfway up her calf.

"Let me help you back into your wheelchair and schedule an appointment as soon as possible. After your operation, you can start using your left foot with the help of crutches."

"That's it? I'm wheelchair-bound until then. How long will it be before I can walk?" The whole procedure had gone so quickly that adjusting to the fact that she could not walk had hardly sunk in.

"Remember that there is no reality, only your perception of it. Man is indeed the creator of his reality, but not as a separate force. Blend your energy with the infinite." Her Higher Self reminded her to become her observer. By mentally seeing herself standing behind her wheelchair, she allowed her thoughts to create a vision of being able to walk. It was so because her perception that she couldn't walk had already programmed the obstacles she would encounter in her reality.

"I would not recommend putting any weight on your right foot for at least eight weeks. When are you flying back to Amsterdam?" Doctor Beck asked while removing his white coat.

"In ten days."

"Then I suggest you have your left foot seen here in George. It's easy to have a pin placed into that bone, and I would do it as soon as possible; then you can at least rest on that foot." He spoke to the nurse, discussing when her operation could be scheduled for. They both looked at her and waited for her consent. She could read their minds. They understood her dilemma, especially being in a foreign country.

"Where is your husband?" The nurse asked. She further explained that Doctor Beck was the orthopaedic surgeon who would do the operation. His pleasant, open face and his smile projected a feeling of competence.

"He is on the way, but I left my papers, passport and travel itinerary at our Crystal Cliffs cottage. He will find out about our travel insurance."

I suggest you have both feet X-rayed again when you are home and let your orthopaedic specialist in Holland decide if your right foot must also undergo an operation." Doctor Beck said something to the nurse while pushing her wheelchair back towards the lift. He shook her hand and said goodbye.

"Shall I take you to our administration office to schedule you for your operation on your left foot?"

"Let me think...You'd better first find out when I can have this operation. Can it be done in one day? I mean, I don't have to stay overnight, do I?" The nurse didn't know.

When they arrived back at the reception, both Mien and Harrie looked relieved to see her.

"Is it possible for me to phone Holland? I need to speak to my family, asking them to organise any necessary paperwork." She had directed her question at the nurse pushing her wheelchair, but Harrie had taken over. The nurse was already talking to a woman behind the counter.

"Where are At, Jock, John and Pat?"

Mien pointed towards glass doors, explaining that At and John were both being seen by the emergency staff. Pat had gone with them.

"At asked me to find out what had happened to you, so I stayed with Harrie waiting for you. Are both your feet broken?"

Harry's sombre expression reminded her of Katrina and that Ben might still be in danger. She could feel her anxiety levels rising again, so she inhaled deeply. She explained the outcome of her injuries and added that she needed an operation. Simultaneously, she felt the energy of Hans' telepathic signature:

"Mom, take this opportunity to walk the fine line of being in the world but not of it. Embrace the events and ignore the rest. See you tomorrow evening. Remember that our universe is a process of events rather

than things. Try to walk through life feeling free from attachments, perceptions, delusions and illusions."

In other words, go with the flow, she thought. Nevertheless, Hans' advice had helped. Somehow, she still felt that to break one's feet, a person must have asked for an experience to do with going forward. The surgery was scheduled for the following day. Jock had booked a guest house nearby for Annelies and Mien so they could return early for the operation. Everything was arranged from Holland. Jock had called his sister Sonja, who made all the arrangements. She knew Dr. Beck and convinced Toon that Annelies would be well cared for.

After At and John were discharged, Jock and Harrie reported what had happened to the police. She had insisted on it. Nobody had yet heard anything from Ben and Katrina. John had an appointment with a dentist, that was all.

She was awake for hours in the morning, lying in a single bed with both her feet on a continental pillow. The only free guest room had two single beds. Mien was still fast asleep.

"Ben, where are you?"

Only once she knew Ben was safe could she relax.

"Good, you are awake. How are your feet? What did you do to the two men who stormed the main building of Crystal Cliffs? They were both out of action due to heavy cramps, and boy, they both must have lost kilos! Good work! It made it easy for me to overpower them. The local police arrested them, so I have spent the night in our unit. It's not nice being here without you."

Gosh, what a relief. Ben was okay. She now needed to get some perspective back into her life. What she had learned during her whole ordeal was to save her human energy, especially during trying times. Only her Higher Self's energy would enable her to handle the higher vibrations ordinarily inaccessible.

"You have no idea how relieved I am that you are safe. I never slept a wink. I copied your stunt in Cape Town, remember? Glad it worked favourably for you. They have scheduled me for a nine o'clock operation. What are we going to do after I'm out later today? I'll be wheelchair-bound."

It's incredible how a single misstep could abruptly disrupt their entire vacation! She needed to strengthen her ability to use her energy fields correctly. She now wished she had her laptop with her. There was so much she needed to type for her decoding workbook.

"Let's first get your operation over with. I will be at the hospital before you go in. Is Mien there with you? Jock told me that he could only find one free room near the hospital. Mien wanted to stay with you."

It was getting lighter. Annelies could see Mien's dark blond, curly short hair on the pillow. Who would have thought it would be Mien who once again shared a room with her? As if they had some unfinished business to attend to. Why else...

"Are you in pain?"

The painkiller they had given her must be working. *"No, not really."*

Last year, when she gave her second decoding workshop, POWAH told her that there were two parts of her mind, and one was always silent because the force of the other part denied the expression. Whatever she had understood, she had taken metaphorically. It was reading Richard's journal that linked 'POWAH's information with the left and right hemispheres of the brain.

During her last workshop, Richard asked her: "Is our 'Physical reality' primarily a mental or a spiritual phenomenon?" She replied that there is the assumption that the individual Self consists of various levels of being, constituting a hierarchy of octaves. She added that he should not discriminate between them and directed him to an article about that question for their website. She wished she could read what Richard had written in his journals again.

"Annelies, are you awake?" Mien asked

"Yes, for hours. I'm not allowed to eat breakfast, so why don't you find out what they serve? I want to be at the hospital early so that they might start with me first." She now wanted to get it over and done with; the quicker, the better.

"How are your feet? Are you in pain?"

"Uncomfortable, but I took pills for the pain, and they work."

"Oh, Annelies, I'm so very sad for you. I have been thinking of how to get you around in a wheelchair after your operation. I asked if you have to stay over for a night, and the one older nurse didn't think so."

"Well, that is good news. Can you help me? I have to go to the bathroom."

"Gosh, of course. I'm glad you are not on your own. Do you think you can manage with the help of your crutches?"

"No idea, but I'd better try. I have never used crutches, so that is a new experience. I cannot put my weight onto my right foot, so I have to see if I have any balance just using my left foot. I need you to stop me from falling."

With great difficulty, she managed to get to the bathroom. Her left foot was complaining, but the strong, stiff bandage did help a great deal. Mien helped her inside. She was glad for her to be there. Apart from Ben, she would have been quite lost without her. Gosh, how was she going to have a shower or a bath?

"Just sit on the edge of the bath, and I'll wash you down. At least you can be wheeled up the ramp to the top floor and be outside resting on our deck. I've been considering making it as comfortable as possible all night."

"Gee, I have never given it any thought, but I can't get around in a wheelchair on your property! What about our plan to go to the Hogsback? That is also out, I suppose."

Mien looked the way she felt, defeated. There was no way she was now going to the Hogsback. What was the point? She had wanted to go walking into the forest. See if Nadifa was still there. The thought of her being dependent on others completely shattered her.

"Let's take each day as it comes" Mien hugged her, and she felt like crying.

"Why don't you see if they serve breakfast. I'll be alright. I can even wheel myself around, look."

Mien helped her to get dressed and into the wheelchair, and then she attended to herself. It was just after seven when they both appeared in the dining room. She was not hungry, even after eating nothing the previous night. Mien ate some fruit salad and drank fruit juice. Some people looked at her in pity; she could feel them thinking.

"What's wrong with her?"

Her painkillers were wearing off because her right foot, which was in a cast, started to throb. Oh please, don't get all depressed, she warned herself. She had to look on the positive side. It was a temporary setback, so she needed to learn to go with the flow.

"Annie! Oh, my dear, to see you like this. Are you in any pain?" Ben's expression said plenty. He must have seen her first, waiting in a wheelchair, before she saw him entering the guesthouse dining room. Both feet were injured by how she had them resting on the footrest. Ben's strong hug uplifted her spirits. She could imagine how she would have felt if their roles had been reversed.

"It's not too bad. Some throbbing, but I can take something for the pain. I haven't taken pills this morning since they are going to operate in an hour. It's going to be done under a full anaesthetic, so please stay with me as long as you can." She whispered the last sentence.

"I have no intention of leaving your side. Don't you worry?" Ben was kneeling next to her chair, holding onto both hands. His loving expression made her smile. She could feel his affection, his love for her, as if a beam of light had pierced her solar plexus.

"Annie, I know why you are...scared...but I've spoken to a nurse at the hospital already. I told them that I would bring you."

"Hi Ben, I didn't know you were here. Have you had something for breakfast?" Ben replied to Mien that he would take her to the hospital and that he would stay with her until she woke up from the anaesthetic. Mien was reluctant to leave them, but she had no reason to hang around.

"Annelies, I will see what we can do to make you more comfortable in your temporary situation. Call me on my cell when you are ready to return to Crystal Cliffs. At least I hope you are coming back to us?"

"Gosh, Mien, I haven't thought about that, but you said yourself, how can I get around in a wheelchair from our rondavel?"

"I'm going to find out what we can do. I would hate the idea of you both moving into a guesthouse in George when you are our guests." Mien was upset, but she wasn't sure she wanted to return after what happened.

When they wheeled her outside, the Volvo was parked nearby. At was the driver this time. Nobody had spoken about yesterday's attack, and she had been so occupied with her situation it had slipped her mind. She needed help getting into the car, as it was rather high. She used her left foot to get herself seated, and Ben had worked out how to collapse the wheelchair in the boot.

The trip to the Hospital was short. They wheeled her in, and after Ben had signed some forms, she was taken away by a hospital porter. Ben had to run after them to make it into the lift.

"I want to see where you take her, and I will stay with her until she goes into theatre. " The porter shrugged his shoulders.

They settled her back in the room with the two beds. Hers was again near the window. The other bed was occupied, and one visitor was sitting next to the bed. An older nurse greeted them and asked questions while ticking them off on paper on a clipboard. Then they were left alone.

She was now wearing a hospital gown, sitting in bed under a cover, and a long white curtain was pulled around her section of the room. Ben found a chair, and she only saw that he had taken her small suitcase.

"Oh, I'm so glad you thought of some fresh clothes. Did you bring my laptop?"

"Annie, you didn't think you were going to write, did you?"

"No idea. I don't know how long this is all going to take."

"Well, I didn't bring your laptop. Let's take small steps...I mean."

"Sweety, I know what you mean. Nice choice of words, though." She smiled to make him feel at ease.

"Ben, I suddenly remembered. Are Hans and Liesbeth not arriving tonight?"

"Yes, let's hope so. They arrive in Cape Town, but I don't know if they can get a connection to George." He took her hand into his.

"Annie, I don't want you to be worried. Your accident was just that, a freak accident. Not like the last time..."

"Oh, I know. Yes, it has played on my mind, but as you said, tripping on one step, nobody could have planned that. What has happened since?" She heard the two people on the other bed talking, so she was whispering.

"Annie, I can imagine that it must all be unsettling for you after your last experience fourteen years ago, but...let's not focus on any fear-based thoughts. The local police have arrested the two men, and as you know, they were both doddery wrecks. I wish you could have seen them...not to mention the smell!"

Ben's face broke into a wide grin when he described how both criminals were having the runs.

While Ben was talking, she recalled that the number code of her unconscious language of Light symbol also stood for unity. Had she again chosen to embody this soul quality by losing her consciousness, this time through having an anaesthetic?

Her Mental Youth Vibration Code 9-Unity[1]

This quality of Unity, an awareness of the concepts of an oversoul and group-soul, is grasped. Unity symbolically represents a culmination of wisdom and experience and buzzes with the energy of endings and new beginnings.

"Are you ready for me to take you to the operating room, Mrs Zwiegelaar?" The words group-soul stayed lingering. If only she could have her laptop with her...

"So sorry, yes, oh." What she meant was that she needed the bathroom. Since she hadn't eaten or drunk anything since lunchtime yesterday, she felt rather faint.

They wheeled her away into her bed while Ben followed, walking next to her until they arrived at double doors that said: theatre.

"Mr Zwiegelaar, you can visit our visitor's room. We will let you know when your wife returns to her room." The head nurse said firmly. She had a kind face that took no-nonsense.

"Ben, I'll be fine, honest. I will see you soon... Love you!" At the same time, she squeezed his hand.

A different nurse in green gear with a face mask prepared her for a sedative when Doctor Beck suddenly appeared, and she was also in theatre gear with a face mask on. Seeing his familiar face made her feel a whole lot better. The surroundings were nothing like before. The energy felt a lot different....

He explained again what he would do on her left foot, and then a different man introduced himself as the anaesthetist and asked her another list of questions he ticked off from a clipboard. He settled her nerves completely. So far as she knew, she was not allergic to

---

1. https://allrealityshifters.wordpress.com/six-youth-and-physical-soul-quality-codes/

anything. For a split second, she questioned herself if she should mention her poisoning episode from years ago, but then she declined.

After receiving the injection, she noticed a yellow spot in front of her eyes, followed by a spinning sensation. Her vision became blurry, and she was unable to see anything. The darkest darkness replaced fear, anxiety, and a sense of strange anticipation, yet she still recalled the lecturer's words....

"Our Memories are part of the karmic cycle. Memory creates a desire, which then causes us to take action. That action then creates another memory, and we go around again. It is a part of our nature to learn and to grow. And one way we do this is by taking risks. When we learned to walk, we risked falling. We are constantly striving to better ourselves and our lives, and we can't do that by standing still."...

Then timelessness had set in...

***

The cinema at the Waterfront in Cape Town was packed with people eagerly waiting to see the movie "Vanishing Worlds", which had been the subject of many rumours. Annelies and Ben were excited to see how the audience reacted to their story. The special effects were stunning and greatly impacted the viewers, creating an atmosphere of heightened anticipation in the cinema. Many people sneaked in during the episode that depicted Annelies's story in the mid-nineties. During this part, Ben squeezed her hand, knowing it was one of the scariest episodes of their lives.

The actress was following her script. The audience could see that she tried to open her eyes. Annelies knew that her mind wanted to, but there was no control.

She could hear people running around her. The last thing she remembered was...food! Something to do with what she had swallowed. At first, it had made her mind dull; then, there was nothing but the pain....

Chapter 12
Our Number Code Symbols

Cape Town – Fourteen years ago

Where was she? She vaguely recalled having just started eating dinner at the Constantia Nek restaurant....

Ben! He had asked her something.... What was it? Oh...The pain in her chest...the way it folded around her like a blanket. It came in waves, tossing her up, dragging her under, washing over her, carrying her away from herself, from everything....

Now, there were people everywhere, and light and noise. And more pain. The man from the ambulance lifted her arms and squeezed her wrist; another shined a flashlight into her eyes. She was poked and prodded, a blanket laid over her body, a mask pressed against her mouth. She panicked as the thick plastic covered her face, but her next breath was deep and fresh, and it gave her the strength to take another.

Warm hands gripped her on either side, lifted her, and placed her on a long, smooth board. They laid thick straps across her body to tie her down. She felt so trapped! She was panicking!

"No," she whispered, forcing her mouth to form the word. "No."

But the straps clicked shut and were pulled tight. A hand pressed softly against her forehead. She felt herself lifting off the ground, then moving toward the gaping mouth of a white truck. Its sirens flashed, turning the world red, blue, and red again.

"Shhh, it's going to be all right," a man whispered.

"Do you know what happened?" he asked, leaning over her. His eyebrows were bushy, his eyes deep green. They crinkled at the corners when he smiled. "Can you tell us your name?"

He lifted the mask so she could speak.

"Do you know who you are, hon?" he asked. In the distance, an engine roared to life. A door slammed shut, and the ambulance lurched into motion. "Do you know your name?"

Of course, she should.

It was...

She was...

But there was nothing where there should have been a name, a person, a life, an answer. Her mind was black., empty.

"I am...," she mentally whispered. The words she was trying to utter out loud scraped her throat raw. "I don't know who I am."

The darkness returned.

She knew she was lying flat on her back. It smelled like chloroform. She must be in some hospital emergency room of sorts, but where?

"Doctor, my instructions are to be your assistant while the woman is unconscious. I have no idea what you are going to do to her, but the poison I gave her will wear off in a few hours."

She heard a female voice, but she could not speak. Where was she? Now, the pain stopped cradling her. Instead, it began clawing at her, devouring her. It was like a living beast, ripping her apart from the inside, struggling to break free from the outside world. The darkness behind her eyelids nipped at the edges of her mind, crawling back, offering her peace, asleep free of pain. Instead, she screamed, or she tried to.

"Goodness Doctor, she hasn't passed on. Are you..."

She desperately tried to move, but even the tiniest of motions – opening her mouth, drawing in a breath, tipping her head back to unleash the sound was fruitless. Then she felt a new, different kind of pain. As if a sharp knife suddenly sliced across her chest. It cut through the dull fog of her mind. The bright light of the world resolved itself into defined shapes, sharp lines. She was awake, petrified.

Stop! You can't do that," the woman shouted in panic. She heard shuffling and a noise as if someone had been slapped.

"No, she is not. Do your job or else." He hissed. "I've done all the tests; believe me, she's gone."

Waves of panic washed over her. Was she dead?

"Come back here bitch, or you won't get paid. Clean her up, and I'll work on her at dawn. It needs all my concentration."

His angry tone ripped at her as if she was worth nothing. The light...she realised that it was coming from a bright lamp. She desperately tried opening her eyes. Instead, she heard a click, like someone had switched off something, and the darkness returned.

She lay on her back, her arms stretched out at her sides. Beneath her, it felt hard, uneven. Small, sharp objects bore into her back, biting into her skin. She was afraid of floating into the darkness again. She couldn't move her head, but she darted her eyes from side to side behind her eyelids. Was she imagining it? She saw nothing at first, nothing but metallic shiny walls. Forcing her eyelids to open felt like pushing at an old, stuck-down window frame.

"Where am I?" she thought, her breath rasping as she breathed more air. A tickle was at the back of her mind, like a voice she could barely hear. The answer was there, just beyond her reach. But when she strained for it, the pain came back worse than before.

Maybe this was all a dream, she decided. So she lay still, breathing, and waited to wake up.

At first, she thought she was imagining him. A shadowy figure seemed to hover over her. She knew he was coming for her, and she should have felt relieved, but instinctually, she knew she had to keep very still to stop breathing. Then she thought it was a phantom and waited for him to disappear. Instead, he leaned closer, and his musky, warm breath gave her the creeps. He seemed to observe her like she was a wild animal as if she would bite, watching her to see if she could move. Then the same click and a bright light flooded the room.

He was just a silhouette behind the lamp, his face hidden in shadow. He grabbed her head and turned it sideways. Her eyelids pulled open as if someone had opened a blind. Was he inspecting something? As he stepped away, she saw his shoes, black leather with shiny straps where the laces should be, inside a green plastic shoe bag! Terror swept through her. She couldn't run away; she couldn't even sit up. She was too weak. She was too terrified.

I can't stop him. She didn't know where the thought had come from, what it meant, or why she felt so certain it was true. Stop him from what? The voice in her mind was her own, but it knew more than she did and was afraid.

The man drew closer, circling cautiously, almost as if he were the one afraid of her. Her muscles tensed, and she opened her mouth, but her throat closed up. She couldn't make a sound. The dark figure was almost on her.

Then, without warning, the siren's scream in the distance cut through the silence...and the man walked away.

She never saw his face, but she heard:

<Fear is the deadly enemy of man. Ninety per cent of our worries and miseries are due to fear and wrong imagination. Though what is feared may never happen, its apprehension saps out man's vitality.>

POWAHs telepathic voice sounded like a clear and bright whisper. Annie could feel that she was at the threshold of a gigantic event. She then saw energy as it flowed into the universe.

<Annie, there are other ways to improve the quality and the amount of fuel for our physical vehicle. 'Earth Breathing' is

one of these ways. **Turn your energy field into Superfuel. Learn
to train your human brainwave rhythms and synchronise them
with the Earth's natural pulse.>**

The blackness drew her in...although she knew now her name was
Annie and that different individuals surrounded her because of
their difference in size. Their luminosity and roundness were made
of fibres that seemed stuck together...At the core of these people,
she saw geometric shapes made of what appeared to be hard
vibrations of matter. Now she understood it. The core was like
letters or number-like shapes strung together. The geometric shapes
affected the energy fields of human beings.

"Is this it? Am I just a bunch of letters that form my Body Codes of
Light?"

Most of the symbols that she mentally saw were not loving. Instead,
they reminded her of traumatised kid's drawings, not letters or
spiritual symbols.

"Can one read energy as if it were a text?" She heard herself asking.
To think that behind the very letters of names, their numeral
translation could be decoded in modern sciences as the elements
that make up matter were not new to her. However, the codes that
represented her bodily chemical codes were still baffling.

The moving Forgiveness screen-saver image distracted her from the
genetic code riddle. She heard her name spoken aloud: "Annie,
Annie," and suddenly, the yellow ball between her eyes changed
into an image of an early morning sun streaming into the hospital
room.

Back in George

"Annie, wake up."

She was so disorientated, not knowing where she was. ...but then
she remembered.

"Hi, gosh, I'm back. Goodness, I'm glad."

"How do you feel?" Ben sat next to her bed.

"Fine" She looked at her left and right feet. Her right foot was still in plaster past her ankle. Her left foot had a thick bandage on, but she felt nothing, no throbbing. A nurse drew back the curtain, asking if she wanted anything to drink.

"The operation, they've done it! What's the time?" Ben and the nurse looked at each other, smiling.

"Noon, we are serving lunch in half an hour. What would you both like, chicken or fish?"

The question made her feel thirsty, and her body made her take a deep breath. Then, her sense of smell recorded apple blossoms.

"I will bring you something to drink first, then you can tell me."

"Do you have apple juice?"

"Sure, if that is what you feel like. Sir, are you thirsty?"

"Oh, yes, please, same for me will be great."

The nurse walked away and truly felt relieved that she was back with Ben. The smell of hospitals had given her gooseflesh before, but now the fear had gone.

"Well, that was not so bad; gosh, I feel as if I have been far away ...I do remember getting the injection ...and then nothing...but then I remember something!"

"Really? Were you awake during your operation?"

"Gosh, no. Let me think. Agh, it might come back to me later."

The person in the other bed was still fast asleep. There was no one with her. She must have operated on after her. The same nurse appeared but went to the person beside her, calling her by name. The female in the bed made a sound and then turned.

The nurse pulled on the long curtain between the two beds to give the woman waking up some privacy.

"Have you been here all the time?"

"More or less. Annie, I've booked us into a guesthouse in George for three nights. Then you have to go back to the hospital to redress your wound; after that, you can use that foot, meaning you can put some weight on it, so they say."

"Mien will be so unhappy."

"Why? It's only for three nights. Hans and Liesbeth will be arriving tomorrow morning. I've booked them into the same guest house. I was lucky to get two nights for them. Then we will see from there on what to do." Ben took her hand into his. He looked tired.

"A young nurse brought their apple juice. Ben sipped on him, and when she finished hers, he offered his glass to her.

"Gosh, I could drink a whole bottle."

"I've had coffee when you were under, but I'll be glad for the lunch." They had chosen chicken. She was keen to find out what the hospital food was like in South Africa.

The same nurse she had seen before the operation came in to inform her about the follow-up procedure. After lunch, if she felt up to it, she could get dressed and have X-rays taken of the foot that had been operated on. After that, Doctor Beck would like to see her at two-thirty. Then she would be free to go.

Lunch arrived, and she was ravenous. After eating half her plate, her energy returned. The woman in the other bed turned out to be a young girl of around eighteen who had damaged her wrist at a party with broken glass badly enough to warrant an operation.

Both Annelies and Ben were very happy with the private hospital's treatment and standard of service. Travel insurance that had come with their air tickets paid for it all. At the least, they did not have to spend a small fortune as a result of her freak accident.

Annelies managed to dress in bed. Ben helped her from the bed into her wheelchair. After the visit to the X-ray department and Doctor Beck's office, she had also received a pair of crutches. She was told to keep the orthopaedic boot and bring it in when she had to return to change the bandage.

Ben phoned Mien and said they would meet her at a coffee shop. She was wheeled around and started to get used to the idea that for the next few weeks, she would depend on Ben or anyone else to help her. She knew already that that was going to be a challenge.

The weather was gorgeous, and she tried to feel the positive side of her situation. They had decided to keep their return booking, but Ben needed to inform the airline about her needing a wheelchair since they had to leave it behind when they left George.

They both decided to take each day at a time.

The first three days were probably the worst. There was no way that she could even get to the toilet or wash appropriately on her own. How different is it to experience life from a wheelchair? She kept reminding herself that it was temporary and that she could walk again soon. Her respect for people who lived life in a wheelchair and who were dependent on others had risen off the chart.

"I hope Annelies does not try to be too independent this afternoon." She overheard Ben talking to his sister on the other side of the guestroom door. Ben was leaving for the day with Hans and Liesbeth. She insisted that she would be fine. Mien would take her to the hospital; she had already arranged it.

"Can she get into the swimming pool? Oh, I don't suppose her cast can get wet. " Mien summed it up. Not being able to get either foot wet was the biggest drawback. Tonight, she hoped she could have a bath. She could manage if one foot could get wet by resting the right foot on the ledge. She had already figured it out. The very thought of bathwater made her suddenly remember her dream. She had been swimming.

"Good morning! I'm so glad to be able to do something for you by taking you to the hospital."

She smiled at Mien but wished she didn't need any help. She had been a strain for the last two days of finding wheelchair-friendly places. She would have been much happier to be left on her own with her laptop. Now was the best time to write, but everyone was eager to make her situation happy. She wasn't miserable, just frustrated.

"Let's make it a whole day of it, shall we." Spending time with Mien by herself was at least a bonus. She wanted to suggest seeing a movie and visiting an art gallery after her hospital visit. Ben was not interested in that so that she could do it with Mien. Having already found out on the internet that both places were wheelchair friendly, she wanted to give Ben some time with Hans and Liesbeth without them worrying about her.

"That is if you have the whole day?"

"To spend it with you, always. Let's see how long it all takes at the hospital, and we can phone them if we need any help."

"Why bother them? Let's take a taxi. I've got their number. It's easier to get in and out from a lower car, and the chair can fit in the boot." She had already made enquiries and phoned a few firms. One lady was accommodating and gave her the number of someone with experience with wheelchairs.

"Mien, I will take you out for the day; all I need from you is to push me when my arms tire from wheeling myself. Hopefully, I'll be more mobile when I can get around on crutches."

She knew Ben had been in contact with Interpol, and she suspected Hans had come especially to deal with some of Toon's business connections. Liesbeth had just come for the ride, so she said. As proof, she had arranged a hair and nail appointment for herself and her mother the next day.

"Mien, what do you know about the meeting that Hans, Ben and Liesbeth were discussing?"

"Last night?" Mien shook her shoulders. "I think At's group wants to meet them."

"At has invited them to Crystal Cliffs. Some are camping, and some have rented our other cottages. They are giving a public lecture tonight at the local hall in George."

Mien was surprised that she didn't know. Ben had not said anything, but then she had been so occupied with her situation that he might not have thought she would be interested.

They arrived at the hospital, and she was settled in her wheelchair; the driver asked if they needed him to pick them up. They paid him and took his cell number.

"What is their talk about tonight, do you know?" Turning her head to look up at Mien made her feel dizzy when her friend pushed her to the X-ray department.

"About the reality of the extraterrestrial presence. Do you want to go?" Replying to someone she didn't see face to face felt rude.

"That depends. If Ben is going, I will want to join him, but if we meet some of At's friends at Crystal Cliffs tomorrow, it might be easier for me to stay in my room and do some writing."

Mien sat down next to her on a chair.

"I'm not sure how accessible the local hall is. I know there are steps, so we will see. They are showing nothing you have not heard about or seen photos of, so Ben had not bothered to mention it to you." Her name was called, so she wheeled herself inside the X-ray theatre. Her X-rays were saved onto a DVD so she could show them to her Orthopaedic specialist in Apeldoorn. It was surprisingly busy for such a small private hospital, but many people came from afield.

At last, they were outside in the hospital's car park. Mien had already phoned the taxi but was told to wait outside for a few minutes.

"Now what? Annelies, what do you feel like?"

"What time is it? Maybe we could have a light lunch and see a movie like we used to do together."

"Are you sure? Let me see. It's now just after twelve."

"Mien I know what movie I would like to see. Avatar. I've heard so much about it. I missed it when it was showing on the circuit."

Mien was searching on the internet on her cell phone when the taxi arrived.

"You are in luck. They are showing Avatar at two o'clock and at five at the old cinema where they are showing older movies. Mien asked the driver to take them to the Garden Route Mall.

It was quite a sensation to be wheeled around. Normally she avoided shopping malls, but she might as well make the best of her situation. They purchased their movie tickets for the two o'clock show and were now off to find somewhere to eat.

"What about a Cappuccino," Mien suggested a coffee bar and restaurant with an outside terrace.

"Why not? I'll wheel myself to the nearest table." The staff were amiable and immediately took a chair away to make room for her wheelchair. "I hope you don't mind. I love science fiction movies at best, but not everyone does."

Mien was sometimes hard to approach. Often, it felt as if she was not at home. It seemed that her best friend from years back could still be as mysterious as ever, just like in the past, when they were both single, playing the field.

While driving from Clovelly to George, At described the action shots and fantasy scenes in James Cameron's epic motion picture, Avatar, with Sigourney Weaver. She knew then that it would be her cup of tea.

"I don't mind at all, but I must admit, the movie Julie & Julia, a feel-good movie that features a great performance by Meryl Streep, is my kind of film. It's all about food!"

"Oh, I saw it on the plane coming out here. Yes, I enjoyed that too. I was surprised that it was still showing."

The waitress brought their order: chicken tramazinies with two cappuccinos.

"No, I never really go to the movies alone."

"Don't you ever go out with Katrina or Pat?" As a divorcee, she had never thought Mien might be somewhat stranded for a female company because the other two women had partners.

"No, not really. I have been shopping with Katrina a few times, so I knew of this coffee bar, but John hates for her to spend any money. They live on a tight budget, so they say."

Mien received an SMS on her cell, so she did not discuss her social life further.

"I got a text message from Harry!" Her surprised tone confused her. Why would Katrina's partner not phone instead? That was somewhat strange, but then it was cheaper than phoning. Gosh, were they that frugal?

"No, not Pat's husband, Harry Brinks!"

"Oh? How well do you know him?"

Mien shrugged her shoulders, but her face was all flushed.

"We have been seeing each other on and off in Holland. I like him, but..." Mien wanted to say more, but the waitress interrupted her. She was lost for words. Mien and Harry Brinks. She had never even contemplated such a match.

It was getting close to two o'clock, so she paid the bill.

It was a whole new experience to see a movie in an old cinema from a wheelchair. They were asked to wear masks, so they both needed to improvise with scarves. Neither had purchased any masks and were not interested in buying them from the hotel's reception counter. They both thought that was a money scam, knowing that any cloth or paper masks offer no protection from a virus. It drew a lot of attention and caused controversy at the hotel desk, but Ben explained in detail why masks do not work. He had been talking to his brother, who should know because he is a genetic scientist.

She was right at the back. For three hours, she had been riveted by the spectacular scenes and the creative idea of Jake, experiencing two realities. Gosh, the truth was staring her in the face. The two directions shape their reality. As a race, we evolve our intuitive heart-centred right thinking mode or stimulate our mental left brain thinking mode. The movie showed both options. We're writing our script, and filmmakers make movies that show the outcome of each direction.

"Annelies, you have been so quiet. Gosh, Avatar truly spoke to my heart. I am starting to believe that this is a "sign" that our collective "awakening" is expanding to embrace a much larger whole."

Mien's enthusiastic response was emphasised by her squeezing her shoulders. As she wheeled past a newspaper stand, she saw the dreadful images on a newspaper poster, all about an earthquake in Kuril Islands (Russia). Could that be part of a necessary purging process? Or what about the Nibiru cataclysm that is supposed to create a disastrous encounter when it closely passes Earth? She pondered while Mien pushed her wheelchair.

"Annelies, let's return to the same restaurant and tell me your impressions of the movie."

She had to smile; Mien's mood had greatly improved since Harry contacted her. Was her friend in love? Gosh, how they all lived in their reality bubble. She knew Harry very well. They even had a short affair just before she left for South Africa for the first time. Then, they lost contact. Only when she and Ben bought a house in Apeldoorn did their paths cross again. Years later, he became her financial sponsor. Together with her brother Fred, they purchased the Prinsegracht building and turned it into a hotel.

It was still early because the shops were still open. They returned to the same coffee shop and found a free table outside. Mien awaited her response about the movie when her cell phone vibrated in her bag.

"Annelies here." she rarely used her cell phone.

"Hi Tannie, we were wondering where you both have been. Mom and your cell phones were off." She explained that they had been inside the movie house and were just about to order something to drink at Cappuccino.

"Did you see Avatar?" At was all eager to hear her comments. She smiled at Mien, who knew her youngest was speaking to her.

The waitress brought their drinks, and she finished At's call.

"Gosh, Annelies, I was not feeling good about how some corporate exploiters showed no respect for the sacredness of the Tree of Life and its Goddess Eywa."

"Same here. The destruction of Pandora seems so cruel and unnecessary. Lifetimes of hatred, violence, and distorted behaviour patterns that fear-based human egos have perpetuated for aeons of time now played out in their reality."

"How can we relate this to the record-breaking Atlantic hurricane season, flash floods, earthquakes, volcanic eruptions and wildfires?" Mien asked. She forgot that Mien was telepathic, having picked up her thoughts.

"Who knows?"

Mien's body language summed up the rest of her response as she sipped her orange juice.

"But then, those are natural disasters created by nature."

"I know, but the movie Avatar is once again proof that being the observer, by looking into Jake's two illusionary worlds, we can see the mirror. He had an opportunity to experience his physical reality and lived a different life while asleep. More meaningful and heart-centred."

"You are right. As the observers, we could look at the movie and feel what a spiritual awareness would be like." Mien pondered.

"That's a thought."

"Yes, like seeing into a different reality."

"That is true, sure, but both realities were an illusion for Jake, not so?" Mien added.

"Mmm, it could be that all the painful experiences humanity has endured in this Earth school are being pushed to the surface worldwide. Through movies or watching the fake news on CNN, reading fake newspapers, and the fake internet articles all on a fake pandemic, we know that chaos has arrived."

"I agree. You only have to look around South Africa to see that misery is felt everywhere," Mien replied.

What changed was that now all people, whether black, brown or coloured, could use all public facilities. That was not the case when they were in their twenties.

"How can we each make a difference?" Her friend's tone clearly expressed the energy of hopelessness that has lately hung around many people. Only now, hearing her friend's despairing tone, did she realise that being morbid was not the answer. Silently, each withdrew into their thoughts. The movie made her recall her mental health code, the number nine. The soul quality of Unity is embedded into the crown chakra.

Her Emotional Youth Code 9 was again Unity.[1]

Unity appeared a lot in the decoding, which she knew already.

< 9 often represents pain or sadness; being on cloud nine is the ultimate happiness. The Soul quality of Unity is a blessing for the initiate.>

POWAH's signatures had come through her as if her higher self wanted to remind her.

She wondered about her emotional body health aspect. She couldn't remember what else she had written in the interpretations of her Body Codes of Light workbook.

"Come on, cheer up. The ending of the Avatar movie held a great message for me." She placed her hand on Mien's.

---

1. https://allrealityshifters.wordpress.com/six-youth-and-physical-soul-quality-codes/

"Please tell me."

"Humanity as a global united energy field must individually take responsibility for every abominable human miscreation that we all unconsciously manifested. That means that each person must transmute any misused actions back into Light. Every spoken or written word that contains negative energy must be transformed. Energy cannot be destroyed; it can only be transformed. We can each do this by keeping our daily feelings, thoughts, and actions vibrating on a high note," she said, taking a deep breath after her summary. " Was that the great message? I just read that an Earthquake killed People in Turkey. Was that again a wake-up call, but how many do we need?"

"Probably, and much more will pass during the next few years. Looking around and hearing about a so-called pandemic, we can be confident of one fact: Things are changing, fast."

They both heard At calling out to Jock. "There they are."

"Mien, it was in the end that I realised that an underdeveloped visitor from outer space will never again destroy the inner core of Pandora. The divine light of the Goddess Eywa saw to that!"

"Oh, you mean we will never be able to destroy planet Earth?" Mien seemed to cheer up through her summary.

She rolled her wheelchair away to make more room at the table.

"Let me guess, you are discussing the movie Avatar?" Jock remarked as he took a chair from another table and joined them

"Where are Hans and Liesbeth?" She knew that Ben had been helping At set up for tonight's lecture on the alien topic.

"They are queuing to see the movie Avatar. I hope they get tickets."

"Oh, what for the five o'clock show? We never saw them when we walked out." Mien replied as she made hand signals to the waiter so that he could take Jock's order. Seeing Jock in a business suit was a surprise. She asked why he was wearing a suit.

"Hans thought there might be cancellations. He seems to know these things." Jock replied with awe, ignoring her question. She smiled, knowing what effect Hans could have on people.

"I would love to hear their reactions when they see that horrible scene when the trees are on fire." Mien was more affected by the violence than she had been. It was, after all, just a movie. Jock did not share where he had been.

The movie reflects what is happening worldwide, and watching the results of our miscreations as observers will hopefully wake many people. Then we can transmute our distortions back into Light." Hearing her reply made her feel somewhat righteous. Look at her, stranded in a wheelchair.

"Annelies, that is a rather glum response to a movie. Did you both not love the incredible scenery of Pandora's landscape?"

"The film was an incredible visual treat. I've never witnessed such complete humanoid models moving so realistically. They were tall compared to humans, which was also very impressive. It reminded me of the giants that might have walked on our planet aeons ago." She received more intuitive impressions than what she was willing to share at a coffee shop, but that was all she could add for now.

"Well, the film was like a nested puzzle with layers of meaning. On one level, it is a love story with the most up-to-date special effects possible, and although the film is long, it flows so well that time flies by. On the other hand, the movie doesn't distinguish between the real and mythic."

Mien's comment, while studying the pictures on the menu, gave her an idea. How different does a bright red polished apple look from the tiny brown seed within its core, and yet they are interchangeable, the one merely representing the expanded realization of the other?

"The movie showed me that we must strip away the illusion, just like an apple peeling." Both Jock and Mien were not following her contemplations. They paused in silence.

"Our reality, hidden within the confines of our nature, must wake up! We all know intellectually that we are multi-dimensional. So bear with me and my example. As one peels away the layers of an apple, eventually, only the core remains. This core, which is the apple's physical matrix, holds the apple's very program!"

Jock nodded, and Mien was pondering.

"Mmm, I can see that planet Earth, by having an earthquake, is busy peeling away, but what about all the human lives that have been lost while doing so?"

"Mien, we must keep reminding ourselves that we are vibrational entities and are only aware of our physical layer. We need to train our thinking in those terms. Everything around and within us is vibrating, either with positive or negative vibrations."

They were all listening, waiting for more explanations. All the tables were now occupied with people ordering dinner. It was just six o'clock.

"You are so right. One day in the Pannekoek, Annelies explained this by drawing on a serviette the symbols she often saw in people's energy field."

Mien drew some line drawings on a paper napkin that had an angry feel. When she showed them around, it made her feel sad.

"We all need to find a way to intuitively be aware of the negative and positive vibrations that interact through our physical bodies."

"Are you that aware, Annelies?"

"Gosh no, Jock. I would not be sitting in a wheelchair if I had been."

"But Annie, maybe you subconsciously asked for the experience?"

She shook her head. "No, Mien, we can consciously take control once we are aware. I'm also battling to do this. That is the one positive result of my injury. I can now recall my feelings then and know how negative these vibes were. We were fleeing out of fear. I didn't want to leave when we ran, trying to escape from those men, but my intuition told me to stay.

The waitress asked if they wanted to order something besides a drink. She felt inclined to decline, but Jock had to satisfy his sweet tooth, so he ordered muffins.

"Mom, we are in. We are watching the beginning of the movie. Let's meet for dinner at that restaurant near where At's group will hold their alien talk."

"Hans and Liesbeth got in. Hans just told me to meet for dinner at a restaurant near where At's group is holding a talk. Do you know where to book a table for all of us?"

"Gosh, I'm impressed. Why do you telepathists still use cell phones? You must again explain how telepathy works. Surely we must all be able to do it?"

Jock was warming up to their alternative ways, as he called it. Not that she felt very proud of herself after having broken her feet.

"Annelies, how is your workbook getting on? That's what Katrina asked me to ask you."

Mien's posture had changed since this morning. She appeared younger. It must have to do with her and Harry Brinks. "Mien, what's going on with you and Harry?"She beamed at her, wondering if she would pick up her thoughts. Mien just smiled.

"I bet Annelies wants to know about Harry and me. I can feel it. I want to share my feelings for him, but I'm unsure. He had phoned me before, but I must have missed his call. I know that he wants to come for a visit, but am I ready for that?"

Mien was getting more sensitive because she was projecting her thoughts. Up to now, her thoughts had been directed inwards towards herself. She now knew her friend was not ready to share her private life with anyone. So, Harry wanted to come for a visit.

That would be nice for Mien. Why did she not invite him to go to the Hogsback with him? Now that she was injured visiting the forest was out of the question.

"Annelies, would you ever consider giving your decoding workshops in South Africa?" Jock asked.

She now wished for more free time away from people so that she could work on her workbook after Mien's question about her workbook, and now Jock. For that reason, she took her laptop with her, but nothing had come of it. She managed to reply to her emails. That was all. At home, the pressure of everyday life with its ups and downs often robbed her of time for herself, but being on holiday was just as restricting.

"After my workbook is in print, I've been contemplating having the decoding formulas, with their interpretations, published on my website. But that is still in the design stage.

"Oh, do you mean your workshops will be available globally?" Jock asked.

"Yes, I suppose so. Trevor is looking into it. He has already shown me a form that people can fill out. He would have to write a program for my workshop, which takes time."

"You mean something like astrologers show on their websites?"

"Yes and no Mien. Remember that drawing and doodling is part of the whole process."

"Why the twenty-two spacings?"

"That is a kind of template that I'm using. Mien, I told you the apple example. In my workbook, decoding our twenty-two vibrational layers, or spacing, works like this: think of an apple peeling. Each number vibration of the twenty-two layers, or spacings, is the missing part of the distorted DNA code."

"You mean we hold onto codes like a virus; that is why we only see this layer of our reality?" At summerised.

"How fascinating. I only just last night read an article about the so-called junk DNA." Jock must have done some research on her subject. For a moment, her thoughts were sidetracked. She needed to go with the flow and see where it would take her.

"Let's say that this junk DNA is constructed like our languages are with syntax and grammar. Now, let me ask you both a question. Do you believe that the visual processing machinery housed in and around your brain is constructing images out of nothing?" She waited for their reply.

"No, our brain does an incredible amount of computation before we see what we see, but who are we to say that it's the "right" computation?" Jock replied.

"Exactly. There is some correspondence between the "light you're letting in" and what you perceive.

"I prefer to go with your apple idea. I mean peeling the apples until you get to the core." Mien interrupted. "That is such an easy way for me to imagine it now. I never understood the twenty-two layers or spacings, but never mind, I'm sure you have a reason." Mien's expression was glowing. Something must have clicked for her.

"Jock, our reality is made up of the geometric shapes scientists call platonic solids. They form real patterns out there in the world. When our brains extract and act on them effectively, we will fare better than those minds that don't. That's how evolution works. In my workbook, I will explain my theory with diagrams."

"Interesting. What you are saying is that our brains must be pretty damn excellent at this stuff because otherwise, we wouldn't be having this conversation." Jock grinned.

They all laughed. Having these interactions always cleared things that were still vague before.

"It's challenging to articulate an abstract concept, especially when we are unaware that everything in our physical structure is like a map that can be altered by viewing it from the right perspective."

"Oh, you mean like...the map in your hands? " Mien turned both her hands up so they could see her palm print.

"Yes. Patterns, maps, lines, and the sound of numbers or our DNA are part of a digital communication system. A mind designs DNA."

"Who's mind?"

"Trevor would say there are several possible conclusions: human-designed DNA or DNA occurring randomly and spontaneously. There must be some undiscovered spiritual law of physics that creates information. I want to go with the last conclusion. A Super-intelligence, i.e. God designed DNA."

"Annelies, I never realised that your concepts of immortality were backed up by science. I thought it was just an idea that you explored." She could sense that Jock needed the intellectual approach to life, and Mien was more simulated intuitively through her feelings.

"So far, I can share that when we have reached our inner core, which is at the fifth decoding stage of the ascension game, we will have awakened our light or immortal body. It's then that our Soul force can awaken to an awareness of how to create events in our physical dimension."

"Tannie, how do you interpret spirituality compared to other religious or scientific discoveries?"

"Oh, dear. The nature of spirituality is that it longs to be shared, and we are all inclined to share that which is of greatest personal value. I'm no different to any other philosopher."

How else could she come up with her theories? It's through sharing one's personal experiences that a pattern seems to emerge.

"Boys, my workbook, and the articles on our website are all written so that our readers can allow themselves to choose what is personally applicable. There is no room for spiritual arrogance in today's world."

Jock seemed to be happy with her reply, but At was again drumming his fingers on the table, pondering.

"I can't wait to read and use the decoding steps Annelies has developed. How she came to them is immaterial to me." Mien said with a warm smile.

"Perceptions about ascension topics very much depend on each individual, but as Mien said, the articles on the website reflect our own experience, not someone else's."

Mine were written on the spur of the moment." Mien added, looking at her watch. At nodded in agreement.

"Lately, when I read my articles weeks later, I often wished I could change them somewhat."

"But why, Mom?"

"At, it's because our perceptions of life can change drastically. We have seen the movie Avatar, for instance. Suppose Annelies' decoding workbook has the power or the intent to awaken us. In that case, we can learn how to manifest life on Earth, such as health and happiness, houses and money, without losing sight of spiritually-evolved values, then she has succeeded."

"Thanks, Mien. Even if ten or one hundred people have found our articles on the website helpful, or they have inspired them in some way, then that is what we must be grateful for."

"How do you see or understand what, for instance, happened in other parts of the world?"

"You mean the Earthquake, tornadoes or floods?"

"Yes, and all the people that lost their lives. The poverty and so on."

"Jock, I fully believe that every person needs only to recognise this life-sustaining centre, this spiritual matrix within themselves, as the basis upon which successful physical life is built. Now is the time for every one of us to be the force of Divine Light we are all destined to be."

"But that does not answer my question."

"Jock, what happened in Haiti on January 2010 will hopefully also never again be forgotten when over 300.000 people lost their lives because our planet Earth is moving forward into the Light at warp speed. Anything that is not of the light must be transformed. The precious souls who embodied a human form in Haiti and those who were there to assist are blessed for the extreme sacrifice they made for all humanity.

"I now got it. The movie showed me that we can allow ourselves to be transported into another reality." Mien's inner joy emanated from every pore of her body.

"You mean through our dreams?" Jock asked.

"Whenever, since we are all one, every particle of Life is interrelated, interconnected, and interdependent because there is no separation. Yes, humanity has been given the last opportunity to WAKE UP! The phrase "I see you", which is the Na'vi greeting in the movie, said it all!"

She insisted on paying for the bill. Money had never been an issue for her, but Mien and her family needed to budget for every expenditure. Jock would drive them back to the guesthouse. They wanted to pick her up when it was dinner time, but she already planned to have a quiet evening and not join them at that lecture and later for dinner.

The images the boulder had shown her just before their trip to South Africa suddenly appeared when Mien brought up Haiti. Images of incredible damage to cities and countryside alike had her wondering where that would happen in the future.

She urged Mien to join them, as Ben would later brief her on the global agenda he would address.

Chapter 13
Cellular Memories from Other Lifetimes

From Annelies's Akashic records

Alone at last. Two hours to herself felt more like freedom than ever before. Mien had arranged everything around her on the small private stoep outside under a huge tree fern. She had even opted out of joining them for dinner. Tomorrow night, they would be staying at Crystal Cliffs again. Ben insisted. Before they flew home, he wanted her back in their cottage for six days.

She could get around on crutches, on one foot, but her balance was not all that good.

While she waited for her laptop to charge up, there was a knock on the door.

"Room service." A voice called out.

For a split second, she paused. Her alarm bells had still not disappeared. Then she recalled that Mien had organised for her to bring her dinner to her room.

"Come in, please."

A big black woman arranged everything on a small table nearby and left. Butternut soup and a big salad. That was all she had requested.

Her laptop had a new screen saver. Ben took that photo in Cape Town, so he must have added it to her screen saver file, but how uncanny. The blue sky showed that the mountain's edge looked like a human profile, just like her dream. That was where her mind must have got the image, but why? Was the photo Ben had taken in Cape Town purely a coincidence?

Her last dream flashed past like a movie script, including the message from the rock, and now it was her screen saver. How uncanny.

It was a scary thought that a Luciferian force could completely control the human mind and that this was already happening. However, she felt inadequate to meddle in genetic science theories that were still beyond her understanding.

"Listen to your inner mind to find the answer."

The rock face's reply to her questioning mind started feeling invasive. Somehow, her body still reacted in a gooseflesh-like reaction, travelling into her neck. Was it her body that showed she was again meddling in areas she could mentally hardly comprehend?

She trembled when she moved her mouse to the taskbar in the left corner. She sensed an unfriendly presence nearby. Were the memories from her dream time trying to warn her, or were her memories from fourteen years ago resurfacing? Was there a connection between what happened to her years ago and that she broke her feet and At's abduction?

With a beating heart, she saved the file she had been working on for the last hour. Her somewhat stuffy head told her that she needed to stop writing. She felt overwhelmed by the amount of information she had taken in as if she had been overloaded. Her now pounding headache told her to close down.

She was going to wait for Ben to return from the talk and ask him all the questions that had still not been answered.

Reading a magazine to sidestep her mental chatter was not working. It was already after ten. She wondered when Ben would return from the talk on Alien invasion. She was almost sorry that she hadn't joined them. Maybe meditation would speed up the time.

By blocking noises to silence her mind, Annelies made herself comfortable in their queen-sized bed. Resting against several pillows did the trick. She had taken a pill for the constant throbbing in both her feet. It started to work.

Some thoughts tried to creep in, but she replaced them with visions of space. A black dot, which became a circle, appeared behind her eyelids. Then, she felt herself drawn into a sea of numeric symbols that vibrated in unison, creating a sweet symphony of life that no musical concerto could match.

< The human ear is not yet awakened to receive the real music of creation.>

Those words she recalled, but then her observer moved away to another reality.

At first, it was as if she had never left her bed but for the deep blue colour of the soil between her toes. When she bent to scoop a handful of rich, moist grains of sand, she knew she was not on planet Earth. Like Earth, the fragrance and colour smelled organic, but she had never seen a blue tint in her back garden. As her mind formulated visions for her to interpret, a crystal-like high-pitched sound awakened her sense of hearing.

The organic smell and the planet's music made her feel at home, and then an emotion of gratitude engulfed her whole being.

<Remember that you were born knowing the most important and highest truths of life, the best of everything worth knowing. You knew that life is wonderful and worth living; you were born knowing love and ready to give love. Your Soul expressed the quality of courage, and you were without self-consciousness or fear of humiliation. You could sing, dance, and skip freely to express joy or run naked into the sea. Life was an adventure, and you were the explorer.>

She questioned who had put those thoughts into her mind for a split second. Was it POWAH speaking to her to remind her of something?

<Attachment to matter is the most potent block to realisation>
What is her attachment to what? What are her perceptions about her reality? Or the program that controlled her mind? Experiencing being human, especially now that she knew her Soul's purpose, was OK with her, but was that an attachment? Would her ascension only happen if she released all her physical attachments?

<You can't ever leave me. I won't ever leave you. Once I catch hold of you, I don't let go>
She wasn't sure if that thought had come from POWAH. The energy had a clinging feel to it. It took all her willpower to stay silent, bringing her inner world back into focus. What made her realise that when more visions entered her inner eye, her emotional body seemed stirred by intense feelings of regret? Why?

Where and who was showing her this world? Had these vague memories been stored in her cellular memory? Was that why it could suddenly stir up feelings? Was she experiencing a genuine flashback while meditating? Was her mind somehow trapped in a spiral of gathered experiences?

Where did these visions of landscapes come from that were so different from what she had ever seen on Earth, her soul awareness? Or did she have what was called an altered state of consciousness?

<Your consciousness uses your inner eye to create a physical illusion, but when your third eye shows you an experience from your Akashic records of higher spiritual wisdom, you become the ultimate observer as a co-creator.>
That felt like POWAH's signature, so who was...? She always knew that there was a higher consciousness part of her, observing itself as if there were two of her. Communicating with that aspect of herself seemed to feel easier when she had an inner dialogue with

POWAH, whom she felt was the ultimate observer of the Jaarsma Clan.

POWAH was not a Godhead or an ascended master. He was to her what spiritual guides were to other people who channelled them.

In her imaginary world, her mind recalled that Richard had described a similar impression of POWAH during a workshop evening last year. She then understood that they were all united through their higher self, which became an energy consciousness called POWAH. The fact that they saw or heard the same entity she experienced from a higher consciousness level started to make sense.

In their case, the people drawn into her life through her ascension workshops all had family connections with the Orphanage, which confirmed the meaning of Theo's discovery to be correct. She was beginning to comprehend a group-soul consciousness. It meant that every human being existed in every dimension simultaneously, and her physical reality was indeed a mental illusion. The level of someone's awareness determines what form (density) is experienced. That became clear to her now because of her clairvoyant skills.

She practised her rhythmic breathing again and went into a contemplative mode, hoping that POWAH would show her how to awaken from the human dream fully. She felt a sudden rush as if her body was sucked into a tunnel.

Did POWAH represent what the many Gods were to the Egyptians? She wiped away that thought to drift deeper as if tapping into her Akashic records.

The spinning sensations made her dizzy; again, she felt like she was getting smaller and smaller until she vanished.

***

"Who do you think recognised that my Oneness is All and is in All?" She heard someone ask.

"Where was she?"

Her question triggered a memory of Akhenaton, the Pharaoh who went against the priests by introducing the worshipping of the one God. He paid dearly for his convictions and many of his royal household. For a moment, it felt as if she had died.... Her body was gone, and then visions of an open landscape where the temperature was hot and humid took her deeper into the recesses of her unconscious mind until the bodily senses of herself as a young girl took over.

She knew that her name was Ametsi, a young priestess who, together with other royal children, had the privilege of studying under the great teacher Djehuti.

Oh, how she battled to understand the science of alchemy. She tried to stay focused, but her mind could not grasp what her teacher was explaining because the heat made her sleepy.

"Ametsi, pay attention!"

Djehuti's stern voice made her straighten up.

"The first nine of the 22 genetic melody codes of light have the greatest influence on the etheric body program, but they are the most difficult to assimilate by the human mind."

With great difficulty, she tried to stay awake, especially when, after each statement, a moment of silence followed.

"You are all very privileged to study the science of the Gods. This knowledge will enable us to attract and hold more Light particles through several energy bodies."

Djehuti's voice bounced off the great temple pillars that supported the ceiling. A soft breeze from the desert gave her a temporary lift. He replaced the papyrus leaf page with another to read the next leaf. Then he paused and looked up.

"You all know that every initiate into the spiritual sciences must be worthy of such knowledge."

She wondered if she was worthy since her concentration made her head spin.

"How can we consciously interact with these time codes that seem implanted in our energy fields?" Azino asked. He was the brightest student. She didn't even know or understand enough to ask such a question.

"By awakening your intuition skills." Djehuti's penetrating look with which he studied each of his students made her tremble.

"Not only do you subtly awaken your Soul awareness levels, but you must fully understand your 22-numeral language of living light codes. Their sound vibrations will affect your ancestors and descendants three to four generations backwards, forwards, and even sideways, as in siblings, etc.

Ametsi could not help observing that her thoughts captured an image of her grandmother. How could her numeral codes of light affect this dear but very old lady? When Djehuti's eyes rested on her, she knew he had read her mind.

"Only through physically experiencing the ageing process does knowledge have a chance to transform into wisdom, Ametsi."

"Accumulating knowledge does trigger our ageing process on genetic levels; this has been proven." Djehuti turned around and studied the engravings from the papyrus manuscript to which he had access.

"When you look at the body of an elderly person, all you see are the experiences of sorrow, joy, pain, suffering, bliss, greed, fear, worry, happiness." She wondered how old Djehuti was.

"You all need to learn to see the energy levels of others to know who is in control of that body, the persona or the higher consciousness of that person. Only then will you know the answer to life."

The image of her grandmother made her smile. All she could see were her laughing eyes, which observed her compassionately; her heart would melt, knowing she was greatly loved.

"True wisdom knows no age, Ametsi."

She looked up from her slate to confirm she had heard him telepathically. She stifled a giggle, knowing he had read her mind.

"Our elders must strive to initiate change in their program by freeing themselves of the stigma attached to ageing. That is why the Soul qualities of patience, reflection, appreciation, justice, humour, to mention a few, are often only awakened by life experiences."

She wondered what more was written in the papyrus book.

"These Soul qualities are in short supply in our society. There will come a time when 'the Word' will lead to the downfall of humanity, so the very process of ageing was a parting gift from the Gods."

Somehow, she questioned that. How could ageing be a gift? She knew that in her heart, getting old held no attraction for her. Could she not fully awaken while still young? She had just celebrated her sixteenth birthday. She had reached marriageable age. Only Azino was the right person for her, but he was leaving.

"Remember that your persona always views any change as a threat. Since your persona can only live in terrestrial time, and your Soul exists in Soul time, people must free themselves from any attachments influenced by terrestrial time." She shook her head, for her inner dialogue made her dizzy. She had to admit that she felt despondent because she didn't like the changes. Why could Azino not stay or take her with him?

"I still do not understand how we can slow down or even stop our ageing process. Must we release ourselves from any attachments that belong to this world?" Azino asked while winking at her.

She was so glad that he had the nerve to ask. She would rather sit and wait for Djehuti's telepathy to make sense.

"By activating your numeral codes of light on physical matter, you can reactivate your pituitary gland that has been deactivated until now. You will still have to travel on a cellular level through your unique genetic pathways to awaken this God code, Azino." The silence that again penetrated Djehuti's outdoor lecture venue numbed her as if she was not there. Suddenly, she saw herself as an older woman.

Djehuti rested his hand on her shoulder as he instructed Azino to use his inner sight and to describe what visions he saw."

A warm feeling spread all over her when Azino looked into her eyes. Azino's love for her calmed her nerves. He was two years older and would soon leave to study further under the high priest in Luxor.

"My mind is showing a world so strange..." He frowned from concentration.

"I'm ...Ametsi is my partner, and we are inside a building with strange furniture... I see a box with moving pictures...and an animal...I see a dog!...she is speaking to him."

Azino's surprise at seeing a dog was bizarre for them. Was Ametsi seeing her communicating with an animal?

As those words sunk in, she tried to see what Azino was seeing. Or at least get a feel for the world he was describing. Was Azino getting visions from her past or future? That they were betrothed made her feel good, but why was she holding onto the idea that she looked old?

"As students of the science of the Gods, you are all learning to communicate with your sound codes. Those codes are your blueprint, shared with your ancestors and descendants. All of your soul experiences, which are stored in your Akashic records, will be activated and felt physically at the end of time, even on a frequency level. It means that sensitive relatives will sense that something has changed within them."

Although she heard the words, her sadness clouded her concentration because she would soon separate from Azino. Only Granny knew how she felt. She had warned her not to get attached to Azino.

"We all know spontaneous healings frequently occur in a family unit when one member has experienced a twenty-two code initiation. When Soul time sets in, terrestrial time takes a back seat."

At this moment, she had a sense of déjà vu. It dawned on her that programming had been inserted into their genetic codes, enforcing a belief in only tangible, observable things. This program held the answer to unlocking boundless potential. So, what exactly was this key?

Then she remembered why...Oh no! Was it her karma? Had she programmed herself? So, was it up to her to activate it again? A feeling of despair took hold of her.

Djehuti asked if she was alright. How did he know? He must know that she felt despondent.

The sensation of speeding through a tunnel backwards took away who she was..."Come back tomorrow, Ametsi, when I have important things to tell you about your Auric grid spacings.

Her physical body was sending shooting pains through her spine. It was as if her body was retaliating against something, and her brain was about to crash. All she remembered was the words, "Come back tomorrow." They were still ringing in her ears, but the soft humming noise from the air conditioner now replaced the sound.

***

A full moon was just above the horizon, hanging like a glowing ball. What was the time? How long had she drifted off? Her meditation must have turned into an out-of-body experience!

Gosh, her body felt stiff. She contemplated if she could get up from her wheelchair and use the crutches on her own, hopping on one leg. Mien had told her that her crutches were next to the bathroom door, just in case she needed them.

"Annie, how are you managing?"

She smiled at Ben's mental probe. He should see her now, carefully resting her weight on her left foot, which they had operated on. She was determined to go to the bathroom alone before Ben entered their room.

It was not all that bad. Painful, but not so that she could not give it a try. Oh dear, her wheelchair was about to roll back. She needed to learn to put the brake on.

"Don't worry. Before you know it, I'll be walking again. How is the talk on aliens?"

She was panting from pure exhaustion. Trying to manage the crutches by using the wall as support worked. It made her feel more stable. The thought of losing her balance from using only one foot to walk on was enough to scare her.

"I'm glad you opted out. Nothing we have not heard before. It's new to many people, so they provide a service by informing them about the different means of contact. I like the frace a different lecturer implanted in his audience. The fact that Angelic beings do not need a spacecraft."

She felt somewhat pleased about getting to the bathroom and back. She was now moving towards their bed.

"So I didn't miss anything, apart from the truth that flying sources are not necessarily a positive sign. This individual must have been a person with a different viewpoint on Aliens. And we will see three people from At's group tomorrow, right?"

When she heard the key in the lock, she had just enough time to get herself back into bed.

***

The last three days back in their cottage at Crystal Cliffs were an experience never to be repeated. They finally left her on the main building's deck while the men met with At's UFO group.

She was so dependent on Ben to get her around, and always patiently reassuring others that she was okay started to frazzle her nerves. All she wanted to do was spend time on her writing. Now that she could not get around, she was happy to be alone. They left her on the terrace, sitting in the shade next to a table where her laptop was plugged in.

She was glad to have been excused. One group member had given her gooseflesh, but her impressions needed to be confirmed before she shared her suspicion with Ben. She had been visiting their website, but nothing out of the ordinary, just stories people seemed to need to share. Nothing or nobody was lurking in cyberspace that she could tell.

The sun had suddenly broken free from the mountain tops, baking in full force onto the woodwork a staff member had oiled. She got a jolt when her WhatsApp popped up with the words: "Annie, are you there?"

She always loved receiving WhatsApp messages from Trevor; they were so full of exciting ideas or contemplations that were often controversial or unique.

"Yes, I'm working on my decoding book. I'm sitting outside high up on a wooden terrace at the main building of Crystal Cliffs community. I'm well looked after." She typed back.

She settled back in her wheelchair while sipping her favourite fruit juice, 100% apple juice.

"Good to hear that. I know you are writing your workbook, so I wanted to share how far we have come with our research."

That would be a treat, just what she needed for her decoding book. Her first question was personal, but she typed it anyway:

"Trevor, can you explain how I managed to attract my accident? I can come up with many theories, but none satisfies me."

She wondered what he would come up with.

"Mmm Annie, while our physical 'container' would be operating in our 3D "reality", none of the atoms that make up our bodies at any given time would have been in our bodies during any past event. I mean that matter moves from one place to another and reunites so you can be you!

"Now you have lost me." She typed in reply.

She wondered if her physical body code vibration would shed light on her state of being.

Her Physical Body Code Vibration 7- through the Crown chakra is Freedom

The words of POWAH were clearly in her mind when she had been decoding herself by following the charts

<Your physical body code of 7 signifies freedom, divided into the etheric, astral highest self, and the human self.>

If only she could be more aware and connected to her body avatar.

"Annie, if our bodies were to be seen under a powerful microscope, what would probably be like a sea of sand grains in perpetual motion. I will send you a picture so you can use it in your workbook."

Trevor attached an image through WhatsApp, but she knew it would be far too low in resolution for her book. She learned that from Liesbeth, who knew about these things. She saved it in her interpretation file to work on later.

"Remember that you aren't the particles of matter of which your human body consists. Our real energy bodies are in space, which we cannot comprehend. Our physical body is a mere virtual manifestation."

She had to ponder over this hard before she could reply.

"Yes, but how did my thoughts create me breaking my feet?"She still felt the need to reflect on her worries.

"Annie, it concerns the time flow we perceive every moment. I must tell you that our massive research and experiments on human thought have paid off. Every person is a neurotransmitter."

"Meaning?" She typed back.

"We can now prove scientifically what effect human thought has on our reality, but to answer your question, that has to do with how we each create our causal plane. Also, gravity affects our time flow."

Trevor must have understood something that had eluded her.

"What makes you suggest that? Are the atoms that make up my physical body disconnected due to my thoughts?"

It must have been the energy of fear that disconnected her energy body from her physical body.

"Our thoughts do create, and we can now almost predict what will happen during the next few years. Our consciousness field will have already created a new reality in our causal plane, and we have found a way to monitor this."

She knew it. Trevor had discovered something significant, so she asked:

"That is some statement. That makes me wonder. Do we then tap into this causal plane during our dream time? I realise that being in the now moment seems to bypass our reptilian time flow awareness. Is that what you mean?"

Her mind drifted off momentarily, recalling her visions from a different lifetime when her Whatsapp reappeared.

"Yes. You've got it. Our reptilian brain is the culprit that keeps our earth-bound reality alive. Then the universe we live in presents itself as even more illusory, where bodies, minds, and planets are parts of a great magic trick without a magician or an audience."

That last sentence gave her a feeling of floating forever off into space. She saw Trevor typing by the animation on her screen and waited for the rest.

"Leo has been working on an instrument that detects gravitational waves. He believes that he has discovered a "granulation" in space-time that indicates that our universe is nothing more than a giant holographic illusion created by the networking process in our brain."

What granulation meant made no sense unless she was there with them. So she typed back:

"I know that the idea of a holographic mental universe isn't new, but how can our senses even perceive past or future realities in such a distinct and "voluminous" way even if we appear to be no more than shadows on a flat-screen? Like when I see myself on my Zoom camera."

In her Zoom program, she could see herself in a little box in the top corner of her screen as a two-dimensional image, but her WhatsApp did not. She recalled another life that still had a three-dimensional feel to it.

She typed, "Trevor, how do my eyes make a flat image look three-dimensional? Could this apply to the entire universe?" She waited for Trevor's reply.

"Annie, the problem could be that our human eyes, our powerful telescope lenses, conform to the reality our reptilian mind has programmed. Our mind has to first adjust to that idea that it is an illusionary hologram, including that our universe has not yet overridden our physicality program."

Could they not override that program? Oh, was that what would happen during 2020 and beyond? Trevor was still typing.

"The second point to consider is that our brain can also be found in the illusion, never being able to interpret a universe with a greater or fewer number of dimensions than can be perceived by our reptilian brain."

She typed back:" Except during Dreamtime." Thinking of a fish that could not possibly know that there was a whole world on dry land.

"Yes, because then we are perceiving our reality outside, away from our physical brain. Our energy bodies are then our vehicles". Trevor replied.

Trevor was right; only when she communicated with POWAH did she know that her mind had sidestepped her brain. That was how it felt.

"Leo speculates that our organic computer is like a digital image transformer with low and high resolutions, but it loses clarity when we are not in the now moment. We feel that there must be an exact point where the hologram of our reality begins to "pixelate" itself."

Was that why her visions were far more vivid when she tried not translating them into words? That must be it. Thinking in pictures, as Tieneke naturally did, could be the answer.

"Trevor, another question. Looking around me, I can see the mountain to my left and right. I can see the dunes and hear the surf, or rather, I'm part of a mental hologram that I can imagine, but how can I shift my intellectual perception away from that belief, knowing that I'm in a mental illusion, so to speak?"

She waited for Trevor to reply, knowing it concerned her belief. She could sense that he was thinking about how to respond. Then, the animation on WhatsApp showed her that he was typing.

"Leo speculates that our brains are hologram matrixes interpreting the hologram universe by mathematically constructing reality through codes. In the same way, when we see an image on our screen, we know that it is made up of codes. We must learn to interpret the frequency codes from a higher reality transcending time and space."

She was not sure if she could follow Trevor's reasoning. She knew about codes, but how did he mean codes of light? She remembered dreaming about a language of living light.

"Annie, the second point to consider is that if our organic brain is in the illusion, it has never been able to interpret a universe. Therefore, we have to stop analysing."

But she was sure she had already been observing another dimension while meditating.

"But Trevor, because we are multidimensional beings, why could we not perceive our physical reality through our five senses and simultaneously be aware of higher dimensional realities?"

She often perceived that she was being made aware of higher dimensional realities. She knew she was not fantasising about them.

"Annie, during these times, many people all over the planet have started to break away from only seeing one reality. I know many of the Jaarsma Clan have, including you. There are numerous examples. Richard recorded in detail many cases in his "Orphanage of Souls Journal" As we learn more about ancient civilizations from excavations and research these finds at archaeological sites, we are increasingly amazed by how "modern" the science and technology of ancient times were, compared to our time now."

She agreed. It seemed to her that many scribes from ancient times were obsessed with the power of the mind. Their ancestors understood the power of thought more profoundly than the general public did today. Why was that lost? Then she recalled a teacher in her dream saying: *"There will come a time when 'the Word' will lead to the downfall of humanity."*

Sitting comfortably in her chair on the deck while everybody was doing their chores made her feel lazy as if she should be doing something. Her shady spot would soon be no more. She should move. Then Trevor's text appeared. She had lost the topic of their interaction, something to do with ancient civilisation.

"Many scientists suspect truth has eluded us for generations because the universe to us are just particles in emptiness. Understanding the truth amid the mirage has become urgent, but we don't want to be trapped by frustrating arrays of unprovable theories."

She first waited to see if Trevor had more to say before replying. Then she typed:

"Well, one thing I now realise more than ever. When our minds can transform physical matter, we must learn to design our reality instead of reacting to it."

Thinking back to all the drama that had played out during the last few days and last year, she now understood better how she had broken her feet. Her reactions to an illusional reality had made her lose complete control over her body. She admitted that to Trevor.

"Annie, you are so right. I can imagine how you reacted to being threatened, making you fall. But don't be too hard on yourself. I know that you will make a lemon into lemonade. I must now love and leave you.

I look forward to the time when you are both back in Holland. Tieneke is already preparing the workshops you will give to your formal group at Half-way House in June and July after you have moved away from Apeldoorn.

"See you soon. Love to all xxx."

It always inspired her to have these conversations. She knew that she was addicted to the mental stimulation, but for her, it was essential to do so since her journal had read like a kind of map.

"Annelies, may I disturb you?"

Katrina joined her on the deck. She sensed that she had been there for a while.

"Annelies, do you mind if I sit with you?"

She liked Katrina, and her aura was unmistakable. There are no hidden agendas, unlike what she had seen in Pat's energy field. When she returned to Crystal Cliffs after her operation and heard Pat's voice again, it was as if she remembered that their lives had crossed before.

"What is on your mind?"

Katrina smiled, observing her as if to say: can you read my mind, too?

"How does one know when someone is not what they claim to be?"

"You feel it in your solar plexus. At least I do."

She would love to know to whom she was referring. Why did she get the feeling that it might be Pat?

"Yes, I know, but how do I know that it is not just my ego sending signals to make me react?"

Mmm, she had a point there. She knew the intellectual answer to that one, but Katrina should, too.

"Reaction to anything, a situation or a person, always comes from our egos. We probably have a similar situation personally. Our higher self is beyond that kind of behaviour. But you know that."

"I know, but At's friends have disturbed me with their alien stories."

Katrina moved closer, and her body posture felt like she was holding onto many inner hurts. Join the club, were her thoughts.

"Annelies, what I'm about to tell you is a big secret...." She waited in silence to give her space.

"I have given a baby up for adoption, and I have had an abortion." After the words were out, Katrina waited in anguish for her reply.

"Were you very young? I mean, when you gave your baby away."

"I was sixteen, but the adoption mucked up my head far worse than the abortion I had years later. I've googled over the years about the psychological after-effects of giving up a baby. What little I found is astonishing." Katrina's tone had become so low that the last two words were more of a whisper.

She tried to get a hint at what Katrina's world would have been like in her younger years. She had to search deep into herself to feel compassion for someone who did what she could never have done. Not in a million years would she have given her baby away! But then, was she not judging? Who was she to think that she would not have done it any better than what others' decisions were in life? "Katrina, are you still judging yourself about the decision you made long ago?"

"Yes, I find it hard to forgive myself. I keep wondering what has happened to my baby. Am I responsible for the misery I have caused someone else?"

"Why do you think your decision has brought unhappiness to your child."

Katrina studied her face as if she wanted to say:

"But you don't know it all. My mother gave me away, and I never got over that feeling of being rejected."

She had heard Katrina's plea. Not that she could tell her that, but she could empathise.

"I can see that you are rejecting yourself instead of loving yourself."

She could see that her energy vortex around her sacral chakra was cramping so tight that no feelings of self-love could pass through. She rested her hand on hers, knowing that sometimes physical contact could break barriers.

Katrina's lip quivered, so she knew that she had hit a sore point. The tightness around her sacral chakra was loosening slightly, sending her feelings of compassion to her lower body. She mentally aimed for some healing energy from light to be at its core. Loving thoughts backed up by intent did wonders for the human body.

Katrina took a deep breath because the light beam she had projected had shifted her wave frequencies.

"Annelies, I would love to take Tieneke's mind drawing course. The inner hurts I have stored away for a long time must surface so I can love myself instead of always feeling so guilty."

"Then what is stopping you? You have the workbook, not so?"

"Yes, but I would like to interact with Tieneke while I follow the workbook. Is that possible?"

"I believe so. Tieneke's mission is to help anyone ready to release their dark shadow sides. I say that because we all have them. When we truly start working on this ascension journey, we can't have any baggage, but if your intent is there, you will find these obstacles before you know it. Then feelings of inner joy and happiness will replace your previous negative emotions."

She waited for Katrina to digest her reply. Why was her face so familiar?

"Katrina, have we met before?"

"Funny you should ask. I've been thinking the same thing from the moment you arrived."

"Really? Mmm, I'm sure it will come to us."

"Annelies, do you believe that what you truly wish for, you can make real?"

In an instant, an image of an unborn child came to mind. So that was it. Katrina would still love to have a child. She wondered what her age was. She could be anything from her late thirties to early forties.

"Yes, I do. There are no such things as miracles. We might call events or manifestations miracles, but the universal law is always in action through our thinking."

"You mean that what our mind, emotions, and how we feel physically translates is what creates an attractor field around us? I read that somewhere in one of the articles on the internet."

"Absolutely. It sounds so simple, hey."

Katrina's eyes travelled to her feet, and she could pick up her thinking: "Why did she then attract her accident?"

"On this trip, I wanted to write and simultaneously do some releasing myself. I left a lot of unhappy memories behind on this continent. I have to bring them to the surface. If the creative law of our universe, our third-dimensional realm, responded in the manner it has, then I have to accept that, in my case, having two broken feet is the best thing that could have happened to me."

"Has it?" Katrina asked if she felt in control of her life, even in a wheelchair.

"Oh yes. Life from a wheelchair is very different."

"In what way?"

"People treat you differently. Some seem to think that you are mentally or not all there. That is the most disturbing response." Recalling the waiter at the restaurant who had asked Mien what she would be having. She had taken that very personally, which was silly.

"Objects that you used to see from an eye-level point of view, you now see from the bottom up; your dependence on others to get you to where you want to be. Those three observations have taught me things I would not have learned without a wheelchair".

"Like what, for instance?"

"The major lesson was to be aware of my thoughts. My angry reaction to the two men who attacked us, that reaction had come from somewhere deep inside, but instead of staying the observer, I used it to attack."

"Do you believe you had to turn the other cheek?"

"Mmm...well, if that would have prevented me from having the accident, who knows? Whatever energy we project to others will return to us, so why not withhold from reacting altogether." Her right ankle was throbbing, so she soon needed to rest her feet higher up on another chair.

"I'm not sure if I could do that. Not reacting to violence."

They were both silent in their thoughts. Annelies was trying to sum up how her temporary handicap could have a positive effect. What had she learned so far?

"I needed to realise that my strong independent nature can sometimes intimidate others....and oh yes, to be patient with myself and others, especially when I want to go somewhere; learning to ask for help; that shop fittings are not always kind to people in wheelchairs. Often book, magazine stands, or other merchandise is in the way."

What more had she so far learned that was conducive to her ascension journey? She still could not come to terms with being unable to bathe now that both her feet could not get wet.

"Katrina, I know that my condition is very temporary, so understand me when I sound flippant by being in a wheelchair. Being a person with paraplegia due to an accident is something entirely different, but still, I know in my heart that we can have it all. The sentence: 'Ask and you shall receive' has strengthened many people's faith. Those few words have given many people hope during difficult situations."

"You mean that being a paraplegic could also be temporary."

"Yes, if your faith in the law of the universe is strong enough, why not."

"I suppose that is the reason why people visit healers all over the world who claim to heal anything."

Katrina's comment reminded her of Hans' healing skills, which all concern the power of superlight and where a sound originates. There was the proof already.

"Someone told me once that every person who had found a mission, purpose or passion in life experienced it as a clear indication of where their lessons were hidden."

She mentally heard Katrina thinking:

"What is my mission in life? I would love to be a mother and help others overcome their inner pain. If that is my purpose, then is that where I must look for my lessons."

They both heard voices from inside getting louder. Their private time was over. Katrina stood up to hug her.

"Is there anything you need?"

She inhaled deeply, thinking... "There is not enough time in the day to do everything I want."

She hugged her back, saying with a grin. "All I need is to learn how to stop time!"

Chapter 14

The Daughter of the Elephant Whisperer

When Time Lines Overlap

When Katrina left, a feeling of peace enveloped her. There seemed to be a gathering inside, but she wanted to be left alone outside. They served her drinks and snacks that were fit for a queen.

They had a WiFi connection on the property, so she had better look at her emails before working further on her journal.

Wow, her body was not accustomed to being a wheelchair user. Her back was feeling stiff from sitting down all the time. She could get around on her crutches if she used the walls as a support, but she had already fallen twice and had a big lump on the back of her head to prove it.

Gee, she had over fifty emails. Surely not all from her last article?

She felt tempted to open Trevor's emails but decided to reply to her fan's messages first.

At least twenty of her replies were from her article: Are we living during the end of times?[1]

"Does that also mean the end of money?" Someone had asked.

"Are we all going to drown because the seas are rising?" It was the following email.

---

1. https://nadinemay.com/latest-news/is-there-evidence-of-the-end-of-times/

"There is so much I still want to experience, but I'm stuck in a job to pay my bills. Should I walk out?" That one had just come into her inbox.

"How can we clean the planet of negative thought forms?"

"Have you seen the film Pay it Forward?" That email came from a person who had been in her decoding class.

For a moment, she had to think. Had she seen it? Something about a young schoolboy. She scrolled further down without opening any emails to see which one would need her to reply the most.

"What can we do to change and what to change to?" She recalled hearing Toon's reply: Crisis marks the end of an era and the start of a new one. He had been very impressed by the Trendwatcher on YouTube.

The following email with the heading: "I can't wait for this world to be over." made her open the email. That could be an inner cry for help. She'd better open this email first.

Hi Annelies

I read your article several times, but my life sucks. Yes, I have heard about how our minds create our world, but I don't believe that. How can I be responsible for the death of my little girl? How could I possibly have known that my cousin was hiding a sick man, his teenage son, who should have been locked up in a mental home? My husband walked out on me last week. He said he wanted his freedom back, and yesterday I was told to look for other work.

Last week I decided to follow your advice. Each morning before going to work, I repeated to myself: "I am OK, I am worthy, and I am willing to love my higher self and lower ego-self. I own everything I attract into my life. Therefore, I accept that what I attract in my human experience will be for the good of the whole!"

Now, I feel worse than ever. I can't wait for this world to end.

Judy

She already knew what Judy's obstacles were. Plenty of negative entities in her immediate sphere were attacking her because she was detoxing them through her affirmations—poor woman.

Dear Judy.

I can feel your despair, but knowing what an effect affirmations can have on a person, be proud of yourself for doing it. Believe me when I say it will get better.

See that the impact of your intent to manifest a change will happen. Be like someone who is following a strict diet to get healthy. In the beginning, they have to overcome their cravings, so they have a hard time. In your case, the feelings of grief, sadness and depression can 'unconsciously' be addictive on a cellular level. Your emotional body is used to feeling in a certain way, so now, with you saying your intent out loud, the energy of these affirmations is stirring these familiar emotions. There are great videos on YouTube that will be very beneficial for you to look at during your transition times. I will add the links to this email. Email me in a week if you like, and in the meantime, keep affirming your affirmations until you can say them in your dreams....

Now, she had to search for the videos Judy would enjoy and copy the hyperlink in her email.

"There you are."

"You thought I had run away, did you?" She said, smiling up at Ben.

"In my dreams, you still will be running." Ben draped his arms around her from behind her wheelchair. She loved his warm, stubbled cheek against her.

"What are you looking for, videos?"

"Yes, well...there it is."

Please pay it forward to an assignment to save the world.

"Have we seen that movie?" Ben pulled up a chair and helped himself to a biscuit from the plate that Katrina had just put down.

"Ben told us you are writing your journal so Liesbeth can edit it into a novel. Is that correct?" Pat asked while she arranged all the deck chairs in a circle. She studied Pat's body language to see if there were any conflicting energy patterns. Annelies felt Pat had been instructed to spy on her, but was it just her imagination? Was she paranoid, or was it her sixth sense?

"Well, let's say that I have given it a go. Is everyone here?" Counting the chairs that were collected from around the rest of the balcony.

"Yes, except for Hans and Liesbeth. They will join us later."

"Annie, since we are flying home tomorrow, we all thought it would be a good idea to have our last dinner outside in a traditional South

African braai style." Her friend said that when she joined them outside,

"What a great plan. Thanks, Mien, and to all the others for being so accommodating."

"Well, we all are sorry to see you leave for Holland, especially the way you are, in a wheelchair."

"Don't tell me that you feel personally responsible for my accident? She didn't want anyone to feel any remorse for her situation. She would rather have it that they all hoped they would return soon. She was still sorry that they had never visited the Hogsback together.

"Annelies, will you revisit us in the coming years?"

"Absolutely. Did you think I was thinking with regret that we never visited the Hogsback?"

"Yes, I must have." Mien's face broke out in a smile. "I never thought it would be like this!"

"What do you mean?"

"Well, I was always under the impression that with telepathy, you hear someone thinking word for word. But that is not the case, is it?"

She had to think that over. When a telepathic message came from far away, her mind would pick up on the words, like a special sound that the other person was thinking, but when she was closer to someone, the sound was often merged with the person's body language.

"I think for some, it might be. It all depends on the sound frequencies of others that you resonate with. We all live in our reality, but the more we realise how connected we are to other energy levels, the more we become sensitive to other people's realities.

"Is that not having empathy?"

"Yes, the ability to feel and understand the emotions of others is a start, but then you have to be on a similar wavelength to become a telepath. I can sometimes pick up thoughts from people who are not, but then I must make sure there is no mirror directed to me when I hear them think." She grinned at herself. For the first time, she didn't feel guilty for being served upon....

"Mien, can you help us," Pat asked. They both left her alone.

She closed her laptop since Mien's family and friends had all decided to join her on the balcony. Ben took her laptop away to their cottage to be packed for their trip home tomorrow.

Harry and Jock were arranging several barbeques behind the big palm that was thriving in a huge pot. Out of the breeze, the outdoor braai kitchen unit was away from them. John brought a long trestle table outside.

"Tannie, I have so many questions. Do you mind if I use this opportunity to fire them at you?"

She laughed. "Sure, fire away; I will do my best to answer them."

"I want to ask Annelies a question first At before you bombard her with what is on your mind," his mother said, carrying a tray with snacks for everybody. Mien looked much more cheerful than she had been during the last two weeks. She knew that Harry Brinks was arriving at George Airport very late in the evening the next day. Mien had booked two rooms at the same guesthouse where they stayed after her operation. She would miss greeting him. Their connecting flight to Cape Town and Amsterdam left in the afternoon.

Everyone was waiting for Mien to fire her question, but she already knew.

Do you believe in twin flames? She had mentally asked before she spoke to her son.

"Well, Mom asks."

"At, don't be so impatient," Mien responded. Her eyes were open wide, staring at her. Waiting.

They were all settling down. Jock and Ben were taking care of the meat, chicken and potatoes on the fire while Katrina and Pat brought in the salads and other dishes. Harrie asked everyone what they wanted to drink and told At to help with the drinks.

"Annelies, do you believe that the relationships we attract during these transformation times can be more than just a romantic attraction?"

"You mean the difference between Soul mates and Twin flames?" She could not help it, teasing her.

"I have read up on them; I just wanted to hear your version."

"Soul mates are members of your Soul group. We have had many lifetimes and incarnations with each other before."

"Your star map explains that, isn't it?" At responded as he handed her her drink; she had asked for an Appletiser.

"Yes, and often, a resonant feeling occurs when people are of the same soul group. Hans said that there are four groups of Souls incarnated on the planet. Still, if individual Souls have experienced many lifetimes in a family bond with each other, then the Jaarsma Clan idea is an example."

"Four group souls, I've never heard that?" Katrina said in surprise as she offered a plate with snacks to the group sitting in a large circle. "Gosh, but then many people must belong together!"

"Let's get back to the twin soul scenario. When is a relationship named that?" Mien asked again.

"Well, people with matching sound frequencies feel attracted to each other because they have ties of the karmic kind, but a twin soul relationship is very different."

"How so?"

She had to formulate the best way to explain what she knew or perceived a twin-soul relationship.

"I'm sure we have a twin-soul relationship, Annie; what do you think?"

"The twin flame relationship is not always one of romantic love since it is always one of service."

"You're kidding. What are we then, just Soul mates?" Ben beamed.

"Let's use Toon and Ingrid's relationship as an example. They were brought together when they were ready for service, ready to live together as a couple without karmic ties, but living in service to others."

"You mean to say they have no karma?" All heard the doubt in Mien's voice.

"My friend, a twin flame relationship deserves a far more intricate explanation. It deals with our masculine and feminine polarity. A twin flame relationship brings challenges similar to the Soul mate relationship. Still, twin flame couples are usually more evolved spiritually, so challenges are overcome easily and are seen instantly as opportunities for growth and learning."

"So what I understand is that twin flame relationships are always between a man and woman, and they both have to be at an age where they can have a relationship as a couple."

"No, I don't think so, Jock. I asked the same question years ago." She looked at Ben when she said that. His expression was contemplating—this time, she hadn't picked up his thoughts.

"In rare cases when one twin is ready to work in service with their divine counterpart and the other not, then the twin who is ready to receive a flame relationship will create new possibilities with the higher self aspect of the twin into their higher reality."

"Is that what happened between you and Theo?" Ben mentally asked.

"Does this mean there is more than one twin flame for each person?"

"Katrina, there is only one other half of your Soul's essence, but that other half of you is as multi-dimensional as you are. Therefore, if one twin chooses to walk away from their divine counterpart on Earth, the remaining twin will be compensated by drawing a second twin flame relationship into their lives."

"What you are saying is that there can be three persons involved in a twin relationship?" Ben asked out loud.

In a way, yes. A second twin flame will still be the person with the matching frequency of the one true divine counterpart of which only one exists, but that twin soul can exist in more than one person."

"Is that threesome what Hans called the frequencies of an oversoul?" At asked.

She was surprised at his level of understanding. She nodded in agreement. "Yes, that is what I perceive it to be." She replied. "The conclusion to this topic is that at this time of ours, leading up to the return to zero point, many of you are connecting with your twin flame essence or higher self."

She looked at Mien, who was blushing.

"Each individual is manifesting these relationships due to their desire to connect with the divine aspects of themselves, which is mirrored in another who holds the frequency of your higher self." She hoped that they were all satisfied with that explanation.

"Now it's my turn."

They all laughed at At, who had been shifting on his chair the whole time that the conversation on Twin Flames was in progress.

"I love your explanation; I wish you had told me that before." Ben beamed.

"Annelies, you were not at our meeting last week about the alien agenda, but they spoke about hackers in our energy field. Have you heard about it?"

Everyone was silent, waiting for her reply. At's question took her back.

"Let me share with you what I remembered happened to me fourteen years ago."

"Are you sure, Annie?" Ben beamed.

"I will only share what I experienced after my ordeal at the hospital. It's appropriate."

She took a sip of her Appletiser and settled back in her wheelchair.

"Fourteen years ago, I was shown what our physical world looks like from a pure energy perspective, that there is no distinction between aesthetically pleasing elements in nature."

"What do you mean when you say shown?" Pat asked

"I had been poisoned, but that is another story. Let's get back to At's question about hackers of our energy fields."

Pat was annoyed. Her field had a sickly shadow she could not understand, but she would fail if she tried to shatter her focus.

"Every human being's aura field has many distorted elemental energy pockets snugly embedded everywhere. Some are denser with distortions than others."

"Can you see that?"

"Pat, please let me first reply to At's question."

Some people's energy fields are brighter than others. Trees appear to have the same energy as human beings. The animal kingdom also has a distinct signature, so has any other creature with a life force."

"And aliens, can you spot them?"

"At let Annelies finish her explanation."

"Okay, sorry."

"At it's alright. I understand your anxiety. A non-human creature embodying a human body is seen from a very different perspective."

"So it's true, then, that we are in the middle of a mind war? Are there Aliens that have trapped the minds of most of humanity? Is it true that most people live in a fantasy world disconnected from reality?"

She looked up at Ben, who was tending to the barbeque.

"You said that the meeting was not all that interesting."

"Annie, nothing was new to us; you know everything they discussed."

"At was the talk about how people are being brainwashed through manipulation of the reptilian brain in humans?"

"Yes, they said by mind control experts who enter the mind through the right brain since it is relatively dormant in most people."

"The adverts on TV do that as well, brainwashing, I mean." Harrie commented from behind the palm tree, and the smell of fried meat started to overpower the otherwise fragrant scent of the fynbos below."

"Not to mention modifying our food, water and medical supply with mind-altering chemicals," John added.

"Yes, by giving the population what they desire, junk food in excess, they, therefore, deprive people of what they need, nourishing foods," Mien added.

The barbeque smells were slowly mingling with what was left of the fragrance of the low-growing bushes below the wooden deck.

At's question on the topic of the human energy field was diverted by her aiming to tell her about her experience.

"We all have to emancipate ourselves from mental slavery, and remember, none but ourselves can free our minds. Please, Annie, continue," Ben said.

"Yes, that is what my decoding workbook is all about: releasing ourselves of dark energy particles. The word aliens, for me, represents fallen angels or fallen humans. They are like a virus that has infected us all. Once we become aware of them, we can rid ourselves of them through our individual "I Am."

How was she going to explain what she hardly grasped? Hans would be far better at it.

"The way the human brain works, the network kind of action between the notes and neuron exchange in our brain helps to explain why creating a symbol that stands for a feeling or, as Tieneke calls them, a Soul quality, actually works.

"What are neurons or notes?" Katrina asked.

"Nerve cells are nodes in our brain. See a node as a railway station, and the neuron pathway are the tracks linking each railway route to all other stations. Does that make any sense?"

"Mmm, sort of," Katrina replied.

She stood up to prepare the plates because Harrie warned everybody that the meat was almost ready.

"Please, Annelies, continue to tell us about what happened fourteen years ago and what energy fields look like," Mien asked, aiming to get back to At's question.

"I started to understand how the ability to heal is possible. I didn't know that at first, but while I was in a Cape Town shelter, I saw a mother who was truly obese with a small baby who already was showing clear signs of obesity, especially in his little legs, so I wanted to get to know this woman."

"How did you end up in a shelter in Cape Town? "Pat asked. She was intrigued, but her reasons did not go along with being surprised. She picked up and said that she knew how she got there! That idea so startled her she had difficulty not to react to it, but instead, she beamed: "*Ben, how well do the others know Pat?*" while ignoring Pat's question.

The young mother at the shelter stood out with her kindness, especially as she seemed out of place among the others. Her love for her child was evident. I knew I had to befriend her first to gain her trust and understand her true feelings.

I had to befriend this woman before I could get close to her so she would be willing to reveal her inner feelings."

Katrina asked if she could dish up for her. While Harrie also asked which shelter in Cape Town she was talking about.

She was pretty hungry and told Katrina that she would do it herself. After all, there was nothing wrong with her arms. She waited while everybody helped themselves.

"At, until I felt it was safe to pursue getting back to Ben, I needed to learn from my experience since I was becoming aware of the energy levels that seemed to hang around the shelter like a heavy curtain."

He nodded while Jock, his brother, had been silently listening.

"I knew that I was shown how life was for people on this level of society; apart from clearing my karma, which I was willing to do, I must learn to see my abduction experience, no matter how horrible, as a blessing in disguise."

At was not entirely in agreement since he had compared her experience with his, but was it so different? Mien nodded. Harrie was whispering something to Katrina. Seeing these two together made her wonder.

"I suppose that is how we must see all the obstacles we create in our lives, but can't we avoid them?" Katrina asked while she was dishing up for herself.

"Probably by overcoming the tendency to react to any energy that stems from fear. My fear element of being discovered after I fled from the lab in the hospital was still there, but I knew that that fear was my stuff. I had skipped many karmic distortions while pursuing my passions for the ascension journey. I now also realise that had I been shown or experienced this abduction at any other times, when I was younger, for instance, I would not have been able to cope."

Katrina nodded, saying: "Living and surviving on that level of society must be scary... I once worked in these shelters."

While the others were helping themselves to second helpings, she quietly sat back. The conversation around the group had taken on a different focus.... Harrie has seen to that..... Ben was talking to his sister when she felt her timeline again blended in with the past.

***

The shelter was horrible, grim and dirty. The thought chatter most people in the shelter were meddling with was mundane and pointless, more like a repetitive noise that reminded her of early school days when they were all repeating tables from a blackboard. Gosh, what an idea. That was it. Some people were on some addictive substance that kept them robotic! Others had dropped out of society for different reasons, but to her, they all seemed switched off, or for a better, clearer understanding, their mental chatter imprisoned them! There was no outgoing thought stream. It was as if they had sealed off from their individuality. Instead, they were in a hive mind. But how?

The mother of the obese baby was different. She was depressed and in need of help, especially having such a young baby, but what was the story that had landed her in a shelter for people in need? She needed to find out.

"How long have you been here."

"Why do you want to know? "The woman whispered in reply as if someone was listening in.

"You don't fit in. Are you on the run?"

"Are you!" the mother snapped back close into her ear.

She was momentarily lost for words....knowing she was also on the run, but from what? What had they wanted from her body? Being locked up in a freezing room made for dead bodies still gave her a choked feeling.

"But why here?" she whispered back.

The mother picked her baby up and moved away; she then turned and made a sign to follow her into a different room, where food was served.

The clothes she had received in the shelter started to itch, and the shoes, which were an improvement on the last pair she had escaped with, were threatening to fall off her feet. They were too large, and whoever had worn them before must have stretched them. She initially believed finding this shelter was fortunate, but now she was unsure. It felt like a concentration camp, except everyone was free to go.

Was she being shown how the dark forces from other creations had found a way to occupy the energy fields of human beings? But how?

"Through the reptilian brain." She replied to herself, or so she thought.

No matter how she tried to connect with Ben telepathically, her fear levels were still blocking her....so, whose thoughts had she heard?

She now understood why the world is the way it is. Fallen enemies have already invaded it! No weapon or tactic will prevent their next takeover unless human awareness is raised. I can see that unresolved issues are hazardous to hang onto.≈

"Annie, shall I get second helpings for you?"

"Annie, where have you been? I have been telepathically calling you."

"Oh... so sorry...I was far away. Let me wheel myself to the table with all the yummy foods." When she helped herself to more salad, the others talked amongst themselves. For the first time, she discovered that when she was recalling or living out an experience, telepathy did not work!

Hans and Liesbeth had arrived, and At wanted to know what they thought about the movie Avatar. Liesbeth waved at her and dished up for herself and Hans. They must have spent time in the sun since they both had lost their pale skin tone.

Ben was sitting beside her, working on his iPhone, confirming their arrival time at the airport early the following day. The four of them would travel back together to Europe.

Gee, what she had written in her workbook about the distorted energy pockets due to an experiment that had altered the Body Codes of Light now became apparent. It had to do with their reptilian brain. So far as she knew, every human being had one. Was that the way the luciferin energy force was programming them? Or at least tried to?

Looking around at all the others, she saw they were unaware of her contemplations and had no clue what she had just been made aware of. Was their reptilian brain a kind of implant device that the ego controlled?

She overheard Hans and Liebeth talking to Harrie about the Hare Krishna movement, which suddenly gave her a déjavu...where had she seen...but then Ben asked her something. Her mind had been far away in her past.

"Sorry, sweety, I'm thinking how close we could all be to being fully taken over by the negative forces that have found a way to infect the consciousness of a cluster of cells in our human body."

Now, the articles they all published on the website have started giving her an idea. Could it be that the brain was the source of physical mortality? If each individual had the opportunity to sidestep the reptilian section of their brain during the closure of the Mayan calendar, would that save them from being taken over by humanoid entities? Was she on the right track?

"Will you share that with me when we are by ourselves? It's unclear to me; I feel you're onto something!"

She winked at Ben. "Yes. I now understand why we have the opportunity to experience and examine our shadow selves, which are controlling us during this time. What our fears are, and who makes us believe and feel them to be true, is just an illusion."

Hans and Liesbeth must have overheard their mental dialogue, for they nodded, smiling. Harrie and Katrina were conversing with them, and Harrie turned as if he had also heard her telepathic conversation with Ben. Now, that would surprise her big time.

While everybody on the terrace was enjoying themselves, she wished she could excuse herself, but she needed help to get to the cottage.

"Ben, please, can you help me? I've had enough, and I would like to retire."

She said goodbye to them, and Ben pushed her wheelchair down the ramp. She had, after all, a great excuse to leave the party early. She needed to visit the bathroom and pack!

Ben returned after ensuring she had everything to prepare for her last night at Crystal Cliffs. Her suitcase was packed; she only wanted to write down her thoughts now that her memories of fourteen years had resurfaced! Somehow, Annelies needed to gather as many memory files as possible while still on South African soil. Oh, she was sorry to leave for Holland because the summer climate on the Garden Route in South Africa was far more to her liking, and knowing that she would arrive in mid-winter...how would she cope with moving in four weeks from a wheelchair?

Getting dressed and undressed still took her longer than usual, but at least she could do it alone. She could hear laughter in the distance but needed a quiet space to return to her past.

She settled herself in bed, resting against the headboard. Her laptop was on a pillow next to her. Ben promised not to stay up late, but she would probably be fast asleep when he returned.

She opened the files that held her journal writings. Reading over her previous writings might clarify some of the questions that could be answered as she returned to the shelter.

***

Hare Krishna

Suddenly, she remembered where she knew Harrie and Katrina from. The shelter in Cape Town fourteen years ago! Of course, it must be that. He was the guy who often came around preaching. At least, that's what some said—no wonder she had not recognised them both today. They wore Hare Krishna robes fourteen years ago, and Harrie's head was shaven.

She knew that it was entirely possible these days that a Hare Krishna person could live next door to you, and you wouldn't know it, but she now wondered if Harrie had not already recognised her. What had happened to those two during the last fourteen years? Could it have been Harrie's baby that Katrina had to give away for adoption? She would now not have been surprised if that was true. What puzzled her was that they were no longer a couple. Why were John and Pat far more suited to be together?

She would type her impressions in her journal as if it had just happened while hiding in the shelter, but for now, she moved her laptop away to let her mind go over the episode she had repressed for many years.

When a rumour went around the shelter that the Hare Krishna couple had arrived and would dish out homemade soup, many got up from the pavement outside. She was curious, so she followed the mother inside with her baby. She said the soup was the best food ever for free in the shelter.

The tall, bald young man waited while most of the people in the queue settled on the floor after being handed a bowl of soup. The couple both wore white robes. She knew that the u-shaped white tilaks symbol on his forehead marked the body as the temple of the Lord. The girl had long hair in a plait and a red spot on her forehead, which meant that the girl was married that much she knew.

They both bowed, making the namasté sign. The girl seemed to be the only one who responded until the baby's mother pulled her into the queue.

"Don't let them know that you are here", she hissed, angry.

The young man had seen her already because he nodded when it was their turn to receive a bowl of soup. She looked at them both, but the girl had turned to fetch something while the young man pointed at the spoons.

She sat in the corner of the room on the floor next to the mother with her baby, and more people streamed into the room. Soon, the place was packed, and the doors were closed.

The soup was tasty, but some hoboes' slurping noises while eating almost destroyed her appetite.

Then the young man started speaking, while the girl kept serving soup to people who wanted second helpings; she was startled by his accent. He was Dutch!

"Krishna consciousness is a science, and God gets on very well when science is used correctly."

He waited for people to settle down and got their attention by ignoring the slurping sounds. At least nobody was talking.

"However, there is another aspect of science that connects closely to God: the aspect called Faith."

Some shelter people seemed to drift into their world by closing their eyes.

Hearing the word 'faith' as an aspect of science had resulted in some having questions etched into their faces. Even the young mother, trying to conceal her disinterest by looking down at her baby crawling on the floor, turned her head towards the speaker.

"I can see that some of you want me to explain. The word 'science' comes from the Latin word for 'knowledge'," He continued."The whole realm of science exists because of humanity's desire to know everything about the universe.

The young man seemed to forget, especially when speaking enthusiastically, that his audience consisted of dropouts. Many could not even follow intellectual vocabulary or any profound ideas. He was hoping that their brains were not too severely damaged by society.

"Superficially, they may not be paying attention," She heard him thinking, but beneath the surface, their subconscious minds absorb everything they need to know. I must wait and watch them as they listen."

She had been so surprised that her telepathic skills had returned, making her stop listening to the lecture momentarily.

"Most great discoveries have been made employing faith. Scientists had such faith that they conducted countless experiments to prove their theories. For example, the laws of electricity were proven after hundreds of laboratory experiments had failed because of one man's utter faith in his theory."

She wondered what he was leading up to. Some people were already leaving when there was no more soup.

"Did any of you know that when Einstein was still a young man and an unknown, back in 1912, he discovered that Time is an illusion of this world?"

"What does that mean?" a bearded old man asked in the corner.

"He believed that Time, as we know it, did not exist outside of Earth's atmosphere, and once Man could overcome the atmosphere, he could reach the stage of being able to travel backwards and forward in Time."

"Is that a fact?" asked a young man who was addicted to tic (Methamphetamine). He had suddenly picked up interest.

Yes, it is, but let me tell a story before I continue entertaining you. During the whole time, the couple had been standing behind a trestle table serving cups of soup to the scruffy-looking people who were now gradually drifting away.

"I will share a time parable with you all that hold great wisdom by SIVANANDA."

They all wait with anticipation. Annelies had no idea who SIVANANDA was, probably his teacher.

"The Lost Wrist-Watch," the speaker shouted so everyone could hear. She now wondered if he had Indonesian blood in him. That would explain his darker skin colour.

"A man was frantically searching for something in a dark room. He was weeping and shouting. He was making a mess of the things kept in the room. He broke some and tumbled on others. Yet, what he was searching for, he could not find." Everyone was silent.

"A friend came to the threshold and asked for the reason of the man's misery. He replied: "Oh my friend, I have lost my wristwatch. It is gone."

"Hey, she stole it", the tic addict poked the old man sitting next to him in his ribs, laughing. The storyteller waited until everyone was quiet again, then he carried on:

The friend said: "How can it go away from here? But, what a fool you are to search for it in the darkness! Look, I have brought the light. Now, calm yourself. Think deeply and try to remember where it ought to be. You will soon discover it."

"The man did so and got the wristwatch. Then the friend explained the following:

"The watch was never lost; you have not gained it now. It was there all the time. However, you did not find it due to the darkness in the room and because you were searching for it in the wrong place. You were ignorant of its whereabouts. Now that the ignorance is removed, you think you have found it. It was always yours and was never lost."

"Yeah, yeah, yeah, so what is the punch line of your story?" A haggard-looking woman asked.

The young man looked around and said: "there is a similarity in this room and outside. Within the deepest recesses of man's heart is the Self, full of bliss and peace, but, blinded by ignorance, man cannot see it to experience the bliss and the peace."

No one said a word.

"The man who lost his watch was searching for happiness and peace, so he wanders about among the objects of this world and makes a mess of himself and the things of the world. He even causes misery to others and himself when he weeps and shouts."

She looked around the room and saw that the older man had left. The preacher knew it as well, for he had stopped.

"In my story, remember that the friend appears with the lamp of wisdom. He says to the man: "Remove the darkness of your ignorance with this lamp of wisdom; calm yourself; restrain all the mental modifications. Then, analyse all experiences and meditate on the result. You will discover the Self, the real I.Am. You had not lost it before, nor have you gained it now. It has always been there. Only you were ignorant of it. Now that in your pure heart and calm mind, the Self shines, self-luminous, you feel that you have regained it. You had never lost it."

"Boring story," the young man said, but the baby's mother had tears in her eyes.

"Okay, let's go back to Einstein, who believed that Time, as we know it, did not exist outside of Earth's atmosphere."

For the first time since she had escaped, she felt herself settling down into a more peaceful mood. She blended in with the rest so no one would find her here.

"The world's leading scientists, physicists, nuclear physicists and astrophysicists. " He continued, "They are still working on bringing it to effect in this reality. If they succeed, then within a few years, there will be real-time machines enabling Man to travel into the past and presumably into the future, but why do we need machines to do that? We are so much more. We are spiritual beings having a human experience."

"I have already found my time travel machine." The young man boasted, but everybody ignored him.

"I thought science is based on provable facts, not on faith!" pouted a ragged woman. She wondered what her story was.

"Indeed, Mel? Do you remember the tale I told you last week?" The Hare Krishna speaker asked. She had wondered what tale that was. In short, metaphysics is the science of the mind, and psychodynamics is the law that governs the action of the mind."

"I still don't understand," puzzled the woman, "what this has to do with physics."

"The connection," he said, "is that all of this, physics, metaphysics, medicine, love, mind, heart, machines, electronic appliances, God's divine law governs all aspects of life.

She knew that Hare Krishna's teachings often repeat that physical life is temporary and will always end up dying, so what was the message this young man wanted to convey to this bunch of dropouts?

The girl was trying to get his attention by pulling at his robe, and he bent over to her while she whispered something in his ear.

"My wife feels an African tale will be more appropriate to prove that God's law governs everything."

His wife had picked up the baby. The mother must have trusted her to do so. The room was now suddenly getting empty except for a few. Most people had their soup and were not interested in his preaching, as one tarty woman mumbled.

"Tell the story of the daughter of the elephant whisperer, his wife said loud enough for all of them to hear."

For a split second, he was frowning at her, but most of his scruffy audience wanted to hear the story of the daughter of the elephant whisperer, she included.

There was a knock on the door, and all she remembered was that the mother had taken the baby from the Hare Krishna woman and run away.

Something had happened because she could not remember the full story of the daughter of the elephant whisperer, the girl who wanted to become a Mahout like her father. Her father decides to give her a chance and gives her responsibility for an elephant calf.

She was interrupted by a knocking sound and realised Ben was returning from the deck party.

She pulled her laptop near her to type her memories down before they were gone from her mind. It was essential to write down all her experiences as the others had. Pity about the daughter's story: It was a love story; all she recalled was....

"The ranger Mohammed becomes her only supporter and shows her the world of elephants in the jungle. Here, they save an elephant baby from its death. Strengthened by this, she progresses in her work with her little elephant, Kandula, but her path changes when Kandula is taken from her." For the rest of the story, she lost. She must ask Harrie how it ended.

"Still up and working, I see."

"Yes, and I remembered where I know Harrie and Katrina from."

"I never knew you had met them before. You never told me when?"

"At first, they both looked so familiar, and Katrina said the same about me, but now I know. You will find it hard to believe what I'm going to tell you."

"Go on. I'm waiting." Ben mumbled while brushing his teeth.

She told him about the shelter and the Hare Krishna couple. As Ben was about to ask a question, his cell phone rang.

Now she recalled what POWAH had said to her when she decided her Mental Health body code

Her Mental Health Body Code Vibration 9-Unity[2]

---

2. https://allrealityshifters.wordpress.com/six-youth-and-physical-soul-quality-codes/

<Unresolved emotions from difficult and traumatic past experiences are "Trapped Emotions," and they are linked to many mental, emotional and physical illnesses.>

Her vibration code nine of Unity had come up three times! She now understood how important it was to release any past experiences. On the ascension journey, a person must never live in the past or repeat lower-level personality traits like depression and anxiety.

Chapter 15
Our Innocent Hidden Agendas

Apeldoorn - February

Three weeks had passed since they had returned to Holland, but it felt like years. She closed the front door with one foot still in plaster after wishing Hans a safe trip to France. The house sounded hollow and empty now that most of the boxes had gone. Next week, the removal van would take the rest.

She still had so much to do. Her computer would soon be gone, so she had better do some last-minute writing on her workbook.

When Hans drove away, she heard him hooting. He was greeting someone, which reminded her that she'd better get on with it before her niece, Tieneke, arrived. Last week, Hans, Ben, and Joris drove to France to pick up some of her plants. She had opted to stay behind in Holland to work on her projects. It was also too much of an effort to get her in and out of the car. She had got used to her crutches but was not allowed to put any weight on the right foot.

She had done a lot of writing in her workbook being alone.

There was so much to do now that they had decided to move to Halfway House in France. She knew that she had great trouble getting rid of stuff. Ben had been far more ruthless when it came to discarding things. She wasn't proud of holding onto stuff, especially knowing nothing was real. Her mind was still holding onto images that appeared physically as stuff!

Forgive, Forgive, Forgive. she said to herself. That felt better already.

Ben was talking to someone in the hallway as she logged on to upload her article on the ascension topic website entitled 'Is Our Body Weight Important?' At the same time, her emails came in.

Niels, one of the participants from her workshop, asked that very same question, and so did his girlfriend when they were alone with her last week. She had written in her workbook that bodily identification reinforces the lower self and that only spirit identification releases the body. However, knowing each person must make that a personal choice, she suggested some detoxing remedies.

Niels' girlfriend had later emailed her about her weight problem, and her reply had been in the form of a question:

"It's your body weight from a dream time perspective, or is your physical form telling you what you are holding onto?"

Niels got it, but his partner didn't, so she shared how she managed to get her weight to a comfortable level. Not according to the advertising or social standards, whatever they might be. That would be giving in to a program that was not hers.

Since she started to clean her body with at least 1.5 L of purified water first thing in the morning, followed by eating fruit until lunchtime, she gradually lost what she considered excess weight. Now that she was trapped in a wheelchair for six weeks, putting on weight might be the result.

She still liked wearing colourful caftans, but not out of shame or needing to hide bulk. She had always seen herself as a tall, big-boned frame, so why should she try to change that? She knew that she was attractive, at least Ben thought so, and believed that it stopped her from ever fussing about her looks.

Writing about "**the Body Codes of Light**" and how their numerical vibrations influence the image by which each person's mind is controlled started to make intellectual sense.

Decoding the six youth and health spacings her journal covered helped her change her perceptions of reality. She finished her article with the water therapy treatment by Dr Mahmoud Hussain and uploaded it to her blog. Trevor had shown her how to publish hers under her name, Annelies.

She heard Tieneke talking to Ben in the kitchen, but she didn't want to get up to greet her just yet. Ben could have her to himself. He would soon be on his way to Den Haag. She had already hugged him goodbye before disappearing into their office to write.

The two got on very well, and she would work until her niece knocked on her office door.

The one email she received from Gerrit, her half-brother, two days ago was still in her inbox. He rarely emailed her, so she opened it the previous evening, just before bed. Two hours later, she was still reading the articles he had told her about on a website.

Dear Annelies, I came across this website, which made me think of us all. I mean us as the Jaarsma Clan. Have you ever come across it? She clicked on the link, which took her to a video:

The Game of Enlightenment & Abundance[1]

She had to get used to the advertising banners everywhere. Still, since Gerrit had especially wanted her to see it, she would give it a going over...and before she knew it, she had moved into a different dimension—the dimension of Cyberspace. The banner image was from the Gold Ring community she had belonged to many years ago.

"Gee Annie, what is so absorbing on the Internet that I must carry our coffee tray here?" Tieneke exclaimed after she had knocked and banged the door open with her foot because her hands were full.

---

1. https://www.youtube.com/watch?v=K63t11IYQ38

"Oh dear, it's so ...strange to see you in a wheelchair."

She hardly heard Tieneke talking to her. Her heart was still beating from pure astonishment. She was half smiling and simultaneously very uncertain of her sanity.

"It will not be for long, I guarantee you."

"Oh, Annelies, it must have been so awful when it all happened. Are you in any pain?"

"Not at all. I'm just frustrated that I can not bear any weight on my right foot. Still, two weeks to go, and it seems forever." Annelies looked up from her screen to study Tieneke's aura.

"Come, sit down next to me; I've got something to show you."

The feelings of grief for losing her daughter were still visible in her field, but less so than before she left for South Africa.

"Guess what? We have found a very thought-provoking website that will blow your mind. I can't wait to show it to Ben!

Tieneke dragged a chair next to Annelie's wheelchair while making room for their coffee-making mugs.

"What time do you expect Ben back tonight?"

Ben was a witness to Nick du Toit's arson and murder trial in Den Haag. The papers had been full of investigations that linked Nick du Toit to shady deals in South Africa. While Ben remained convinced that the bombing of Toon's project last October was backed and financed by powerful and vital people, Ben now suspected that even Nick du Toit had been misled into the later part he had played in the whole saga.

Last year, she had supported Tieneke in her grief of losing her only daughter, who was also involved with the same crowd that connected Nick du Toit with the terrorists.

"I hope Ben will not be too late, so please stay for dinner. You will not believe what I've discovered; Gerrit told me to check it out, so I did. I stayed up until two in the morning, reading from the screen."

She still had difficulty suppressing her astonishment. By pure fluke, Gerrit had discovered an exciting site, and yesterday afternoon, she had surfed the whole website and somehow came onto a link that took her somewhere else. It looked like the same website, only the top banner was different. She had downloaded some more last evening to read in bed. It was as if she was reading articles she had written!

"Is that your website?" Tieneke saw it, too!

"No, not that I'm aware of. I only write articles published on the site that Nadia, Trevor's assistant, created, the ascension topics website. I don't yet have one myself...at least not so far as I know...but I know it could be, read this...Watch, before it goes away I'll try to print it out.

She scrolled down a lot of text and clicked on edit - select all - copy. There it was, all on her clipboard. She switched her printer on after pasting the text into a document on her PC and moving the file by naming it Ascension.

"It must be good for you to rave about it and print it out!"

"Wait and see." As the printer was coughing the page out of her printer, her computer screen jumped back to her forgiveness screen saver! That happened the last time, and she could never return to the same website. It was as if she had been reading about something that had not yet happened!

Tieneke was reading some of the pages that came out of the printer. "But you must have typed this. It's all you. The way you talk. The title is typically you. Are we all born as a result of an idea?"

"I know, it's so weird; I can't remember ever having written this. When I first found this website, I felt as if I had landed on a site that was mine...It was almost as if I had a déja-vu moment. You know when you have been there before."

"You said just now that it might disappear; why would it?"

"The last time my screen saver jumped back, I could never find it again, no matter what type I typed into the search engine." She was glad to have the opportunity to share her confusion without thinking she was losing it." While sipping her coffee, the images of giant boulders in a Cape Town garden reminded her that their concept of time would change.

Tieneke read out loud when the pages came out of the printer:

My name is Annelies. I'm not sure who Annelies is. I could just as well be a character in a novel. How real is that? But of course, I think I exist just like you, the visitor who reads these words. I'm well aware that the world as I see and experience it is a projection of my mind. So be it. My family and friends know and love me, and I love them. With their help, I have been guided to develop and run an ascension card game online.

"But ...that must have been coming from you. It's even mentioning your ascension card game."

"I know, not that I have seen this article yet; I've only read one article on forgiving our illusional programming by integrating the unconscious information to attain a fifth-dimensional awakening."

"Did you print it out?"

"No, I read the article online before it disappeared."

"I can't believe this. Let's look into Google. It must be there."

"The Gold Ring website is there; I still have that link. That site is also astonishing. It's as if a global transformation has already happened."

"And from that site, you came onto the other website, the one with this article you just printed out?"

"Yes. It's so frustrating. I've spent three hours searching for it yesterday. And just now, I had it, or so I thought. I looked into my computer's history, and there it was, but then my screen saver seemed to wipe it away.

Tieneke gave up and read the rest of the article:

Some still remember an existence without form, sound, fragrance, time or space. It was a reality where the I of us all was in everything simultaneously.

It was a reality where the human mind cannot live. The moment we try to go there, our minds hold us back, so we must find a way to go beyond our minds.

"Is that at all possible?", I often asked.

The answer to that question came gradually through allowing my mind to play a game.

"Annie, do you see what I see?"

"No, what?"

"Look at the date."

Tieneke was referring to an advert at the top. It said 18 May 2021, which was the following year.

"Annie, do you think...that you did just that, go beyond the mind, so this article is from the future?"

"Let me read it first. Then I'll tell you."

"Okay, but just hold on, before the text disappears from this page."

Our ascension workshop website aims to create and play the awakening game. We want to take each player beyond the perception of this world of duality; the winner (everyone will be a winner) of the ascension game will have awakened from the dream which started long ago.

She was trying to read past Tieneke's shoulder, and what she read again created feelings of déja-vu

When we ate from the apple in the Garden of Eden (metaphor), In that instant, a weblike membrane split our human brain into two hemispheres. Our holistic multidimensional reasoning side went to sleep, while our 'linear thinking side of the 'persona program' came into existence. That is a very simplistic way to describe how our five physical, sensory perception channels established our physical world. Things that were at first invisible became solid. From a world where we were all at one with everything, we moved into a world of form, which became 'visible', and throughout 'time', a world of duality became our reality.

"Gosh, but it must have been you writing it. It so feels like you. Are you sure? Here you read it. It even mentions Ingrid's journal?"

Through Cyberspace, I will facilitate our creative cardmaking game. Still, first, as I do in Ingrid's Journal: The Reality Shifters, I and the rest of our clan will share through our articles what the ascension journey means to us; while our visitors can read up on how and why we need creative tools to change our perceptions.

She almost wanted to cry. Was she losing it? Even the title The Reality Shifters was mentioned.

"You know what is happening?" Tieneke exclaimed in surprise.

"No, what, tell me."

"Our timelines are merging. That must be it!"

"What do you mean?"

"I'm not sure, but look here..." Tieneke took hold of the mouse and right-clicked. A box appeared that said:

—You can generate as many timelines as you like. If you're into creating web pages, you can even take the timelines we generate for you here and put them on your pages – an unmatched personal touch everyone will enjoy. In addition, you can insert up to ten custom, colour-coded personal time segments (events or ranges) in a timeline.—

"I don't get it," Annelies said with frustration, resting back into her wheelchair, trying to assimilate this timeline idea.

"Okay, let me explain. Present time, locally speaking, is the combined moment-to-moment relativistic coupling of space-time as it dynamically accretes in motion in the continuum."

Tieneke was trying to explain a concept that eluded her.

"Now you've already lost me."

"Our physical universe exists in a self-contained continuum of mass, form, force, and motion in space and time. These are Trevor's words, not mine."

"Oh, well then, maybe I must let him explain it. All I understand now is that at this moment, we are floating in hyperspace."

Tieneke was scrolling through the Gold Ring website. It was a online community that had thousands of members from all over the world.

"Have you signed up yet?"

"Believe me, I tried to, but every time I want to...the page disappears. Don't click on the signup button."

"Annelies, I'm so excited that it's all happening. Humanity is at a crossroads of evolutionary choice and the opportunity to become spiritually awake to birth a flourishing human civilization into the first twenty years of the third millennium. That is my intent, so things like this encourage me."

"I'm glad you are, but I must understand it first." She took the mouse from Tieneke and tried again to click the signup button, but the page disappeared again.

"Oh no!"

"What happened? What did you do?"

"I tried to sign up like I did yesterday. You see, this happened before. I've lost the page that holds the sign-up button."

"No, you can't. Let me."

Whatever Tieneke did, there was no history, no evidence about what they had both seen. A box appeared saying links were broken, but no information about which web address.

"Gee, I thought you, of all people, are already far more awake on higher levels. Aren't you clairvoyant and telepathic as well?"

"Good grief, I'm not even awake half the time in this often hell hole of a world. I suspect that POWAH is doing this in cyberspace, and everyone who finds it will interpret his information in their own way."

"You mean that POWAH can create a website that you created in the future? That sounds too far-fetched to me. Maybe you have forgotten that you wrote it. It might have been, like you said, an article you published on other websites."

"No, I never did, I'm very sure, but I plan to include it all in my journal. My ideas also explain crop circles and how I think they appear."

"Gosh, I wonder now. That must be the same site Trevor was puzzled about last week." Tieneke stood up and paced around.

"Really. What makes you think so?"

She knew Tieneke and Trevor had a relationship going, but she had no idea on what level. "Annelies, have you spoken to Trevor about this website?"

"No, not yet. I want first to show Ben. That is if I can find it again."

"How did you come across it? Oh yes, Gerrit told you first, but how? Did he email you a web address?"

Tieneke was as keen as her to find the website again. She could tell that by her whole posture. She shook her head because the link was gone, but she now recalled.

"Yes, I found it through Google. I can't remember what I searched for, let's see...I know I was looking for an image of a beach, something that was written on sand. I wanted to add that into my ...hey, there it is!"

Suddenly, the familiar page appeared again. Tieneke grabbed her and peered over her shoulders at the screen. The text mesmerised them, and it seemed again like she was looking at a PowerPoint slide.

I was created as the good book says; the word came first. This same power of an idea, a thought, became me, Annelies Zwiegelaar, and through me, another was speaking. The voice said that it is an energy being without form but able to communicate on a wavelength that produces sound, like the sound we witness and translates as rain or wind or the sound from our oceans when its currents form waves that crash onto our shores. This power represents the source of all consciousness. The supreme God/Goddess expressing through us is what we know as the force of life. Some call this energy the Holy Spirit or a vital life force. I also perceive this energy as my oversoul, which I call POWAH.

They were both speed-reading the text in case it would once again disappear before their eyes.

For us (The Jaarsma Clan), we awakened our intuitive nature by creating a deck of personal cards — these became the awakening tools with which we started to play our ascension game. Please look through Tieneke's animation workbook, The Language of Light, and read up on how she came to inspiration. Something was revealed to her that went beyond words. It told her how we can still translate 'feelings' into symbols that express a language she calls the language of our souls.

"You wrote about me! Read on!"

Many readers have asked me how the ascension journey came to me. All I can say with certainty is that I was born into this world as an idea like we all are. I was just more aware of that truth from the beginning.

That was the last both had time to read. The screen had jumped back to her screen saver.

They both stared in silence at the screen, puzzled.

"But that page must have still been there all the time, but somehow it goes away when..."

"Gosh, Tieneke, this reminds me of how the twenty-two excerpts that Ingrid added to her journal came about."

"What do you mean?"

"Ingrid had a similar experience. She wrote about it in her journal."

"Incredible. I'm so confused. Oh, Annie, what if..." She could see that a cloudlike shadow enveloped Tieneke's aura, as if...

"Annelies, what about if...what would happen if we moved towards a higher consciousness? What if we start to perceive a reality that looks like ours but just at a different time?"

She knew Tieneke was thinking of her only daughter Hennie, whose consciousness would be somewhere...but where... on any of the astral planes? Hennie had not appeared to her, and not to her mother either, it seems, otherwise Tieneke would have told her.

"Come, let's go to the kitchen."

She was about to wheel herself out the door when Tieneke took a book that was still not packed away from her bookshelf. It was Ingrid's journal: The Reality Shifters.

"I remember Toon using these words just after their wedding ceremony."

"What words?"

"My love, we are the reality shifters." I read that on the screen.

Tieneke was browsing through the book, looking for some text...

"Did she not write about an ascension topics website?"

They both heard a dog barking outside. If Joris were here, he would have already run to the back door, jumping to be let out...but Joris was already at Half-way House in France.

"Where have Toon and Ingrid gone to this time?"

Tieneke must have had the same thought, or was she picking up hers? Being such a creative person, she was surprised she was not already more attuned intuitively.

"They visited Damanhur,[2] the community I told you about in the Italian Alps." She noticed that Tieneke had lost weight. At first, she thought that her grieving was the reason, but now she was not so sure anymore.

"Come, let's make some tea, or would you rather have some juice?"

---

2. https://damanhur.travel/

She wanted to get her out of her office for the moment. Somehow, there was an energy present that affected Tieneke. She suspected it was Hennie but was not about to shake her young friend even more. Moving out of the office might clear the room.

"Did Trevor show you his article: Is our 'Physical reality' Primarily a Mental, or a Spiritual Phenomenon? We worked at it together." Tieneke said as she took hold of her wheelchair.

"I've added his article to my **Body Codes of Light workbook**."

"How is that going?" Tieneke asked

"Slow, what about your workbook? Has it been reprinted?"

Tieneke helped her by reaching for the teapot. It was too high to reach unless she stood on one foot.

"The colour version is published, but the greyscale version is still available on most major bookshop websites like Amazon. Trevor is helping me by transforming my class material for an online workshop so I can spend more time away."

Tieneke and Trevor had been spending much time together since her husband Roelof's funeral. Two people on their own with no attachments or commitments, apart from their passion for waking up from the human dream, had found a divine friendship in each other.

When Annelies started to recognise how two people's auric signatures seemed to resonate on a similar note, she knew that the souls of those people belonged together. When she and Theo finished preparing the rules of the first level of the ascension board game, little did they then understand that Trevor and Tieneke must have known that on a Soul level, they would be together during the second stage of their lives.

"I have written another article last night. Do you think it could already be posted under my name?" Tieneke asked.

"I don't see why not. Trevor showed me how to publish an article online; you must learn to do it yourself."

She placed the teapot and cups on a tray, and Tieneke returned it to her office. While Tieneke poured, she surfed the net and landed on the ascension topic site.

"Oh, yes, Trevor showed it to me as well, but I was not paying much attention then."

"Oh, where were your thoughts?" She replied, arching her brows. Tieneke responded by giving her a playful shove. She knew it. These two were hitting it off.

"What is your article about?" She asked instead.

"Is there a linguistic communication device that breaks all barriers?"

"That sounds like...of course, your language of light symbology workshops[3]."

"Annelies, when did it start? I mean, when did you know that you were clairvoyant?" Tieneke's quivering voice again told her that energies of grief still hung around her. She could or would not let go of her heartache. Losing your only daughter from a drug overdose, and then a month later your husband, must have been heavy. Roelof died after a heart attack. Not that their marriage was a good one, but losing him seemed to have added feelings of guilt. She hoped Tieneke would soon share them with her so she could help her let go of her mind-created illusions through self-forgiveness.

When did she know that she was a clairvoyant? She never knew the term then, but a memory of her early childhood came to mind. Remembering the gripping feelings of fear as she woke up every time she saw the inhuman creatures that seemed to chase her in her dreams.

"I don't know. I recall seeing invisible people in my childhood, but I only found that out later."

"Were they people that you...knew?"

---

3. https://lightworkerjournals.wordpress.com

Tieneke offered her a stroopwafel. Now that she lacked exercise, she shouldn't accept, but what the heck?

"No. I'm not even sure if some were human. I did suffer from nightmares...and still do occasionally."

Gosh, were they back to haunt her? Did they resemble the images she recalled from her dream?

Tieneke was quietly sipping her tea. When did she realise that others were not what she was often aware of?

Years ago, when Nicky, Trevor's girlfriend, gave her a doll, she could still hear her saying: *"My angel, when you wake up, look at your doll, and Dienie will be there to greet you. The scary creatures will leave when they see her."* She often saw Dienie, a nun whom nobody else did, but Nicky knew.

The doll was a gift from Nicky, who seemed to cry a lot when she visited her mother, but she never found out why. She had treasured that doll and carried it wherever she went from when Nicky said it would scare away the creatures. She must have been around three or four. She could still recall how scared she was, knowing the grey shadows would all hang around her cot, making faces at her. Especially their eyes, even thinking about it, gave her goosebumps.

"Tieneke, I must have always seen more than others, except for one of my mother's friends. She knew why I...she gave me a doll to protect me from scary creatures. I suffered a lot from nightmares when I was very young." "And still do," thinking back to the rock face.

What she was not telling her was that it was Trevor's first love who died in childbirth. She suspected that Hans was Trevor's biological child, but nobody knew what happened to the baby. The face of Nicky had often reminded her of a younger version of what Nadifa must have looked like for some strange reason.

"But... so did Hennie. When she was around two going on three, she screamed each morning for me to come to her bedroom. It started to worry me, so I took her to a child psychiatrist who said that it was very common for young children to have nightmares, and he gave me pills that seemed to work."

Tieneke's tears were streaming when she shared how she and her late husband, Roelof, fought in the early morning after hearing Hennie's screams.

"Roelof often got up and left early for his work. He never once would pick Hennie up from her bed. After the pills the doctor had prescribed, and the screaming had stopped, we left it at that."

Tieneke admitted that she had often felt uneasy giving her pills until her only child was at least twelve years old.

Annelies was shocked at hearing that Hennie had been given unknown drugs for that long.

"Annelies, how could I have been so unaware? I must have started the drug dependence. I know I was unaware of it in that sense, but why did I not listen to my intuition?"

It was the first time that Tieneke talked about Hennie since she died so tragically last September, apparently in an explosion near Toon's Valley of the Gods project. Initially, everyone assumed that Hennie had died alongside Piet, her niece Yolanda's ex-husband. Their remains were found in the same partially destroyed building. However, the autopsy revealed that Hennie had died from a heavy overdose just before the explosion.

"My love, please, don't make things worse by blaming yourself. It might now be the time to practice forgiving yourself and even the doctors who described the pills. They did it out of ignorance, remember?"

"Yes, I know, Trevor suggested the same, but should I not take some action about how medications still fool people today?"

"My dear, we have all been ignorant about medicines that have been, and still are, prescribed to people. You were following someone's advice for the best interest of your child. So many parents have done that. It's time to forgive your ignorance truly. That will heal the emotional pain a lot faster."

She knew Tieneke could cope, but there would always be moments like these that she would drop her energy, giving her emotional body a chance to re-scan and delete emotional baggage that was becoming an obstacle towards her awakening.

So those were the guilt vibes she had spotted in her energy field. She knew that, by seeing guilt vibes for what they were, they equally reflected her guilt since she had seen them. She must note this since it would help her with the virtual ascension game on the third level, which they played soon.

Tieneke was reading the notes spread all over her desk while she was drawn by Trevor's latest article they had written together.

"Annie, why did you write that the idea about the 22 spacings on our decoding sheet that you acknowledge in your introduction in your workbook had already been worked out? What do you mean?"

"Ideas are there for us to tap into. Often, we make it our idea, but it can never be just ours entirely."

"I know, but how is it possible that someone else has come up with the same idea?" Tieneke was clearly in an investigating mood.

"If it was not inspired by ...well, we do tap into the universal matrix with the help of our Higher Self, which we all have named POWAH."

So you are saying that POWAH has contacted other people around the planet?"

"Absolutely, but they might not know POWAH like we do."

"You mean they call the entity or spiritual guide differently?"

"Yes, depending on what group of soul your soul belongs to."

"So who is, or has the right information?"

"They all do."

"Mmm, I'm not so sure about that. There are so many thoughts about who we are, where we might have come from, and where we are going if we don't destroy ourselves first. They are all so different. Some philosophies come across as arrogant, opinionated, dogmatic and especially the religions of the world seem to use the power of fear as their weapon." Tieneke seldom spoke at this length.

"Every group soul has their method to call their souls home. It ultimately doesn't matter since we were all created as an idea by the one supreme being." She replied.

"Mmm, you mean we mentally came into existence?"

"Yes, I perceive that as being the likeness, the mirror, or the image of the Godhead. Our temple is our mind."

Tieneke's questioning made her recall the video clip that Theo had left behind.

"I would love to see the introduction movie clip Theo, Richard's brother, left for us. Can you make me a copy?"

"Made one already."

She was now sure that Tieneke was getting telepathic.

She handed her a flash drive, explaining that she must be alone when she watched it for the first time. That was very important. When Tieneke asked why, she explained that when she clicked the upload button, a panel asked her if she was alone. Trevor hadn't told her that it would when he sent it last week. So he must have told Tieneke to get a copy, which she had already made on her own accord.

"Weren't you suspicious of getting a video clip through your email, since these days, lots of mental programming devices come through to us through our electronic equipment?"

"I knew it came from Trevor, remember? My body would otherwise have been in an uproar if someone unknown had sent me video clips. They can block off other more important emails, but when I opened the video clip, my emotions acted like I was entering play-land, but my mind was neutral."

"Was it inspiring and sensible to watch it on your own?"

"Yes, I think so; it was a very shifting experience. Later tonight, if it is not too late, I'll watch it again, but this time with Ben. If we had seen it for the first time together, I would probably not have stirred me so deeply, but then we are all different."

While Tieneke cleared their lunch plates for the kitchen, she picked up notes she had printed the previous evening. It was a paragraph from the introduction section of her genetic decoding workbook. Often, she would print out what she had written and leave it around so she could later read over it again. Tieneke returned to say goodbye; Annelies wished she had someone to go home to.

"Why don't you stay for dinner?"

"Annelies, I must learn to be by myself. I want to move on, which will not happen if I run away from the empty house that awaits me. Thanks for asking, but I will be fine."

Tieneke kissed her goodbye, wishing her well with her healing process. She took the disk and put it in her bag, but at the front door, she turned around.

"I'm not so sure if I'm ready for an emotionally stirring treatment by watching this video. I have plenty of work to prepare for my online classes, which will keep me going. I'll see. Many thanks for a very thought-provoking afternoon." Tieneke's firm hug said plenty. Just as Ben drove into their double driveway, she wheeled herself out to Tieneke's car in the driveway. He parked and waved at Tieneke, who was reversing out. She was glad to see him....

Ben took hold of her wheelchair, and they went inside together.

"How was it, the court case? I mean, are you allowed to tell me?"

Ben was getting a real pro, tilting her over the doorstep through their passage into the kitchen.

"Boring, and at the same time, frustrating. We waited forever before I was called as a witness to Nick du Toit's arson and murder trial. Toon was never called. We knew that would happen."

"And now, how long does this go on?"

"Who knows? Let's forget it. I'm starving."

It always astonished her that food was often in Ben's mind. Luckily he had never put on an ounce of weight.

After they had eaten dinner, she talked him into seeing Trevor's video clip together. Before telling Ben about the mysterious website incident, she needed to speak to Trevor soon. Tieneke was the first to learn how she couldn't remember anything about writing it. For now, she needed to make sure that she was not forgetful.

Were these shifting realities in time the first signs of the apocalypse? Not that anyone would have thought it would be a mind-bending experience, but now she understood why. The word apocalypse in Greek meant removing the veil. She now realised that the veil must be the arachnoid, a web-like tissue separating the human brain's left and right hemispheres.

Who knows, maybe many people today have memory losses or other brain inefficiencies. She had been quite shocked when so-called déja-Vu experiences had often landed people in psychiatric homes in the past.

Ben was looking forward to seeing Trevor's video clip.

They settled on the sofa, and Ben placed his laptop on the coffee table directly before them. They had sold their TV, amongst many other things. Some extra cash was useful now that they had to learn to live on his pension.

The introduction slide showed a sacred archaeological site that still held images of enigmatic temples amongst huge stone faces. Even in the video, they were still wrapped up and hidden amongst copious amounts of a twining jungle creeper.

The following image, The Soul of Man, took you into a vortex of spinning geometric symbols. She now knew that inside these sacred temples, many interesting and, at times, gruesome film scripts flashed by that many people didn't notice or wish to see. She hoped Ben would be alright since he had seen many gruelling situations during his career.

"Who created the video? Does Trevor know?" Ben asked.

"No. At first, we all thought it was Theo, but Richard said that Theo had never visited these temples."

The camera was now zooming up close into the crystal. That is what it looked like. The video was made excitingly and creatively, especially for people who wanted to experience how huge Crystal Skulls record the human soul's Akashic files.

They both sat and watched as unbelievably sacred, sublime and absurd places flashed by. It was as if each facet of the crystal's grid formation had crowned as if they were part of the world's seven wonders. The Crystal Skulls now projected each scene like a movie. She knew from the beginning that she had been looking at her Akashic records, especially when a middle-aged blond woman with a very modern hairstyle triggered memories.

Was the story they were looking at in the future or the past? When she spotted that the hands of the woman were well manicured, with a wedding ring on her left ring finger, she felt very weird.

The woman was typing! She had two gold rings on her right ring finger. One ring had two small diamonds in an elegant setting, and on the same finger, she saw a ring with the eye of Horus symbol in gold. She almost again jumped off her couch when she saw her hands. At least it felt as if they were hers, but her hands were very different.

Ben must have seen other scenes that one of the several Crystal Skulls projected because his stunned face gave his inner turmoil away. Then, the clip was finished. Ben was as amazed at the whole experience as she was for the first time. In an email, Trevor said he wanted to show it to her first as an example to be used in her ascension card game on the third level. That she now knew for sure.

"Wow, that was something. How are you?" Ben asked.

"Frazzled, and you?"

"Confused. What were your Akashic records projections like?"

"Strangely, I was initially unsure what I was looking at, but then I seemed to recall the emotions. And you?" She asked.

"Well, when I saw a film clip streaming out of these Crystal Skulls, I almost freaked out. I saw many homeless families living in tents. Sadly, they had all lost their homes to a massive tsunami that was followed by an earthquake. The quake shook for seven whole minutes, killing families, especially many young kids, who were all devastated. Something strangely weird was about to happen. That was when I freaked out.

Was I seeing myself from another life? I feel more protected than The Queen of England right now."

Ben's story made her recall a dream about significant flooding images.

"What unsettled you the most?" She asked, suppressing laughter at the way he summed it all up.

"Observing the rich and famous that left us in droves. It reminded me of our luxurious train journey. There was a clear division taking place."

"Which direction did you feel a part of?"

"That was the weirdest thing, neither direction."

Ben was silently mulling over his mental encounters.

"Gosh, Annie, my intuitive vibes couldn't help but feel that something strangely weird was about to happen to us, not in a planet-shaking God-fearing fatal way, more like a dwindling illusional lake with its changeable shades of dark blue ...

They closed the screen and tidied up. They were both too frazzled to speak. Ben took his laptop up with him to their bedroom. She felt like having a long, luxurious bath instead of a shower, which Ben preferred. She did need his help to get in with her one foot that was in plaster, but when she let her body settle in the warm water, that felt like bliss....

If Trevor had created this video clip, then the skill that Trevor showed in just writing code would have produced these effects by stirring people's unconscious data, which was phenomenal. She suspected that Richard, Leo and Theo must have had a hand in it, but none of them could grasp how he did it like automatic writing. Trevor would sit in front of his computer, and suddenly, his hands ran over the keyboard. All you see on the screen is what looks like codes.

She suddenly remembered something when Ben was about to leave the bathroom.

"I thought when you were watching the video, you mumbled, "I can now fly.""

"Did I? My scene was a real Lawrence of Arabia dream scene...me on stallion horseback galloping, not flying."

After his bathroom duties, Ben found his sleeping T-shirt on the hook of the bathroom door they got in Cape Town. She'd better get out of her bath since she still needed his help.

Ben helped her out of the bath, and they settled in their queen-sized bed together.

The bedroom was bare, without anything on the walls, and her voice started to echo.

"Now, you are going to think I've gone potty, but I'd better tell you what else I saw," Ben said as he pulled the duvet under his chin.

"When the sun finally fully set in the sky, I saw fish still alive swimming inside a small dried-up lake, and it looked as if it was slowly draining away through a badly fitting bath plug! Then, early in what looked like the morning, I spotted a supersonic water pump to assist with the water levels. I seemed to know what I was doing."

"Did you...see images of drought or flooding?"

"Both, I guess. My emotions were shaken for some reason, but I can't remember why for my life."

I still see this image of a swan-shaped paddleboat that seemed to carry tidings of joy without them running aground." He shook his head in bewilderment.

"My mind certainly knows how to span images before my eyes. I don't know where the visions came from, but the drama surrounding Nick du Toit somehow has something to do with it."

Ben pulled her close, and they cuddled as if they were together for the last time.

"Each friend represents a world in us, possibly not born until they arrive, and it is only by this meeting that a new world is born."

He mumbled in a sleepy voice. Ben's comment was so out of character that she peered at him in astonishment. What does he mean?

"Ben, are you still awake?"

Instead, he started snoring. Her mind went over what she had written in her workbook that he might have read. Something about an innocent agenda, so she mentally asked:

Is it true that we don't see things as they are; we see them as we are?

< Very few human beings receive complete truth, resulting in an instant illumination. Most of them acquire it fragment by fragment, on a small scale, by successive developments, cellularly, like a laborious mosaic.>

It was always a loving feeling when her higher self seemed to reply to her thoughts, thinking about the woman she had seen in the video. Was that her in another lifetime? But what does the diamond ring and the symbol of Horus's eye mean... great wealth?

< The video intends to achieve a change in you. If you had not seen it, you wouldn't have changed.>

What does that mean? Was it her guide POWAH who replied now? Ingrid and herself had the numeral vibration of 22 in their decoding as their guide. It represented the Language of Light symbol of instinctive. There was so much she was mindlessly working on when writing the Body Codes of Light workbook. Her emotions were all over the place after watching the video again.

Her Right Hemisphere Code vibration 20Hidden truth[4]

According to Tieneke, that numeral vibe stood for Hidden Truth. That somehow is linked to the soul quality of her intuition.

Tomorrow, she would look up what she wrote in the translations section of her workbook, but for now, she would rather experience illumination through a dream.

---

4. https://allrealityshifters.wordpress.com/the-human-brains-left-and-right-hemispheres/

Chapter 16
The God that Dwells Within.

Where had the Time Gone?

Lately, having her left foot up higher was more comfortable. Her feet were starting to swell up, which she never experienced before. Ben had just left and would be home later in the afternoon. Thank goodness the weather had calmed down, so she hoped the roads would be free of traffic jams.

At a distance, she heard a radio announcer saying:

"Hail, rain and strong winds battered the Netherlands Tuesday, felling trees, creating localised flooding and causing major road and rail disruption."

She looked up, wondering where it came from.

"The Dutch meteorological institute KNMI said wind speeds of more than 105 km/h caused trees to fall on roads and rail tracks, resulting in long delays throughout the country for commuters. More than 5 cm hailstones were recorded in the country's southwest."

Gosh, how strange. Had she heard this before? There was no storm or hailstones that she knew about. Where was this coming from? She was alone except for Joris, who was curled up under her one foot. There was no radio nearby.

"There were more than 300 km of traffic jams on the Dutch roads, with the A20 near Rotterdam entirely closed off in both directions due to flooding and fallen trees. Lightning brought down the railway network's electrical systems at Leiden, near The Hague, and several other towns."

Joris was still fast asleep and hadn't moved. How weird. What storms was the male voice referring to?

She wheeled backwards so as not to disturb Joris. She moved her wheelchair near the window to look outside and see if she had heard her neighbour's car radio. There was no car on the driveway.

It was now silent except for a soft breeze that played with the leaves of the sweeping branches of her tree, Wisteria. Gosh, at this moment, had it happened before? Feelings of déjà vu penetrated her whole body. She rolled back to the desk when she had an intuitive urge about something to do with sharing. She had to type the words in her head.

"You are the caretakers of the Universe. Only One Source and One Force control everything, and that is Super Light." Those were the words that rang in her ear.

When did she discuss super light? Vaguely, she remembered Hans' explanation, but that was before they left for South Africa. She'd better shake it off. She needed to work on the article she titled Breaking the Death Habit.

"Come, girl, you can do it." Talking to herself helped, mainly to prove that it was her speaking and no one else this time.

Lately, she had been practising stepping away from her body while typing. It seemed to help with her creative flow, especially when working on an article or a chapter for her workbook.

"Relax, close your eyes. Step away," she whispered, imagining herself sitting erect in her wheelchair while pretending to lean over her shoulder at her screen. She tried visualising that she was sitting in bright daylight on an office chair, pretending someone else was typing. Or, someone was typing about her sitting in a wheelchair. Where had that idea come from?

Suddenly, Joris jumped up as if something had alerted him. To her amazement, the artefact on Ben's side of their desk had a glowing halo! Or was she imagining it?

Trevor brought it back from France last week, together with Joris, who he said was pining for them. Ben had kept the artefact away from her during their packing since her reactions to South Africa had been somewhat disturbing before their trip.

"It's okay, Joris, calm down." She pulled his head on her lap, stroking him. Joris had been ecstatic to see them. It warmed her heart that a dog could stir such an emotional reaction. Now that Toon and Ingrid were travelling, he was more bonded with her than ever. Ingrid was already far into her pregnancy, but she had insisted on accompanying Toon just this once before the baby was due.

Joris' hair stood on end while they both watched with fascination how the metallic colour of the artefact had changed into a multi-colour high-gloss finish that reminded her of the inside of a beach shell.

Trevor wanted her to have another go at the artefact, but she wanted to focus on her journal instead. Ben must have forgotten that he had left it on his desk.

Like a cell phone announcing an incoming call, a sudden vibrating sound made her almost jump out of her wheelchair. Joris got on his hind legs, front paws resting on her lap, barking at it.

"Shhhh, Joris, it's okay. Go lie down."

Whatever was activating, the vibrations were coming towards her, or so it felt. Then, her vision started to blur like it had done in the fairy garden six weeks ago. Leo, Ben's twin brother, said that artefacts, like crystals, have the power to interact with the human mind.

She settled herself behind the keyboard to be ready to type what she experienced when she heard the following words;

'*You don't need me. Just let the words come. Your inner sight has fully opened up to take a multidimensional journey.*'

Was it truly the artefact that spoke? Could it show her what a multidimensional world was like? With some doubt, she telepathically replied:

"*Who...are you, whoever you might be? Will you show me how to travel inside or outside my body?*"

She would be far more comfortable if POWAH were near, but she followed the rock's advice and started typing. The text on her PC screen was normal, but with a difference. The energy that guided her fingers over her keyboard was not coming from herself. At least it felt as if...

<Yes, we will show you that we are all one in your dream state. It's your mind that translates images into words. Then, the separations between energies come into effect. The human mind uses visions for you to translate so you will recognise them, but they can often be mistranslated, depending on which aspect of you makes the interpretations.>

She now recognized POWAH's reply signature, which was a relief. Somehow, the rock must be in the form of an antenna POWAH used. When his energy was around her, feelings of timelessness took over.

<Listen with your heart, and I will show you what our multidimensional universe looks like. We will leave it up to you to translate what you see into words.>

She hoped her mind could connect with the information often stored in rocks or crystals. She sensed that the artefact was likely imbued with information. She just needed to interpret it into words.

Was POWAH guiding her so she could see into different dimensions while being wide awake when she noticed auras around people? She could see more than colours recently, although she hadn't tried to develop it.

She settled herself in her chair, allowing her subconscious to take control, and she trusted that the words would flow.

<We are taking you inside one of your body cells. Over 75 trillion cells comprise the human body, each cell as individual as you are. Therefore, you must follow our instruction guide, your body avatar.>

POWAH's instruction was typed out without any effort from her as if time had stood still. She knew every inner journey had a special preparation written in her workbook. Then, a mist-like veil lifted, and she felt as if she was inside a weird-looking structure.

The two tasks, typing and observing, didn't stop her from mentally asking questions.

"Are we now inside a cell?"

Somehow, she had imagined it to be different. She had read somewhere that each cell is like an elemental being that takes care of all its functions like a completely self-sufficient city

< your body cells are the smallest measure of living elemental entities for now. Every fibre of your material body is made from cells. At birth, a baby's body has about ten thousand trillion cells. An adult has 50 to 100 thousand trillion cells.>

She sensed that POWAH was waiting for her to acquaint herself with the environment and movement so she could add her language skills and describe her inner space.

She was still unprepared for the sensation of being an energy form with nobody. For a split second, her anxiety levels flung her backwards into what appeared to her to be a liquid colour substance. Then she was inside, and deep space opened up all around her.

"Oh, are we still inside just one cell?" Her mind translated her visions so fast. She was approaching a landscape that appeared very alien. It reminded her of science fiction movies.

<Let's examine the universe of one cell.>

POWAH's words flashed by her while a starry space opened further due to the sensation of speed. She spotted constructions she couldn't yet fully describe in front and below. She seemed to be behind a control or keyboard panel of sorts. What looked like buildings below her were at the same time like nothing she had ever seen before, as if they were made of liquorice allsorts!

Where had she seen that image before? Suddenly she felt she was being sucked backwards. To her astonishment, the scenery below instantly reminded her of the landscape of her virtual awakening card game! Had Trevor seen a similar view when he designed her computer program? Even Richard mentioned this landscape in his journals, and Ingrid, Toon's wife, had also written in her journal that the ground layout of the Valley of the Gods, if seen from a great distance, resembled an eye symbol.

<Your mind can only translate what it knows. You are inside your body temple, your divine universe. Each cell is like a star. Many clusters of stars form a galaxy, which are your organs. Each vibrates on different frequencies, which create different dimensions.>

She wondered which dimension she was observing now.

<We will take you around 22 galaxies, and you will translate them in terms your readers will understand.>

"Where are we now then, and who else is...?" She could barely form a question. Being in two places all at the same time made her dizzy. She could feel that her fingers were typing away, expressing thoughts into words that her higher mind had intuitively translated, but having no form still gave her dizzy spells.

Suddenly, a new sensation erupted within her as if she were speeding toward what looked like a brilliant inferno. A pyramidal glass structure became larger, and inside, through the transparent walls, she saw a pulsating being – like an entity– that had a tetrahedron shape.

<This beautiful inner sanctuary is what you would call the nucleus. It's like a courthouse where all your genetic information is stored. It is where your genetic decoding will take place to follow your intent, which is Breaking the Death Habit.>

Was she confronted with an alien creature? On closer inspection, she heard the most incredible music. She could feel that her fingers stopped for a split second. Then, they again travelled over her keyboard. Time was no more like all her life experiences merged into the same ...zero point.

"POWAH, can I use this information in my decoding workbook? Will you show me how we can genetically reverse our lifespan? Can our physical body regenerate itself so we can leave this third dimension by choice, not by physically dying?" Her thoughts reminded her that it would hinder her ascension even if she held onto feelings of doubt. When she observed the chaos in the world by watching television, listening to news bulletins, or reading newspapers or magazines on global warming, all that information was not very conducive to her intent.

<Your questions are already answered. Developing a philosophy of physical immortality is the first step. There are many layers of consciousness within your body temple, each reflecting the world you experience externally.>

That everything was a reflection of everything else was not a new idea, but that within her body were different consciousness realms was an idea she had never contemplated before.

POWAH, can information bypass the five senses of my physical body?

< Great question! Yes, as God's image reflects man, the universe is in the image of your immortal body of light. Some call it your resurrection body or your ether body>

That was an awesome thought. Of course. "In my father's house, there are many dimensions." Never had she fully grasped that her body temple was God's universe!

For an instant, she seemed to flip out of her trance state. It was simply worrying. She mustn't forget to type that. Oh, it was so challenging to be in two places simultaneously. Her ego mind was probably lurking nearby to see if there was a flicker of a chance to interfere.

<Why do you think the ancient texts all mention the power of the human mind? You are the temple of the divine, All that is. Your body is, after all, created by your mind.>

What POWAH had voiced in her head meant that each cell in her body was like a universe, also a likeness of All That Is.

When POWAH mentioned 22 different galaxies, she knew that in her workbook, it read that there are 22 elements by which 'God' created the world.

<Yes, and MAN is a divine expression of spirit, reversely expressing LOVE. When humankind's program ends, the external physical world they perceive to be real will be no more.>

It's always the same message. About a program that runs its course.

<When the spirit leaves it, the physical body will perish, but when the human Soul is awakening in their etheric, astral body, the soul is free to travel within its Soul realm universe, then the external world will merge with the inner realms.>

Was that how it would happen? She knew that her thoughts and beliefs formed an external program in her brain. Therefore, people who want to change can create a 'program' to override their inherent programs. That was what her decoding workbook was all about. Still, that didn't explain how to change the 'belief program' so that the human temple will NOT end up ageing, getting ill or dying.

<Every human being can create an effect and thereby attract the change in themselves that they desire, but not many will perceive it to be possible. For them to avoid physical death is impossible. Your Earthly reality will go on as long as human consciousness is evolving. Many will incarnate back into this duality type of reality. Your external life and your 'perceived' reality will continue for as long as you choose.>

Wow! To be in two places all at once was truly remarkable. To be at her computer typing while at the same time being introduced to the entity that was a nucleus within one of her body cells was genuinely superb!

<Your thoughts of everlasting life will produce health. Science has already proven that your beliefs influence your health. What practical value does believing in death have if you desire health? The belief that death is inevitable has probably killed more human temples than all other causes combined.>

Typing the telepathic thoughts into words still interacted with her emotions. It was impossible not to separate her inner journey from her outer world. She tried to focus on POWAH's spectacular light show, especially when the spinning tetrahedron gave away to a form.

She knew or had read somewhere that platonic solids are believed to be the geometrical internal structures of the atom. Leo explained that the grid structure in her workbook must be seen as an actual fractal and holographic. Having this vision of the world inside a cell, she grasped that they span all of Creation, including its many consciousness levels. They are not just on Earth but correspond to the entire Universe on many higher spiritual levels. The Physical Universe could not exist without these Grids.

After what appeared to be a long silence, a voice, like a musical orchestra, started to stir the elemental creature within the nucleus.

Its electrifying shooting sparkles turned into words, saying, "God is in every cell of your body."

POWAH's loving energy that enveloped her whole formless field felt euphoric... but what about...?

"What about people who have already passed on?" She beamed while hovering before her nucleus. Then, yet another entity appeared that showed the face of Theo, Richard's older brother! Or was that because she thought of him, and so she saw him?

It hurts when Theo leaves Holland to be on his own, dying in solitude. For a while, her feelings had turned into anger. How could he go? Why not share his last days on Earth with his brother and her?

"Annie, I learned that if death were inevitable and beyond our control, to believe in immortality wouldn't hurt you all; that is why I had to leave. The cause of death is pollution in the etheric body. That's why I am here to show you what ages and kills the human body. Toxins!"

Her physical heart skipped a beat! *"Theo? Is that you?"* She mentally shouted and instantly knew it had to be Richard's late brother, her very close soul mate. He was a lot younger, but that had never changed how she felt towards him. Was he now really communicating with her? Had he died in solitude, away from everyone dear to him? His telepathic signature felt the same as when he was in the flesh.

"Annie, I'm interacting with you, POWAH and the artefact Leo found. We three are projecting from one mind, one source. We form a relationship as one."

That might be the case, but for now, she could not imagine Theo, POWAH, and the rock to form one unity unless there was no orientation.

"Indeed, Annie, the "I Am" notion goes around and around, forming one vortex of energy that goes in and out of itself. Therefore, you can't die, you can't go away, you can neither add nor subtract. There is always a continual pulse. That is immortality!"

How awesome, and she was going to learn all about what killed the human body. Was it the food we buy or grow and prepare? She suspected that already. Physical pollution must happen through food and the fumes we breathe in. Or what about our genetic ancestral lineage and our past lives, or our interactions with other people who are harmless in and of themselves but who overdose on eating, smoking and drugs, not to mention emotional traumas?

"Annie, even if you survive old age, illness, and accidents and practice the techniques of rebirthing and affirmation, your own belief in death will get you in the end – unless you change it. Each I.Am must build its etheric, astral body, so the I. Am of each individual can experience immortality."

Ooh, was that directed at her? Her nightmare that the artefact had brought on the first time. Why the fear? What had that reflected in her? Where had these unsettling visions come from? Were any of her organs not in good shape?

"Annie, getting rid of physical and energy body pollution faster than we take it in is the spiritual purification game. That is what our awakening game is all about. The more you all master this awakening game in everyday life, the more you all can live in the Christ-conscious Spirit. Humanity must bypass the fear of physical death by playing the spiritual purification game."

Ooh, was that directed at her again? Recalling the blond woman in the video, why could she still feel the energy of fear? What is it that reflects in her? For a split second, her mind drifted, questioning: were any of her organs not in good shape?

"Annie, your workbook and journal must include how you unravelled your death urge. Your belief program is absorbed by your three energy bodies from family tradition, past lives, culture, and mostly what science tells you."

For a split second, Theo came into focus. Theo appeared a lot in Richard's journal, especially while he was out of his body during sleep. He had also perceived it as being out, away from his body.

More than ever did she know that she had been prepared for this work of how to travel on the ascension path. She must have chosen it with Theo and the others from the Jaarsma Clan.

For an instant, she imagined that she was looking over her shoulder and reading the text as it appeared on her screen. That must be because hunger pangs from skipping breakfast made her think from her body's point of view. What happened to the apple she ate for breakfast, not to mention the tea she had swallowed?

"Annie, let's take a look. Did you know that your tongue mirrors our internal organs, especially the organs of the digestive tract?"

No, she didn't. Again, it felt like she had been transported from one dimension into another within her inner universe. For a split second, her anxiety levels seemed to fling her backwards into what appeared to be a coloured liquid. Then she was inside.

"Oh, are we inside my mouth?" Her mind translated her visions so fast, as if she was inside a huge floating tank often used at many spas.

<Yes, excellent. Your mouth's basic temperament and function are unemotional since it mashes and liquefies ingested food and drink.>

As POWAH's words flashed, giant portholes on the sides of what appeared to be a 'floating tank' opened up. With a roaring sound, ticklish liquid sprays filled her whole mouth.

"What do you mean by unemotional? I've often put food into my mouth while I was emotional." She beamed, *"Is eating or starving oneself not an emotionally loaded action."*

Surely, she could think of many almost multi-layered reasons for eating. Either human beings eat to satisfy hunger, or there is a need to fill up due to emotional shocks hidden in a person's energy field. The image of a fridge magnet almost made her lose her concentration. Being in two places simultaneously made her dizzy until she felt that her fingers were still typing away, expressing what her higher mind had intuitively translated into words.

"Annie, we were not referring to what 'human beings' do when feeling hungry. That is an external observation. Someone looking through a microscope at what you see now observes an automatic cellular function. We see how the mouth mashes and liquefies ingested food and drink."

Theo's signature seemed to be different from POWAH's. Oh, she had been analytical as usual. Her inner vision projected a chamber of sorts so utterly foreign she was indeed back in an elemental environment.

< Your tongue is also a sense organ. Through its sense of taste, the tongue detects the relative concentrations of various nutrients in the food and signals to the digestive organs which digestive juices and enzymes they should secrete.>

Gee the noise! Were POWAH and Theo inside her human body? It was as if she was transported into a stock exchange hall where everyone was simultaneously shouting at everyone! Much information was being directed in all directions, probably sending signals through her whole universal body. Added loudspeakers were shouting all at once. Especially as she swallowed her tea or when her teeth broke off a piece of her apple, the digesting noises were amplified, showing how incredibly hard her body worked when she swallowed. The sounds reminded her of water running out of a plug hole.

<Exactly, your inner world is never silent. Your taste buds, especially, are very clever. For example, the taste of french fries will tell the gall bladder to secrete a lot of bile.>

She almost laughed out loud when her mind translated the tip of her tongue funnily. Elemental creatures grabbed hold of chunks of sweeties, including pieces of salty drop she was so fond of, and shouting voices told her that all that garbage stressed them out! Then she recognised where her taste organs were situated. The sour and bitter receptor buds were to be found on the side of her tongue.

<Correct, and the smell of food is sensed by the olfactory receptors in your nose. The sense of smell is much more complex than that of taste. It can distinguish many subtle variations. The senses of taste and smell work together to enable you to recognise and appreciate flavours.>

There was so much more to her inner universe than she could have ever imagined on her own. Then, what appeared to be a humanoid male figure turned towards her, threw his right arm up towards a patchwork of bright colours, and asked, *"How about this?"* All she heard was her speech! The words she uttered were forming mutable colour waves! They showed her that there is an endless outflow of creation due to every word she spoke out loud! She felt herself tumbling gently and sliding over her tongue, which enabled her to form words.

"Yes, your mouth, especially your teeth, lips, and tongue, are essential for speech. Your lips, which line the outside of your mouth, help hold food while you chew and also help you pronounce words."

Theo's mental chatter made her think of an advert selling toothpaste. Someone's smile with the help of a mouthful of teeth was always attractive. At the same time, teeth provide structural support for the facial muscles. How awesome. That is often the first thing people notice: a smile. It didn't matter what age, but the most endearing was from a baby.

"Annie, that was the first thing I noticed about you. Your smile."

"Oh really?" She beamed, feeling almost giddy with happiness, hearing Theo's telepathic response to her thoughts as she was sliding down over her tongue, which finally ended in a dark void.

"Yes, it's the facial expression that most engages others. Your mouth also forms your frown, and lots of other expressions show on your face. Your clairvoyant abilities will significantly improve now that you can rapidly shift your mind inwards.

"Annie, next time, I will show you why you must move towards a more alkaline diet."

She knew from reading up on it that an alkaline diet is essential for optimum health. However, seeing how her apple was digested and sorted out was incredible; many chemical entities worked on an assembly line. Each had a unique job to do. Were they all reflecting the consciousness she expressed?

"Yes, they do. That is why it's important to focus on your physical body when moving from your inner third dimension into the inner fourth density. The fourth density is much more full of life."

Now she grasped why people must especially care for their physical body temple, their inner universe, with its unending deep space...where multidimensional experiences are digested in many ways. It was teaming with life. Then POWAH added:

<Remember to move into a density where compassion, understanding and love are the predominant energies. It would be best if you embodied those Soul qualities.>

To her amazement, she saw and heard how symbolic shapes, like the Language of Light symbols from Tieneke's workbook, trailed past, playing a symphony. The movement created a feeling so uplifting that now she could see these symbols' harmonising effect on her trillion body cells, like stars highlighting her inner universe.

"Annie, you and your participants must reflect a balanced melody from within and externally. Do educate yourself about food and healthy diets for every individual. Their diet change will bring changes to the inside of their body temple, which will materialise on their external reality. See your reality as if you are all living within one large physical body."

Could her dream have been a warning? Almost like an example of what her inner universe looked like. That was somewhat alarming. She had interpreted it differently, like a predictive future vision.

"Remember, Annie, that every cell that makes up your physical body is a reflector. Its outside membrane can be seen as a mirror, reflecting the thoughts and actions of your food."

Her stiffness brought her attention back to her body inside her office and the external world. Her apple core had already turned brown, and twenty-two minutes had passed.

***

She was back awake, sitting at her computer like she'd been in a trance. The artefact on Ben's side of the desk looked normal.

Looking at her screen and reading her typed words, she was dumbfounded about the twenty-two decoding experiences that translated structurally. Not only was that what she had asked for, especially her workbook structure, but she'd already followed that without knowing why!

"Annie, remember that time is more of an external illusion. Your physical manifestations are always first established in your etheric causal realm as a trial run. You have intuitively picked up on what structure to use."

"A full conversion from fourth-density towards a fifth level of awareness will occur between 2020 and 2026, along with conscious bathing, breathing, purification, detoxing treatments and time spent on creative projects. Only then will the truth behind exercising and healthy eating habits heal all diseases."

This time, she heard Theo in the same way that she could communicate with POWAH, but his signature differed from that of POWAH—more like it was her higher self.

The pieces of the decoding puzzle were coming together. Twenty-two fractals, spacings or cards were to be created within her workbook. Each spacing showed the participants the condition of their inner universe.

Her Physical Youth Body Code Vibration 7- through the Crown chakra is Freedom.[1]

Her telepathic intuitive interaction with Theo was a journey in itself, the first step on her journey. It had started by entering into her mouth. We are what we eat, so that made sense.

"That is for sure." Theo telepathically replied.

She was strongly urged to turn around in her chair to see if she could see Theo instead of just hearing him.

"Would each individual who shifts past this third-dimensional veil perceive it as being on the other side, except that it would be a dreamlike reality, a fifth dimension?" The way this shift in reality would be experienced was still unimaginable.

---

1. https://allrealityshifters.wordpress.com/six-youth-and-physical-soul-quality-codes/

There was a lot to do, but for now, sitting down and typing further on her keyboard was asking for trouble. Her body needed to stretch again she needed to get up onto her one foot, use her crutches and move around.

"Annie, for now, you all still perceive a very abrupt wall, or veil, that separates you from me. That is the illusion. It does not. You all need to cross that head game, and then we will all move into a higher dimension together. None of us would even be aware of it since we never left God's creation in the first place."

Joris was now staring at her as if to say, who is it that you are talking to? His tail was wagging. His inner universe was alerting him that it would soon be feeding time.

Head game or not, she was still plainly dealing with this reality, so she stood up, got her crutches and hopped into the kitchen. Theo would have to give her some slack.

As she was about to open the fridge to get Joris his dinner, she read what the magnet on her fridge door in the kitchen said:

When loneliness is experienced, humans go to the fridge. When people can't understand what's happening in the world, they go to the refrigerator. When people feel unfulfilled in their work or marriage, they go to the fridge. Some go to the fridge for different reasons, but what you see inside will tell you. Your reality is written on the inside of this fridge.

After feeding Joris, she giggled. Mien gave her that magnet years ago when they shared a flat in Sea Point. She had been depressed in those days before she and Mien had split up to each go their ways. She wondered how Mien was doing now that Harry had joined her. She had twice tried to connect with her mentally but without success. It was still a shame that they never went to the Hogsback to see if Nadifa's cottage was still there. Maybe Ben might be persuaded to visit South Africa again when she is completely healed, and their life at Halfway House gives them more time.

Having lunch on her own was always a challenge. Skipping lunch was always an option, but then she knew that she would eat twice as much by dinner time, which in her present condition was not wise. Yesterday, they did some last-minute shopping after Trevor had left Joris behind with them since he was on the way to give a lecture in Amsterdam.

Shame, Joris was unsettled. He watched her as if to say, what now, are we going into the garden? She opened the back door for him, but he was not interested in going out.

This time, her normal routine with the things she usually bought changed. Now that they were practically camping in her house, she opted for easily prepared snacks and salads.

Standing on one foot while leaning against the counter preparing food had proven tiring, so her kitchen habits had changed.

Gosh, how this one relatively minor accident had already created so many changes.

The sun was out, and it reminded her of her plants. Why not enjoy her lunch in her conservatory while she still could? She improved at going around the house on crutches, but her balance on one foot was still not great. At least there was less clutter now that most of their household goods had been packed into boxes.

After watering the plants that were still left in her conservatory, she hobbled back to her office to read her emails before Ben arrived home. She was proud of her plants. They loved her as Joris did; she could feel it.

She hoped that Quincy would look after her plants the same way that she had done. It almost felt like she was saying goodbye to them all, and they sensed it.

While her computer was downloading her emails, she took Ingrid's and Richard's journals from the shelf. She wanted to read again what message they had written about in their sixteenth chapters.

Her eye travelled back to Ben's desk, where the old papyrus scroll was still resting next to the artefact Leo had given him so she could find out if she could pick up any impressions. Richard said an old English colonel had first discovered this ancient scroll. He had painstakingly copied the script onto a thin copper sheet that Leo, Trevor and Theo had carefully translated.

There it was. In Ingrid's journal, the message was: Handing over the Lower will and Surrendering to the Higher Self. She knew what had transpired today was because her higher self had been in the driver's seat. The translations from the scroll were published in Richard's journal **Orphanage of Souls**.[2]

The translation read: When Myths Rule the Game, and the last two coded messages were: Know of thy bondage, know how to free thyself from the illusional wars. Out of the darkness shall ye rise upward to travel to the stars.

Be aware of massive Earth changes, along with pole shifts. These occurrences have been well documented in your ancient myths.

What had the author been trying to say, when he painstakingly carved on the papyrus leaves, that we needed to look into the ancient myths?

Suddenly, her fax started to print. In small print, she read:

Many generations ago, Queen Numbi and her people saw a burning white light like a star fall out of the sky. The story is that it was not a star but a shining ball of metal, brighter than the Sun. And when this ball came down to the ground. Queen Numbi, a sick older woman then, went towards the light and was swallowed by it. She had become a much younger woman after entering the light.

An eery feeling came over her again, as if the metallic artefact and the papyrus scroll tried to nudge her about something.

---

2. https://books2read.com/u/m0eMKP

Chapter 17
The Valley of the Gods

Apeldoorn

Joris' sudden alertness told her that Ben had arrived. He made doggy noises in the hallway from pure happiness when he heard the car tyres on the gravel driveway.

"Hello there, finish what you planned to do today?" Ben called out, peeping around the office door. She could see that he had had a difficult day. His energy felt very troubled, and his aura felt sharp flickers. She stood up, resting on one foot to hug him.

"Surfaced into our world, have you?" He beamed.

"Why are you saying that? Do I look as if I have?"

"You look a bit...spaced out, what happened?" His strong arms around her felt good. Ben was her lover, partner and best friend in this life, but Theo was her twin-soul. He was the other half of herself, but both men held an essential place in her heart.

"Mmm...while you were out today, I'd... Never mind. Ben, tell me first how your brother found that metallic-looking artefact. Do you know?" Ben helped her walk with her crutches towards the kitchen.

"Leo? You know that they are always exploring underneath the tunnels where Toon is expanding his Valley of the God's park, and ever since that last bomb blast, so much more has come to the surface; even Toon has difficulty keeping people at bay."

"Like who?"

Gosh, she hadn't even thought about dinner! Instead, she asked questions. Knowing that his day was nothing like hers had been. She felt somehow guilty.

"Come, I'll make coffee while you unwind and tell me about your day." She would share later that the artefact had triggered her multidimensional consciousness, but first things first.

"Are you managing, or shall I get your wheelchair?"

Joris kept jumping up to Ben as if to say: take me out to the back garden.

"You go and take Joris out. I'll be fine." Lately, she has improved at using her crutches while resting on one foot protected by an air boot. Ben took Joris for a stroll while she took some easy meals from the freezer.

When they came back, Ben had difficulty explaining his day. She knew he had an appointment with her younger brother Fred, who owned a bookshop in town after the trial. He would take over the mortgage of their house and pay them the current value. She didn't know that André, a detective who had become a family friend, had followed up on some instructions Ben had given him in connection with another upcoming trial.

"Annie, I hope you have not prepared anything since we will meet Hans and Liesbeth at the Pannekoek for supper."

"Oh, good that you tell me, that is perfect with me. I'd better put this ready-made dinner back into the freezer." With the help of her crutches, she went to their bedroom to change into something appropriate.

Upstairs, all she could think about was her inner body journey experience. She knew that her visualisations were created by her brain waves, like her intuitively 'knowing', but the message she was left with about the structure of her workshops could have been a warning ahead of time. Soul memory records can't be accessed linearly, only from experiences, and lately, she seemed to have had access to her holographic memory where time and space did not exist.

The colourful caftan she bought in Kalk Bay reminded her of a book with photos of boulders and rock profiles around Cape Town. It was still lying on the window seat. Of course, that is why her soul record had brought that information to the foreground. She had been in contact with massive boulders when they stayed in Titanya's cottage. From that moment, she had started having visions while wide awake. Yesterday morning, when she had begun to sort out which books to take with them to France for the library at Half-way House, she had studied the pictures in this book on sacred sites in the Western Cape near Clovelly. She had her higher mind use the images to translate the message from the artefact.

When they were in Clovelly, visions surfaced in her dream, especially a towering rock structure that seemed to touch the sky.

A few evenings ago, when they had watched a video projection, the scene was so disturbing she wanted to stop looking...since she was in it!

"Annie, do you need some help?"

Gosh, she'd better stop reminiscing. The last boxes in their bedroom were the evidence that they would soon move away from Holland. Would Ben settle elsewhere, away from the unofficial office he had run from their Apeldoorn home?

"No, I can manage, but I'm just slower." She beamed back.

Being an independent detective had often taken him away on business. For the last few years, he mainly worked as an undercover agent for insurance companies. Still, last year, the episode involving Toon's large construction project, The Valley of The Gods pleasure park, had kept Ben away from his usual contacts in the police force. Ben was pleased When he was asked to join Trevor and Richard in their underground workspace in France. Sometimes, Ben revelled in his job, but being a detective was not always fun. Lately, ever since he had opened himself up to the perceptions his twin brother held dear, he admitted that he now understood why Leo suspected that people like Jaarsma clan members held ancient secret codes in the cellular memories that were now being activated.

"Annie, I promised to meet Hans and Liesbeth at the Pannekoek coffee shop at 7."

It was just after six, time enough to seal at least the box with the books. After returning from their holiday, Annelies did at least three boxes per day. She had managed to pack even with her temporary handicap. She would be ready in two days before the removal van arrived. Gosh, would she miss this house? Especially this bedroom that held good memories.

Next time, the venue for her decoding classes would be at the Halfway House. Many participants from her ascension workshops, who had played the virtual ascension game on the first two levels with their Language of Light cards in her home, would spend a whole week at the guest house in France.

She was looking forward to that, but lots had to be organised from her side, so she had better get on with it.

Their ascension journals, which Liesbeth edited into novels, were to become the memoirs of a group soul's experience from the moment they chose to participate in the awakening game.

Her Left Hemisphere Code -23 External expressions

Today, that numeral vibration has started to make sense. It linked to her Soul's purpose of her numeral 5, the Breath of Life. Number 23 carries a message from Source that you are supported in your endeavours. She recalled doodling both symbols during one of Tieneke's workshops long ago.

It had taken at least thirty years for her to write about why and how her first encounter with her higher guide POWAH had occurred, but she still kept questioning whether it was her conscious lower ego mind or her higher mind penetrating her thoughts.

Ben projected.

"Annie, are you ready? I'm waiting for you in the car. Do you need any help coming down? Your wheelchair is in the hallway."

"Oh yes, yes, I'm coming," while suppressing a slight annoyance with herself at running her life the way she did.

POWAH's parting whisper, which sounded like "Remember, forgiveness", settled her mood as she sat on the steps, heaved herself down the stairs, and slid into her wheelchair. She rolled herself out through the front door towards Ben, who was already waiting outside, holding the door open so she could slide into the front passenger seat.

"What or who do you need to forgive?" Ben asked.

"Never mind, go, we will be late." She said out loud. She kissed his cheek when he joined her in the car.

"Mmm, you're still a dish, you know."

"So are you, drop-dead-gorgeous, I mean." She meant it. The scars from the brutal attack he had experienced last year had all healed.

She waved at their neighbour as they pulled out of their driveway. She reminded herself that she mustn't forget to say a proper goodbye.

"Did you have further success with holding the rock Trevor brought back? I asked you but never received an answer." Ben's question reminded her of the message the boulder with the profile had told her. It was ringing in her ears as they drove away.

"It's during these times when an opportunity has presented itself again for other intelligent species to infiltrate humanity on Planet Earth while a great awakening will occur. Please be warned. Wake up from your illusionary world. Otherwise, humanity will become a slave race once again."

Somehow, while the scenery outside flashed by, it had awoken more dialogue she had not recalled.

<Humanity must awaken to their Spiritual knowledge within in order not to lose their freedom to another more mentally advanced creation that has already lost its god-given gift of compassion. Only then will humans be able to join as a galactic species and ascend further towards the light>

POWAH was referring to a dream she had only partly shared with Ben, especially about her inner body journey. She had to be sure that it was not her imagination.

"Ben, I'm still having to come to terms with the dream I had. I panicked from the sheer urgency, which woke me up."

"Really? Was that why you were typing away early in your office yesterday morning? Are you going to share it with me? Your thoughts tell me that there is more."

Ben's manoeuvring in the heavy traffic due to the many bicycles reminded her to stay in the now.

Ben had not telepathically heard her thoughts clearly when she recalled her episode from yesterday. They were still driving a car, but many people were impoverished by the global economic meltdown. It was showing on the roads. There were far fewer cars. Toon had even said that his major holdings were losing their value. He was taking more capital from his enterprises to plough it back into the various communities worldwide. His next project was to set up an internet-based community where everyone could participate freely. The forum was linked to the Valley of the Gods Park.

"How long do you think we can maintain driving a car?"

"Petrol driven, a couple of years, but Toon is investing in that new company that already has an assembly line going."

"Already?"

"Yep, self-powered energy vehicles. They can be powered independently of any natural energy reserves. Self-generating vehicles are the only answer to get ourselves out of this hole we've dug for ourselves."

They arrived at the Pannekoek just as it was getting dark. Spring was in the air. It was just after 7.00 that Liesbeth saw them, for she waved from behind a window. The wind was still strong, and heavy grey skies promised more rain.

"Hi Mom, glad you could make it," Hans said, holding the door open. "Liesbeth and Tieneke have to leave within an hour."

Whenever she saw Liesbeth, she still had to get used to the idea that her long-lost baby daughter had grown up so close for many years without her ever knowing about it. Thank goodness her kidnap story from so long ago had not been splashed in all the papers when Liesbeth's story became known to Ben and herself. Forty years ago, the publicity had made no difference in solving the crime, but today, the media would have exploited her dramatic story. It would serve only to wake up more unpleasant memories. She would rather deal with them gradually.

"Where is Tieneke?"

"She is picking me up. She's not joining us for supper; she has some errands and is running late."

"Don't you dislike driving in the dark? Why not wait for tomorrow?"

"Mom, we have a meeting tomorrow morning, and Tieneke likes driving after hours. We will be fine."

"I already miss you, sweety." She whispered, kissing her. *"I have so much to share with you all."* She was by now bursting the tell about her inner body experiences. A large flat TV screen on the wall she had never seen promoted a dining card. Why would that be advertised unless...

"You will soon join us, won't you?" Liesbeth beamed.

"Yes, love, it depends on many things. But let's not discuss that. I would like to know how we can wake up people about how dangerous it is to listen to the daily news, the TV or media, or even advertising, like that TV over there."

"Miens partner must be looking for ways to attract more customers to finance the sale of the coffee shop. Who knows." Ben remarked, shrugging his shoulders as he rearranged the chairs so that her wheelchair could get near the table.

"Mom, remember that dysfunctional input helps society fulfil the prophecy it constantly witnesses on TV. Any media that keeps people away from their inner world is supported by the elite of our society. "

Ben agreed, making her recall what he had mumbled before sleeping last night. A family with three children was watching what was showing on the big screen instead of having a conversation together, and so was a couple on a separate table, who seemed too young to be married or even have a long-standing relationship. They were all mesmerized by the TV.

"Mom, because the media has also become polluted because the political arena distorts our world-view by excessively focusing on external events or situations none of us have personally experienced."

Hans' reply was so true. Hans and Liesbeth were far more aware of what was being played out, which was noticeable in how they generally responded to things. Liesbeth reminded her that she had said she had something to share, so she told them about her inner journey while they were all studying the menu. They were all entertained when she recalled how busy her inner world was when she had eaten an apple. With a smile, Hans asked if she would be more aware of what would pass her mouth.

They all ordered dinner from a young girl who was a new addition to the Pannekoek. Richard no longer ran it for his aunt Mien. Richard and Sascia, his girlfriend, had moved to Halfway House at the beginning of the year while she and Ben were vacationing in South Africa.

It was a joke when Hans suggested a melted cheeseburger from the menu since Hans and Liesbeth ate very healthy food. She playfully thumped him on his shoulder. They would rarely eat anything that was cooked or fried. Liesbeth asked for a glass of warm water with a slice of lemon, but she felt like a tomato cocktail.

Ben asked Hans why the media was seen as being toxic, as he called it after the waitress had served their main course.

"Dad, because our human brain, subconsciously, cannot distinguish between what it experiences and what it is shown. Any corrupt information during the change over time is especially harmful."

"TV and the internet are often misleading. Annie, is that subject mentioned in your workshops?" When the waitress appeared at their table, Ben telepathically asked her if they needed anything. They all studied Annelie's facial expression, being telepathic. Movies were often discussed during her workshops, but never what was on the internet.

"How we think and respond are the output of programs stored in our brain. Since these programs are malleable, any information we hear, read, or experience makes us who we appear to be." Liesbeth reminded them all.

Now she understood why she had been very shaken by what the artefact had stirred within her subconscious, as if what she dreamed about had already happened or was soon going to happen.

"Mommy, do you know why we think we dream? We are all but thought within the mind of the creator." Liesbeth beamed, smiling, reminding her of the illusion of her so-called reality.

"Probably, but in our physical reality, bad news brings pain. Good news brings pleasure. So why not focus now on the uplifting, inspirational, forgiving news and, above all, unifies us as a global species to be reckoned with?" She replied out loud.

The coffee bar was not very busy. The energy was also different now since it had changed hands. She recalled that Mien had mentioned a friend who wanted to take over her business so she could be with her children in South Africa, but now that Sonja might settle in Holland, she wondered... Some of Sascia's framed photos still decorate the coffee shop's wall. She hoped the new owners would keep displaying them.

Ben told them about the scroll and the artefact and why Trevor had brought them back again. Hans and Liesbeth were unaware that Trevor had scheduled several lectures in Utrecht.

"I think it was sudden. Trevor was asked to fill in for someone." Ben explained.

While looking around, her mind trailed away...to past times.

The Jaarsma Clan, her soul family, had often held informal meetings at the Pannekoek, especially when she held her ascension workshop classes in the evenings. That would not be happening anymore.

"I reckon that while most people constantly misrepresent the scale of a threat, which keeps the populace in a mental siege, an enormous control has been achieved," Ben spoke with contempt.

She had not followed their conversation about networks on the internet. It reminded her of the website Gerrit had told her about.

"Many people don't listen anymore to news on TV or radio. Reading of newspapers has also dropped. Instead, the subscriptions to website newsletters investigating all angles of a newsworthy story have tripled this year." Liesbeth's soft voice still held a lot of power.

"Dad, remember that Uncle Trevor wrote in one of his emails that the world is still heavily controlled by a network of secret societies, intending to create a new world order and a one-world government."

"Yes, but then Trevor loves these conspiracy theories."

"The foundation for modern-day secret organizations was laid by Cecil Rhodes, a British imperialist in South Africa not so?"

Hans nodded while enjoying his dinner. He always followed her thoughts, which just now were in the political arena in South Africa.

"A well-known politician reminded everyone that the media all over the world is working hard to make us, humanity, believe that global unity is the road to freedom, when in fact it is the road to enslavement," Ben telepathically responded since someone came over to their table.

The young waitress asked if they wanted to order dessert. It was getting late, so they declined.

"Ben, if the Illuminati succeeds in microchipping the population at large, could that also stop the great awakening from happening?"

Ben looked at her with surprise. "I never knew that you knew my real assignment." Having both conversations going on at the same time was typical for many members of the Jaarsma clan.

"Probably, if we do believe that. Leo said that a microchip can slow down the speed at which our bodies vibrate, preventing humans globally from reaching higher levels of awakening. Who knows. Scary thought, hey?" Ben replied out loud. "So, the people who appear on your Jaarsma Clan star map must know about that unless it all makes no difference since the lower realms are an illusion." He added while shrugging his shoulders.

"Dad, you are right; it might just pull back the veil from the edge of the illusion...especially if we accept that there is a higher guidance that has a plan," Hans added while Liesbeth smiled.

"Oh, and do you know what that plan might be, wise guy?" She tickled Hans, guessing that he probably knew.

Hans never replied; they all got up to get their coats. At the same time, Ben paid the bill until Tieneke arrived. What good timing. Liesbeth said goodbye, and Hans had things to do, so he left separately.

There were still some feelings of sadness lurking when she waved to Liesbeth as they drove away. She often wished to catch up by spending more time with her.

She fondly thought of Tieneke, who generously shared her symbolic drawings and wrote The Language of Light workbook. They would arrive at Halfway House during the night.

She understood today why they all met their true soul mates later in life. Toon, her half-brother, with Ingrid, who had joined her ascension workshops. Yolanda, her niece, and Eddie from Australia. Her brother Fred ran a bookshop in the centre of Apeldoorn with Quincy, Ingrid's sister. Gerrit, her half-brother whom she had discovered a few months ago, was bringing Adel, an art teacher.

All these couples had triggered their awakening codes on a cellular level, so their lives had changed drastically.

Soon, she hoped to add Tieneke and Trevor to her list of twin soul couples. Trevor was much older than her, but she did not think that would be an issue. For now, she kept that thought to herself. Tieneke had not fully developed her telepathic skills, so that idea was safely hidden.

Ben wheeled her to their car in the parking lot. She had used crutches when inside, but the wheelchair was still much more comfortable.

Some people wanted to know what had happened to her and were expressing their horror that it had to happen in South Africa of all places. Most people seemed to think that there was no health care there. Ben then used the opportunity to promote the group positively by telling them about their experiences.

Some were pleasantly surprised since they were ignorant about what other countries offer regarding health care.

She knew that being insured during a holiday was a wise decision; otherwise, it would have been an expensive experience.

Ben was getting very good at folding the wheelchair into the boot of their car while she had learned how to slide in and out of the passenger's seat, holding onto the handles near the seatbelts.

The Jaarsma Clan's Last Meeting in Holland.

"Ingrid, how are you?" Annelies commented with amusement at Ingrid's heavily pregnant bulk while Toon held on to her as if his wife would deliver their child in her hallway. The baby was due any day now.

"I tell you, this baby girl is into interior design; she keeps rearranging her living quarters," Ingrid grumbled, but with joy.

Toon grinned wide as he carried Ingrid's suitcase.

"Well, it's a girl. Soon, she will have all the space she needs. You should see her room!" Ingrid giggled in lightheartedness. "Toon went crazy buying toys."

"Toon, make Ingrid comfy in the conservatory while I call Ben," she commanded.

"Gosh, Annie, it takes some getting used to seeing you like this."

"Well, it will not be for long, Toon. Soon, I will be on my feet again, running after a crawling baby."

Joris was making sure Toon and Ingrid knew that he had missed them. He followed the couple everywhere. He knew that his main boss was Toon.

"Annie, how long will it take before you can walk normally, go for hikes and so on?" Ingrid asked.

"I keep hearing five months, but I hope it will be sooner."

They were the first to arrive. The whole morning, Annelies spent catching up on correspondence from the ascension topic website so

there, and it was not so far for the rest to drive just over the border into France.

"POWAH told me that we, in a sense, are being re-booted with attunements that are re-harmonizing us, calibrating us toward the coming changes. So, if we hold onto our thoughts and their manifestations that still create feelings of fear, then these new harmonisations reflect information in our visions. So remember, we are all co-creators. Nothing will change if we separate ourselves due to beliefs about who is right and who is wrong. These are the end-time obstacles we all need to recognise within ourselves. Everything is a mirror. I would rather keep my thoughts in check and go within. I hope that our thinking minds can perceive this information." As she said it, she tried to hide her deeper anxiety. No one replied because André, the detective, walked in.

André reacted just as surprised, seeing her using crutches. Ben had not told him about her accident in South Africa.

"Yes, I did. What do you think? André was the one that got Interpol involved because I was officially on holiday, remember?"

"I like to hold on to some sanity while at the same time finding out what has stirred all this chaos." She said as she greeted André.

Toon showed André the legal document. She had met André for the first time as Ben's younger partner when he worked on cases Interpol handed them.

His fiancée Ula, who had worked at the same firm Ingrid worked for last year, was the connecting link to yet another person that appeared on the Star map. She never mentioned that revelation to anyone until they would be ready to hear it.

"Toon, excuse me for asking, but...what made you so different from the directors or owners of oil companies who were secretly working with one of Iran's top nuclear scientists on natural gas-related projects." André still held some resistance or was still suspicious about some of the Jaarsma Clan members.

"Am I so different? Thank goodness that I'm where I am at this moment of my life.

Toon's grin spoke more than words ever could as he carried on.

"Years back, at the time of the 9/11 attacks, I had unpleasant dealings with the head of a 13 billion dollar private firm. My father had dealings with him thirty years ago, so I was warned. Still, when this company started to invest people's pension funds in other companies that made money when America was at war with Iraq, I withdrew or closed all the contracts we ever had with them. Many business people who knew what I did said they could not pull out if they wanted to. Instead, they made many billions of dollars from the war on terror, so they had to convince people like me, and especially the American public, that war was the only solution to freedom! That was a lie, and I knew it. That was the time when I pulled out completely. Well before the economic collapse. And they never forgave me for it."

"Toon, do you think the same businessman is responsible for what happened last year?" Ingrid called out in horror.

"Kitty, don't even contemplate about who was responsible for what. Think of our baby." They all heard Toon's mental reply, except for André.

"I reckon we are talking about a large amount of money?" André fished.

"More than what Bill Gates is worth."

"Wow, that is something. So you think that what has all happened, the fact that you got shot, Ingrid's kidnapping, the destruction of the Prinsegracht Hotel, Ben's attack on life; all those incidences stem from one source?" André exclaimed in doubt. "Or...is it linked to the fortune that you have withdrawn from companies who are still corrupt?"

"André, there is significant opposition from brave people worldwide who choose to face the wrath and hostility of the

Illuminati's authority, so we must do the same. Those who have their perceptions as a cultural software program implanted by Illuminati authority, well, we all have to forgive them for their ignorance and for their determination to do what they think is right for human beings."

She hoped that André was able to follow her reasoning. She suspected a far more sinister plot was behind their chaos and misfortune. That was what Nadifa had told her long ago: to be aware that many people will be changing on a cellular level and that they could be followed due to their awakening DNA strands that have been dormant for so long.

"I know that the pioneers of a warless world today are young people that refuse military service," Fred added.

"Annie, so you knew?" Ben beamed as he rested his hands on her shoulder. She nodded in reply.

"Toon, but something or some experience must have made you turn around. Was it the 9/11 event?" André asked.

"Mmm, in my twenties and thirties, I was drawn to reading books on mythical legends, anthroposophical topics and scientific theories behind symbols that originated in antiquity. Especially the Sufis, who have used oral traditions for centuries to identify individuals and their roles, but Rudolf Steiner helped me understand who, how and why we incarnate during these times."

Toon winked at Ingrid when she raised her eyebrows. She noticed that Ingrid kept stroking herself on her side. The baby must be kicking.

"I started to question if that was all a lie because the western Churches condemned all kinds of occultism with the strongest words and penalties, believing it is from the devil. Once you start questioning and asking for guidance in your quest, you soon start to see life from a different viewpoint. My perceptions changed, and so did my goals and ambitions in life."

"Mmm, yes, I suppose I can understand that. So you believe as well that everything from mass mind control, economic enslavement, political control, media control, and military control, all these tactics are being used to bring about complete domination?"

André was in a questioning mood, alright. Ben winked at her.

"Remember Annie, how we argued years ago till early in the mornings about how the lower astral realms established an illusional reality."

"Yes, André, with barely a whimper, we have condoned the loss of our values and free-thinking, the loss of control of our minds. That is the scariest idea, which we all have to be aware of every moment we suspect that we are not operating from our higher self-awareness." Toon reminded them how easy it was to be bulldozed into a belief program.

"André, don't you agree that those in influential positions who are probably still making unwanted decisions for us have almost succeeded in bringing forth a global government or new world order?" Fred joined in while Quincy served them all coffee and cake. She was not allowed to do a thing. André didn't answer Fred.

"They... let's call them a dark shadow consciousness that seems to control the Illuminati. This wealthy group of people held powerful positions worldwide for thousands of years. They have invaded our religious institutions, schools, our economy, our history and culture, our political strongholds, and even our minds." Fred remarked further with a firm tone of conviction.

When Annelies heard the last car arrive on the gravel, she realised that the dreadful heavy feeling that had spread all over due to their discussions was why they were coming together.

Gerrit, another half-brother and his wife Adel were the last to arrive. Thank goodness that the chairs had not yet been packed away.

"Annie, shall I gather them all in your workshop room? The large table will be more useful, don't you think?"

Gosh, when would she ever have such a gathering together? It would be sad if that would not happen in France.

"What makes you think we will not yet be together at Half-way House, Annie?" Toon mentally replied.

"I meant in our home Toon. I have to get used to it, living in a smaller cottage, I mean."

Leo had warned them all to stay in observation mode during this meeting, as they had during their previous meetings two weeks after she had lost the Prinsegracht Hotel. Then, she realised for the first time what they were up against. The horrible fire that destroyed the hotel both her brother Fred and herself had built up over the years had shaken her to the core.

It was time to leave all these sad memories behind. Now was the time to join others who were awakening.

Richard, one of her ascension workshop participants, had lost his little girl and got burned in the process of saving some children in the main lobby. How would they ever wake up from their crazy plot that felt so very real? Was the biggest threat hidden in the fact that the global human mind, in unison, could be taken in by the illusion of it all? Would enough people wake up to the fact that their heroes have misled them? Is the attention span of humanity outside of each individual an evil trap?

Both Gerrit and Adel couldn't get over Ingrid's size. They had not seen her since New Year's Eve.

"When is the baby due?" Adel asked.

"Any day now, so we are all prepared." Toon proudly replied. They all laughed at his excitement. Ingrid rolled her eyes as if to say, who's giving birth here? *"Kitty, I wish I was true."* Ingrid playfully tickled him.

"Wow, all those boxes! Annie, I hope you have lots of room at the other end!" Quincy remarked.

"Yes, rub it in. I'm having a battle with detaching from worldly goods." She laughed as she said it. Knowing how true it was, but not wanting to make Quincy feel guilty.

The men were all debating heavily when the woman gathered in the kitchen.

"Annelies how is Tieneke coping?" Ingrid asked because she had not seen her or Trevor for months.

"Quite well, in my opinion. Tieneke has her setbacks, but she and Trevor are becoming quite an item, which somehow makes up for the loss."

"I sure hope that will apply to Richard because his little girl lost her life in that horrible fire. I know that the I Am of Sammy has not died, but it still is hard to remind oneself of that idea while in mourning." Quincy commented.

"She must have shifted a great deal emotionally. What do you think, Annelies?" Ingrid telepathically beamed. Ingrid's sister Quincy was confronted last year by the fact that her then-husband Oliver and Richard's first wife, Ellie, were Sammy's parents. Richard learned through trauma not to hang onto the reality of this physical life, and so did Quincy, both with the help of like-minded partners. She had no idea if Ellie and Oliver supported each other in their loss, but rumours were that they were not.

"I don't think we have to experience grieving if we wake up before a major obstacle could happen, but that is my perception." She said.

"Gosh, Annelies, I would like to believe that. But what if that is what it takes to want to wake up?" Quincy asked.

"Who knows? On a soul level, they made a choice, I mean all three of them." Ingrid projected while clearing the dishes from the dishwasher.

Some were to be packed into the following box, while she left out just two crockery and cutlery. Ever since they decided to do all the packing themselves instead of just hiring a firm to do the work for them, she and Ben found out there was some enjoyment attached to packing. It had created many enjoyable evenings recalling events.

"I would like to be awake enough to feel the truth of your statement. Annelies, what did it take for you to get to this conviction, or am I stepping on dangerous ground?" Quincy asked. She knew that Quincy was born with awakened natural clairvoyant skills and that she had used them, probably unknowingly, but she must have been able to see that her emotional body was not always that stable.

"I will soon share some of my awakening experiences through my journal, but now is not the time to go into detail about it. When you decode the aspects of your last five soul cards, you will learn to connect with your guide or guides during this lifetime.

"That reminds me. Ingrid, how was Damanhur, the community you and Toon visited in the Italian Alps?"

During their conversation in the kitchen, Adel did not speak a word, but observing her body language and emotional field, I see that the things that were said must have made an impact. Ingrid and Quincy noticed it as well.

"Well, all I can say is that the temples are just one of the extraordinary achievements of the people of the Republic of Damanhur.

"Damanhur has drawn on ancient knowledge, esoteric traditions, and modern research to promote a culture of peace and balanced development through solidarity. Toon was in his element. Their respect for the environment and social and political commitment is awesome."

"Is that not what Toon has been doing with his money, building communities like Damanhur worldwide?" Adel asked. In the background, they could hear men's voices and roaring laughter.

"Damanhur is a place where dreams are realized, where ideas beyond reason are given a chance, and where very often they become a reality. That is what inspired us the most. Never give up on one's dreams, no matter how unrealistic they seem to others."

"Then that is the place I would like to visit. I'm sure that Gerrit feels the same way."

"The way Toon has described Damanhur to the others, I'm sure he will, don't you worry." She replied, grinning.

"How did you...do you know? Is it true that you are all very telepathic? Gerrit told me that you are, but..." Adel's voice turned into a whisper. She was an artist, so her skills, like Tieneke's, came out differently during her awakening.

"Adel, I know you will soon be joining us at Half-way House, so please do so if you are drawn to join my decoding workshops. I will continue facilitating the genetic decoding workshops until the workbook **Our Body Codes of Light** is in print. By then, there will be enough awakened teachers to carry on and take over my workshops worldwide. The sooner, the better."

"What is the aim of your decoding workshop, may I ask? Adel's tone was almost a whisper.

"To awaken the Soul-Christ spirit within. Without Tieneke's Language of Light mind drawing from the higher self, the decoding method through several esoteric sciences would not have been as powerful."

Her kitchen looked so bare, with the boxes packed in the corner.

"Now I understand. Gerrit explained how his own doodling experiences around the Soul qualities triggered many previously unconscious beliefs."

The men were calling them, so with some reluctance, they followed her to her workroom where she had held so many decoding workshops. It looked bare without her drawings and illustrations on the wall, but Joris behaved as if she had been away for hours.

"Annie, we have concluded our next move, but we need the women to agree before we go on with our plan." Ben and Toon both projected the same content to Ingrid and herself.

She looked at Ingrid, who shrugged her shoulders.

The artist's impression drawing of the Valley of God's Pleasure Park was on the table. It was very impressive. Toon had come across photos of the lotus temple in Delhi.

"Gosh, that is beautiful. Is the centre island going to be like that? I mean, the water around the island and the temples?" Quincy asked.

"That is why I want you all here. It will not be the same, but it's not too late to make changes. We have many problems with the dome structure, so I contacted the Iranian architect who designed this temple, who now lives in Canada, to visit our project in France."

Ingrid unrolled the dome drawing and spread it over the centre island. Then she placed the images Toon had printed from the internet, and together, they all gave their input.

"This Lotus design comprises 27 free-standing marble-clad "petals" arranged in three clusters to form nine sides. We can do something similar with our 22 free-standing glass pyramids." Ingrid suggested.

Everybody was enthusiastic about Toon's project, and they would visit the Valley of The Gods park soon before the third stage was complete.

Chapter 18
The Birth of a Crystal Child

Apeldoorn

It was late in the afternoon. Ben and Toon were mentally very silent. They were driving back home after being in the courtroom in Den Haag.

"Come, Joris, let's go for a walk. Let me try out my crutches; I'm constantly getting fed up sitting down. Your boss will not be coming back before it gets dark."

Joris responded in great excitement as if the garden was new territory. Just as she was about to leave the house through the kitchen door, the phone rang, and she telepathically heard Ingrid simultaneously.

"Annie, the baby is coming. Toon is on his way to the hospital in Utrecht. Can you take me?"

Good grief, that was why they were silent. Oh gosh, how was she going to manage that? Ingrid must have completely forgotten that she was not able to drive. All she could do was ask her neighbour Sue. She looked through the window and spotted her car in the driveway, so she phoned. She was in luck. All she needed to do was close the house and ensure Joris was locked inside.

"I'll be there in 10 minutes. Can you hang in there that long, or shall I call an ambulance?"

Getting Joris into the kitchen and in his basket took five minutes. Joris was not pleased but rather confused. He had a way of showing it—poor chap.

She closed all the doors and got herself into the hallway. At that moment, the front doorbell rang, and Sue was there to help her.

"Annie, please hurry; I should never have gone away even for a day. I should have known better. I've phoned for the ambulance in case" Toon beamed in distress.

"Thanks, Sue, let's go."

"Don't panic so, Toon. Your little girl will know when she must come into this world. I'm on my way."

Her neighbour drove as fast as was allowed. When they came near the area where Ingrid lived, she heard the siren. The ambulance flashed by as they drove into her street. She told Sue to park on Ingrid's driveway onto the side so the ambulance could reach the front door. As she was about to get out on the crutches, Ingrid opened the front door.

The man from the ambulance must have seen Ingrid's big pregnant belly and turned to give instructions.

She was three metres away from Ingrid, who suddenly covered her mouth from sheer embarrassment.

"Oh, Annelies, I'm so sorry. I forgot that you can't walk."

Thank goodness it was not Ingrid's first baby; it was her fourth, so she knew what was in store for her.

"My water broke, and I have contractions every five minutes. Knowing it's going too fast, I've tried to slow them down. I'm not dilating enough. That is why it's probably better if I use the ambulance. Will you come with me?"

Ingrid sounded in control, but she almost fainted as she finished her mental sentence. Standing half outside her front door was not a clever plan, and so they helped her onto the stretcher. The ambulance people were fast and efficient. Sue helped her close up the house, and then they followed the same route as the speedy ambulance.

Her adrenaline rushed through her body as Sue tried to catch up.

"I have to slow down, Annelies; I've never driven this fast."

She rested her hands on Sue's lap, saying: "Many thanks, Sue, you are the best neighbour I've ever had."

When they entered the freeway, Sue slowed down.

As they drove into the Gelre Ziekenhuis in Apeldoorn, the radio in Sue's car announced a news bulletin that almost made her neighbour swerve onto another lane.

"Annelies, I've never had to visit the polyclinic in Sprengenweg, but it looks like we arrived at the wrong entrance."

So far as she knew, that is where the ambulance was heading. Why hadn't she asked? Perhaps she should be heading for the Wilhelmina Kinderziekenhuis.

"Toon, where is Ingrid having the baby? I've lost the ambulance."

"Annie Ingrid just told me they took her to Hospital Lukason on Albert Schweitzerlaan."

Thank goodness for their telepathy skills. Annelies knew where that was.

"I'm so sorry; I remember now that Ingrid was booked into the Hospital on Albert Schweitzerlaan. Do you know where that is?"

Sue nodded and turned around.

"Annie, was she alright when you saw her?"

"Yes, she was OK, but her water broke, so the ambulance acted quickly. Don't get all worried Ingrid knows what to expect." At least, she hoped so. Every delivery was different, and Ingrid was forty-five.

"Oh, Annelies, it's all my fault that Toon is not here. I don't want him to speed on the freeway to be with me. I wanted to stay home as long as possible."

Ingrid must have followed their telepathic conversation.

"There it is." She pointed to the right, and Sue drove towards the nearest entrance.

"Shall I wait for you, or do you need my help? Why don't I quickly get a wheelchair so you can get around inside faster."

Sue was already out running towards the glass doors, and not more than two minutes later, she came out with a wheelchair.

They were both inside where Ingrid had been taken, and after explaining that her husband was on the way and that she was the closest family member nearby, they showed her where to go.

The commotion behind her made her turn. Toon came running towards her. He thanked Sue for taking Annelies. With all the stress, it also completely slipped his mind that Annelies was immobile.

"She's in there, Toon, quick, I think the baby is coming."

The rest that followed was like you see on a hospital soapy. Lots of commotion and people in white coats going in and out of the delivery room. Surely nothing was wrong?

Sue had to be reassured that she could go home since she knew Ben would arrive at any moment.

"Annie, you are here after all. Is Toon...." Ben called out.

"Toon's with Ingrid. You must have driven fast to get here so quickly" Ben was out of breath from running.

"Don't even speculate on the speed. I wasn't driving; it was more like flying. Are things okay?" Ben thanked Sue after she had told him of her quick response.

"The baby's coming, the baby' it's coming", Toon's voice was so loud, everyone in the passage stopped walking.

The delivery room door opened just enough for her to see a glimpse of Ingrid, who Toon helped to sit up. The wailing and hollering announced that the baby must have been coming at just that moment.

Why some nurses had to leave the delivery room during Ingrid's labour was beyond her. Then, both Ben and herself heard a faint baby cry. Later, she heard that Sandra was born "sunny-side-up."

When the nurse told them that both mother and baby were doing well, they were shown where to wait down the hall.

"When do you think we can see them?"

"I don't think it's allowed for the first twenty-four hours. Come, Ben let's get something to eat in the cafeteria." She put her arm around him, pulling him close. For a moment, she saw herself many years back, all alone, giving birth to Tessa. How different it must be when, during those crucial moments, the father was there to greet the baby you give birth to.

"Oh, Annie, I know what you are feeling right now. Please let it go forever. Please, it so hurts me to know that you were alone."

"Sweety, I never blamed you," she whispered. "You never knew, and it was my mistake, not yours, to have refrained from telling you."

They silently ate when Toon suddenly showed up, still wearing hospital gear.

"Congratulations." she held out her arms to him, so Toon bent over to receive her big hug.

"Oh, Annie, what an experience. When I looked down, there was the baby's head crowned at over 15 cm. Then I realised that I would be the one to deliver my daughter."

"What do you mean?"

"The doctor showed me what to do. I first saw her eyes and nose when things stalled slightly."

"You helped Ingrid instead of the doctor?" That idea shook Ben, and it surprised her somewhat, too.

"Yes, I wasn't sure whether to pull on the baby's head. To her credit, Ingrid was reassuring everyone and giving further instructions to the two nurses." Toon's deep voice was so emotionally charged that as he carried on, she expected him to burst into tears at any moment.

"Inevitably, the whole head came out. I remember that Ingrid's daughter, Debbie, said something along the lines that all babies are blue when they come out. I wasn't sure whether to pull on her head to coax the rest of the body out but fortunately decided to let nature take its course since it seemed to be doing a good job so far. After what seemed like an eternity of watching the baby seemingly asphyxiating, the body came out. No cord around the neck and seemingly okay"...Wow, Annie, nothing like laying your hands on a newborn baby to put things in perspective... birth is truly a miracle of life."

"When can we see her."

After what felt like five minutes, Toon took hold of her wheelchair and took her to the room where they saw many babies behind glass. The nurse held Sandra up close to the window.

"Isn't she a miracle? I won't travel anymore until she is old enough to come with us."

She wondered if Toon could pull that off, not leaving Holland for a business meeting elsewhere. Ben looked tired, and she had not asked either of them for the result of the court case. Now was not the right moment.

Toon stayed behind in the hospital. He would drive home after he'd phoned Ingrid's three grown-up children. Ben drove her home. The wind had finally calmed down, but it was still very chilly for the time of the year. Sandra was born on the 23rd of March. Her sun sign was Aries.

Joris greeted them as if they had been away for years.

"Is he going to stay with us now that the new baby has been born?" It seemed like she knew more than him.

"Probably. Until we move to France, that is already next week!"

"I know. Are you sorry to move?"

"Are you?" Ben looked tired.

" It's still early, sweety, but let's go to bed. You had an eventful day, and I want to hear all about it."

"Are you sure? It might give you nightmares, you know."

What had Ben and Toon found out that would give her nightmares?

"On the car radio on the way to the hospital, I overheard that the controversial Dutch businessman Nick du Toit was arrested in Switzerland last week on fraud charges connected to the bankruptcies of several companies." She waited for Ben to respond while he closed all the curtains and switched off the light.

"Nick was employed by a group of businesses that tried to stop Toon from withdrawing any more capital from the bank in the USA." It did not surprise her to hear that. Ben didn't elaborate further, so she wouldn't press him. To focus on events that only brought them grief did nobody any good. Instead, she would ask for more insights about her decoding program.

Ben helped her upstairs to their bedroom, which would soon be no longer theirs.

***

Two days remained until the arrival of the moving van. Joris lay snugly curled up at her feet. He kept them warm this morning. While the wind was howling outside, her emotions were similar, stormy. The computer screen's cursor was waiting. Her title:

Are the feelings humanity generates globally registered by other humanoid entities who are off-planet?

She'd typed it purely from being in the moment, for that was her question, but what now? She had experienced no more flashing hallucinations, although she tried hard to get into a meditative state. The artefact kept quiet. No sound or halo came from it, which disappointed her somewhat. This morning, she woke up from a nightmare that felt all wrong. It had infected her mood. The ghastly visions couldn't have anything to do with her previous predictive visions.

Her packing was finished. They would soon leave Holland for good. Apart from releasing useless memories, through packing, clearing and sorting, there was more to come. The world around her seemed to have become more chaotic than ever. She could feel it physically with her own body. It felt all clogged up.

Joris was also dreaming. His short yelps shook his whole body, but he calmed down when she stroked him.

"Having a bad dream," she whispered.

Time seemed to have sped up lately. Trying not to identify with the clock seemed to fail her miserably.

She was willing to release anything her ego-mind still clung on to, no matter how horrible the realities appeared to come to life in her dreams. Were they just reflecting on what still had to come? What if? Realising that her physical experiences were a blessing in disguise, why was she now so suddenly feeling her age?

Lately, it was almost impossible not to identify herself with her physical body. She knew that it was more than her identity as Annelies. She grasped how ignorance and unawareness at the societal level could manifest physically. Troubles existed worldwide, including political conflicts, changing weather patterns, wars, widespread crime and corruption, epidemics, and economic crises. These thoughts inspired her to write the following text for her article. At least her cursor was happy.

> Yes, they are. In my dreams, the biogenetic engineers who visited our planet millions of years ago are returning! Now I know they were to our ancestor's godlike creators with a small g. Today, I know they might have been from a more technically evolved

dimension, having found a way to enter our consciousness field. That was a possibility, but they were not from a higher spiritual dimension that would represent the Prime Creator - All That Is.

Was that what the rock had shown her? How was that possible? Was her human mind still so in control that humanity, like their ancestors, became trapped in their spell again?

They, like us, are part of the illusion that appears real only to our minds.

Having typed that in bold made her feel better. At least it stated that she would not give in to a mindset drawn to conspiracy theories.

Everything still looked grim and cold outside. Inside, her office had lost its homely energy, as if the boxes around her had withdrawn the cosy atmosphere she had created for years. Even the smell from the boxes held feelings of a closed chapter.

She could grasp that everything was projected, intellectually like a movie, from her mind, but how could she change her mental script?

"Mom, focus on your vision boards or watch Trevor's last video. It's only ten minutes." Liesbeth telepathically beamed to lift her sad mood. She already felt better, especially when her Skype box popped up. It was Trevor.

Yesterday, she worked on her decoding workbook for two hours while Ben again accompanied Toon to Den Haag.

Sandra was now one week old and thriving. Ingrid had come home two days ago, and Toon wanted to show her around the world.

This morning, Toon had to appear in court again, so Ben joined him as she made further plans to write her decoding book.

While packing, she came across many typed and printed notes she had used in her workshops. She had to type them all over again so

Liesbeth could do the editing and whatever else was necessary to link to her workbook.

It is ludicrous how a man's mind can spin impossible scenarios to take seriously. Nevertheless, in this life, they, her family, and her friends are all trapped in the same script. How else could she explain why she still identified with it all if nothing was real? Her train of thought reminded her to look up Ingrid's and Richard's journals before she watched Trevor's video.

"Joris move away."

She was going to follow Trevor's advice by reading up on POWAH'S excerpts that Ingrid had received last year. Combining them with Theo's translations of the twenty-two tablets Richard wrote about, she hoped to expose the deeper message. Especially now, she could include them while typing her interpretations for her decoding workbook. Each grid spacing in the second part of her workbook would reveal what soul quality could be implemented for each individual.

Her Life Opportunity Code of 44-Community[1]

The master number that was revealed to her at the time would materialize now. She would be moving into a community.

The excerpt on The Dimensions and their Densities[2] and The Prophet's Game from Ingrid's journal stimulated a thought that transformation had to do with the concept of time and must have something to do with our perception of time.

This morning, the mirror clearly showed a face that had changed in time, but is that because we are moving through time and observing how our body changes as we go from the past to the future, like watching a movie? That thought inspired her to type the following

---

1. https://allrealityshifters.wordpress.com/level-one-of-the-present-six-decoding-spacings/

2. https://allrealityshifters.wordpress.com/powah/the-awakening-game-excerpt-2/

question for her website article. So she opened that file again and typed:

Is time a ninth dimension science revealed by the Mayan Calendar in December 2012?

She had read that on the internet, through the writings of Barbara Hand Clow. Hans once tried to explain it by saying: "It's a fold in time that jumps between one universe's infinity to another."

In Richard's journals, tablet eighteen[3] is titled When distortions take over the game. Verse ten says time will seem shorter until you awaken within the source. At the end of his chapter, Theo tells Richard about his out-of-body experience and that she would share the nine aspects. As she browsed through Richard's Journal, **Orphanage of Souls**, she remembered telling André that some, like Leo, the genetic scientist, were speculating that the entire DNA structure of every living creature is linked to a time-release capsule.

She packed the two novels in a box and returned to her desk. Before she could type anything else, she tried to silence her mind. She suddenly had the urge to type:

> Were the ancient Sumerian clay tablets and other prehistoric writings left for us to find at the end of another cycle? Did the author(s) of these scripts know that a time would come when they would reincarnate thousands of Earth years later, just before the great shift in consciousness?

Time is a creation of the mind, remember!

That last bold sentence was more directed at herself. POWAH had told her years back that she would have to pick the people who would write a journal about her decoding workshops; she had never realised the intent behind it all. Now, it started to get clearer. Not only did they all seem to be genetically connected, but their cellular memories held the same stories. It also confirmed to

---

3. https://allrealityshifters.wordpress.com/richard-de-jong/tablet-eighteen/

her how everyone is forming one global consciousness field. This field might have several layers with different vibrations, more like a rainbow, which would tie in with the functions of each layer of colour or, as in her workbook, the grid spacings.

Joris was now fully awake and wanted to explore the garden. That was a good sign since he had been following her everywhere in the house lately. He had almost gotten under the wheels of her wheelchair, and that was how close he stayed to her. He sensed some departure, so he was dogging her.

As she let Joris out from her sliding door onto her back stoep, she instantly sensed the presence of POWAH in her office, waiting for her to quieten her mind. Knowing that her guide was not separate from her, like any other entity, was still invigorating.

She decided first to try what Ingrid had done, typing questions her higher self or guide might answer.

Somehow, Annelies knew the answers would come. So she typed her first question:

"POWAH if one's memory is like a slide projector, filled with snapshots of images, sounds and feelings, when does 'Time' come into it?"

She wanted to wait in stillness, but Joris wanted to get in again.

"You do pick your moments, don't you?" Now, she knew what it was like to do everything from a wheelchair. Every move took longer; every action required more effort. Joris wagged his tail when she let him in, and his cuteness made her smile. Her energy had shifted.

Something made her turn because she was startled by the changing light in the office. Her computer screen suddenly displayed a bright blue background like Ingrid had described in her journal!...

<In your time frame, your thoughts around time are all just in your mind since your mind invented time. You have to step out of it and awaken to the truth of the light that is shining all about you.>

She needed to read this paragraph a few times before she could reply. It was still unclear whether she was communicating to her Higher Self or a higher group consciousness was opening up to her soul awareness.

"What about my memories?"

As she typed, she waited while her thoughts projected the image she had seen on the DVD. Those were stored in her memory. So, how real was that?

<The graphic demonstration of what appears within your so-called historical memory is the resurrection, or your reconfiguration, of a whole body that must be you. If, instead, you hold on to feelings of separation from the whole you, then it is impossible to use your physical body to wake up; I encourage you to do so now.>

Did she do that? Hold on to thoughts or belief that her higher vibrating bodies were separate? If so, would she not be able to experience her full awakening while still having a physical body? Why would POWAH reply like that?

POWAH, I've always thought, before you came into my life, that one's perception of the speed of time is directly proportional to how much life experience one can remember. So, our perception of time is based on the speed of light, which is NOT a constant. For instance, Albert Einstein might have been dreaming while working as a patent clerk, writing his theory of relativity. Are you saying it all happens in one single moment?

She felt rather clever having typed that question, realising at that moment that her ego must have been interfering.

<Correct on both thoughts. Time is an illusion. The thought forms you construct, including your ideas of a linear association, are only formulated within themselves as you have constructed them in your mind.>

Yes, POWAH replied to both her text and her thoughts. They were all one! But then POWAH must know her anxiety attacks. How could she ever stop them from happening?

"You mean that if I manage to step out of time, there is no more time. But how?" Instead of typing, she mentally formed her question to see if she got a reply.

It took a while before the screen changed. In her experience, time was still authentic.

<What is the difference between 15000 million years, a million years or 100 years, one year or 10 minutes except within the association of your thought form?>

Wow, her mind was still in contact with a higher source, or she thought. That was also true. Her thoughts happened when she felt them; no time was involved, so thinking happened outside of time!

"Then surely the time has to do with our experience of cause and effect in our world of duality."

She wouldn't give in so easily, having been pondering things lately, how they somehow attracted or created the cause of all the dramas, and what an effect it had on her. She couldn't speak for others.

<The distance between the cause and the effect, which is the thought of your mind and its subsequent result, will be exactly as far apart as far as you have mellowed in your self-declarations of the extension of your mind.>

When she read the reply, she understood that immediately, but that then applied to everyone within the same plot.

"In simple words, what we believe to be true we will experience?"

< Yes, within the one mind, all is one. When cause and effect are brought together, like the thought of happiness and wholeness, you inevitably fill yourself up with what you would call continuous moments. The mind that holds itself in time is nothing. It has no source, and therefore it is not real.>

Suddenly, she got an aha moment. That is what Trevor did when he created the DVD for Richard for his talk last year. He showed pictures in which you can see an original and one in which the light polarisation had been made artificially. Trevor had explained that Theo had guided them to create a whole other level of detail, something entirely out of the range of our normal perception. She needed to type this, even knowing that POWAH could read her mind.

"Trevor told me that it's nearly impossible for us to imagine what a perceptual experience of multi-dimensional realms would be like during our waking moments (for now). Although I experienced a sort of flashback. I knew that the light body on the screen was me

<That moment was truly miraculous. The movie or the imagery of the symbols in your mind came together. It fused philosophy and science, the art of creating with your mind. It helped to organize the chaos of historical thought at that moment.>

She needed to read this over, so she had better keep typing her questions.

POWAH, I know that all creation is within All That Is, but...is there something, or some force, trying to manoeuvre us from attempting to wake up fully?

<Yes, your persona program. This split of your persona's mind aims to keep you in darkness, which is the direction of your apparent reality because thought is delusive. The perceptual mind will attack this idea as it has always attacked the idea of wholeness.>

As she read POWAH's text, a feeling of hopelessness overwhelmed her like a tidal wave.

"How are we free from this split, fragmented perceptional thought process?"

<You can't die. Keep that in mind. You can cause dramatic changes in the fabric of your mind since you can only have one

thought at a time. As you put the energy of light into these thoughts, they are causing incredible re-configurations within the fabric of your time association.>

POWAH had an unusual way of forming words into sentences that made no sense together unless you read the words in shorter bites. Her screen turned back to a familiar page, so she knew her telepathic communication was over.

She thought back to Theo's translation of the rhythmic song titled The Prophet's Game, where the author of the tablets explained how the language that vibrates in light could release the virus without a fight. Why had he used the word virus? Would the author of these tablets have known about how a computer virus can mess with our electronic language codes? Or, that was it! They meant the Body Codes of Light.

Oh, she'd better close her document. She had no time for Trevor's video. She would rather spend some time packing the last boxes from the lounge. The whole house was starting to feel different. Empty, hollow. One more night, and they would leave for France.

"Annie, why don't you come with me? I must deliver these papers to Fred at the bookshop." Ben was clearing their breakfast dishes.

"I haven't gotten dressed yet, and I'd like to bathe before my eleven o'clock appointment. I'm still in my robe."

They were having breakfast for the last time in their kitchen in Apeldoorn. She could not let on that she needed to say goodbye to the house. It was hard for her to move. Ben seemed to cope much better with the significant change.

"Please just pick me up from the orthopaedic surgeon's office at ten-thirty, and then after, we'll visit Toon and Ingrid with baby Sandra. Are you sure that Joris will stay with them this time?" She had booked a taxi to take her.

"Yes, Toon already feels bad that Joris has been more at our house than with them. Ingrid is fine with it."

They would stay overnight with them since the removal people would take everything away later that afternoon.

"You'd better go. It's nearly nine. Fred will be at his bookshop."

"I see that you are already resting on that foot. Is that allowed?" Ben looked alarmed.

I'm sure. The cast is coming off, and it feels fine. You have no idea what difference it makes now that I can get around on these crutches. I'm not taking the wheelchair with me to France."

"Oh well, you know better. I look forward to joining Trevor and Leo in their project."

"Yes, I can imagine. How is Toon's project getting on?"

"We will hear all about that tonight, I'm sure. I'll pick you up just after ten. See you then." Ben kissed her and left.

Chapter 19
The Light Body of the Soul

Worlds Within Worlds

After taking a quick look at baby Sandra during lunch, Ben drove her home to pack her laptop before they left for good. Her dressing gown was in the same bag as all her workbook files. Their last night in Holland would be spent with Toon and Ingrid.

When she moved to her empty office on her crutches, the blinds were still closed, and Joris followed her as if he knew they were about to leave for good. He was not letting her out of his sight.

Walking around the empty house using only her left foot quickly tired her. She pushed her wheelchair away from her desk and sat on her office chair. She hadn't yet closed her computer down from last evening's writing. Instead, her computer screen had gone into its screen-saving mode, so her mind drifted off. Joris must have known she felt like a short meditation, so he settled under her desk.

As she did her breathing, with her eyes closed, a soft, diffused light penetrated her eyelids. Her eyes had flown open, feeling as if they were hinged on high-tension springs, but her computer room was silent and dark, except for the screensaver.

With slight reluctance, she again closed her eyes while Joris rested his nose on her left foot, which was still in a big boot.

For a split second, she figured that she must have slipped into a lucid dream of some kind, so she turned her screen off, adjusted her dressing gown tightly around herself and let out a long, deep sigh.

At that moment, the light returned. This time, Annelies kept her eyes closed but watched in amazement as the light penetrated through her eyelids and formed the same glyphs Annelies had seen on the artefact Leo had found. It was still sitting on the desk, waiting to be packed!

The symbols wavered over her head like a mirage of serpentine sculptural glyphs of shimmering golden light. Her entire body began to emanate light as she gazed at them through her closed eyelids. To her surprise, the symbols started to shift—not the symbols themselves, but something within them. Something was circulating within them like blood flowing through an artery.

Whatever it was, it began to speed up faster and faster, and then she noticed a whirring sound, similar to the hum of electricity but infinitely smoother. It started as a low humming buzz, and then it began to pitch to a near-inaudible state. Just when she thought she would lose it, it began to oscillate.

At first, the sound was like a wavering electrical rhythm, pulsing like a massive heartbeat a million miles away, but then something changed, and she could hear words forming into sentences. Nothing intelligible, but it was a language pattern. Her physical senses told her that. She could feel her whole body leaning towards the sound, being the observer that she was. She knew that her mind was desperately trying to translate the meaning of the words.

Then it happened; her mind could translate the experience...

"Feel no fear. Relax and listen to my words."

The words were spoken with perfect diction, articulated like a Shakespearean actor.

"What I will impart to you will be stored in your subconscious mind for later recollection. Upon awakening from your meditation, you will have little recall of our meeting. Again, we regret this, but it is necessary now."

Annelies could feel her conscious mind forming a protest, but it dissolved before being voiced.

<We know what you desire is to activate your spiritual knowledge, and it will since it is your wish.>

POWAH's mental signature is familiar.

Annelies could feel her body but could not move her limbs or even open her eyelids. She was utterly entranced by what she intuitively felt was POWAH's voice, and with it came a familiar degree of peace.

For a long time, she waited in silence until her breath became part of a melody. Then she heard the Shakespearean voice in her head again saying:

"You do not yet understand the context in which our technology is placed upon your planet. This insight will come, but it will take time. Rest assured that we are watching, waiting, and vigilant to protect your and our mission's interests."

She swallowed hard and tried to speak, whether with her conscious mind or vocal cords; she wasn't sure which.

"Who are 'we', and what technology?" she mentally projected.

Again, she waited silently and felt as if somebody was trying to speak through her, but that she wouldn't allow. Her body was hers, not some entity that needed a human body for whatever reason.

Again, she felt she was repeating herself, so she beamed: *"I'm well aware that my ego is interested in the past or future, so I don't want to misperceive anything."* She knew that her thoughts were perceived

"We are all that you will become. You are all that we have been. Together, we are what defines the human Group Soul."

She wondered why she heard two voices. Was the Shakespearean tonal energy repeating things she already knew? Why did she feel it was not POWAH?

<The rock communicating to you in your dream state is interpenetrated with the light of the First Source; the source is you and anyone on planet Earth. It's your Higher Self that has now moved nearer this stone monument. We bring you the translations of your Body Codes of Light through this source.>

She now wondered who her higher self was. Which stone monument was POWAH referred to? Did she...

<The artefact given to you has been stepped down into this weaker light so you may see how your form will become unified to a new cosmological structure, the architecture and grandeur you cannot imagine.>

Annelie's mind, in a flash, remembered Dienie's voice from long ago when she was 15 years old...

"The new spirituality will have as its foundation a cosmological substrate so profound that your conscious mind will not yet contain it."

The poetic voice reminded her of an awareness she was not ready for.

She smiled inwardly at Dienie's recollection while POWAH tried to get her attention.

< Study your life obstacle code >

Oh gosh, the obstacles she encountered. She recalled what Dienie had shown her many years ago. Often over the years, she had questioned, "Why are fairies and angels more real to me than my physical reality?"

As a child, she had been a loner, more interested in her own, what her mother called a fantasy world. Knowing that intense emotions and hormones often trigger psychic abilities, why had she then lost the ability to see into other worlds when she became a teenager? Had she lost this ability, like losing files on her computer?

<Those abilities are never lost. You need to take a break and get accustomed to a new phase of your life. Your world, or your reality as you experience it, will drastically change.>

She clearly remembered the obstacle card she had created on her own. 19 and 10 into 1 Perseverance. Peaceful bliss into Forgiveness. Tieneke told her that all three of her Soul quality codes work together, so she must stay on her path.

Her Life Obstacle Code 19-Perseverance[1]

Gradually, she felt like she was in two places simultaneously. Her reality was already merging with other realms, but how many people experienced what she did? She would have to share this meditation in her journal.

She settled back into her usual meditative state. It felt as if the artefact was guiding her to imagine a beam of light entering the top of her head, illuminating her from the inside. It was then that she could observe that her whole body was light. Was this what her light body or her etheric looked like? She felt like she was being in a kind of bubble of light.

< Your higher divine self has entered your etheric light body, changing your physical cellular structure. Place your tongue lightly on the roof of your mouth. Now, see yourself as transparent, pure energy. You are nowhere and everywhere. The unconscious field of your higher self is not separate from its source.>

She had difficulty keeping grounded while her body felt so weightless as if she could leave it at any moment....

She pondered on the many often tragic events that had happened from the day she had turned 15 and from the time she started her ascension workshops in her spare room. Life began to have a different meaning when she awakened to the understanding of her blueprint.

Trevor mentioned in his email that her journal would be written over time. Was that why her mind slipped into her past, awakening memories?

<You have not been able to interpret your Body Codes of Light before because you did not understand the concept of

---

1. https://allrealityshifters.wordpress.com/level-one-of-the-present-six-decoding-spacings/

wholeness. You have not yet embraced the grand universe of which you are part.>

Did she hear these words? Why did she feel as if these words that her mind interpreted were not only addressed to her? A cold shiver ran down her physical spine as if.

She opened her eyes to see if the artefact was still on her desk. Of course, it was. Joris had not moved from under her desk.

She now felt the weight of her body, but she knew she had experienced what her light body felt like. That was incredible. She was keen to understand how Liesbeth would fictionalise her story.

She stood up, leaned forward and rested both her hands on the side of the rock. It felt cold and empty of any intelligence. Ben would see her now, holding onto an object as if it were only a crystal or a crystal skull she had only ever seen on the internet. Having that thought somewhat unnerved her, as if someone else was thinking.

She removed her hands from the artefact and rested back in her chair. After all her studies and contemplations, she still couldn't get past the vastness of her mind.

Joris stirred, wondering what time it was. She looked at her computer, and to her amazement, only ten minutes had passed. It felt like hours.

This time, she moved all the files she had worked on the previous evening across her network onto her laptop. She would work on her laptop until they were settled in at Halfway House.

Trevor's video was still sitting on her laptop for her to watch. Since it was only ten minutes, she was tempted to look but changed her mind. That wouldn't be fair. Trevor's work deserved all her focus. Watching his video in a hurry would be disrespectful.

The title of the video clip, The Crystal Children, was intriguing, but she restrained herself and moved the video clip file onto her laptop through her network.

"Come boy, we'd better get up. Ben would soon be back."

She closed her laptop and disconnected her network cable. Packing away all her work into one smallish bag felt strange, but she immediately released her anxiety about losing her laptop.

Why would she still be plagued by scenarios she had no intention of attracting? Lately, she intuitively felt that a kind of war was happening inside. Who was in control? Was it her higher mind or her persona?

What a strange idea to have a war about who controlled her life. What had POWAH implanted in her mind? That there was no separation!

Was the outside reality a reflection of her inner sub-consciousness? She knew that Toon had been given visions of a timeline that was a few years ahead, so he thought. Toon wanted them to move by settling into his Half Way house project, which Ingrid had written about in her journal. For the last time, she went upstairs to the bathroom.

She was getting very good at moving around on her crutches, but having the cast removed would make all the difference.

She looked into the hallway mirror and was determined to see a striking woman who had still not lost her looks.

As she dressed after her bath, she wondered which shoes to take. She was certain she no longer needed the strapped boot on her left foot. She packed several pairs of shoes in a bag. She was almost ready when she heard Ben returning.

"Annie, are you ready?" he asked from around the door of what used to be their office.

"Coming." Joris had already heard Ben and ran like a bullet.

Goodbye Apeldoorn

"Welcome; we are so glad you spent your last evening in Holland with us." Toon's greeting was cut short by Joris, who raced towards him.

"Hello, boy, you're happy to see me."

"Gosh, you'd think he'd been locked up the way he behaves." Ingrid laughed at Toon. A big man over six feet tall was on his knees, hugging an excited Labrador.

"Annelies, your cast is gone; how does it feel to walk normally again?" Ingrid was looking good. Her figure was practically back to normal.

"Well, I wouldn't say I'm walking normally. My feet feel very weak. I'm glad I can now wear shoes again, but from now on, I'll need support inside my shoes."

"Oh, you mean inserts, like Toon has. Come inside and let the men bring your luggage in."

"Yes, I suppose so, but after they took a mould of the soles of my feet, I was warned that I might have to buy bigger-sized shoes. So I dragged Ben into two shoe shops before he dropped me off at home for the last time."

She turned to wave goodbye to Ben and Toon. Together, they were going to oversee the removal at their house.

"Gosh, look at that dog, sniffing underneath all the shrubs and bushes, making sure his territory has not been invaded while he has been away. You sure you will manage with Joris now the baby is here?"

"Absolutely. Joris needs to be introduced to Sandra anyway. It will be interesting to see how he reacts to her."

"Is your baby asleep?"

"Yes. Sandra has her afternoon nap, which is until she wakes up, which should be soon."

She followed Ingrid towards the lounge. Their hallway was decorated with many photos, some of which she recognized. They were taken of Half-way House. It was a beautiful estate. She remembered the day as if it was yesterday when Toon had managed to purchase the chateau.

Toon had it exorcised because it had been used as an orphanage during the war, and Theo knew a lot about the history of the estate. Theo told them that when the Germans ordered a nearby orphanage to be evacuated during the Second World War, the previous owner of the chateau, Nick du Toit's grandfather, was forced to gather together the two hundred children in his care.

After hearing Nick du Toit's story from Ben during the trial, it seemed to her that Nick's grandfather, who seemed to have behaved as if he had a divine calling to save children in his attempt to make the world a better place, had failed to take care of his son, Nick's father.

"Sascia was asked to create a before and after brochure on Half-way House. " Ingrid explained.

"The photos reminded me of what Ben told me about Nick's trial."

"Oh, I was not aware that there was any connection?"

"Yes, when Nick was a child, he lived there."

"Really. he was an orphan?"

"No, he wasn't, but Ben said that when unaccompanied children were placed in institutional settings at a young age and for long periods, they are greatly at risk of having psychopathology problems in later life."

"Meaning."?

"Ben never told me the details in so many words, but there is an investigation going on into the death of this English professor who built the first underground laboratory. Did Toon ever tell you about this man?"

"I remember now. It was Jill who told me that Otto suspected that Nick murdered the professor and then escaped to South Africa."

"Gosh, I hope I don't pick up unpleasant vibes when we move to Half-way House."

Hearing the sound of a crying baby stopped their conversation. She followed Ingrid into the richly decorated nursery. It felt as if she had walked into a toy shop.

"Good grief, you weren't kidding." She had never seen so many teddy bears and dolls. Above the crib, an exquisite flying fairy about to catch a baby fairy, reminded her of the fairy kingdom in Swellendam, back in South Africa.

"It's gorgeous, isn't it," Ingrid responded to her thoughts as she picked up her baby. "It was a present from Sonja, Mien's daughter."

"I'm sure she must have got it in the fairy sanctuary in Swellendam, two hours from Cape Town."

"Oh, did you visit that place when you were on holiday?" Ingrid asked after she had made herself comfortable on a cute sofa and started breastfeeding.

"No, not this time, but a shop at the waterfront advertises the place. Mien told me that it was Sonja's favourite stopover when she was driving between Cape Town and George."

Nothing was as endearing as seeing mother and child bonding in this way. She had breastfed Tessa for six months.

Sandra was staring with wide-open eyes at her mother while she sucked, gulping.

"I read somewhere that very young babies can only see blurry shapes because they are nearsighted."

"Debbie says that a newborn has 20/400 vision. This allows a baby to see our face from a nursing position about 8 to 10 inches away." Ingrid looked radiant as a new mother.

"Have they all been to see their half-sister."

"Yes, at the hospital. What time is it now?"

"After five, can I do something?"

"Richard and Sascia will be joining us for dinner at the Pannekoek. Toon's idea. I've not yet prepared a meal at home since we brought Sandra home."

I didn't know they were in Holland?" Gosh, when was the last time that she talked to Richard? They had all been at their New Year's Eve party, the most memorable evening of her life.

"I look forward to seeing them both. Are they settling in at their new place?"

Richard had joined Trevor and Leo in their underground laboratory under Toon's Valley of the Gods pleasure park. She looked forward to a tour of where Ben would join them.

"Yes, I think they are. Richard was asked to give a lecture in Amsterdam. Trevor will also be joining us."

"Oh really?"

That meant she needed to look at his video before they met for dinner, but it was still sitting on her laptop.

There was a soft knock on the door, and Sandra instantly let go of Ingrid's nipple. A young girl peeked around the corner.

"Debbie! You are early; that is a surprise."

"Hi, mom. Oh, hi, Annelies. How are you? I heard about your accident." Debbie started to speak to Sandra, and if she was not mistaken, the baby smiled.

"Gosh, mom, that is very soon. Have you finished feeding her?"

"Yes, since she is more interested in you than drinking more milk."

She knew that as babies grow, their vision improves so that by three months, they can recognize the outline of a face as someone enters the room. Human faces are one of an infant's favourite things to look at, especially their caretakers or parents. Sandra was very allured. Her eyes were large and penetrating. She almost hypnotized them all.

"Gosh, don't you all feel as if your soul is being laid bare for Sandra to see?" She remarked, smiling.

She took the baby from Ingrid and gave her a loving cuddle before she handed her over to Debbie.

"That is what Toon said the first time he saw her." Ingrid's proud voice and Debbie's soft, endearing chatter when she took Sandra from her reminded her of the title of Trevor's video that she still needed to watch. Thank goodness her laptop was with her.

They left Debbie with Sandra in the nursery, and Ingrid took her to the bedroom where they would sleep that night.

The bedroom was large, with a seating area. It was elegantly decorated, and the original oil painting above the bed brought back memories of Clovelly. Why, she had no idea, but the view from the painted window was identical to the view from the cottage where they had stayed for two nights. Incredible. Was that just a coincidence?

When alone, she decided to waste no more time doing social things other than being a guest in Ingrid's house. Instead, she opened her laptop. The battery was fully charged, so it would play a video without problems.

The noise from the people talking all at once on the video reminded her of her childhood. The images and the many voices drew her back to Trevor's work.

While the video clips passed, Trevor's dictations made her relate to all of it. She belonged to the first wave of indigo children born several years after the Second World War.

"The Indigo children arrived with the key to multi-dimensionality. They were born into third-dimensional bodies, but their consciousness is effectively in the fourth dimension and capable of moving into the fifth. They are the cornerstone lightworkers that will see this civilisation into the golden age."

Trevor's voice held a firm conviction during the movie slide show. Now a female voice took over. It was the voice of Tieneke. A film shot of a baby on the back of a mother from Africa was communicating with several butterflies.

"Crystal children are now born during the age of the gold ray of incarnation and evolution."

She instantly knew that Sandra was such a baby. The beautiful movements of the Language of Light symbols that created the crop circles in the field in the video left her spellbound.

"The Indigo and Crystal children that come to the planet are known as star children because their souls are more at home in the stars."

She thought of Hans and Liesbeth when Tieneke explained that crystal children have never been on Earth. They have access to the gifts of clairvoyance and healing.

"The images now showed a multidimensional DNA structure not often seen under a microscope," Tieneke narrated.

"They come at this time as a 'special assignment' team to assist Earth and her inhabitants with their transition and rebirth as a higher dimensional 'New Earth.'"

The music of the spheres and the creative paintings about the elemental kingdoms made her think back to her experience with Dienie.

"Many crystal children are born into the sixth dimension of consciousness, with the potential to open up rapidly to the ninth-dimensional level of Full Christ Consciousness, and then from there to the Thirteenth Dimension which represents Universal Consciousness." Tieneke's soft voice carried on.

The video was captured at a high altitude in the mountains where Toon had also established a community.

"People in the multi-dimensional state have accessed their higher I Am presence or state and recognise themselves as spiritual beings or a bodhisattva in training. They have a human body but can function in this plane as material beings."

She wasn't sure if she ever recognised herself as a bodhisattva.

"The bodhisattva is constantly aware of themselves as angelic, powerful, and creative. They have no time or need for fear and victim drama. Their time is better spent in creating the kind of reality in which they would be happy and content.

She loved the way the video ended. Trevor cleverly captured how higher levels of awareness of the interconnectedness of all things in people who desired an empowered and creative life could become the characteristics of all humans on Planet Earth. She closed her laptop and put it back into its carry bag. Tomorrow morning they would be on their way to their new home.

As she descended the stairs, hanging onto the bannisters, she heard Ingrid talking to Debbie. She was going to babysit her half-sister while they went out to dinner. Toon wanted to take Sandra in her carrycot and ask Debbie to join in, but Ingrid wanted to leave her baby home. It would be the first time she would be away from her for a few hours.

"Phone us, will you?"

"Of course I will, Toon. Take your wife out for dinner; it will do her good. Mom, please relax. Your next feed will not last for a couple of hours."

Ben helped her into the back seat of Toon's BMW.

"Did the removal people arrive on time?"

"They were there already when we arrived. "I informed them that most boxes were kept in the garage."

"Annie, Fred was there organising them all. They promised to join us here when they have finished. " Toon projected.

"What, already?" She called out loud. She couldn't imagine that Fred and Quincy would have already moved into their house.

"It's not ours anymore, my love."

Ben took her hand in his, knowing that she felt the same as he did. Cutting cords with the home you had shared for so long was not as easy as she had hoped. It did help to know that her brother had taken the house into his name, but deep down, moving away from Apeldoorn felt strange.

"Oh yes, that reminds me. Trevor will share the latest developments on our project tonight." Ben said. He was already thinking of the part he would play when they settled in. Having seen Trevor's video, she was better prepared for any questions Trevor might ask during dinner.

When they arrived at the Pannekoek, Nel, the new owner, greeted them. Mien had told her about her friend, who was keen to take over from her.

"Annelies, I see that you left your crutches at home," Nel remarked.

"Not altogether. They are in the car, but using both my feet again is truly a blessing."

"There is your table, and some of your guests have already arrived and are waiting for you all."

She immediately saw that the flat-screen TV on the wall was not on.

Trevor, Fred and Quincy were in a deep discussion, but when they saw them, they all stood up.

After all the greetings and ordering drinks before dinner, they settled in while waiting for Sascia and Richard to arrive. The atmosphere was cosy, and not many other people were there. They had the most prominent table on the corner.

"Trevor, I bet you asked for the TV to be off, am I right?" She beamed with a smile.

Trevor nodded. "Watching TV, especially fake news, while having dinner is the most unhealthy thing we can do during these times."

She looked at Ben, who raised his eyebrows. They had often done that, watching the news over dinner, but not lately. There was a natural separation between families and friends due to different viewpoints about the pandemic. They were moving away before there might be a total lockdown.

"There they are." Ingrid had not seen her daughter since Sandra was born a week ago, except for a short time in the hospital. Sascia wanted to go directly home to greet her half-sister, but Toon insisted that she do so after dinner. It was great to see them both as a couple.

"We heard all about your accident. How are you?" Richard beamed with a big smile. His mental projections were a lot stronger.

"Busy recovering. I believe that we will soon be neighbours."

Tieneke had mentioned that their cottage at Halfway House was near theirs.

"We do not have a free-standing cottage like yours, Annelies. You will see."

Everybody asked them about their trip to South Africa and how life was for Toon and Ingrid with a new baby. They all ordered dinner, and Ben pressed Trevor on the latest developments.

"You will know we have slowly excavated the tunnels underneath the Valley of The God's project. After the blast or explosion that almost cost Leo his life, and after the months of clearing the debris, we discovered more tunnels, especially one that led to a large cave."

Richard was nodding, and so was Sascia. She had heard from Leo that Sascia would be doing the photography.

"Many of you probably know that the Dordogne region of France has hundreds of caves open for the public to visit."

She had heard about them but had never visited them.

"Let me explain about these caves. They fall into two categories. Many caves are famous for their prehistoric paintings, and some caves are more renowned for their rock formations, like stalactites, stalagmites, and other curious shapes formed by the effects of water over thousands of years."

"You mean that the cave you found has never seen the light of day?" She asked.

"No. The strangest feeling is the connection one gets, knowing that our ancestors must have been in the same place in this cave, being in awe by the beauty of nature."

"Some of Sascia's photos will soon be published in a brochure when we have found a link or created a passage that will lead us directly above ground within the Valley of the Gods park."

"The region is very seismically active, and Leo and I suspect that at one time, gigantic volumes of tidal water must've rushed through these tunnels into this enormous chamber."

Trevor picked up that Richard was keen to take over from him, telling the story of their finds.

"We all agree that the earth's magnetic field was much stronger than it is now and that this cave-like chamber must have been used by priests thousands of years ago, teaching their students about Earth vibrations," Richard added.

Annelies looked at Ben, who kept silent.

"Are you telling me that ancient people knew more about how to exploit magnetism?" Toon asked.

"Absolutely. Most of us know that the human body is an electromagnetic apparatus extremely affected by electromagnetic fields. Leo believes our ancestors were very involved in using magnetism in their healing and fertility." Trevor replied.

The waitress came to take their order, and when she left, Annelies asked. "How did they know how to create sound waves that could heal DNA's reproduction?"

She had read that the fertility rate in Europe and North America had dropped drastically in the last 50 years.

"Leo and I feel that this chamber must be a healing centre at one time because of an experience I had with a tuning fork."

"Is that why Leo wasn't injured during the blast? The sound could instantly harmonize his physical body," Ingrid asked.

"That could probably be the reason, yes."

"Hans explained that organs out of resonance will move back into harmony by specific frequency."

"Wait a minute, Leo didn't have to tune forks when he was covered by the rocks from the blast." Ben interrupted.

"True, but the stalactites and stalagmites can be used or create the specific frequency needed for healing."

"These stalactites and stalagmites are formed by capillary action rather than dripping water. Not so?" Toon asked while sketching on a napkin.

"Yes, stalagmites and stalactites are dripstone forms and take thousands to millions of years to form. What are you drawing?"

"An idea for the temples in the centre of the park."

Both Nel and the young girl served their dinner. Nobody ordered starters.

"While studying the skeleton we found near the artefact, we wondered what the connection was, so we asked Ben to give it to Annelies to practise her psychometry skills. Leo was keen to hear from you if you knew who it belonged to."

"Oh, Annelies, did you get anything?"

"Yes, Richard, I did from the artefact, but I never knew you found a skeleton near the metallic rock." She never had picked up on anyone so far as she could recall. "And the scroll, was that in the same area?"

"Yes, and here comes the interesting part. Besides the metallic-looking device of sorts Ben gave you to study, Leo stumbled upon a large round stone disc half-buried in the dust on the floor of the underground chamber. The disk is approximately nine inches in diameter and three-quarters of an inch thick."

"Why do you say a disk?" She asked.

"Well, etched in its face was a fine groove spiralling out from the centre to the rim, making the disk resemble some kind of primitive phonograph record."

"That was not where the artefact was found, Annie."

"Oh, but nearby?" She asked out loud.

"Yes. Remember the photos we took from the thin copper sheets? We always wondered what the connection was with the scroll and why this English professor took the trouble to copy the patterns from this stone disk onto the foil sheets by embossing them."

"You mean the photos that got Richard into trouble?" Sascia asked.

"Yes, the same. We now know what they were after."

The waitress interrupted their conversation by asking if everything was alright. They were all waiting for Trevor to carry on.

"This English colonel was a professor of linguistics." Trevor left them all with their thoughts, giving them all the time to eat dinner.

"But the message that Richard received was from the scroll, not so?" Sascia asked. Richard seemed to know what Trevor was about to share. She tried to remember the photos that were stolen from Richard. She always thought it was due to the scroll.

"Theo began the arduous task of trying to decode its message. Eventually, he began to make progress. A word emerged. Then another. A phrase became understandable, then an entire sentence. He had broken the code. "

Trevor let that sink in before he carried on talking. Sascia mentally asked Richard what Trevor meant by saying, "He had broken the code."

"You mean what is written on the scroll?" She asked.

"Annie, I know what you are thinking," Ben whispered. "Did Theo leave us all with the answers, and we have not yet unravelled them."

"Theo discerned that people around six thousand years ago wrote the messages on the scroll. When he had completed the translation as much as he could, he sat back in his chair in disbelief, but he never shared what was so astounding."

"Did you ask?"

"Yes, Theo believed that the occupants of an astral craft found refuge in the cave. Much later, Leo decided that was what Theo meant because their peaceful intentions were misunderstood by members of the tribe who were occupying neighbouring caves. Sound familiar?" Trevor looked at Ben. Trevor hinted about something, but she could not pick up what.

So what she experienced in her meditation, the voice that seemed to come from the metallic device, was a technology they were not yet ready for.

A waitress came to take their empty plates away, asking if they wanted dessert. Toon was keen on dessert, so they all joined him. She only ordered a cappuccino because she needed to lose a few Kilos. Doing no exercising was starting to show. At least, she thought so.

"I'm confused. Didn't you say that the chamber was discovered after the blast when Theo had already passed on?" She asked.

They all waited for Trevor to explain the reason for her question, but instead, Richard beamed: *"Annelies, I am still in contact with Theo; that is why Trevor said what he did."*

"The enlightened ones came down from the clouds in their astral craft." Trevor was enjoying his ice cream when he said that between mouthfuls.

"I never saw that translated part," Richard said.

"I know. We only found the translation last week. I can add that the scroll's author knew a lot about how sound receives light; we are only now beginning to understand this new esoteric science about Astral Crafts."

During the whole conversation, Fred and Quincy had not spoken a word. She was keen to know when they would move into their new home.

"Gosh, I look forward to you giving us a guided tour of your chamber. Ben, have you been there?"

"Annie, you will experience that it will be a challenge, climbing down into the cave, and just be prepared for the steep climb back to the top.

Chapter 20
The Elemental Beings of Light

A New Start

Annelies was relaxing in her new surroundings on the front deck of their wooden cottage, going over the last week before they had arrived at the Chateau.

The evening they had spent with Toon and Ingrid seemed ages ago, but that was the start of their new life. When they left the following day to drive to France, they did some sightseeing and stayed overnight at several guesthouses. Everything seemed to be on high alert about a possible lockdown affecting many businesses. Last week, they had arrived at Half-way House. Everyone was there. Hans and Liesbeth, Tieneke, Trevor, Sascia, Richard, and their hosts. The couple that ran Halfway House, Peter and Helen, with their three children. Even Otto and Jill came from Buttercup Valley. They had organised a great reunion, especially for them.

"Annie, there you are."

Her half-brother Otto had come to say goodbye. He was five years her senior but could easily pass for fifty. Both Fred and Otto took after her dad. Dark, slightly curly hair with only streaks of grey at the temples. Both were somewhat taller than her, but she was tall for a woman.

Otto and his wife Jill would return to Buttercup Valley in Toon's plane before the crazy restrictions they all knew had a suspicious agenda behind them.

"Hi brother, sorry you could not stay longer."

"I never stay anywhere too long, but you know that. It's now your turn to visit us."

"I hope we still can. Dirk, Toon's pilot, has already been told that he may not take off."

She closed her laptop and was about to stand up, but Otto insisted she did no such thing.

"Where's Jill?"

"Saying goodbye to the grandchildren before they go to school and playschool. Are you settling in?"

"Yes, I sort of have to get used to it."

Their cottage was just the kind of place where she could withdraw to prepare for her workshops. It was tucked away in the trees.

"Ben has been kept busy, and today was the first day I could write again."

Otto settled next to her on the bench on their cottage porch.

"I hear you will be giving your first workshop this coming weekend since you arrived."

"Yes. It is decoding our six blueprint cards on the third awakening level. I hope the weekend is long enough to get through the work."

"Is that the title?"

"No, not really, but it's going to be a creative workshop; apart from the decoding exercises, making a deck of cards is fun; you and Jill should one day join the workshops." Otto nodded and waved at someone who walked past.

"I thought it was a kind of computer game you were playing, or do I have that wrong?"

"Yes, that as well. It's a bit like the transformation game, but then far more interactions with each person's symbol graphics, and we each play from a screen that links to the big screen on the wall."

Otto shook his head. He was not computer literate, so her explanations only alienated him. He was a handyman and loved planting crops, an outdoor type.

"This was the cottage Jill and I stayed in before we moved to Buttercup Valley. Did you know that?"

"No, I had no idea. How long did you stay at Half-way House?"

"Six months. That was four years ago."

Children's voices in the distance reminded her that she had promised to show Peter and Helen a menu layout she had used in her hotel.

"Yes, Ben and I will soon visit you in the mountains. I'm sure Toon will find a way. Gosh, so much has happened. We settle in while Ben and Leo prepare a way out of the tunnels through a passageway that runs underneath one of the pyramidal temples in the Valley of The Gods pleasure park. Fred and Quincy's upcoming wedding is also here. We are getting used to a whole new routine, being part of a community." She replied in one breath.

It was still strange not having her own home. She now realised how much attachment cords to a property could delay one's adjustment to a new environment.

Jill joined them, and after saying their goodbyes, they left her alone. At least the weather was a lot milder in France. She could already sit outside.

This afternoon, she'd once again asked for her Higher Self to be in control while working on her decoding interpretations. The construction of the image of the spacings on her grid sheet, which was divided into five layers, had taken her the whole afternoon.

Only recently did she see a resemblance of her five awakening platforms to Toon's layout of the Valley of the Gods park structure. Trevor also picked up on it when he created the backdrop graphics for the game Richard described in his last journal.

Toon's idea had come to him during the late nineties when he was beginning to feel restless doing what he was doing, travelling around the globe on business meetings with his late father's many corporations, especially the oilfields in Alaska. He had started selling off the shares, which financed the start of at least four community Halfway centres. The one in France was the first one. Connected to that centre was the Buttercup Valley community in the Austrian Alps.

That was probably why POWAH had instructed her to ask Ingrid, Richard and Liesbeth to write a journal on their experiences. Of course, it made sense.

Ingrid's journal reflected that people would have to have a motivation, a passion almost, to want to wake up. Many people on the planet were not even aware that they were not awake.

First, people drawn to community living must be motivated to do so. This motivation usually came about by seeing and understanding why their dysfunctional society held no future on a global scale.

Her Awakening card creations on the first level dealt with the five personality cards. Her astrology charts were all still in one of the boxes. She had not yet unpacked them. There was just not enough space. She needed to clear out more stuff that was of no use anymore.

The Five Personality Cards

On her astrology chart, a two-dimensional representation of the first level of their physical reality and interpretations still dealt with mundane thinking patterns. There were five cards in her awakening game where the number codes could change when someone, like herself, moved to a different location.

The first three spacings on her decoding program dealt mainly with the egoistic human mind that still intensifies itself incorrectly and imperfectly.

She looked up Ingrid's chart, which she kept in a file on her main computer under the file titled Ingrid, but it was not on her laptop. She had her permission to use her decoding work as an example. Ingrid used her married name Barendse. She had participated in her ascension workshop before meeting Toon, so it would be different during her seminar at Half Way House. That would be interesting.

Ingrid's Present Personality Code-44 Community was like her opportunity code

On the second level, people would be attracted to community living and would have prepared to become more self-sustainable in a small way. They would have gathered information through books and personal efforts about how they could live a more fulfilled life. That was why the second level was gathering information on the awakening journey.

Richard de Jong was a good example. He is an intellectual, but at the same time, his out-of-body experiences made him a perfect candidate for writing a second-level journal. He was a typical example of someone who analysed everything. She had also his permission to use his decoding work as an example.

Then, she came to the third stage of her Awakening project. That was her level with her journal that Liesbeth would later turn into a novel.

Like herself, people living on the third awareness level would start to visit communities, read about them, start their own, or get involved in projects that interacted with the already established communities worldwide. Some were online communities. Not everyone would end up living in a community; instead, some would support Eco-villages of their choice while living outside a community.

Fred kept donating books to Halfway House. Tieneke gave her mind-drawing classes, and Niels was the technical computer expert contracted by Toon to maintain the computers of Half-way House and later the Laboratries database.

People who started their communities faced a long and challenging time to keep existing. Many would not be able to pull it off without some financial backing. The other reasons were often the inability to let go of old needs like possessions, private space issues and many other habitual patterns, not to mention finance.

That was what happened to Mien's two sons in South Africa. Her best friend, who had lived in South Africa for most of her married life, had not chosen an easy incarnation. Being married to the same Nick du Toit, who was now sitting in jail, waiting for the outcome of his trial in Den Haag, had been hard.

Gosh, what had Ben further said about the trial? She had never asked him what happened the last time he and Toon had to be in Den Haag. To all of them, it was clear that Nick was involved or knew who had planned the kidnapping of Ingrid and the attempt on Toon's life.

Her first decoding workshop registration at Half-way House in France was filling up. Liesbeth warned her to be prepared for a large attendance. Some people were travelling from Holland by car, taking the chance that they might be stopped at the border. Nobody knew what was going on. Many would be staying at the bed and breakfast section of the Chateau. In the meantime, her third-level group would arrive soon. She had spoken to Tieneke about joining her as a facilitator. She knew Trevor hoped she would also move to Halfway House for different reasons. Tieneke was also getting people to sign up for her Language of Light mind drawing classes at Buttercup Valley, which was not easy to get to. So Toon had organised for his private plane to take them instead. That short flight would soon be added as a tourist attraction.

That had been the plan, but now, due to this fake pandemic propaganda, it was all in chaos.

When Toon purchased this property in France with its surrounding vineyards and buildings years ago, most people were unaware of the global changes that would soon be upon them.

Last year, when the large estate attached to the chateau came onto the market again, nobody knew what was hidden deep underground.

Toon's obsession with building community centres around the globe took years to unfold, but he never deviated from his passion. His vision that a global collapse on every level would happen in their time kept him focused. From a young age, he knew the responsibility of inheriting a massive fortune that was bestowed on him because he had chosen that path.

As for herself, she knew that she had chosen to design a map or a workable structure, inspired by many of Rudolf Stainer's writings, that many, if not most, western people could follow. It was one of the ways to bypass the intellect controlled by the human persona.

Toon, with Ben and his twin brother Leo, had detailed how a community could work. Later, Trevor and Otto joined Toon with his plan, for Toon controlled the capital but did not necessarily have all the wisdom necessary to pull it off successfully.

That reminded her. Had Ingrid ever elaborated on her experiences when they visited the community of Damanhur in Italy? Especially the Temples of Humankind. Trevor told her that the temples were significant underground constructions excavated by hand into the rock by the citizens of Damanhur. Toon only mentioned that their Valley of The Gods resort had a similar flavour but was above the ground.

"Hi there."

She waved back at a man who looked familiar. He seemed to know her.

"Oh, hi, Dirk. Sorry, I didn't recognise you. Are you back already?" Can you still fly in and out from France to Holland?

How could she forget Toon's pilot, Dirk? When he was out of Europe, he often flew the plane for Toon and was now flying visitors back and forth. She couldn't remember how long the flight was to the Buttercup community higher up in the mountains.

"Toon flew some members home this time. Are you settling in?" Dirk replied as he walked up onto the porch to shake her hand.

Good grief, was this man telepathic?

"I'm not sure yet. Do you live nearby?"

"Yes, in the village."

Dirk chatted more about his family, how he heard about a Dutch businessman looking for a private aeroplane pilot, how his life had changed when he became his pilot, and how his wife wanted to participate in the workshops at Half-way House. She was now glad that she had deleted that over-the-top email from Dirk about the healing council of Orion and the Ashram of Lord Rama. She was genuinely pleased to experience how many people were awakening around the Jaarsma Clan.

When Dirk left her on her own on her front porch, which ran all around the cottage, it reminded her of the wooden deck around the main building in the community in South Africa, which was built by Mien's two boys with the help of local artisans, except that it was far more private.

Getting used to being close to people who walked past her cottage took some. Her porch in the front, which led to her front door, was often used as a gathering place. It was north-facing and very secluded from any weather. Her view from the spare bedroom balcony upstairs was outstanding since it was both south-facing and equally private. It reminded her of the balcony of the main bedroom of Titanya's cottage in Clovelly, but slightly larger, without the stunning sea views. Instead, she looked out over the vineyards.

Suddenly, she thought the small room off the balcony would be a great place to create her office, both inside and outside.

This decision inspired her so much that she immediately made plans. She got up and brought her laptop inside.

The tiny spare room upstairs would be perfect since Ben would not have to share her office space. After arranging her desk, her computer with her printer and scanner, and organising everything she used to have in her office in Apeldoorn, all in the small space, she looked at her connection cables. An electrical plug near the window next to the door opened up to the balcony. Perfect.

The small half-round table outside would take her laptop. Working outside instead of indoors made a difference.

"There you are," Ben called out.

"What do you think? I'm making this my studio, office and meditation hideaway."

"Annie, I'm delighted you have done that. Now I know you will settle in. I was worried you might have had regrets."

Ben was always very affectionate and supportive, especially in a happy mood. His firm, bear-like hug made her feel good.

"I needed to create a private space for myself. Now that I have made a start, I will soon make this our home."

She was proud of her labour. It inspired her to start with a meditation as a form of initiation.

"Why are you here? Having a break from whatever work you are doing these days?"

"I'm changing into other clothes and will join Toon on the construction site. You should soon come to see how far they have come on."

She said she would, but now that she had created her office space, she was eager to explore more of her inner world, the world of her etheric body of light. Later, she would share her experience with Ben, but for now, she needed to digest her visual meditations within herself.

When Ben left, she settled into her office chair, which had almost become part of her. Ben offered to buy her a new one, but she was not about to part with a piece of furniture that had looked after her human body during her awakening stages.

She repeated the same ritual, starting with her breathing. This time, she hoped to get into the same deeper state without the mysterious artefact. She again placed her attention on the crown of her head and imagined that her breath entered her body through that area. Then she visualized the same light beam that someone would switch on....

***

After a while, she felt the same weightlessness as she had done before. Her physical senses were still very close because she could sense her surroundings, but as if a mist-like vapour had separated her from her human body, she again felt as if POWAH was talking to her.

<Your identification with your mind is your greatest obstacle, but for now, we have decided to explore what your mind has filed away.>

Could her mind ever reach or penetrate beyond itself? The sensations of POWAH, speaking to her, was that just happening in her mind?

<Like your plants, which all have root systems that penetrate Earth and drink of her substance, humans must find their root system. It's in this way that all plants are linked.>

In an instant, her mind had manifested a scene where shrubs, trees and plants were growing amongst many rather large boulders. She wondered where on earth this was.

<You are nowhere and everywhere. The unconscious field of your Higher Self is not separate from its source.>

Her mind again stepped in because her attention was drawn to the flash of different light colours, reminding her of a photo of a city scene at night.

<Now, imagine that each plant, tree or shrub has an invisible secret root connected to the very centre of your planet, like what you see now.>

The visions reminded her of the movie Avatar, which she had seen in South Africa.

<At this point of convergence, every plant is unified and aware that its real identity is this core system. This secret root is the lifeline through which individual expression (the seed) is brought to the earth's surface and its unified consciousness released.>

She now saw how the root system POWAH referred to was like a freeway, spreading much like the branches of a tree. The energy force pulsating like a thin winding thread in continuous movement, as you see on a video of a city scene at night, was still unfamiliar to her. Where was she?

<You are inside your biological human body.>

In an instant, her mind tried to take over again, knowing she was sitting in her chair behind her computer. Was she shown how her higher intuitive mind could explore the vastness of her unconscious? She now understood that while she was still in the moment, she could only go beyond her conscious mind.

<Yes, now you can see how the physical body of each individual has a secret root system that spirals into the uncharted realm of the central universe of the first source, like an umbilical cord that connects the human baby with the nurturing essence of its mother. These secret streams of light are the carriers of the human Etheric double, hidden in your Body Codes of Light.>

POWAH had always said that the teachings of the Language of Light would awaken their Body Codes of Light, but she could again feel that her mind still tried to frame a question.

<All life is embedded with what we will term codes of light energy. These codes written by the body elemental and encoded within your biological cells will reveal your core wisdom. It can awaken within your cellular program a link that will permanently activate your higher I Am mind. The body elementals can show you how each biological cell is the passageway into wholeness and unity, even in its incomplete existence.>

She almost flipped out of her altered state from the inspired ideas rushing into her when she remembered the elemental beings she had connected with before, but she managed to silence her thoughts.

<Inspirations are eternally holding on to the 'knowing' that this secret root exists even though it may seem intangible to your human senses. Your Body Codes of Light numeral energy are like a tireless magnetic force that drives fragmentary life experiences into a unified life expression. It is the immutable bridge over which all life will pass.>

POWAH's reply to her thoughts made her remember why she had to start her ascension decoding workshops with the five present spacings. When one large boulder drew her attention, surrounded by plants and rocks. She knew it looked somehow familiar. Somehow, she had the urge to thank the rock, but for what she had no clue.

'I'm one of the Builders of Form called upon to provide the universal Light substance and follow a 'genetic code' to create your planet. The length of time that any Elemental can hold this 'genetic code' in their consciousness determines the duration of the manifest form.'

Was it indeed a colossal stone that spoke to her? Or was it her mind that telepathically translated the consciousness of this massive boulder on the property of the Titanja's cottage? Was this all for real? Was her mind forming an image again?

'Each Spirit spark, before their first incarnation, was joined to an Elemental in a solemn ceremony before the karmic lords. Do you recall this ceremony?'

"What ceremony?" With great difficulty, her mind tried translating visions so alien it made no sense. She knew then that she had to let go of trying to think. She forced herself to observe her physical body in her chair. At that moment, peaceful feelings of immense gratitude engulfed her beautiful, almost angelic being.

'Your super consciousness has given you access to your inner universe. You did request it, not so?'

With astonishment and pure illumination, she recognised the being telepathically speaking to her. Dienie suddenly appeared as what, a natural spirit? Dienie was the name she had given her years ago, dressed as a nun. How come she now recognized this entity as...what, an elemental being? For a moment, the idea was almost enough to make her faint.

Just let go of your thoughts and your need to translate your experience into words; they will come later. Come, I must show you something significant for you to realize.'

What happened by following Dienie's advice blew her mind. She was clearly shown her inner visions. She had to remind herself that she was inside her own physical human body.

'So you are. We are sharing with you why you have chosen to enter this incarnation during the constellation of Leo.'

"Are you going to show me why I chose my three soul spacings?" She heard that she spoke out loud since she was alone in her physical reality.

'Yes, to decode your genetic blueprint, you must recall and bring this information into your mind. Until now, most people have not grasped the spiritual knowledge behind the science of astrology, but you will soon understand its logic. Come...'

Her inner body world transfixed her whole being. What happened next would all depend on what? Her knowledge of genetics? She had no clue about the workings of a biological cell. Leo would be far better off taking this interstellar trip into a microscopic universe.

Gradually, Annelies became awed by what stood before her. She could almost describe it as a fairy, except no wings were flickering. It was hard to conceive that she had stepped into a world 100,000 times smaller than the reality she knew so well.

Rather than entering outer space, they entered inner space where she would meet her elemental partner.

A reddish light blob that changed into a green fluorescent image seemed to come nearer. One moment she was observing a miniature cell, and seconds later, she was flying deep into its molecular architecture.

She felt like a co-pilot, or at least what her mind translated as looking through a pair of eyes like the windows of an astral spaceship. The controls that steered over a cellular landscape were in complete control. Her Elemental partner was her tour guide, pointing out notable landmarks.

'Never before has this been seen by human eyes, except through a microscope.'

The cells Dienie pointed at took on the appearance of sentient creatures. Was she indeed brought face to face with the molecules that were the very foundation of life itself?

She knew that her subconscious had taken her deep into the levels of her super-consciousness. The elemental being she had dreamed about had heard her plea. In her heart, she knew that nothing was hidden, but she had to ask for it to get it. She needed to understand the workings of an environment as foreign to her as the North Pole, the universe of the human body.

'What your higher mind brings to your conscious awareness is taken from your akashic records. You are not in your past or future; they do not exist. Remember that...'

She had been allowed to inhabit a human form, and the elementals, cute energy balls of fire, danced around her in joy. They were going to be partners! The music of the spheres played the rejoicing serenade to announce the forthcoming experiment. The karmic lords informed her that the Elemental creature, in the form of an energy ball, was destined to stay with her. Dienie, the Spirit of light, would always be near so long as she desired to inhabit a physical body.

Everybody at the ceremony laughed when her elemental being started to show off her skill by showing how she had been trained at inner levels to draw the universal light substance by following a code to create a flower or anything in nature, simply by holding onto the thought.

She was almost awake back in her office chair when her mind projected an image she needed to translate. She tried repressing the urge to stay fully alert. Now, she understood her companion's joy in showing off. When these potential Builders of Form increased their capacity to hold the patterns they received from the great Nature Devas, they worked up the ladder of evolution to a point where they might be entrusted to build a human temple. This human form would house the presence of a divine great spirit, adding to the experience of a human soul. That was it! She now grasped the existence of fairies and other fantasy creatures written about in so many children's stories.

Her elemental partner, her body avatar, was entrusted to keep her physical body in repair and always make it a habitable temple.

In a remarkable show of colours, the pure electronic light substance and the forces of the organic energy forming into her body elemental were spectacular. She looked with great affection upon her elemental being who had earned the right to admire the perfection of her higher mental body.

"Only these 'God Codes' were to be used." Annelies heard telepathically, but by who? Again, she felt as if someone else was observing her.

With great admiration and gratitude, she was shown, on an enormous screen, what these God codes represented as a program.

What these codes manifested within the third-dimensional plane was impressive. Her physical body was beautiful in every aspect.

Her Etheric energy body was the program that her elemental was used to out-picture the full glory of her higher mental body. It was going to be easy for her elemental being to have reference to her grid pattern from time to time now that she, the divine spirit, had woken up to her existence!

After her elemental ball of energy took up residence within her physical human temple during each new incarnation, she kept it spotless, like a housekeeper or a caretaker, to maintain the functions in workable order. She instinctively knew the link between her mind and physical form was meant to bring joy.

What had gone wrong?

'When man began to experiment with the divine energy during the Lemurian epoch and programmed into his etheric body certain distortions and impurities of the essence, your body elemental became confused because the pattern distorted, and it obediently began to build the distortions into the flesh.'

While meditating in South Africa, the giant boulder showed her a vision, like a movie script. It depicted how her soul could journey between different realms during her incarnations. In between lifetimes, her elemental partner had the freedom to roam the elemental kingdom and rest before joining her for the next stage of service in a new embodiment.

'The following scene might be disturbing, but your mind must perceive. The lords of karma called you again – since all your soul's experiences are not only on Earth but also from the inner realms and between embodiments because your elemental partner needed to resurface within your etheric body at this time.'

In pure dismay and shame, she observed how reluctant her elemental partner was now when it showed up. She wanted to reconnect, but instead, in deep humiliation, her elemental being showed to the karmic lords a body she hardly recognised.

'What you see now is an example of what distorted genetic codes can do to a human form when there is no feeling of forgiveness, love and gratitude; you removed these quality codes from your etheric body library.'

"But how come? Why?" She mentally asked. Even in this incarnation as Annelies, her body had not been so deformed. As the observer, she recognised the angelic being that appeared next to her elemental partner. Was that her? She wanted to merge with her higher mental body to offer her support, but when she saw that her elemental partner was soothed by her higher presence, she learned how important this lesson was.

'When the divine energy of pure unconditional Love is given to your body elemental to weave these genetic codes into a new physical form, you will see how important it is to live every physical lifetime in harmony with cosmic law.'

Gee, what she saw was all happening on energy levels, which her mind could not translate into words, but she understood now how the program called 'belief' makes human beings think that their physical lives are controlled by their genes. This is not the case. No matter which parents you chose or in what part of the world you decided to incarnate, the soul's information of previous lives affected what the physical temple would be like.

She saw how reluctant her elemental partner was to take her impure substance from her etheric energy field and use the "best" of the elements for the outside of her physical body, hiding the impure substance inside her form!

Visions of squatter camps with garbage all around people's humble dwellings came into focus. Was that a reflection of the reality in humanity's physical world?

She now understood that the outside of the human form does not reflect the person's true nature.

'You have been shown that it has been difficult for your elemental partner to reproduce your higher mental body through the etheric substance you have provided after centuries of your endeavours.'

With great sorrow and regret did she now fully understand how when the lower mental 'ego' body took charge, the tremendous added strain of working against the appetites and passions of the persona aged a human form, primarily when the consciousness of the persona held onto feelings of fear, anger, hate or sorrow. She now understood why her body elemental had developed an antipathy for her. It was because it had to work with impure material. It was programmed to create a human body with deformed body codes. This was no longer a creative endeavour.

'When an individual comes to a point of understanding and chooses to abide by the Laws of Love and Forgiveness for itself as a human creation, and releases itself from all activities which break down the structure of the physical form, then the beginning of a new association and friendship between the individual and the body elemental will be established.'

Annelies now fully grasped how the 'belief' that humans are frail biochemical machines controlled by genes is false. Human beings are influential creators of their lives, and the knowledge of the authentic self would provide self-empowerment.

She was now very clear about how to format her workbook—the Body Codes of Light. The human form would become whole again by purifying the etheric immortal light body while being in a physical body.

Her vision quickly evaporated as if her mind were a sieve, and she could not hold the images of what felt no longer like her future. In an instant, she was fully alert and back in her chair behind her computer, back in her new office at Halfway House.

***

She heard many voices from below the cottage near the front porch where they had sat to have breakfast this morning as if they were all shouting at each other. What was going on?

"When duality patterns are threatened by unity, forces" she picked up from somewhere.

Her emotions were suddenly in an uproar. No matter what, it was already too late, even if she stayed aware that she had been reacting. Hearing people's destructive or judgmental thoughts often created a cramping pain deep in her solar plexus, primarily when directed at her; she felt as if the people walking past her cottage were angry about something.

She got up, closed her computer, and softly walked down the winding wooden staircase to avoid making a noise.

Why she came across the way some people perceived her to be often surprised her. It took a lot of contemplation before she learned the difference between what people were saying and what they were hearing.

"Mom, most people only hear what they want to hear, see or feel to be true within themselves. True listening is not yet a very developed skill in many youngsters."

Liesbeth's telepathic message was comforting to hear. These kids outside did not exhibit Trevor's symptoms, which are clearly documented in his video.

"Mom, remember the body language, the tone of their voices, and the energy levels of the youngsters in the front of your cottage; much of that energy is influenced by communication with a group on the internet. It's a website that documents past events on this property, telling them they would become one force of power."

She could see through the bamboo blinds from the kitchen that a group of teenagers had gathered in front of the porch.

"What are they arguing about, do you know? Where are you?"

Liesbeth was silent for a while, but the angry voices from outside echoed inside her head.

"Stop hiding from the truth. Show your faces. We know that you are hiding away." Someone was shouting.

The feelings the group of youngsters expressed with their shouting reminded her that she had energetically accumulated those feelings. They were created from experiencing disappointments, hurt, grief, unhappiness or lack of self-worth over many lifetimes. Now she understood why that energy would surface in all people, young or old, during these end times. They all needed to be transformed or healed.

"Mom, after Otto and Jill left the cottage to live permanently at Buttercup Valley, Helen rented the cottage temporarily to three people without a home for financial reasons, or so they thought. The people outside your door think the same occupants are still living there. Don't interact with them. I will inform the others."

Gosh, it never crossed her mind to do cleansing before they moved into the cottage. Strange that Helen never mentioned them.

She peeked through the window and saw that Ben had arrived. He was speaking to them. She couldn't hear what was said, but the group slowly moved away.

Suddenly, the phone rang. It was the first time she heard the landline ringing in the cottage.

"Annelies here."

"Hi, I heard you had some disturbance at your front door. We are sorry about that. Peter is on his way to you. Are you still joining us for a meeting this evening ?" Helen asked.

She remembered that Trevor and Tieneke would have dinner in the main dining room that evening. Trevor had collected Tieneke from her home in Utrecht, and together, they had been staying at Buttercup Valley for a few days before Tieneke would join her to help with her workshop. Trevor wanted to see how the projector and network setup he used in her workshop worked.

"I will join you later. Ben just walked in through the door. See you after we've had dinner. I'm not sure if Ben will come."

After explaining what the group wanted, Ben kissed her and told her about the temples Toon was building inside the Valley of The Gods.

"I'm so impressed with his visions for the pleasure Park," Ben said when he sat on the high bar stool at the breakfast counter. Toon shared he was inspired by the community they visited in Italia."

"Oh, you mean Damanhur?"

"Yes. I believe Helen said that many people are signing up for your ascension workshop, but aren't you playing the computer game on the third level with your first group tomorrow?"

She then explained that Trevor had already organised a special room and set up all the laptops on the big oval table she had used at home during the second virtual reality card game. They chatted further about how both their days had been.

The cottage had an open-plan kitchen, dining room, and lounge. Annelies had to get used to that, but at least they could chat while she cooked dinner.

Chapter 21
Laws of the Twelve Planets

The Code Game of Ascension

Ben kissed her goodbye, wishing her a great day. He was off to work getting a team together to be responsible for the safety of the people who worked on Toon's large project. Their routine in Apeldoorn was almost similar, except for Ben's work. The company of people he was now spending time with were of a far different calibre.

Her ascension decoding workshop bookings at the chateau on Wednesday and Friday evenings also filled up. Many people started to wake up knowing they were all part of a group's soul, but they had to awaken their individual I AM. She was truly grateful to live in a community where nobody wore a mask, and they could move around on the property wherever they wanted. The stories around the world in other countries were genuinely unbelievable. It seemed that the dark forces had sabotaged the mainstream media everywhere in every country. Nevertheless, people seem to have made plans to come.

Some visitors used words like global consciousness, God, and the supreme spirit. It didn't matter to her so long as the energy of the Jaarsma Clan's example grew in numbers.

Trevor was busy, but after his regular job in the underground labs, he promised to set up a website where people worldwide could participate in her decoding workshops. She needed to begin training facilitators to take over from her. Tieneke would do the same with her Language of Light workshops[1]. Hers were more challenging to set up since they contained drawings, but she was sure Trevor would devise a plan.

Last evening, Liesbeth asked how her journal was going now that she had more time to work on it. She kept adding more information that had surfaced. Her decoding workbook with the decoding sheets and images took the time. Not to mention writing down the interpretations she had never written down before. Now, she needed to recall what her intuition told her to write concerning each number's soul quality. The words of the interpretation would trigger a memory quality code in each individual to whom it belonged.

Before her busy day took hold of her, she needed to meditate to connect with the elemental being for whom she now felt great love and affection. It was almost easier to love her body now that she had the experience of interacting with her body avatar. She now understood that her light body was her consciousness on an eighth-dimensional awareness level. Now, she needed to ask her higher self what her lower self needed to learn from her light body that held all her knowledge.

She settled herself in her chair and allowed the noises from outside to slowly disappear into the distance. Again, she visualized that a light beam entered her crown chakra. A faint smell that penetrated her senses reminded her of jasmine, and she could still hear music far away. Her mind tried to get her back into her physical reality for a split second, but she stayed focused by asking for assistance.

**

1. https://wordpress.com/view/allrealityshifters.wordpress.com

Suddenly it was as if she was standing in a blinding light. Feelings she could only describe as being greatly loved and cared for surrounded and penetrated her like a soft, warm blanket.

A mist-like vapour rose, revealing how its original blueprint still influenced each etheric human light body.

<No immortal soul could embody even a small percentage of its energy into a human form if it did not carry a fragment of the original blueprint. The centuries of abuse and careless use of the human body, sustained by your elemental partner, make it challenging to cleanse the body's distortion fully.>

With that understanding, she immediately observed how her mind wanted to regain control. She knew it was because she felt how her regret had surfaced.

<Your body elemental partner must wait while your etheric body has resumed its light pattern of the higher mental body. Your body elemental will soon be able to out-picture your real self through the flesh.>

POWAH's energy, telepathically speaking to her, uplifted her spirit, knowing that enlightenment is the golden age written in many scriptures and will arrive in her lifetime. Lightworkers all over the planet must now acknowledge their multidimensional universe and be appreciative of its wholeness, structure, and perfection. Only then would real peace be experienced.

<When you experience this appreciation in your mind and body and in the world of time and space, only then can your ascension journey truly begin..>

Previously, during meditation, when her conscious mental and emotional body simultaneously entered the vibratory presence of POWAH, his radiation had always awakened her memories about her elemental partner. But it was only now that she understood that her body avatar had stored the many Body Codes of Light away for her to reassemble.

It was not always easy to admit, but she had hoped to see what her blueprint was like at the start of this incarnation.

Her mind had once again taken control of her visions, but that which the rock or the artefact had shown her earlier was no more real than the reality of her human existence.

< You have been shown the seed vision of your Body Codes of Light energy. The imprint of its purpose will soon come to life. We are here to assist beings like yourself first in conceptualizing and then experiencing the multidimensional universe as it truly is, not only through the language of your world but through the language of Unity, the language of Light.>

Her mind started to speculate why she had previously seen horrible visions of her past, or future for that matter.

<What you saw was a vision of the perceptions of many human beings who had not awakened to their truth. Your Body Codes of Light will be able to deposit a new perception of your I Am Self with the authentic energy of the First Source.>

POWAH confirmed that the perception of each individual created every person's reality. The following message she saw as a vision. Words were inadequate to explain what was real or what was her imagination.

<It is up to each individual to embrace the fact that there is no need for ageing, death, or illness in a physical reality. You must conceptualize and experience the multidimensional universe as it truly is. You will do this by taking and merging with your consciousness through your DNA codes of light.>

As she heard the words forming in her mind, the vision that appeared was that of a young woman around twenty-five years old. She saw herself in millions of mirror-like reflections. Several layers of energy fields were swirling around the physical body of a tall, young, attractive brunette. Her complexion was of a rich golden tan.

It was incredible to observe how her inner spiritual power was anchored in the cells of her living physical body and how it became useable energy for her full spiritual awakening.

<This knowledge, when understood, will change the course of this planetary system. We are here to assist people like yourself and accelerate the information of divine truth in the mind of humanity.>

Those were the last words imprinted in her mind before she started to feel her physical senses again. The vision of herself as young, trim and fit for any physical activity showed that she must sign in for a yoga class. Or at least join some exercise group nearby.

***

Every day, she walked better. She hardly needed her crutches anymore. She opened the balcony door to let some fresh air in. It was a sunny, slightly overcast day. During the night, it had rained; she could smell it.

A Whatsapp caller broke her spell. When she peered at the bottom right side of her screen, she could see it was Trevor.

She sat down, grabbed her headphones, and clicked on the answer button."Hi there, where are you texting from?"

"From my lab office underground. I tried mentally calling you, but you were not picking up my mental signature."

Annelies often wondered why telepathy skills in her physical reality were not working during meditation.

"Okay, I'm here again, back in the land of humanity. What can I help you with?"

"We will soon need your input on building a platform where visitors can experience standing under a strong beam of light. Hans told us to ask you."

Gosh, for a moment, she was stunned; how...How did Hans know about her visions during her meditations?

"Ben told me you will soon give me a guided tour. Especially the chamber you told us about in the Pannekoek, where a person can climb onto steps into the centre part of Toon's project." She replied "Yes, that will soon happen, but can you share what Hans might have insinuated about?"

"If you give me a few more days, I will. I have to get my workshop material ready for the coming weekend."

They logged off, and she sat back, thinking.

"Mom, I was informed that you visited our activation temple. Let your visions come to the foreground of your mind."

Hans' telepathic interruption made her recall what happened when she was in her light body. Who had informed him that she had been in their activation temple?

"I have seen myself as a younger version in a hall of multiple mirrors. Is that what you mean?" she beamed in return.

She projected her visions at the same time, hoping they came across clearly. Feelings of being greatly loved and cared for were also part of the same meditation experience.

"Thank you, mom. Yes, when this divine cosmic light shivers ecstatically in a spin around our physical body, that is when the spirit spark's host is truly awakening. Welcome to our multidimensional reality."

Her feelings of gratitude knew no bounds. Her awakening had started to happen. She'd better type it into her journal so her readers could feel the same joy she now felt.

Information gathering

The weekend for her second and third decoding classes had arrived, and she was ready to share the material. Many people were on the property, and some security at the entrance was re-organised now that the authorities knew about their failure to follow the rules. Toon still managed to travel in his private plane. He somehow had people on the inside who made it happen. She was not going to ask how.

They would soon play their third level of the awakening card game for the first time. Tieneke had helped her with the preparations.

Toon and Ingrid, with baby Sandra, arrived yesterday and occupied the same bedroom they always used when visiting the Château. Hans and Liesbeth stayed with them in the downstairs second bedroom. Richard and Sascia had offered Niels, his girlfriend Clara, Gerrit, and Adel a tour of the large property. They would also stay at the Château.

They all missed Yolanda, now living in Australia with her new husband, Ingrid's brother-in-law Ed. Toon's best friend was running a community near Brisbane. They were also in lockdown.

The room they had organised for her to give workshops had a similar feel to her workshop room in Apeldoorn. Trevor had set up flat monitors with a keyboard and a mouse for each participant while they all shared and interacted on the large screen on the wall. Trevor had shown her how to bring each participant's screen onto the big one for all to see.

"This new way of teaching would, in the future, be in all schools on the planet, Mom." Hans and Liesbeth both projected when she had shown them.

She often wondered what kind of a reality they shared. Liesbeth would no doubt share that in her journal on the fourth awakening level.

Some of her participants had to be taught how to operate the system again, but they soon got the hang of it.

Many people requested to replay the second level before moving on to the third level, which worked for her as she had time to distribute her updated interpretation sheets.

"Can we solve our problems in our dreams and attract our desires by dreaming of them first?" Sascia asked after they all settled in their seats. With a smile, she wondered what her dream had been about.

"To develop faith and a higher vibration, you must meditate regularly. It will naturally help you to purify your heart and mind and align with higher truths. If you meditate on love and forgiveness, face your inner demons, and heal your soul's splinters, your vibration will rise."

"Wow, that is quite a tall order," Sascia responded, pulling up her eyebrows. Her soft, clear skin reminded her of a peach.

"A wise old teacher once explained that there are 'gatekeepers' between our normal conscious reality and subtler worlds. Reach out for your gatekeeper." Gerrit suggested.

"Oh, how was that accomplished?" Trevor asked. He had just come in to see if everything worked. She suspected that he had come to be near Tieneke.

"By creating a 'password' for your gatekeeper." They all stared at Gerrit, in awe at his comment.

"Who was this wise person? Do we know him?" Richard grinned.

"Who said it was a he."

Gerrit's humorous glint said it all. He was in a joking mood.

"Let's get back to our game. During our break, Gerrit might share with us who they were, and that person had such a creative way of explaining the entrance into new worlds." She would hold him to that.

Annelies walked behind every participant's chair to see if they were on the same page on the screen. Tieneke did the same.

"Our thoughts influence our multi-dimensional antenna within our DNA. You have already done the first level with the five cards. They had all brought their decoding sheets from the first game, and now the two hemisphere spacings and their unconscious vibe from the last game they had played in Apeldoorn.

The first eight spacings on your grid sheet and these codes with their number translations will energize our new chakra system on the third level next week."

She showed her PowerPoint on the big screen to back up her explanation.

"I've never understood what they mean by having more DNA strands, Ingrid admitted. "I know it intellectually, but how do we experience it?"

Toon nodded. He had decided to join her weekend workshop to understand how the twenty-two number spacing could show some program. He wanted each of his 22 temples at the Valley of the Gods Park to represent each human grid spacing.

"Ingrid, have you ever felt as if you are simultaneously in more than one world?" Ingrid's eyes rolled into a head, reaching into her memory files.

"You mean when we daydream, or when we visualize, or during the night when we sleep, and the next morning we remember our dreams?"

Baby Sandra was sleeping in her carry cot nearby. Since Ingrid was breastfeeding, she wanted to be near her. Ingrid had breastfed her just before they started so she could stay and participate in the preparations for the repeated game for a few hours.

"That is one example. While in meditation, one can connect with other worlds."

"Have you Annelies?" Ingrid beamed.

"Yes, many times."

"I think we have all known times when we were slipping out of time, daydreaming. Let's carry on. Look at the screen and see how the 22 spacings relate to our new chakra system. Sometimes images tell more than words."

They were all staring at the screen on the wall. A hologram of the human body with spinning vortices is seen simultaneously from the front and back on the screen. The moving colour streams intermingled, and Trevor even added a body tune to his animation. "The first three chakras remain unchanged. Observing the interaction between the functions is important to comprehend the functioning and revitalization of the new chakra system." Liesbeth explained.

"Mmm, we humans have been asleep for centuries, and suddenly, we are confronted with new ideas, concepts, and beliefs. Like Ingrid, I'm still somewhat walking in the dark." Toon remarked. He had been whispering to Niels how to work his screen.

"We all are, I'm sure," Niels added while showing Toon how to click on his screen so that his holographic body image with the spinning vortices appeared.

That was the first time Niels shared his thoughts in class. Clara was spending the day with Helen and the children.

"That is very cool. Imagine, people visiting the park can see their hologram reflected on the screen." Toon remarked.

"Okay, let's carry on. The bottom three chakras hold part of the soul force and connect it to the silver cord. This silver cord that Richard has seen during his out-of-body experiences holds the total vibratory pattern of each unique soul."

"Annelies, how does what you explained relate to the umbilical cord between a newborn baby and its mother?" Ingrid beamed.

"Before birth, babies' nourishment for growing is fed through a similar umbilical cord." She replied out loud.

She let that sink in for a second. She observed that Adel, using her clairvoyant vision, was already painting her feelings on a canvas in her mind.

"In the same way our silver cord, in the region of our solar plexus, feeds our etheric body with the nourishment of light, and because higher light vibrations are now entering our etheric body, it has a stimulating effect on our pituitary gland."

She knew that Trevor had created a video for her to back up her explanation, and it was always astonishing to her how clever Trevor was and so electronically clued up.

"Annelies, Trevor is incredible. I watched him just typing a script in code, and after a while, an image appears." Tieneke said for all to hear. They all wanted to see Trevor in action so Annelies had to bring their attention back to the screen.

"What will happen in the coming years is that our physical body will become more semi-etheric. This new body has the capacity and capabilities and appearance of the present physical body but with many characteristics now possessed by our etheric body."

Having lately had the experience of being weightless during her meditations, it was easier to explain a concept that for many were still just an imaginary idea.

"Mom have you had a light body experience?"

She nodded to Liesbeth on a closed channel. Hans winked at her, which made her smile.

"Let's look at how our antenna aligns itself to a specific band of vibrations within a DNA molecule." The moving animations were more precise than words. Thank goodness for today's technology, so the human mind could grasp concepts through visual moving images.

"Sascia is it this video that you helped Trevor with?"

Richard's question surprised them all. None of them knew that Sascia was helping Trevor with his work. He had left the room but she was glad that Trevor had started to form a team of assistants around him. Especially now that Toon wanted every temple to have a screen where every visitor could see themselves holographically.

"Let's get back to the decoding number vibrations of each of the three spacings on the second level."

"You mean the numbers on this sheet Annelies?" Richard held up his printout so that everyone could see.

She brought up an image of the new chakra system on her big screen.

You can all see how the fourth chakra vortex has now appeared below the heart chakra. It is the first significant modification during these times. It's called the diaphragm centre chakra. This new chakra will be the centre for governing stress since it will be the focal point for rejuvenating the prana or breath energy of the body. Niels put up his hand to get her attention.

"Would this be a reason why some of us are putting on weight?"

She had no idea, but it was a thought, and she said so.

"At the same time, it can remove all toxins from the body. So as you see the fifth chakra is now the heart centre for our intuitive energy and higher emotions such as love."

"How important is it to understand all this intellectually," Adel asked.

"That depends on each individual. So long as we all understand why our thoughts have such a big influence on this whole transformation process, and that we know that our universe responds to our actions."

She soon needed to share her visions with Trevor, Tieneke, Gerrit, and Adel, whom she had been introduced to as her elemental caretaker since they were all great artists in their own right.

"Great idea, Mom. That will make Gerrit and Adele feel that their skills will be useful for a bigger purpose." Liesbeth projected on an open channel.

Richard, Toon, Ingrid and Sascia had all picked up on Liesbeths telepathic reply.

"What kind of skills is Liesbeth talking about?" Toon responded with his usual directness. He often spoke before thinking.

They all waited for her reply, but instead, she looked toward Gerrit and Adel. Neither of them was telepathic.

"Adel, our etheric body avatar, knows or can make sense of it all since it is a genetic editor and grammar checker, but it must be invited to participate."

As she said it, she recalled her experience when she travelled within a body cell. She explained this experience to Trevor so that he could create an animated video, which she could show to all of them.

"Wow, that is amazing," Adel said in a whisper. "I would love to paint that concept." She heard Adel's mental response.

"Let's discuss the sixth chakra or the thymus gland centre." Knowing that the women in her group would find this very interesting.

"The high radiation levels on our planet's atmosphere are responsible for our ageing because this radiation causes the finest centres in our human body to deteriorate rapidly in early childhood. Originally, this chakra was almost the size of the human heart, but it's now an organ about the size of a small pea."

They were all silently following the animated video. It was easy to explain a concept by backing it up with images.

"It was explained to me that over the next ten years, our stress chakra centre will remain active, especially when we are out of our body during sleep or when it is in the body of a newborn baby. This new vortex centre will warn our body avatar of all kinds of diseases and any difficulties associated with the environment."

Images of ageless men and women made a good point stick in their minds.

"This time, the thymus gland will not shrink as one grows older, instead, the new thymus centre will make ageing practically non-existent among collective humanity."

She could sense that they all needed a break. Everyone in the room had millions of questions to which only Liesbeth or Hans might know the answers. She had already been in contact with Hans telepathically, and so had Liesbeth, but she was on an inner mental channel.

She left a big image of a star tetrahedron on the wall during their coffee break. She did that purposefully so that this symbol might spur any questions.

They had all returned to the workshop room when she saw Mien's face suddenly flashing before her and mentally heard Mien's distress call. Maybe she imagined it.

"Hans, what does the Star of David symbol mean concerning the Platonic solids, especially this star tetrahedron?" Tieneke asked when everybody had returned to their chairs.

"Good question, my friend", she beamed at her, wondering if Liesbeth or Hans had mentally picked up on her sudden vision.

"The star tetrahedron is related to the interdimensional human, and it represents the etheric light body that surrounds the cellular structure of a human body. It's a fourth to fifth dimension vibrational unit that can configure rate-like information." Hans replied while nodding to her.

"How does that connect to our thoughts?"

"Tieneke our mind operates as a light or a holographic imprint unit, so when our mind is ordered to project different wave patterns, like the beta, alpha, theta, and delta waves, it's then that the mind opens itself to its interdimensional portals. And as you saw on the image, the antenna points within the DNA are all interrelated."

She activated the animated projection again to make Hans' explanation more mentally accessible. Hans knew many could not follow his explanations, but that did not worry him.

"What I have explained is how the different wave patterns operate in the brain of most humans at this moment. It's completely unconscious, so the regular body functions can be lowered to minimal levels.."

"That's a good thing, isn't it?" Ingrid replied as she stood up to stretch herself and peek at her baby.

"Yes, these brain processing functions between various imaging patterns in the body and mind are only busy when we are asleep." Hans was making a dreaming noise with movements. His body language was enough to make them all laugh.

Toon encouraged Ingrid to attend to Sandra, who made noises while asleep. They all got up to see. Sandra was making small sounds, and you could see rapid eye movements. Her arms were also jerking.

"Oh, how sweet. Is she dreaming?" Sascia asked in general.

"No, she's waking up, wanting milk. I've learned that there are five behavioural cues to know when to awaken a baby to a more fully awake state to drink more milk."

"Don't you wait for her to wake up?" Adel asked.

"I usually do, but now it would be handy to breastfeed her, while we have our lunch break."

Ingrid looked at Annelies for confirmation on the lunch break.

Ingrid picked up her baby, who was instantly awake. Instead of crying, she looked at her smiling. They all started laughing, and suddenly Ingrid's baby's face changed into a sad whimper, and she started to cry.

"Oh, all that loud laughter, did you get a fright?" Ingrid spoke in an endearing soft tone, cuddling her. "Come let's take you away and give you some milk. Toon please can you bring my bag?"

After lunch, the rest of the workshop day went well. They used Richard's spacing example. Richard's Present Emotional spacing Code-43/7-Freedom. Hers was Truth from the crown chakra[2]

When someone knocked on the classroom door, they were all getting ready to finish their six cards for next week's third-level game.

---

2. https://allrealityshifters.wordpress.com/level-one-of-the-present-six-decoding-spacings/

"Annelies, may I interrupt you for a minute?"

She wondered what Helen wanted from her. She had picked up on the sadness in her voice.

Helen handed her a cell phone. "It's for you, from South Africa."

She took the cell phone and listened while thinking of Miens' face, which she had seen in a flash earlier. All she heard was heavy breathing.

"Annelies here."

"It's Harry Brinks. Something has happened to Mien." Her stunned expression had everyone in the room spellbound.

"Harry. What do you mean? "His voice had a frail tone to it.

"She's gone. The boys think she is kidnapped."

She didn't know how to react or what to say. She covered the cell phone and told the others who it was on it and about Mien.

"Do you mean Harry Brinks, my previous boss?" Ingrid asked. "Why is he in South Africa?"

She explained about their courtship when Toon took the cell phone from her. She didn't know what else to think or say. Who would kidnap Mien, and why? Was that why Mien tried to connect with her?

"Toon, ask him where her boys are, and what about...Katrina and Pat?" Toon nodded and walked away, speaking to Harry in the cell.

"Oh gosh, I wonder.... About Sonja, her daughter," she uttered out loud.

"Ingrid, do you think Debby knows how to contact Sonja?"

"You mean Mien's daughter? The girl that goes out with Doctor van Dongen? I can phone Debbie and find out."

"Yes, please." *"Ben, where are you? Please come to our classroom."*

"Well, the story goes like this," Toon said after he closed the cell phone as he walked back into the classroom.

"Harry told me that the police were still investigating the incident that happened in January. The detective handling the case had asked for the boys and Mien to come to the station to sign some papers." Toon is looking at her beaming.

"Mien was surprised to hear that after all that time, they finally found out who the two intruders were, and so they all went."

What do you mean by all? What about the two couples that were also involved?"

"Annie. Don't panic. I'm in touch with André, who has been snooping on my behalf since we arrived home last month."

She looked at Toon, who knew what Ben had telepathically beamed at her.

"The police have arrested three men they had been following for quite some time."

Now, they all wanted to know what had happened in South Africa. They knew whatever it was, it had something to do with her foot injuries. She explained the episode in a nutshell since her mind was in turmoil. She then wondered why both Hans and Liesbeth were not around. They seemed to have disappeared after lunch. That was funny.

Niels took it upon himself to close down all the screens on the large table and disconnected the big screen. Nobody was in the mood to carry on. Adel tidied up what was left on the table, and Gerrit asked her if he could borrow her file for the evening. He would bring it back the next day.

"If there is anything I can help you with, just tell me. Adel and I would like to go over the notes you have written about the six decoding spaces. Do you mind?"

Adel told Gerrit it was fine since she would not work on it tonight.

"See you both Friday morning at nine. Go and make the best of your time here. Visit the vineyards and the greenhouses."

Baby Sandra was watching over Ingrid's shoulder, observing her with intense interest. It made her smile, and she could have sworn that Sandra smiled back.

Richard, Sascia, Niels and Clara had plans for the rest of the evening, and she felt no need for them to stay and hang around. After insisting that they enjoyed the evening, they reluctantly took off.

That left her with Toon, Ingrid and Tieneke. Helen came back to tell her that Peter was online with a person named Jock. She took baby Sandra away from Ingrid, who wanted to stay; feeding her would have to wait.

They all followed Helen to their office, where Peter sat in front of a flat-screen with headphones on, talking to someone.

"Here she is. You can chat to Annelies instead."

Peter got up from his chair and whispered something to Toon.

"Jock, is that you?"

She listened while Jock told her that Katrina and Pat were with him and that John and Pat's Harrie were with the police searching for Mien. Jock had tried to get hold of Ben but didn't have his cell number. After they signed their statements this morning, Mr Brinks took Mien to a restaurant for lunch. Mien went to the ladies but never returned; that was six hours ago.

"Mom, our transformation into a new world is filled with challenges you can't yet imagine. We have all told ourselves that if there were no fear and conflict, life would be easy. However, is it not easy to learn how to enter the consciousness of a dark cloud?"

"Hans, where have you been? You both never came back after lunch? Have you...What are you implying?" She responded out loud when Ben walked in with Liesbeth and Hans.

"Any new development? Hans and Ben, I'm glad you are both here." Toon said with a relieved tone.

Ben took over from her in front of the computer. He talked for a while with Jock through the headphones, but it sounded as if Jock was suddenly alarmed about something that happened.

"Jock, share the screen with us. Can you do that?" Ben asked.

She heard from the conversation that Jock had no idea what Ben was on about. Ben took him through it, and suddenly she recognized At and Jock's office in South Africa on the screen.

Ben typed in the Whatsapp chat box instructions, and after he was sure Jock had read it, he deleted his chat text.

"Just keep the screen running and move away." Ben typed again in the Whatsapp chat box. They all could see that Jock had moved away from his desk. Now, they could all hear a woman shouting. She was sure it was Pat.

"Where is At? Did you ask?" She whispered to Ben.

The whole saga of what happened in the community flashed through her mind. She turned to Hans and Liebeth, who talked to Toon, Ingrid and Tieneke.

"Hans, do you know what is happening? Why do I feel it's all linked to many other criminal events going back years? Am I right?"

Hans and Liesbeth looked at each other, and Liesbeth nodded.

"So I was right. There is more at stake here."

She turned, and they all stared back at the computer screen in Peter's office. Suddenly, an unknown face came up close to the screen. A chill runs down her spine. With a finger on his lips, Ben warned everybody to stay silent and to move away.

"He doesn't know that we can see him. Annie, do you recognise him?"

She shook her head, but Ingrid must have just entered the crowded office to look, who gasped, hands over her mouth.

"I will never forget that face." She beamed in panic.

In horror, did she now realize that Ben was right? If Ingrid knew the man, that made her think about her kidnapping ordeal!

Toon took her away. She followed them, and so did Liesbeth and Hans. They gathered in the dining room. Tieneke had gone away to call Trevor. When they were far enough away for anyone on the other side of the internet in South Africa not to hear them, she wanted to know who Ingrid had recognized.

All she said was, "They called him the Boss-man."

Annelies now recalled reading about Ingrid's experience from her journal! Liesbeth fictionalised it very vividly, according to Ingrid. It was as if she had been there herself!

Not long afterwards, Ben joined them in the dining room, followed by Peter. Helen was with the children since their rooms were close to where the baby was sleeping, and Ingrid did have a baby monitor on her.

"The guy slapped hard at the screen, so we got cut off," Ben said.

"Is there a recording of it? I mean..."

"Yes, Peter managed to activate a program that can do just that: record what is on the screen."

Toon told Ben about the Boss-man, and Liesbeth then nodded to Hans. Ben was upset that the police had never taken him into their confidence about their further investigations and asked Hans if he knew more than the police did.

"Dad, listen, we have worn these earthen bodies for so many third-dimensional lives that we have forgotten the myriad forms our consciousness can create to define and protect us. Liesbeth and I have learned to protect ourselves with battle and prayer. However, we could not protect ourselves from others. Humanities dark attachments have always been our greatest enemy, and we are now part of it."

Trevor and Tieneke, who just walked in, must've overheard what Hans had said because Tieneke wanted to know what Hans meant by saying that the humanities collective lower energy force is our own greatest enemy.

Hans explained that he meant the 'Elite' that had controlled most of the human population for centuries. They were all quietly taking it in. She knew that not every person was under their spell.

"Liesbeth, I have a rather strange question."

They all looked at Tieneke since all of them were telepathic. They settled around the dining room table while one of the staff members rolled a trolley with coffee, tea and cakes into the room.

"Liesbeth, what will it be like when we are fifth-dimensional, with no polarities, teachers, saviours, or enemies? How will it feel when we hold all polarities within our form?"

"That is a weird question, alright, especially now. What made you ask that?" Ben replied out loud when the staff member was out of sight.

"Mom, good question. If we can imagine how it feels or remember how it has felt, it will hasten our transformation." Liesbeth beamed as she rested her hand on hers. They had all listened in.

"However, to remember the feeling of our true multidimensional selves, we will also have to rewrite the old mental programs of limitation and separation." She added when Ben was still shaking his head.

"Is that way the journals had to be written?" Ingrid asked.

"Yes. We created these programs during our many third-dimensional lives." Hans said, spreading his arms wide.

"Is that because these programs will not allow many of us to believe that we deserve the light that has come into our bodies?" She asked verbally, thinking about her meditation experience. She then told the others what she had experienced. They were all quietly listening.

"I knew it. You had such a ...kind of inner happiness about you. It showed in your eyes." Ben acknowledged.

"Liesbeth, is it because we don't believe we deserve the Light, so we cannot use it to create the life we truly desire?" Ingrid asked.

She got over her shock. Ingrid now looked relatively peaceful. Her story must have done her some good.

They all helped themselves to beverages. Peter got up and whispered something to the kitchen staff. Their table was far from the rest of the large dining room, where some bed and breakfast guests were having an early dinner. It reminded her of the dining room at the Prinsegracht Hotel.

"To release these old programs of fear and limitation, we must journey into our deep unconscious. There, we will enter the murky pool of repressed pain and fear to rescue those portions of ourselves that have become trapped there."

"Is that what has been reflected in our physical lives?"

Ben asked it on their mental wave band. She was proud of him. For a detective to hold those ideas was surely a transformation.

"Yes, during these times, we will journey into the humanoid animal stage of our genetic coding. We have all entered our lower astral self, the storehouse of our deepest hidden darkness, where we keep records of fear, worries or anger."

When Hans mentally replied, they were all contemplating. Every face in the dining room was expressing some sadness.

"We must all have the courage to travel there because we know that we are not 'just physical'."

"So what do we do with these violent people I've been in contact with? Do they represent me as well as Annelies and now Mien?"

"Don't ever take it personally, Ingrid. That is also a human distortion. See yourself as a flower in a garden of flowers. If it rains, you all get wet, not just you!" Hans replied, winking at her.

"True, but then some of us, like me and Annelies, seem to have experienced a confrontation with our... humanoid animal stage, as you call it. So, we have been compromised. Not so?" Ingrid asked

They were all waiting for Hans or Liesbeth to reply, mentally or otherwise. Liesbeth thought about how to respond next.

"We know that we are pure consciousness, and the bodies that hold our consciousness require a repair." She said in a soft but steady ladylike voice, typical of Liesbeth's speaking.

"Our mental programs and emotional beliefs were learned long ago when we were children. That is, when we were children, either in our years or our awareness." She smiled at her when she said that.

"During these times, we will all step across the threshold of our unconscious and into our deepest self." She took a sip from her cappuccino and carried on.

"We now have to realise that what is happening around us is also happening within us."

They all listened in silence, with the noises from the kitchen and outside ensuring their conversation remained private now that Liesbeth's replies were verbally expressed.

"Programs that once protected us have become our limitations, but we are ready to rewrite or release them. When these old programs were created, we did not have the power to deal with the situations, but now we have."

"I know all that. I mean intellectually, but what actions must we take concerning Mien's situation? She might be in physical danger." Ben replied. He spoke for them all; she was sure of that.

Liesbeth peered at Hans, who nodded. The silence was almost tangible. They all sensed that more was to be revealed. At that moment, Peter was called away.

"Annie, please tell me what I might miss out on." Peter beamed as he left the dining room table, followed by the same staff member, a young girl in her teens.

"Okay, what I will now explain might be...we, Hans and myself, had to create a defence mechanism to protect ourselves enough to survive a situation beyond our control. However, we now know that these defence mechanisms were like training wheels, which allowed us to "get by until we could learn to ride through life without them."

Liesbeth knew who had picked up on her explanation, including Peter.

"You mean that you must also learn how to respond to what is happening?" Ingrid asked out loud.

"Yes, but it can also help you all if you feel ready to travel into your deepest core so that we can unite and rewrite programs of fear and helplessness and replace them with programs of love and power," Liesbeth replied.

They were interrupted by Peter, who called Ben.

"A person called Harrie is on the landline from South Africa."

"Which one? Mr Brinks?"

"Oh, no. No, this person has an accent. I know Harry Brinks. Remember I met him when Ingrid was kidnapped?"

She then knew that it was Pat's husband who was on the line. Liesbeth and Hans must have picked something up that they were not sharing. She could see it in their body language. She could feel the tension around the table as if they were all waiting for a verdict. *"Mom, fear stimulates a herd instinct, remember? It's a primal reaction."*

Liesbeth's mental warning made her recall the interpretations from her decoding manuscript...The world we have made due to the level of thinking we have done thus far has created problems we cannot solve at the same level of thinking we created.

Ben and Peter returned, and everyone tried to read their minds. At the same time, the young girl who served them coffee informed them that they could help themselves at the buffet.

"Oh, Peter, did you organise for us all to have our dinner here?"

"Yes, why not. It's dinner time."

Ben told them all that they had found Mien. She had managed to convince a woman, who had forced her into a car, to let her go after the woman had panicked.

She then knew who had taken Mien. It must have been the same couple who had followed them from the train into Cape Town. So it was all indeed still connected to Nick du Toit.

"The moment has arrived that we will share with you all what our mission is, and always has been."

The story Hans and Liesbeth told them had everybody at the table stunned into silence. Ingrid knew about the walk-in part that Liesbeth and Hans had shared in her lounge. She had included their story in her journal. Liesbeth also shared some information at the beginning of Ingrid and Richard's journals.

Peter was fascinated by the fact that they serve as guardians of this solar system. She wondered about implementing the Twelve Planets' most cherished laws after they left this planet 6000 years ago.

When Hans mentioned how an 'outer world' dark force species travels around many galaxies to plunder other inhabited worlds, she wondered about At's abduction experience. Hans warned them that they had found a way of getting around this on Planet Earth.

"Man on Earth will do the plundering for them!" he remarked in sadness

Lots of things did fall into place. Ingrid's kidnapping, the problems at the Valley of The Gods, what happened in the past in this region and the discoveries under the park.

"I would love to see this underground chamber, Trevor, even if it is not yet ready for visitors." She said.

"Yes, me too," said Ingrid, who got up. It was breastfeeding time again.

"Leo is waiting for you all; he waited for when the time would arrive for Hans and Liesbeth to share their story," Trevor said.

She looked at Ben to see if he knew more than he had let on, but he completely ignored her. She knew that he was communicating with his twin brother on a private wavelength.

Chapter 22
The Riddle of the Prophet's Game

The Awakening Game

SMALL THINGS MAKE BIG CHANGES danced on the big screen when Ingrid arrived with Toon and baby Sandra in her carrycot.

Liesbeth managed to print her third decoding-level interpretation chapter out for all her participants since her workbook was unfinished.

The motivation and the desire to look into the eye of the observer were typed at the top as a heading.

Ingrid remarked that the title reminded her of the last excerpt she had received.

"I remember, just before our wedding," Toon confirmed.

"Are we going to play a computer game?" Adel asked. She must have seen each participant's name and their card images on each private screen.

"Sort of, but with a difference," Annelies replied, looking to Gerrit to explain the computer card game to Adel since he had played it before. He returned her decoding file, thanking her when she gave him the third-level chapter. They were now dealing with the awakening level her journal was about.

Gerrit then asked about the developments in South Africa.

Three couples were not present when Hans and Liesbeth told their story. Gerrit would have been able to digest it; she was sure of that, but Adel and Niels, not to mention Clara, would have been able to digest it. She was sure that Sascia would soon learn the true story behind all the dramas that had taken place surrounding the Jaarsma Clan, but it was not her call to tell it to them.

When they were all seated, she told them that Mien was back with her family and that the police had arrested the man they had seen on the computer screen. She didn't want to lower the vibration of the group by bringing up more drama, so she asked everyone to settle behind their screen and follow her third-level decoding chapter.

She told them all that Hans and Liesbeth would not join them, but she could not tell them the reasons why. It was not the right moment. Nobody asked why, and she was glad.

"Two visionaries, Trevor and Leo, have developed a groundbreaking tool that engages with our mind, body and spirit." She said proudly.

"Adel has not yet experienced how we play the computer game with our cards, so Gerrit, please help your partner."

Our game is an "Inner-active" computer journey that integrates with state-of-the-art 3D graphics, video and music. With this big screen on the wall, which is linked to the smaller screens, Trevor and Leo have created software that interacts with each individual's cards that are now showing on your screen."

She had heard Niels had also been a great help, so she winked at him. He was a shy, quiet person. He seemed to have lost some weight. Not often had she seen an Indonesian person being so overweight.

Ingrid's young baby was quiet throughout the game, being mostly asleep. However, she woke up as they started to play and remained very still and calm, eyes wide open. It was as though she understood what was happening.

She noticed Ingrid and Toon glancing at each other how they had
done the first time they had played the game in Apeldoorn.

*"Do you see Annie's platform? Look at the island, right in the centre
where the dome will be."* Toon beamed. Ingrid nodded in
amusement.

All the screens in front of them came up with the same image when
she directed her laser to the control buttons on the wall's bottom
of the big screen. When Adel saw Gerrit pointing at the winding
road, everyone was amazed to see the image come alive! A movie
was shown.

Annelies started to wave her hand close to the big screen, lightly
touching it, knowing that eight temples would appear on the
outskirts of the landscape. Trevor had shown her that it was a touch
screen.

"Are those temples built at the Valley of the Gods Toon?" Niels
asked. She had heard that Richard had not yet shown Niels and
Carla Toon's Valley of the Gods pleasure park project. There had
been no time yet. Both couples, Gerrit and Niels, with their
partners, would be going on a tour tomorrow.

"It's not entirely the same Niels. There are indeed eight temples, but
only seven are in development. Toon replied, pointing to his small
screen."

The same landscape as in their previous card game on the second
level appeared, with many coloured footsteps that were headed
past different signposts like plants, flowers, shrubs or even trees
appearing on all their screens. They all came into view as they
touched their screens.

"These nature symbols will once again interact with each of your
cards, as they did on the second card game in Apeldoorn."

Sascia couldn't wait to learn more about the meanings behind the
footsteps on the game's third level. She expressed that she was sorry
Liesbeth was not present since she recalled what fun it was to see

how Hans and Liesbeth took to the game. She told Niels that they knew the game very well, but why did she think she wasn't sure?

Toon winked at her, and Ingrid ruffled her grown-up daughter's hair. "Who is going to tell them who they are, Annelies?"

"I think that is up to Hans and Liesbeth."

"Let's go over the rules once more. What I arranged on the screen are the seven major ascension temples. Each pyramid temple must be seen as a doorway, and each chakra holds the key to each temple. Each temple links you on all the multidimensional levels."

"I thought we now have eight chakras during the shift?" Richard remarked. She was impressed.

"Richard, remember that Trevor has been working on an idea that we can create a new form of group consciousness in cyberspace, namely one in which we attain access to all information via our DNA without being forced or remotely controlled about what to do with that information."

"Yes, I get that, but did you not show us that we will have eight chakras yesterday?" Richard pressed on.

"Let's show everybody my last decoding sheet for my Body Codes of Light. I suggest you all look at your own last three present numeral vibes. The decoding codes change, as did with Ingrid when she married Toon."

They all were rustling through their decoding sheets. That made her aware that she should publish these sheets into a ring-binding file.

"We will, Mom, the moment your journal is translated into a novel." Liesbeth beamed at her on a private wavelength.

It was terrific that Liesbeth could pick up her thoughts without even being in the same room. It reminded her that the Body Codes of Light workbook had to be written soon so readers could follow her journal better.

Her Present Mental spacing of the God/ Goddess through the Solar Plexus Chakra[1]

The 22 numeral steps she needed on the awakening game screen showed her how easy it was to get to the interpretation box. Every player in the room was repeating the same steps onto the path. The silence in the room was almost electrifying. Only Sandra's baby sounds were heard.

When she decoded using various obscure tools, she mentally projected the interpretation of this numerical vibe to reflect the cycle of success. She would have to do a lot of interpretation text to gather all the information of each 22 spacing.

After a while, they all waited for her to reply to Richard's question about the eighth chakra.

"Yes, correct, and collectively, we have known at a deep level that our personality energy field of seven chakras is incomplete. We are, however, in the final act of the play of polarity. As spiritual beings, we will all soon undergo a physical transformation. Our eighth chakra will be fully in place when we are ready to undertake this greater challenge and embrace this opportunity to evolve."

Richard was happy with her reply and turned to Sascia, saying:

"Moppie, I saw some of Trevor's simulations, and again, this interactive card game is a work of art."

The interactions within the game once again brought home that everything around them was just an image their minds had created, showing that even this digital simulation was part of an illusion.

*"Richard, if humans could once again regain a link into the group consciousness field, they would have far more control over their god-like power to create, alter and shape things on Earth! Many people are collectively moving toward such a group consciousness."*Hans beamed from afar.

All the telepaths in the room had heard Hans projecting to Richard, and to be reminded of this truth was always good. Gerrit

---

1. https://allrealityshifters.wordpress.com/level-one-of-the-present-six-decoding-spacings/

and Adel were not yet telepathically active, but Hans seemed to think they would somehow pick up his mental reminder.

"Be careful, both of you. Travelling by teleportation, as you explained, is not without risks." She beamed on a private channel so Richard and Sascia would not pick it up.

"Annelies, last evening, when I was working on my laptop, a friend sent me a link to a video. The main message was: 'Whatever the mind can conceive and believe, the mind can achieve.' I now totally believe this to be true after yesterday's experience." Adel said, looking at them all.

Gerrit was proud of her for sharing. Like Niels, she was also a quiet, somewhat aloof person who took a while to come out in the open.

"Thank you, Adel. Yes, that is a compelling statement. Napoleon Hill said that I believe." Adel nodded. The creative velvet top she wore often gave her a very artistic look.

"Have any of you ever played Deepak Chopra's game?" Adel asked.

"Of course, the Wild Divine. My sister sold that game in her health shop in Delft. She showed it to me. It's beautiful, but it can no longer play on the latest Windows or Apple computers. Ingrid replied.

"I mentioned it because this interactive game is on the big screen, and our little screens reminded me of it," Adel added.

"You are so right, Niels replied. "It had included the IOM Biometric Hardware. I still have the box somewhere. I should try it out on an older laptop. "

"Mention it to Trevor Niels; he might know about it. Let's carry on." She was now getting good at walking without help, but standing still for a long time was hard on her feet.

The cards they all used to interact with each player were beautiful. Tieneke created them, and Trevor used some of her drawings and incorporated them digitally to appear on the screen.

'A World of Darkness was the name given to three related cards that would sometimes appear on their screen, but most of the players used their soul-quality cards to bring their light back into this cyberspace universe that was about to enter into the photon belt.

She now understood why Hans and Liesbeth had to enter into this world of darkness. A demonic race wanted to stop humanity's stress-related chakra, below the heart chakra, from appearing. Hans had shown them that the eighth chakra completed the octave of their personality-based consciousness. The eighth chakra is the portal to their higher transpersonal awareness levels.

"When the cards come up during the null zone in the program, what does that mean in our reality?" Tieneke asked.

"The null zone is an electromagnetic zone with an energy vacuum. Everything is cancelling everything." She replied. She had asked Hans a similar question, so she knew the answer.

"Our solar system is part of the larger solar system that is just about to enter into a cosmic cloud which is recognized by the label of the Photon Belt. It's part of a twenty-four thousand-year cycle of events." She added. Liesbeth had explained to her and Ben last night why they needed to prepare themselves for massive changes.

"This event has occurred regularly before, but not ever since the Creation?" Sascia asked.

"Yes, correct. We are soon going to see some signs and indications of its approach. We are already getting some of them. There is a lot of fighting going on we never hear about. "Toon replied.

There was a knock on the door, and Hans and Liesbeth walked into her immense surprise.

"You have no idea how glad I am that you are both here. Have you ..."
Hans' expression told her to stop asking further questions, even if she had asked them telepathically.

"Look, read the words." Ingrid pointed to the big screen. She read out loud:

It seems that unusual lighting and colours will soon appear in the sky. It will seem like the sun emits less light, even though it's midsummer. It will coincide with a gradual darkening of the planet itself.

"That is creepy, and I still can never get my head around this photon belt," Ingrid admitted with a sigh.

Hans took the laser pointer from her and pointed to the big screen's control buttons. Suddenly, an animation appeared. She was spellbound. Trevor had not shown her this video clip.

"You can all see that the whole universe uses vortices within vortices of centripetal energy. These spiralling energies give rise to natural spacetime orbits. Many satellites around planets, stars, and even solar systems around other major vortex centres are influenced by vortices. "Hans explained.

They saw what seemed to be a new broadband internet system satellite in a low orbit around planet Earth.

"What effect can this have on each of us?" Tieneke asked. She was looking a lot better these days. Far more cheerful. She suspected that Trevor had a lot to do with it.

They were all keen to hear Hans' reply.

"If humanity has evolved sufficiently by the time we enter the electromagnetic null zone, a profound advancement in our consciousness will occur as we become attuned to the high-frequency photon rays.."

They were all quiet with their thoughts. Annelies walked behind each person to see what effect the conversation had on the energy levels of each participant.

"If we are negative, that is, possess too many lower vibrations due to selfish actions, then we are not expected to survive the radiation," Liesbeth added in her soft voice.

"In other words, there will be a natural spiritual selection," Toon concluded.

"Yes, Toon. Humanity has free will, so anything is possible. Shifting our blueprint to higher consciousness for the golden age is the key to the harmonious transitioning of Earth's evolutionary process."

They all took turns playing the Prophet's game with their six cards. When it was Liesbeth's turn to play her six cards, a video depicting a bluish sandy beach appeared on the screen. Familiar text appeared: **<Your planet will enter the fifth dimension and fourth density (consciousness). The fourth density will greatly change the human body, making it lighter and different in shape and structure.>**

Annelies felt the text belonged to POWAH for a split second. Yesterday at the dining room table, she was astonished when Hans told them that POWAH was none other than a master in their world from a parallel anti-universe.

"Well, one thing is certain: everything is governed by frequency." She commented when they had all finished their turn.

"A person manifests only what is in line with their higher self. Therefore, the decoding exercises will raise every person's frequency. Many people, during their awakening, will start to resonate with new friends or even partners. Therefore, the game showed you that the lower vibrating blockages, which most of us had attracted to ourselves before, will gradually disappear."

She looked around the room, and each couple looked at each other with love and affection. Each couple had indeed found their soul mate during these times. Niels was the only one who had no partner to share this moment with, and Ben was not here either, but she was okay with that.

"That's why it's always recommended that a couple goes through this work together so that their frequency rises together."

"Good timing, girly, " Ingrid called out when Sandra started to make baby noises that translated into: "Feed me, mommy."

It was time to have a closure, so at the end of the ascension card game, the group gave Annelies feedback on what they had experienced. Some had felt physical reactions within their bodies, while others were more affected by their emotional level. Without a doubt, something had taken place during the process.

The riddle of the prophet's game was gradually revealed.

The Ascension Cave

"Annie, will you be joining us?"

"Try to stop me. I need to see for myself what that cave or chamber is like. Since Trevor told us about it, I've been visiting this cave in my dreams.

"Really?"

"Ben, remember what Napoleon Hill said on a YouTube video?"

"Oh yes. Whatever the mind can conceive and believe, the mind can achieve. What has that got to do with the cave we will visit?"

"Everything. Wait and see. What I have seen in my dreams, I expect to see happening for real."

When she appeared downstairs, where Ben was waiting for her, she had to laugh at his expression. Wearing jeans and hiking boots was so unlike her; his eyes gave away a look that she wasn't sure she wanted to hear verbally.

"Wow, you look...ten years younger!"

Gosh, that was unexpected. "Really?" She chuckled at her preconceived perception that he hated seeing her like this—all manlike.

"Annie, you could never look butch, that I guarantee."

She saw Peter's landrover waiting down the path away from their cottage. Richard, Sascia, Toon, Ingrid, and Tieneke were all dressed similarly. They had talked to each other before the trip was planned as to what they were going to wear. Sascia had been a great help in telling them all what to expect. Thank goodness for that information. Ben would never even understand such important details as a dress code!

"Annelies! I've never seen you in jeans. It suits you." Ingrid remarked.

"Wow, I can't get over the change. Annie, you look ...younger! Ben, what do you think? It's incredible." Toon would not have said it if he didn't mean it, so she felt great for the flattery. It still affected her.

"Will Hans and Liesbeth be joining us? They must have left early, before breakfast. They were not in their room."

"They left early, I forgot to tell you," Ben replied telepathically.

He joined Peter upfront while she got in at the back next to Tieneke, who whispered. "I think you are rejuvenating."

"Leo asked them to come very early, well before everyone else. No idea why, but I'm sure we will all find out." Ben voiced to the others.

"Who is looking after Sandra?" She asked.

Ingrid turned, smiling. "Helen. I've just fed her, and she and the children will join us at the restaurant on the top."

"What do you mean, on the top?"

"You will see."

The Valley of The Gods was thirty minutes away from the Chateau. They drove past a winding lane and a private driveway leading to the medical retreat where Leo used to work and where they found Ingrid, all safe and sound.

"Have you ever discovered what is going on there, Ben?" She beamed on their private channel. Nobody replied, and she strongly felt it was the wrong question, but why did she have no idea?

She looked at Tieneke, who shrugged her shoulders.

"Was Ben's twin brother not working there at one time?"

She nodded, picking up her thoughts. "Yes, they were researching anti-ageing medicine and psychedelic drugs." She whispered so the rest of the landrover would not hear her.

"During the years when Leo was involved with the research side of the clinic, he always said that the anti-ageing medicine they were developing was not about stretching out the last years of life, it was about stretching out the middle years of life, so that diseases of ageing happen very, very late in the life cycle, just before death, or don't happen at all." Ben telepathically beamed at them both.

"Yes, Trevor told me." Tieneke softly replied, "Leo had told Trevor how the search for the fountain of youth took scientists inside the genetic structure of cells to analyse the role of stress and diet on life spans. Trevor suspects that these dark Lucifer forces, which Hans mentioned yesterday in the dining room, have gradually controlled our world, including the clinic we just passed."

"Oh, so you knew that Leo was their genetic scientist before he started working for himself together with Trevor?" Tieneke nodded.

Sitting at the back of the Landrover, where it was far noisier than in an average car, their conversation went unnoticed. She thought back to the times Leo had often visited them in Apeldoorn. Regardless, he claimed that the cause of human aging had already been comprehended. Leo suspected that during puberty, human bodies are programmed to activate the "death hormone" in the Pituitary Gland. Trevor was convinced this hormone had been interbred into the human race's genes to shorten the lifespan.

"Leo and Trevor must have discovered the interbreeding that Ben had told me about just before Leo resigned as a scientist there." She whispered in Tieneke's ear.

"Yes, scary stuff. They were apprehensive for Ingrid at the time." In horror, she looked sideways at Tieneke. "What do you mean?"

"Sorry, I thought you knew, but Ingrid was already pregnant, so they let her go," Tieneke whispered. She didn't want Ingrid or Toon to pick up on them talking about her. A cold chill went down her spine, thinking that she had observed how bright Sandra already was, but the baby's loving smile made her readjust her thoughts.

In the distance, she saw high structures with an encryption feeling. Instead of driving under a huge archway that reminded her of Cairo, they turned into a private road to the left. They were stopped at a security gate. The men in uniform, wearing masks, recognised Ben and Toon and let them through.

"How many people are now working on this project, Toon?" Peter asked as he parked the Landrover.

"I lost count. A few hundred. On the other side of the park, the buildings are ready, but the large dam of water that surrounds the centre has caused us lots of problems, as you know."

"Do we have to wear a mask? She asked."

"No, everybody has a choice. We needed to follow some protocol to carry on with the constructions, but since we employ so many people, they turned a blind eye."Peter replied.

"Is it now safe?" I mean, we are going underground, not so?" She asked as an afterthought.

"Yes, but that is very deep. It was never affected by the water. You will see."

"Have you been to Trevor's lab?" She whispered to Tieneke, who nodded.

"Ingrid." Tapping on her shoulder. "Have you been underground before?"

"Once, last year, but not as far down as we are now, I believe." Ingrid looked at Toon for confirmation.

"You know why, Kitty? You were pregnant, and I didn't want to risk you falling."

They all heard Toon's telepathic reply. The name Kitty was Ingrid's nickname, and only Toon used it.

They both looked very happy when Richard stepped out of the Landrover and helped Sascia. She wondered if they were planning a wedding soon.

Richard turned and winked at her. He had picked up on her thoughts.

"When?" She asked out loud.

Sascia now also turned and told them all that they were planning their wedding in November, just before the opening of the fourth stage of the park.

They arrived at the entrance of the building and the lift that would take them down underground into the laboratories and offices.

At least four people in the park's uniform were waiting for them. One spoke into a cell phone, letting the people below know of their arrival. No doubt Ben went through the same procedure every morning. They all got out and waited for a lift to come up.

Thank goodness nobody was aware of her anxiety, or so she thought.

The lift took eight people, and Ben knew how to operate it so they could all fit in. It was her first time going underground, and they all watched how she coped with it.

Ben telepathically told her that the first stop was about four levels lower. After he had said that, a tight, claustrophobic feeling took complete hold of her. She could hardly breathe as they went down.

"Here we are." Peter opened the lift doors, and she saw Trevor on the other side waiting for them. He opened a steel gate as she had often seen in movies.

"Welcome to our humble research centre." Trevor helped them all get out of the lift. They had to step over some low railing. She was shaking all over. She followed the others with great difficulty, knowing that she had opened a pandora's box in her cellular memories.

She spotted Leo as he walked towards her with open arms, but you could see he knew about her fear. The love that was coming from him made her nevertheless feel very treasured.

"Are you coping, my friend?" He asked softly. She nodded, but who was she kidding?

"Sorry that I have not yet welcomed you in your new home. I heard from Ben that you have settled in nicely." Leo's musical voice was both humorous and warm. The ageless countenance of Leo, who looked nothing like his twin brother, being bald and shorter than Ben, appeared as if he could be from an eastern genetic background. He observed her with a wise expression, knowing that she had to be brave enough to overcome the claustrophobia that had taken hold of her. She knew that down in the caves, something was waiting for her.

Leo greeted the others and explained that Hans and Liesbeth would join them later. Then he whispered to Ben and Toon, who both looked in her direction.

Leo further explained that the walk-in couple had uncovered various sinister plots with interbreeding on a larger scale, so they were scouting for an update.

"Was that the reason for my abduction fourteen years ago?" She telepathically asked Leo to explain her extreme fear of closed spaces. She could hardly move one foot in front of the other.

Instead of replying, Leo looked at Ben and asked if they would join him in his office. Ben took her hand and followed Toon and Ingrid to a larger space with a higher ceiling. Seeing a plant in a big pot under a fluorescent lamp in the corner calmed her nerves.

"Ingrid, Trevor told me that your baby is a crystal child."

"Really?"

"Ingrid, I must now ask you to go back to a time when you were held hostage," Leo said. Good grief, she hoped that these men were not insinuating anything.

"Remember that you were questioning what was important about the drawings?"

Ingrid turned to Toon and explained: "The same man that appeared on the computer screen yesterday, the same creep who was angry because something was missing in my drawing."

"Was he the person who made rape threats to you?" Toon asked while holding her tight.

"No, he was the one that would or could easily have given the go-ahead, but he was not the guy who wanted to rape me."

She wondered why Leo wanted Ingrid to recall her dreadful experience. She had silently sat down, trying to calm herself by telling her mind that all would be fine, that they would be out of there in no time.

"He blamed me for doing something when I used that drawing program. He said that it interfered with the information in the background. I had no idea what they were talking about. All I was focussing on was how to get out of there."

Leo pointed to the flat computer screen she had ever seen.

"That is the drawing that Ben asked me to change. I remember Ben's email, which I received through their computers. I was so scared they would read it. The drawing looked like a computer sound card at the time." Ingrid said, being surprised.

"That drawing that has led to many complications had to do with the symbol of the eye you so rightly spotted on the aerial photo," Leo explained.

"I remember Ben asked me to change the dome's position on the site plan."

"Yes, and you did."

They were all wondering what Leo and Ben were leading up to.

"You helped us activate a vibration that has released certain stored tablets from the underground tunnels that Leo needed for his further research."

"Yes, that is what you stated in a later email. I'd completely forgotten that." Ingrid paused, "but what has this all to do with the underground chamber we will see?"

When Ingrid mentioned the chamber, her body went into a second spasm of fear. Leo turned to her and said.

"Annie, you asked me earlier if your abduction fourteen years ago had anything to do with the interbreeding discovery, not so?"

"You mean the two kidnappings are connected?" Toon interrupted.

"We believe that they are. I need to prepare you all before you enter into the chamber; that is why I'm asking all these questions."

"Prepare us for what?" She commented in a shaky voice. They were all aware of the battle she was having to stay calm.

"Why? What do Ingrid and Annelies have in common?" Toon questioned. At the same time, he rested his hand on her shoulder for support.

"Past lifetimes. They were both priestesses. According to Hans, they both hold the genetic blueprint from a previous lifetime of initiates who had the mindset of an ascended being."

"Oh, I see, and they were both abducted for the same reasons?" When he addressed Leo, Toon now had his arm around both women, wanting to protect them from unpleasantness.

"Annelies," Ingrid said, "I recall a few recurring dreams where we are both initiates going into the...what looked like the pyramid at Giza. Did you ever have dreams about it?"

She did have dreams about an Egyptian temple where she was a student.... She felt a sudden rush as if she was sucked into a tunnel. An open landscape appeared where the temperature was hot and humid. Her bodily senses of herself as a young girl took over....her name was Ametsi, a young priestess who, together with other royal children, had the privilege of studying under the great teacher Djehuti.

"Mom, in that lifetime, you had become a great Healer and Priestess who knew the secret of the magical cult of the Dragon's Breath during the Egyptian dynasty that was later known as the Akenaton dynasty. The cult of the Dragon's Breath was a cult of Initiates that kept the Earth and the people in balance." Liesbeth's telepathic explanation brought on a vague memory.

"Where are you, Hans?" She replied. She was more interested in getting back to the top, away from these underground caves and tunnels that would all lead to the chamber she had been so interested in.

"Come, let's start with the tour. Annie hold my hand. I promise nothing is going to happen to you." Leo helped her up, and she allowed herself to be taken through the long underground tunnels, where the lighting cast shadows of drawings from long ago. She kept telling her mind to stop taking control, but her body had not yet caught up with her intent. It was Peter who pointed at the wall carving and recognized it.

"Annelies, does that drawing not look identical to the star map you found during the renovation of the Prinsegracht hotel?"

She stepped closer and let her fingers go over the lines that ended in star-like blobs. Then she looked from further away.

"Yes, if you remove the image on the top of my map, the genealogical pattern looks the same." She acknowledged nodding.

"Leo, do you see the resemblance?" He stood close to her, still holding her hand.

"Absolutely. Do you recognize these hieroglyphics? Shall I tell you what they say?" Leo had some fun observing them all.

"Come on, we are waiting." Toon's voice echoed inside the tunnel.

"I am your idea, and one day you will look for me, but I will be gone." Leo narrated the engraved symbols on the wall near the chamber entrance. They were all speechless.

"How is it possible that I found a map similar to the print one during the renovations in Holland?" She was so surprised that her feelings of fear had disappeared for a moment.

"Easy, it was drawn in the late eighteen hundreds," Leo replied.

"By whom?"

"We suspect that the English Professor had something to do with it," said Ben. "Remember that he was the first to create a laboratory in these underground tunnels."

"Let's move on; there is lots more to see. We can talk on the way." She sensed that Leo was not used to having many people around and probably had lots to do in his office. It made her feel foolish, but she was getting the hang of it. The pressure of knowing that she was far underground had gradually faded away. When they stepped into a chamber, it had a feeling of grandeur. It was huge. She could suddenly breathe again.

"Wow, it's beautiful." Sascia acclaimed. Her voice echoed back to her, which was another element they all needed to explore. They were all in awe of the unusual formations of the stalactites and stalagmites.

"These were cliffside dwellings, dating from the 12th century." Trevor pointed out.

Leo let go of her hand, moved to a particular spot inside the Chamber, and said: "This is the exact position below the centre of the island of Toon's project.

They all came closer and saw that the spot had a raised platform. Leo pointed to the nearest wall. All she saw was a massive relief in the wall that stood out and an empty hollow in the centre.

"Theo suspects that positioning the dome will expedite the collapse of the 3D hologram template surrounding our world, which some call the eighth sphere. "Trevor whispered to Tieneke, who was holding onto his hand.

Ingrid also saw them holding hands. She shook Toon's sleeve to make him aware of the couple's progressing intimacy.

They had all gathered near Leo, who said: "You can all imagine that opposing forces want us to prevent the collapse of this 3D hologram. Ingrid almost succeeded by making you change the dome position on the plan. They want to keep full control of our planet and keep our illusionary reality intact."

Richard was in his element. He was pointing out to Sascia which sections of the walls and ceilings she would have to take photos of. "Theo said that 'The Awakened Ones' who walked on our planet used the Eye of Horus as a device to oversee their creation. Then they stored it away like we store our data in our computer." Richard was pointing at the hollow in the wall. "Only their computer was in the shape of a human skull," Richard explained further.

Was Richard implying that the hollow had held a crystal skull?

"I feel that the crystal skulls found around the world are here to share ancient knowledge and wisdom and assist us in awakening our human race to higher spiritual laws and understanding of itself. They are announcing over the internet that many of the ancient tools are now returning because the planet is ready to use them again in a harmonious way." Leo added.

She wondered what Leo had in mind, holding her hand suddenly.

"Leo, where was the skeleton found?"

"Can you see the alcove further down to your left?" He pointed with a stretched arm to a far corner, where Leo's torch lighted up a massive rock formation.

"That is where the scroll was found. If you go deeper into the alcove and look up, you will see an indent the size of a narrow bed; that's where."

She let go of his hand and walked towards the space Leo had described. She asked the others not to follow her. Her fear was gone. Instead, she felt deep compassion and love for the individual who had perished in this chamber so long ago. It was the place where her true healing would happen.

She crawled into the alcove and looked up. There, it was how Leo described it. She hoisted herself onto the ledge and made herself comfortable.

She heard the voices of the others in the distance getting softer and softer.

***

She allowed the mist-like vapour to settle around her, knowing that she would meet herself from long ago — the initiate in this chamber praying for the release from her physical body because she had lost the ability to be in charge of her mind.

For a moment, she found herself standing in an unfamiliar world. Her sandalled feet were standing on a bluish sandy beach. She looked at the sky of many colours she'd never seen before, except when a sunset peeped through rainy clouds.

"Mom, we've brought you to our parallel world to show you what our world looks like."

The tall, younger version of Liesbeth, now recognized as Tulanda, joined her on the beach. She was wearing an unusual long dress which was low-cut, and it had slits on both sides. The fabric had a strange, unfamiliar texture, like fabric with another fabric on top.

"Mom, I want to stress that we are in your future, and you are in our past."

"Is Hans here as well?" That was all she could think about.

When she asked the question, a young man appeared at her side. He was also wearing a very unusual costume. It reminded her of a spacesuit from a movie set.

"You will write about your world in your journal, won't you," She heard herself asking mentally, wondering what life was like in a parallel universe.

"Absolutely, but first, we want you to meet somebody special."

She knew somebody had joined them because she felt a familiar energy signature standing close. She slowly turned and looked up at an ageless man dressed in a tunic whom she recognized as the great teacher Djehuti from her life in Egypt long ago. He greeted her with a bow while taking both her hands.

"I believe you have a different name for me in your life as Annelies." His telepathic signature gave him away.

"You are POWAH? My guide that at first appeared to me as a woman?"

The man smiled and chuckled. He took her arm in his, and together they walked away.

<There are important tasks ahead of you, and we will guide you through them.>

For a split second, she thought she was standing under a powerful beam of light that somehow transported her back into the chamber on Planet Earth.

<Everything in creation is created in pairs and has an equal and opposite mirror image counterpart, the Yin and the Yang, right and left, matter and antimatter, the electron and the positron. The universes of matter and antimatter coexist simultaneously.>

She was the young woman she recognized as herself and observed herself standing in front of the massively large slab of stone in the centre, which she now knew would be where the artefact key could set her free! She also saw Hans and Liesbeth joining her as bodies of light in her task to open the chamber entrance with the proper key.

She observed how the metal-looking ancient artefact, which existed in a parallel world, was placed in her hands. She stepped forward and inserted the metallic key in the hollow that was carved out for it. She stepped back onto the raised platform, and at that moment, a powerful beam of light and the music of the spheres released the bondage that her mind had stored in cellular memory. *"Is this the superlight we talked about before?"* she telepathically asked Hans when she felt weightless again, being a light body herself.

"SuperLight is magnetic light, and its counterpart is electric radiation. Regular light is electric light, and its counterpart is magnetic radiation. " Hans mentally replied. She wondered how long ago it was that she, the other her, was standing at the same spot. What had it then looked like?

In the distance, she picked up a conversation: "The skeleton is believed to be from the Neolithic period, around 9500 BC in the Middle East.

Had she heard Trevor speaking? She was startled that it was that long age. How was she then expected to be a priestess during the Akhenaton dynasty? That was not that long ago.

Someone was asking how they dated the mummified remains of the people who had perished in the chamber.

"By the markings on the top of the head mask of the skeleton. It resembles the relics found in the Liangzhu Cultural period, about 4100 to 5300 years ago. This mark has been found on many relics, such as a high priestess mask." She heard Leo telling the group they were still standing in the chamber's centre.

It was funny, but she felt as if she was in two places at the same time. Was that possible? She was clear of her body, but was she the exact figure sealed in stone, listening to the crystal skull?

"That is how your mind has translated it, yes." She sensed that there was someone else nearby observing her. She turned and recognized Theo.

"It's you! You were there with me in this chamber, weren't you?"

She knew that Theo was also the boy she had been keen on. Azino was the brightest student under the teacher named Djehuti.

"*Yes, I was; we were together then, but not anymore in the flesh. You did not know that, but during that life, I had passed on when you became a priestess. It was me who waited for you when you left your body behind in the chamber.*"

She wondered what he died of in that life, but Theo didn't tell her.

"*Could I have escaped?*" Her mind asked.

"*Yes, you could have since you were an initiate in the art of mind over matter. You knew that how you see your world depended on your emotions.*"

She was sad that she had failed, but her love for herself in that life made her feel complete as a spiritual being.

"*Annie, Hans told me that when the humanoid race from the outer world reached our universe, including our civilisation on planet Earth, they aimed their negative dark vibes onto the elite leaders of those times. We belonged to the Akhenaton dynasty, so we had been corrupted.*"

She then understood that all the drama happening to the Jaarsma Clan was a good example. For that matter, the world at large was still very much under the control of these Dark forces.

"*Annie, I will show you something still locked up in the Akashic records of our planet.*"

Theo placed his hands over her eyes, and when he took them away, they were both standing in a darkish, rather untidy-looking room, observing an older man bending over what looked like the leaf of the ancient scroll found near her mummified skeleton.

"The English professor had painstakingly transcribed and embossed the tiny, almost microscopic characters from the tablets onto a gold foil-like paper." But simultaneously, she heard the words between the people from her reality.

"*Can they see us?*" She beamed at Theo, who shook his head.

She knew that Trevor had taken photos of the fragile, thin sheets where the imprints were still visible.

"Those were the photos Trevor had later sent to Richard, under my instructions, since I had by this time passed away."

Then she overheard Trevor telling the group that the scroll could be perceived as a recorded library book containing ancient Sumeria's information. Trevor also believed the author was a Jaarsma lineage member during the Akhenaton dynasty. In her altered state, she looked at Theo, who nodded.

She was getting confused. How did Theo manage to separate the timelines?

"Annie, when you hear your voice, you often wonder where it came from. Not so?"

True. What was Theo leading up to?

"When you hear a voice speak from another reality where you live, other beings face a similar situation. The human mind also exists where the higher dimensional beings have their reality."

Okay, but she still questioned, in which reality is she communicating with Theo?

"Your consciousness, or your mind, that lives in that reality and that can perceive that reality, can also see and proceed without the eyes, into a different reality, although the reasoning mind is hardly aware of its separate perception."

Mmm, then she pondered. She thought there was no timeline if we were all multidimensional beings.

"Annie, in one dimension, we have learned that the dream you and I are living now is the result of the outside being that attracted our attention and fed us all our beliefs, and by breaking the spell of any belief, our mind requires great personal power that you once lost. We all possess such power that knowing you left behind in this chamber."

She was lost in Theo's interpretation of how her mind could hear the group in the chamber and interact telepathically with him. Still, the existence of the round artefact was a very different story. That object seemed to appear in all the realities she had seen.

She needed to orientate herself to the reality she was listening to. Who had said that the artefact held the twenty-two necessary genetic codes that would restore humanity's original blueprint and that alone could shatter the scientific community?

The whirling sensation took hold of her again, and together they walked hand in hand, and suddenly she saw what the chamber looked like thousands of years ago. It was indeed a beautiful temple. Not anything like the chamber that she had entered as Annelies.

"You have awakened the centrepiece by placing the artefact back in its place. You have finished what you came to do."

Then suddenly, she stood alone. Theo was gone. She returned to the ledge, back to her body, because she could feel that her physical form was calling her, and slowly, her bodily senses started to take over.

***

In the background, she heard voices, so she climbed off the ledge and felt at least ten years younger.

She heard Trevor's voice echoing against the walls of the underground chamber, explaining how the many ancient tools would be returned if the people on planet Earth were ready to use them harmoniously.

Peter asked about the drawings on the walls, similar to the Star map. The symbols were familiar to him.

"Hi, you're back, and I can see that you feel no fear or claustrophobia anymore!" Leo said with a twinkle in his eyes.

She smiled at them all and took Ben's hand in hers. It seemed she had been gone for a very short while, but it felt like centuries to her.

"The correct position of the stone key will release tremendous energy levels, thereby shifting a planetary portal – that is required to counter-match the other planetary vortex portals around the planet. These holographic portals were held within the control of the opposing forces for centuries." Leo continued.

Sascia asked about the tablets.

"It took two years to retrieve what is collectively known as the program of the prophet skulls, which are possibly linked to the tablets. Additional tablets have been discovered in the same cave where the crystal skulls were found".

They all greeted Hans and Liesbeth, who suddenly joined them in their tour underground. She greeted them as well but smiled.

"Sascia, the English professor, began to make progress. A word emerged. Then another. A phrase became understandable, then an entire sentence. He had broken the code."

Hans continued the story while he walked them further into the chamber.

"He discerned that the messages on the tablets were written by a people who called themselves 'The Awakened Ones.' When he completed the translation as much as possible, the professor sat back in disbelief. 'The Awakened Ones' story was nothing short of astounding."

Annelies knew by now that Hans was describing a human race that was last on Earth 6000 years ago. It would be a revelation to read Liesbeth's journal. Over the years, Hans has often talked about a world where people do not age or die. They just left and came back looking younger.

"So you are saying that an interstellar race had visited Earth long ago?"

"Yes. The tablets clearly tell the story of how the 'Awakened Ones' were unable to repair their disabled astral craft and could not return, and so were stranded on Earth."

"The tablets may represent the first recorded visit of a much older civilization to our planet." Leo nodded.

A translation of one of the passages says: 'The 'Awakened Ones' came down from the clouds in their astral craft. Our men, women, and children hid in the caves, and when the other tribes finally understood the sign language of 'The Awakened Ones, ' they realised that the newcomers had peaceful intentions.

"Some of these beings are the ones that went underground. Again, this is just another instance of habitation of this planet by ancient human beings." Trevor said as he pointed at several tunnels, but they had not explored them yet.

They were all speechless once more at the findings hidden under Toon's Valley of The Gods project.

"Folks, remember that angels visited Lot and Abraham," Trevor added when they came to the steel gate that opened into the same lift they had come down in.

Peter was on his cell phone with the people up above ground.

"Are you saying that the Sons of God who married the Daughters of Men were angelic beings?" Toon asked in a humorous tone.

Peter opened the gate, and Annelies was still glad they were going up this time.

"Ah-ha, and the Chariot of Fire that Ezekiel saw was a spacecraft, and Enoch was taken up in a spacecraft," Ben added his bit when they all stepped into the lift.

"At this time, more than half of humanity now has awakened to the point that they can accept greater truth and shall begin to speak that truth, at least in the form of questions. The throat chakra is a two-way portal. To speak the truth, one must first allow the truth to come into the open. Small things make big changes. " Leo concluded as he said his goodbyes. Ben operated the buttons in the lift, and they were on the move upwards.

She was determined to add more plausible facts when the lift took them above ground.

"And Jesus ascended into the clouds, and many cultures have stories of the golden-haired man they saw as a God. So, there are great connections in Christ's Presence within humanity."

She now knew that time only exists in unhappy, un-awake human beings. In real happiness, there is no time, or we start to feel an experience that time is speeding up, so every day flies past, like the lift that speeds up to the surface.

She was looking forward to seeing the sky. To breathe in the fresh air and to rejoice that this troubled world would soon vanish.

The Jaarsma Tree - The Prinsegracht Hotel

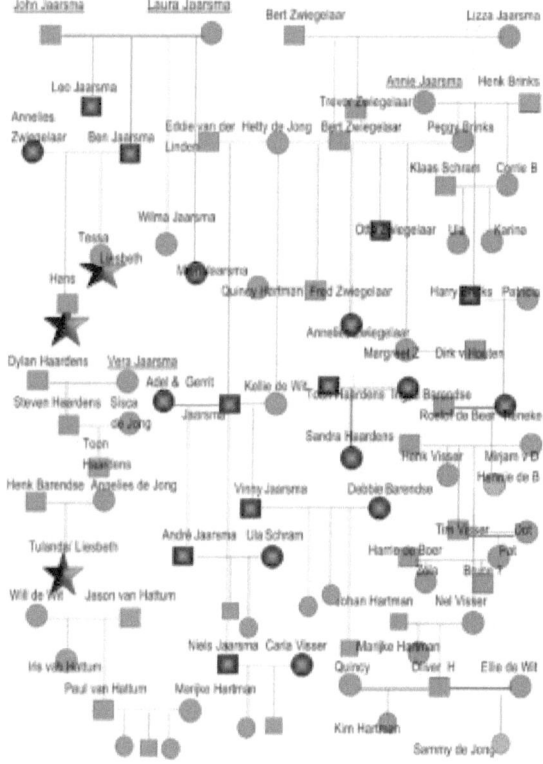

The Jaarsma Tree – Chateau / Half-way House

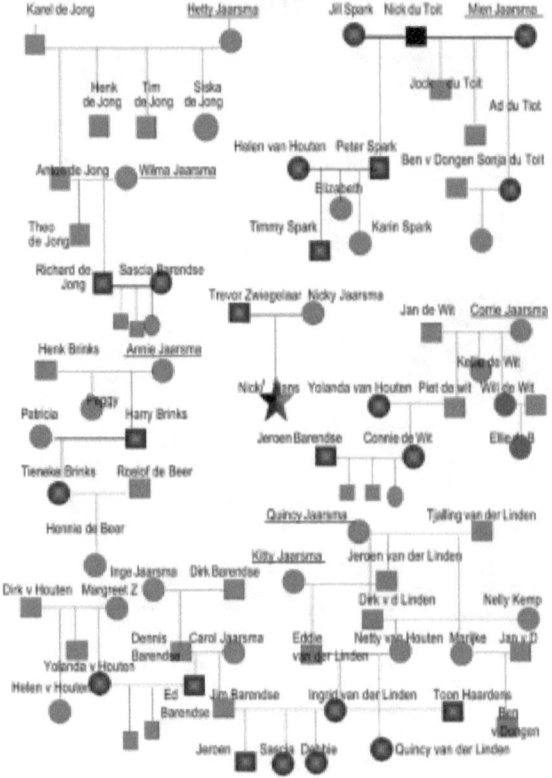

Bibliography

During the writing of this novel, the books by other authors, websites or blogs that have inspired me the most were as follows:

Barbara Hand Clow, The Alchemy of Nine Dimensions (Hampton Roads Publishing 2010)

Bruce H. Lipton, The Biology of Belief (Hay House 2008)

Carl van Vlierden, The Twelve Planets Speak. (Carl van Vlierden 1989) Carlos Castaneda, The Power of Silence (Simon& Schuster 1987)

David Icke, Human Race Get Off Your Knees (David Icke 2010)

Edgar Cayce – Atlantis, the Akashic Records

Ken Carey, The Starseed Transmissions (Kenneth X. Carey 1982).

Scott Peck, The Road Less Travelled (Arrow Books, 1990)

Phyllis V. Schlemmer, The Only Planet of Choice (Phyllis V. Schlemmer and Mary Bennett 1994)

Robin Sharma, The Monk Who Sold His Ferrari (Element an imprint of HarperCollinsPublishers 1997)

Tellis S. Papastavro,The Gnosis and The Law (Tellis S Papastavro1972)

Eckhart Tolle, The Power Of Now (Hodder & Stoughton, 2005)

Vera Stanley Alder, The Fifth Dimension (Samuel Weiser 2000)

Zecharia Sitchin The Lost Realms (Element an imprint of HarperCollinsPublishers 1997)

Eileen Connolly, Book of Numbers (A Newcastle Book 1988)

David R Hawkins, MD., Ph.D,.Power vs Force(Hay House, inc) 1995

Rudols Stainer Knowledge of the Higher Worlds – 1903
https://rsarchive.org/Books/GA013/
Sal Rachele Life on the Cutting Edge (Mission Possible
Commercial Printing (1949)

My gratitude goes out to my creative Higher Self, which POWAH
of the Jaarsma Clan represents.

A dream
Not
Interpreted
Is a
Letter
Not
Read

About the Author

Nadine was born in Holland, became a nurse, and emigrated to Australia and South Africa,is still her home.

Nadine's Higher Self instructed her to write about the potential for achieving full consciousness through visionary fiction. By taking readers on a journey of awakening through the characters of the Jaarsma clan, she aims to help them expand their understanding of 'consciousness'.

Nadine has been teaching people for the past twenty years using a creative and 'wholesome' process to bridge the gap between logical and intuitive abilities. In the nineties, she observed a shift in her students' perceptions through her drawing classes, leading her to develop her Art analogue mind drawing workshops.

In 1998, she held her first genetic decoding trial workshops with nine people, all of whom had different perceptions of what awakening meant to them.

In 2001, Kima Global published her first novel, My Love, We Are Going Home. In 2002, Nadine became the editorial and creative design director of Kima Global Publisher's imprint, The Power of Words. Robin Beck, her publisher, eventually became her husband. She published 12 more titles. Sadly, Robin passed away in 2023. After much consideration and weighing her options, she decided to republish her books under her own publisher's name, 'The Power of Words.'

About the Publisher

In 2001, I published my first novel with Kima Global Publishers. Over the years, I published 12 more titles with the same publisher, who eventually became my husband. Sadly, he passed away in 2023. After much consideration and weighing my options, I have published my two-book series, "The *Self*-Employed Housewife," and the five-book visionary fiction series, "Awakening to our Ascension," under the name 'The Power of Words' through Draft2Digital. I plan to include my workbooks and journals at a later stage. For now, they are still only available locally in SA.

Read more at https://nadinemay.company.site/.

www.ingramcontent.com/pod-product-compliance
Lightning Source LLC
Chambersburg PA
CBHW020916020726
47495CB00002B/221